For the first time Aeron allowed himself to sense what he'd known from the moment he felt the stone's influence.

It reeked of evil.

It was powerful and majestic, a conflagration of energy that defied his senses. But it stained him to stand so close to it. There was a conscious malevolence behind its splendor, an ancient, aching hunger that shrieked for Aeron's willing soul. He knew that if he set his hand on the dark stone, he would be lost forever, consumed and filled with something older than time and unspeakably, irredeemably evil.

Coming in 1999 . . .

FORGOTTEN REALMS®

The Shadow Stone

Richard Baker

THE SHADOW STONE

©1998 TSR, Inc.
All Rights Reserved.

Cover art by Les Adwards; cover design by Dee Barnett
First Printing: September 1998
Library of Congress Catalog Card Number: 97-062376

9 8 7 6 5 4 3 2 1

ISBN: 0-7869-1186-7
8587XXX1501

U.S., CANADA,	EUROPEAN HEADQUARTERS
ASIA, PACIFIC & LATIN AMERICA	Wizards of the Coast, Belgium
Wizards of the Coast, Inc.	P.B. 34
P.O. Box 707	2300 Turnhout
Renton, WA 98057-0707	Belgium
+1-206-624-0933	+32-14-44-30-44

Visit our website at www.tsr.com

For Kim

Thanks for putting up with me.

Special thanks to Julia Martin, Steven Schend, Dale Donovan, Phil Athans, and Peter Archer for helping me to get a handle on the Realms. What a long, strange trip it's been.

One

Aeron Morieth glided toward the sun-dappled clearing, stalking through the green undergrowth of the forest floor. It was a warm day, and the emerald canopy overhead sealed the heat beneath the moss-grown trees; not a breath of wind stirred the leaves and branches. Sweat stained his homespun shirt and trickled down his back. Moving without a sound, Aeron raised his bow and drew back the arrow until the rough fletching scraped against the corner of his jaw, just under his ear. Eyes narrowed, he sighted along the shaft. He'd get one shot, and he didn't want to miss.

Twenty yards away, the lean hare sensed danger and sat up, its nose quivering. With the quiet perfection of long practice, Aeron released the bowstring. The weapon strummed softly in his ear as the gut string burned his fingertips. The rabbit kicked and jumped, shot clean through just behind its forelegs.

Aeron straightened with a satisfied grin. Rabbit, squirrel, and other small game were plentiful in the meadows of the Maerchwood. In the hot, lazy days of summer, he could bag three or four rabbits in an afternoon's hunt. He broke out of the underbrush, blinking in the burnished-gold light that illuminated the glen, and trotted over to dress his kill.

The sun was hot in the clearing. Aeron shook the sweat from his unruly halo of golden hair and paused to strip his coarse linen shirt from his torso. He was a slight youth, no more than five and a half feet in height, with a wiry and resilient frame. Keen intelligence gleamed in his dark eyes, set wide apart in a proud, confident face that showed signs of elven blood. He drew a wide-bladed hunting knife from a sheath at his belt and knelt by the rabbit.

Sweat streamed down his face as he cleaned the small carcass. In the southern heartlands of Chessenta, the Maerchwood never grew very cold. The summers were invariably long, hot, and humid. Aeron had lived with the sweltering summer weather all his life and was about as used to it as one could get. He finished dressing the hare and looped a rawhide thong through the cleaned carcass, slinging it over his shoulder. Whistling between his teeth, he stood, brushed himself off, and set off for home. The Adder River and Maerchlin, Aeron's home, were ten miles away, but he could easily make it in a couple of hours.

Heading northwest from the clearing, he followed a long ridge of hills for several miles. The ridgeline rose clear of the woods, providing a rugged but serviceable path into the heart of the Maerchwood. Aeron ran in the sunshine, his torso glistening with perspiration, bounding from rock to rock. The ridge gradually tapered away into a jumble of thickets and deadfalls; Aeron turned west and followed a dark, swift stream for two miles more before he picked up a forester's trail that led back to Maerchlin.

The trail wound alongside a slower stream that ran west toward the village. Here Aeron encountered signs of settlement again, stump-choked swaths cleared by loggers and vacant trappers' cabins. The people of southern Chessenta had been harvesting fur, timber, and game from the edges of the Maerchwood for a dozen generations.

The Morieths had been among the woodland's first settlers, more than three centuries ago. Aeron often wondered what it must have been like in those days. In his ancestors' time, the Maerchwood was two or three times the size of the woodland he knew, home to ancient elven courts and untold secrets. Aeron had spent more than one afternoon dreaming of the old mysteries and forgotten deeds of the ancient elf realms; the Maerchwood was in his blood.

Aeron settled into a walk as he got closer to home. Despite his stamina, the heat was wearing him down. About a half-mile from the forest's edge, he rounded a sharp bend in the trail and found himself face-to-face with three young men of Maerchlin, coming the other way. Phoros Raedel was the son of Lord Raedel, the master of Maerchlin; Miroch and Regos were highborn kinsmen of Raedel's, and his constant companions. They were big, aggressive fellows, several years older than Aeron, and he'd been bullied by them more than once. Regos was passing a wineskin to Raedel as Aeron blundered around the bend.

Aeron stopped in his tracks, recognizing his danger. It was too late to avoid Raedel and his friends; he'd walked right into the middle of them. He scowled, berating himself for not watching where he was going. The warm rustle and hum of the forest died as the older lads exchanged crooked grins and blocked his path. This was a familiar pattern. Raedel and his friends would think of some torment for him, and he'd fight back with the fury of a wildcat, but numbers would carry the day. Or he could accept whatever humiliation they dealt him and delay the inevitable . . . but Aeron decided he wasn't going to give Phoros the satisfaction. He squared his shoulders and defiantly refused to drop his gaze. "Well? What do you want?" he demanded.

"What have we here?" said Raedel, his face stretching into a cruel smile. He was a tall, well-muscled young man, his body hardened by years of weapons training in the keep's practice yard. His face was square-jawed and heavy. He and his companions carried crossbows over their shoulders. Aeron guessed they were going shooting, which was a bad sign for him; it was likely they'd been drinking all day and were looking for trouble. Raedel glanced over at his companions. "Look, fellows, it's the elf boy."

"Where have you been, elf boy?" said Regos. He was the strongest of the three, but he was a follower.

"Let me pass," Aeron stated flatly. "I'm no elf, and you know it." It didn't help that Phoros's words found their mark. It didn't show much in Aeron—his ears had the subtlest of points, and his light frame and quick mind might have been inherited from elven forebears—but the Morieth name was suspect in Maerchlin. Lacking any living kin, Aeron had spent much of his youth lashing back at his taunters.

"You heard Regos," snapped Raedel. "Answer him!"

"I spent the day hunting, my lord," Aeron replied, repressing a sneer with the title. Raedel's father was nothing more than a glorified brigand who'd seized Maerchlin with his sword fewer than forty years ago. Money and men at arms didn't make a lord, not as far as Aeron was concerned. He tossed the hare to the ground as proof of his words.

His sarcasm wasn't lost on Raedel. The young lord widened his stance, blocking the path. "Hunting? In my father's forest? Who gave you permission to do that?"

"Use your eyes," Aeron said, nodding at the skinned rabbit. "Small game isn't against the law."

Raedel's face darkened. "I say you *have* been poaching my father's deer. And you'll have to pay for that. Don't you think so, my friends?"

Miroch, the third fellow, moved past Aeron to cut off his retreat. He wasn't much taller than Aeron, but he carried fifty pounds of beef high on his torso, giving him a curiously top-heavy appearance. He drank deeply from his wineskin. "Stinking elf boy poacher," he pronounced. "Ought to cut off his stinking elf ears, I say."

Aeron backed away, trying to keep the older lads from surrounding him, but there was nowhere to go. "You know Kestrel would have my hide if I shot one of your precious deer, Phoros. Now, let me go!" He looked about, planning a retreat. The stream was to his left and a dense thicket to his right. No one else was in sight, and the relative safety of Maerchlin was still some distance away.

Raedel caught Miroch's arm and dragged him back. "Wait a moment, Miroch," he said. "Of course Morieth hasn't done anything wrong." His eyes were cold and keen as he looked at Aeron and stepped to the landward side of the path. "Please be on your way. Don't pay us any mind."

Aeron hesitated. Raedel wasn't done . . . not yet.

"Is my leave not good enough for you?" Raedel added, arching an eyebrow.

Steeling himself, Aeron stepped forward, edging past the three young nobles. The stream bank dropped away almost under his feet, but he refused to get within reach of any of them if he could avoid it. He kept an eye on all three nobles as he walked past, not caring if he looked defiant.

As he passed abreast of Raedel, Regos grunted and launched himself forward, arms straight out to shove Aeron into the water. With a snort of surprise, Aeron ducked and twisted away. Regos sailed high, stumbling over Aeron and knocking him to the ground before he crashed down the short bank and sprawled into the stream. Aeron grinned with momentary triumph, then scrambled to his feet.

Too late. Raedel's broad hands clamped down on his shoulders, hauling him to his feet. "Oh, no. You're not going anywhere. I think you owe Regos an apology," the young lord hissed.

Below them, Regos kicked and sputtered. "By Tchazzar, I'm going to kill him!" he shrieked as he regained his feet. Blood streamed from his mouth, where he'd apparently struck a rock in his fall. He thrashed his way up out of the water and drew his knife from his belt. "You are dead, you stinking half-breed!"

Miroch seized a fistful of Aeron's hair and pulled his head back. "Want to cut his throat?" he asked. "Or maybe cut off his elf ears, then cut his throat?"

Raedel snorted in disgust behind him. "He doesn't have elf ears. See? You can hardly see the points." A moment later, he added, "Maybe we should *give* him elf ears, fellows. Would you like that, Morieth?"

Aeron's heart hammered in his chest. He twisted against Raedel's iron grip, but he was held too securely. Regos scrambled up the short slope and approached, steel gleaming in his hand. Absently he drew one sleeve across his face to wipe away the blood, pausing as he glared into Aeron's face. "Hold him still," he said.

Raedel seized Aeron's right arm, and Miroch his left. They set their feet and leaned into him, locking his torso like a stone vise. Regos grinned and abruptly struck Aeron with the hardest open-handed slap he could manage, snapping the helpless captive's head to one side. Dark spots danced in Aeron's eyes and he tasted blood in his mouth. For a long moment, he couldn't see or hear anything.

When he came to his senses, Regos was standing close, looking past his face. One hand clamped the side of his face, and the other hand . . . Aeron felt the cold kiss of steel by the side of his head. A hot sting slid across the top of his ear. A small, pale sliver of flesh pattered from his shoulder and fell to the muddy earth. Warm blood trickled down his neck.

He bucked and screamed in rage. Regos cursed and tried to tighten his grip. "Stop moving, damn you!"

Miroch leaned away from Aeron in distaste. "Hey, watch the knife! You're getting blood on me!"

For an instant, Aeron felt Miroch's hold on him relax. Howling with fear and anger, he stamped his foot down on Miroch's and wrenched his arm away. Miroch yelped and released him. The knife scraped across his skull as Aeron struggled, but he didn't stop. His left hand darted to his belt, and he drew his hunting knife. As Regos tried to capture his arm, he brought the knife up in a lightning slash that laid Regos's arm open. He turned and ducked just as Raedel's heavy fist crashed against his head. Aeron staggered and nearly fell, still held up by Raedel's other hand clamped around his arm. Raedel drew back for another punch, but Aeron reversed his knife and rammed it into

Raedel's shoulder. The nobleman gaped and fell away.

Aeron clamped one hand to his injured ear. Miroch hopped backward and sat down with a thump, holding his foot. Regos leaned over, holding his injured arm. The blade with which he'd cut Aeron stuck in the ground, quivering, its grip slick with Regos's blood. Beside him, Raedel reached up to touch the hilt of Aeron's knife, buried in his left shoulder. A spreading stain of bright red marked his elegant white tunic. He looked up at Aeron, dazed. "I'm going to kill you for that," he stated.

Aeron backed away two steps, vaguely surprised by what he'd done. "You cut me first, you bastard," he rasped. "You got what you deserved!"

Phoros Raedel dropped his good hand to the hilt of a plain long sword he wore at his belt. He drew the blade with a ringing rasp of steel against wood and brass.

Nothing short of murder was in Raedel's face. Aeron retreated another step, and the hot forge fueling his resistance suddenly failed him. Phoros means to kill me, he realized. Abruptly he turned and fled toward the village. He darted and leapt down the trail with the swiftness of a panicked stag, not daring to look behind him.

"Come back here! Come back here, damn you!"

Aeron didn't look back. He kept up his sprint until the older lads' voices faded into the forest behind him.

* * * * *

Half an hour later, Aeron burst out of the forest into a small holding on the edge of the woods. Gasping raggedly, he came to a jarring halt, his chest and legs burning. The house where he'd grown up was a rough-hewn woodsman's cabin, sealed with mud and thatched with straw. A small farmyard penned goats, chickens, and a handful of pigs nearby, and around the house plots bloomed with green, even rows of radishes, turnips, and potatoes.

A brown-haired girl in a blue linen dress straightened up from scattering feed as Aeron staggered into the yard. She was a year younger than Aeron, with a lean and athletic build. "Aeron! Where have you been? You . . ." Her voice died as she spotted the dusty red streak of blood on the side of his head. "Oh, Aeron. What happened?"

"It was Raedel," he panted. "I think I'm in trouble,

Eriale. Is Kestrel here?"

"He's splitting wood behind the barn." Eriale picked up the hem of her skirts and hurried past Aeron, circling the barn. Now that Aeron had a moment to listen, he heard the dull *tchunk!* of an axe biting wood. "Father! Aeron is back!"

The rhythmic strokes fell silent. A moment later, Kestrel ambled into the yard, dusting off his hands. He was a small gray man, only a few inches taller than Aeron. Like the younger lad, he had a wiry frame, but he seemed more weathered than fit. His coarse mustache and dark, close-set eyes gave him the appearance of a sea otter. When Aeron's parents died, Kestrel and his wife had taken him in for the sake of old friendship; he and Eriale were all of Aeron's kin now. "What's the trouble?" he asked. "Swords and spears, lad, what happened to you?"

Aeron leaned over to set his hands on his knees, still trying to regain his breath. "I ran into Phoros, Miroch, and Regos on my way home," he said.

"The lord's boy and his friends?"

"Yes. They'd been drinking. I tried not to provoke them, but . . . they started in on me. Regos fell into the stream, trying to shove me in, and that angered him past all sense. He drew his knife and said he was going to dock my ears. Make me look like an elf."

Kestrel scowled. He carefully drew back Aeron's hair and examined his injuries. "Damn. He notched your ear, all right. You'll carry that for the rest of your days. And there's a long cut on your scalp, too. Did he slip?"

"Yes. I mean, I struggled, and that made him slip." Aeron narrowed his eyes, thinking of what might have happened if he hadn't got away from them. Swallowing, he looked up to Kestrel's face. "It's worse than that, Kestrel. I think I'm in terrible trouble."

"Why? What did you do?" asked Eriale. Like a real sister, she usually delighted in making mischief for Aeron, but Aeron could tell by her voice that Eriale was more worried than she let on.

"Aye, Aeron. What else happened?" said Kestrel.

"I lost my temper when Regos cut me. I used my knife. I laid open Regos's arm . . . and I stabbed Phoros."

"The lord's son?" Kestrel's eyes widened in horror, and he drew in his breath. "Aeron, did you kill the lord's son?"

"I don't think so. I hit him in the shoulder, pretty high,

and he didn't fall. He drew his sword after I got him, though, and he said he was going to kill me." Aeron found he was shaking with repressed emotion from his encounter. "Kestrel, I'm scared. What are they going to do to me?"

The woodcutter paced away, rubbing his face. He didn't say anything. Aeron glanced at Eriale. She was watching him, her face pale. "Aeron . . ." She struggled to find something to say, and bowed her head. "They might hang you. It's death to take up arms against a noble."

Kestrel turned and nodded. "People might think you had a good reason to defend yourself, Aeron, but I can't imagine that Phoros and his friends are going to tell the same story you just told. That will mean three accounts against one . . . and your knife as proof of whatever they say."

"I was defending myself!" Anger boiled up to replace the fear that had galvanized Aeron into flight. "Regos scarred me and laughed about it! He'd have done worse if I hadn't gotten away from them. What do I have to answer for?"

"I know I always told you to be honest, boy, but use your head. Who's going to decide your fate? Lord Raedel, of course. These are his lands, and you're his subject. He's never denied anything to that son of his. He might not have you executed, but I can't see you going free."

Aeron whirled and stormed away, pacing in an anxious circle as he tried to think with his mind instead of his anger. He imagined himself standing in the cold stone hall of Raedel Keep, heavy iron shackles on his wrists and ankles. The old lord would be sitting above him, on the wooden dais he used when he held court. *Aeron Morieth, I sentence you to swing by the neck until dead. Carry out the sentence, constable. . . .* Aeron's knees buckled and he leaned against the farmhouse, his head spinning. They'd kill him for what he'd done. Or, if he was lucky, maybe they'd just bury him in a lightless hole of a dungeon and throw away the key.

"Come on, lad." Kestrel knelt beside him and threw an arm over his shoulders. "I don't think you can stay here."

"What? What do you mean?"

The forester grimaced. "This is the first place Raedel's men will look, Aeron. You've got to get away from here."

Aeron's head reeled. "You mean run away?"

Kestrel nodded soberly. "Aeron, I've tried to do right by

your father. Before he died, he asked me to look after you, to raise you like you were my own boy. Lord Raedel sent him to the gallows twelve years ago. I'll be damned if I see you hanged, too."

"I don't want to hang, Kestrel."

"I know the way the castle lads treat you, Aeron, and I know you. Whatever happened, you did what you had to do, and it's wrong to die for that. But now you'd best get moving. I figure we've got a quarter of an hour, maybe a little more, before the constable rides up here to arrest you." Kestrel rocked back on his heels, surged to his feet, and raised Aeron by the arm. He looked over at Eriale. "Fix up a sack of food, a waterskin, and a bedroll of some kind. And get a knife, too. He'll need a new one."

"Right." Eriale nodded and ducked into the house.

"And get a second sack ready!"

"You're coming with me?" Aeron asked.

Kestrel shook his head. "If I do that, they'll think I put you up to it. That'll smell like a revolt to Raedel; he remembers who your father was. No, I'm going to send Eriale with you so she can tell me where you're hiding. I can always tell the count she's gone off to visit her mother's kinfolk in Saden."

"What are you going to do?"

Kestrel sighed heavily and looked toward the stone towers of Raedel Keep, across the river. "I'm going to go down to the castle and try to set this straight. If it turns out right, I can always tell them you panicked and ran off when I left you. If I can't smooth things over . . . well, you'll be glad you're not here."

* * * * *

Three hours later, the long afternoon was coming to an end. The sky had taken on the color of beaten copper, with red streaks marking a storm front pushing in from the south. Aeron and Eriale rested by an old trapper's lean-to, about six miles southwest of Maerchlin. They hadn't spoken much during the march. Aeron couldn't bring himself to talk about what had happened, and Eriale's gibes and barbs fell flat when he was so preoccupied.

"It'll be dark soon," Eriale said, standing to gaze up at the sky. The lodge stood by a long field that stretched away to the west, and the red and gold of the sunset blazed in the soft tasseled grasses. Eriale had changed into breeches and a rough shirt not dissimilar from what Aeron wore. It was much more practical for hiking than her skirts. "Should we build a fire?"

Aeron glanced around at the watchful woods. "I've seen wolf tracks in this part of the Maerchwood. And troll signs, too. It might be a good idea to have a fire."

They scoured the forest floor for suitable firewood, gathering dry pine needles for kindling. As darkness fell, Aeron managed to get a good fire going. They broke into their supplies and roasted a hen over the campfire, singeing their fingers and faces as they ate.

"Do you think the constable's looking for you, Aeron?" Eriale asked after they finished. She busied herself with banking the fire to burn all night.

"Raedel would never let me go," he said bitterly. "I stand up to him, and I'm going to lose everything for it. It doesn't seem fair, does it?"

"You're safe as long as you don't go home," she said quietly. She looked up at him, her mouth tight. Aeron and Eriale had grown up together, family in fact if not in blood. He could read her moods with some accuracy. Eriale was a level-headed girl with a strong stubborn streak, confident in herself and those close to her. She didn't worry without good cause, and Aeron could tell she was working to keep her concern from showing. She tried to put on an optimistic face. "Perhaps Father can get Lord Raedel to hear your side of the story."

He shrugged. "I doubt it, Eriale."

"What will you do?"

"I can live off the land as long as I need to." He reached behind him for his quiver and emptied it into his lap. Fifteen good arrows, two only fair, and the makings for a dozen more. He selected a rough shaft that was almost done and began to pare it carefully with a sharp fletching knife.

Eriale watched him. "All by yourself? No one to talk to, no friends?"

"You and Kestrel could come visit me from time to time. As for friends . . ." He met her eyes. "I don't have many anyway. No one in Maerchlin has much use for the last of the Morieths, not after my father pushed Lord Raedel into setting Oslin's soldiers on us. You'd have a lot more friends yourself, Eriale, if your father hadn't taken me in."

The forester's daughter smiled sadly. "People misjudge you, Aeron. They don't know you like I do." She spread out her bedroll by the fire and drew a thin blanket over her shoulders. "We'll probably need to move again in the morning. Better get some sleep."

"As soon as I finish this arrow." Aeron turned his attention to the fletching. He lost himself in his task for half an hour or more. Eriale rolled over and started snoring softly. When he finished, he stood and walked away from the fire to gaze at the stars. By night, the forest was alive with the sounds of movement. Animals rustled as they moved through the brush; frogs croaked and called to one another; nocturnal insects chirped and buzzed quietly. In the distance, a hound bayed mournfully. Aeron smiled, closing his eyes to catch every song of the night. The hound bayed again, several others joining in a rough chorus.

Hounds?

Aeron's eyes flew open, and he wheeled to stare into the forest. It was hard to be certain, but he heard them to the west and slightly north, back toward Maerchlin. The dogs barked and snuffled, the sounds of their approach gradually growing into a continuous gabble of grunts and howls. He smacked one hand against his forehead and bounded up to shake Eriale awake.

"What? What is it?" she asked sleepily.

"The constable," Aeron said. "They've got hounds on our trail!"

Eriale sat upright, cocking her head to listen. "They can't be more than a mile away!"

Aeron turned and started stuffing his pack. "Come on! We're going to have to run for it!"

Eriale scrambled up. She knelt beside the fire and scooped great armfuls of earth over the embers, smothering it. "They'll know we were here," she said over her shoulder. "There's no way we can hide all the signs."

"I know," Aeron said. He slung his pack over one shoulder, grabbed his bedroll, and stood. "Got everything?"

Eriale crammed her blanket into her pack. "Let's move."

They set off toward the south, heading deeper into the Maerchwood. Aeron moved fast in the darkness. From his unknown elven ancestors, he'd inherited exceptionally keen night vision, and he could see quite well by starlight or moonlight. Eriale kept up with him as best she could, but she didn't have his acuity of vision or endurance, and she stumbled over thick roots and tangled undergrowth time and time again. He hadn't gone a mile before Eriale began to rasp behind him. "Aeron, slow down!"

He halted on the edge of a small clearing. The moon was rising in the east, casting a silver light through the tree-tops overhead. Very little reached the forest floor. He caught Eriale's hand in the darkness. Behind them, the hounds were baying with excitement. They'd found the campsite and picked up the new trail.

He rested one hand on Eriale's shoulder. "Let's get off the trail. They might miss us." They stood on the shoulder of a tree-covered ridge, surrounded by impenetrable shadows and scant traces of silver moonlight. Aeron caught Eriale's hand and led her uphill. They crashed through thick briars and undergrowth, scuffling through thick layers of fallen leaves. To Aeron, it sounded like the passage of an army.

At the top of the ridge, Aeron turned and looked back to the west. He could make out angry lantern light bobbing toward them through the trees. They were close enough to hear the cries of the hunters. Aeron squeezed his eyes shut and pounded his fist into his hand, trying to think. How could they lose their pursuers?

"Aeron, they're right behind us," Eriale said.

"They're still on the trail. Come on, let's get down the other side of the ridge." He turned and started sliding down the hillside, kicking up dirt and dead leaves as he snaked down the hill's reverse slope. Eriale followed, a few steps behind. The weak moonlight didn't illuminate this side of the ridge at all. Aeron's night vision was keen, but he needed some light to see. He lurched and stumbled as the slope steepened under his feet.

Aeron tried to arrest his descent, but suddenly there was empty air under him. He yelped in surprise and fell, tumbling through darkness, branches and briars stinging him like whips as he plummeted down the hillside. He fetched up hard against smooth, dressed stone. The impact knocked the wind out of him. A moment later, Eriale fell heavily nearby, gasping in pain. After the clatter and rush of the fall, the sudden silence was disorienting; it took Aeron a moment to gather his senses.

Eriale sat up, a little more fortunate in her landing. "Aeron? Are you here? Where are we?"

Aeron raised himself on one elbow, rubbing at a badly barked shinbone. "I'm here, Eriale." As to where they were . . . he looked around, trying to make out their surroundings. Gradually he realized it wasn't completely dark. A shimmering faerie-light hovered in the air, casting an argent gleam over the place. They were in the ruins of a stone building, overgrown with green vines. The glossy marble was veined with dark moss and strands of silver. The stones seemed unusual somehow. As he peered closer, he saw they were delicately scalloped with a fine tracery suggesting living trees and animals, a bas-relief of the forest. "I think we're in an old elf tower," he said in a hushed voice.

"I didn't think there were any so close to Maerchlin." Eriale traced the old lines in the stone. "It's beautiful."

Faint and subtle, the old stones gleamed like soft silver in the moonlight. Despite the clamor of the approaching hunters, Aeron reached out to stroke the cool and perfect stone. Foxfire danced on his fingertips; he could almost hear the faraway cry of elfin horns in the forest, inhale the scents and sounds of vanished starlight. "Who were they?" he wondered aloud. "Where are they now?"

Eriale could not reply. Her eyes wide and dark, she stood rooted to the spot. With a soft gasp, Aeron realized that he'd been holding his breath, afraid to break the faerie dream around him.

Dogs howled and bayed on the hillcrest above them. Slowly Aeron rolled to his knees, then pushed himself to his feet. "They're still on our trail. Keep moving."

Eriale nodded and drew back from the stone wall. She turned to pick up her pack, then halted. "Aeron, wait."

"What? What is it?" He glanced over, alarmed by the strange tone in her voice. In a jumbled gap in the opposite wall stood a white wolfhound, an ethereal shadow of gray and pearl with dark, intelligent eyes. It watched them without moving. Eriale slowly backed away as Aeron straightened, facing the apparition.

"What do we do?" she whispered.

Aeron started to reply, but he noticed the spectral illumination was growing brighter. The entire place was glowing with pearly light. He blinked as a tiny mote of coruscating radiance danced and darted a handspan in front of his nose. The sphere retreated in the blink of an eye, hovering beside the white hound, and then it began to grow, expanding and dimming until it had the outline of a man-shaped white radiance.

The light brightened one last time, and then flashed silently, revealing a tall, thin man with fair skin and long silver hair. He was dressed in pearl gray hose, over which he wore a soft white doublet embroidered with silver designs. His face was long and expressive, with a sad wisdom hidden in his perfect features. He reached down to stroke the white hound's head. "*Cuillen de fhoiren, Baillegh,*" he said softly, in a voice like liquid music.

"Aeron, he's an elf lord," Eriale whispered. "We've trespassed in his house."

Aeron glanced at her, then back to the tall elf. "Who are you? What is this place?"

The elf gazed into Aeron's face with a hint of a smile. He started to speak, grimaced, and then tried again. "I am called Fineghal Caillaen, though some know me as the Storm Walker. I have been waiting for you, Aeron Morieth," he said. An odd inflection weighted his speech, as if he hadn't spoken a human language in a very long time. "Who is your companion?

"This is Eriale, daughter of Kestrel the forester," Aeron replied. A moment later, he realized the import of the elf lord's words. "Waiting for me? How do you know me?"

"The Morieths are known to us of old," the elf answered, ignoring the rest of Aeron's question. "Why do they hunt you? You seem too young to be an outlaw."

"I wounded two noblemen. I'm just a commoner. It's death to take up arms against a lord." Aeron had the uncanny feeling the elf prince could read the truth of his words, seeing the events he alluded to. The baying of the hounds grew louder, and he could hear men cursing and calling out as they came nearer. "Damn, they're almost on us," he hissed. "Come on, Eriale. We have to flee!"

The silver prince raised his hand. "None will find us here if I do not wish to be found." He looked at Eriale, and back to Aeron. "You and your friend may shelter here tonight under my protection. I will see to it that no harm befalls you."

Aeron turned to look up the hillside. Red-faced soldiers

in Raedel's colors picked their way down the slope, dragged on by hounds that strained at their leashes. He quailed in fear as he realized the soldiers must be close enough to spot them, but the eerie silver radiance seemed to attract not the slightest notice. "Why don't they see us?" he asked.

"An enchantment on this place," Fineghal replied. "I'd better help the hounds along, though. They're not so easy to fool as men." He lifted his hand and muttered a liquid phrase under his breath. Silver motes danced around his hand. Aeron was acutely conscious of a thrumming in his heart, a prickling sensation that tickled the center of his chest. He realized he had sensed Fineghal's magic at work. When the feeling faded, he had a sudden and fierce wish to bring it back.

Outside the moss-grown walls, the hounds bayed louder and surged ahead, sweeping past the ruins of the elven tower and crashing off to the north. In a matter of moments, they had vanished into the silver night. More than a dozen men had almost walked right through them without even glancing in their direction. Aeron breathed a heavy sigh of relief as they disappeared. "Will they be back?" he asked aloud.

"Not tonight, they won't," Fineghal replied. He returned his attention to Aeron and Eriale. "I seem to recall that humans require sleep," he said. "Rest now. In the morning we can decide what must be done." He gestured with one hand and whispered softly in the elven tongue. Despite his resistance, Aeron found his eyes growing unbearably heavy. Beside him, Eriale sank slowly to the stone, laying her head on her pack. He didn't remember reaching the ground.

Two

The warmth of a golden sunbeam against his face woke Aeron in the early hours of the morning. He opened his eyes. Cold stone lay beneath him, and above him the green branches of the forest wove a tangled skein of light and shadow. For a moment, he was completely disoriented, but then the events of the previous night returned to him. The ruins of the elf tower seemed unremarkable by daylight. The silver tracery and elfin aura were gone, and the stones were simply mossy old stones again.

He pushed himself to his feet, stretching. Eriale stirred close by, raising her head and blinking at him. "Aeron? Where are— Oh, I remember." She sat up, clasping her arms and shivering. "Was it all a dream?"

"I don't think so," Aeron said. There was no sign of the hunters, and all he could hear were the normal small sounds of the forest—birdcalls sweet and high, the gentle sighing of the upper branches in the breeze, rustling and motion all around him as the forest began to wake. The ruins faced the sunrise, sheltered against the green hillside like a jewel in the hand of a gentle giant. He felt surprisingly well rested, considering the fact that he'd slept on a hard stone floor. "Do you think Fineghal's nearby?"

"The elf prince? I don't see him, or his hound." Eriale stood and looked around. "What do we do now, Aeron? Do we wait for him, or do we move on?"

"I'm not sure where I'd go even if we left now. Raedel's men might have missed us last night, but they won't give up so quickly."

Eriale nodded. "I hope Father's all right. The constable wouldn't have been happy to find us missing."

"I'm sure he's fine," Aeron said confidently. Inwardly, he was very concerned for Kestrel, but it would do no good to share that with Eriale. With a sigh, he reached down and shouldered his pack. In the warm light of the morning sun, the astounding encounter of the night before seemed nothing more than a dream. Aeron wanted to linger by the elf tower, to see if their mysterious host might reappear. He'd never dreamed that he would meet an elf, let alone a lord of elven-kind, so close to Maerchlin. Ancient ruins, elven magic . . . he'd dreamed that someday he'd see these things with his own eyes. If I leave this place, he wondered, will I ever see them again?

He ran his hand through his hair, sighing. Despite his curiosity, it was best for Eriale and he to move on quickly and make the most of their lucky break while the hunters were off their trail. "Come on. Fineghal's not here, so I guess we're free to go."

Eriale frowned but agreed. "Where are we going?"

"South, I think. All of the Maerchwood lies ahead of us in that direction. There's a lot of forest to hide in."

They picked their way out of the tower, circling once to take in the full extent of the wreckage. Aeron decided it must have been a slender and graceful structure in its day, easily as tall as the turrets of Raedel Keep but much more elegant. It seemed sad that it stood no longer. With one last glance, he squared his shoulders to face the day's march.

"Aeron!" Eriale reached out for his arm and pointed back at the tower. There, on the fallen wall, sat the white wolfhound of the night before. It seemed much more solid and tangible by daylight, as if its ghostly form had returned to its own rightful body. The hound barked once and trotted down from the old stones, heading south. It paused to look at them, wagged its tail, and barked again. "I think she wants us to follow her," Eriale said.

Aeron glanced around. The forest he knew, the forest he'd grown up in, still surrounded him. But the old elven ruins and the white hound beckoned to him, emblems of a mystery he'd never suspected. He turned without a sound and trotted after the wolfhound, Eriale just a step behind. The hound led them deeper into the forest, choosing faint game runs that Aeron might have missed without her guidance. She stayed well in front of them, sometimes pressing so far ahead that all Aeron could make out was a glimmer of silver in the shadows beneath the trees.

After an hour's march, steep walls of moss-covered rock rose on either side of them. The sound of rushing water grew louder as the hound beckoned them on, now prancing eagerly. They finally emerged into a bowl-shaped gorge. A tall cascade plummeted down the opposite wall, pooling beneath the wet, gray rock. Cold and clear, a stream ran south out of the vale, sluicing over a flat sheet of bedrock at the base of the escarpment. Above Aeron, the forest clung to the lip of the gorge, and an ephemeral rainbow shimmered in the morning light. He gasped in delight, sensing the cool spray on his face.

Sitting cross-legged before the misty plume, eyes closed and hands folded, Fineghal waited. He glanced up and rose to greet his hound as she barked and played in the water that ran past his feet. "My thanks, Baillegh," he said quietly. Then he turned to Aeron and Eriale, springing lightly from boulder to boulder as he came down to meet them. His garb had changed in the daylight to a deep green and russet brown. Aeron could still sense the otherworldly aura mantling the elf lord, but it struck him now as a sense of health, vigor, or rightness—Fineghal *belonged* here. "Welcome, Aeron Morieth and Eriale of Maerchlin. You honor me by accepting my invitation."

Aeron couldn't think of any gracious response. Instead, he asked, "Where are we?"

"This is my home. Or one of them, anyway. All of the Maerchwood is my home, but I require some place to abide. I took the liberty of coming ahead, but I see that Baillegh showed you the way." The elf's expression was difficult to read, wry and self-deprecating, yet not bitter. He gestured behind him to a small satchel that lay beside where he'd been waiting. "If you have not yet eaten, I've some breakfast to share."

"Thank you, Lord Fineghal," Aeron said. "I'm hungry."

Fineghal held up a hand. "Please. I am simply Fineghal, and I'll have no one at my table call me lord." He sat down on a low shelf of stone, and Aeron and Eriale joined him. From the satchel, he produced a number of small cakes, apples and pears, honey, cheese, and a flagon of fruited wine. While they ate, Aeron related the story of his encounter with Phoros and subsequent flight. Fineghal listened, his eyes never leaving Aeron's face.

When Aeron finished, Fineghal looked toward the north and Maerchlin. "They hunt for you still, Aeron. Fortunately they can't find your trail from the tower to this place."

"Another enchantment?" Aeron asked.

"The tower was a place of refuge many years ago. Those

who came to it in need were not meant to be found or followed." Fineghal seemed lost in his recollections for a long moment before he returned his attention to Aeron and Eriale. "So, young Aeron, what do you intend to do now?"

"I can't go home," Aeron said. "I can't even stay close by. I'll have to go somewhere far from here. I'd thought I might live off the land until things calm down, but it might be years before I can return to Maerchlin."

"If ever," Fineghal replied. "You have no kin?"

"No, my—er, no, Fineghal. I was orphaned when I was young. My father, Stiche Morieth, led a revolt against Lord Raedel twelve years ago. He was hanged for it, and many other people with him. Including my mother."

"It seems hard to believe that the Morieths could ever come to grief in Maerchlin," Fineghal mused. "I remember a time when the Morieths were held in great honor, both by your people and by mine. In fact, there were Morieths who married elven folk a long time ago."

Aeron grimaced. "Phoros and his friends used to call me a half-breed for that."

"I can see traces of elven blood in your features. It must have been hard for you, Aeron. In my experience, Chessentans are not forgiving of such faults."

They fell silent for a time, listening to the wind in the trees and the rushing of the water.

"Fineghal, you said the tower was a place of refuge," Eriale asked. "What did you mean by that?"

The elf glanced at her. "Centuries ago, the Maerchwood was home to Calmaercor, a small elven realm akin to the great kingdoms of the Chondalwood or distant Cormanthyr," he said. "In those days, elven lands such as Calmaercor were scattered across all of Faerûn. But the elven folk have many enemies—dragons and orcs, giants and goblins, and even human, with their lands that grew up around our borders. The people of Calmaercor fought the troll kings of the mountains that men call the Riders to the Sky, the fire creatures of the Smoking Mountains, and finally the power of ancient Unther. Our forest, which once stretched from the Adder Peaks to the Sky Riders, has been burned, logged, and settled a piece at a time. And we have been diminished while our old foes have grown more numerous.

"Unlike the elves of Myth Drannor or the hidden fastnesses of other lands, we didn't place our faith in cities or fortresses. Instead, we built watchtowers to hide our people in times of danger. The first were built to thwart the trolls and salamanders, but as humans migrated into what is now Chessenta and brought axe and fire against our forest, we hid from them as well. In time the towers all fell, sniffed out by human sorcery and pulled down one by one."

"What happened to Calmaercor?" Aeron asked.

"Two hundred years past, we decided to withdraw from the Maerchwood and leave these lands to the Chessentans. I am one of the few who remain."

"Why do you stay?" asked Eriale.

Fineghal straightened and swept one arm out to indicate the cascade, the glistening rock, the rich forest. "I cannot bear the thought of leaving," he said. "I miss my people, but having lived under these trees all my life, I can't imagine living anywhere else. There is magic here still."

"You must have lived here a long time," Eriale said.

Fineghal looked up at the sky overhead. It was as bright as burnished brass, promising another day of summer heat. "As humans reckon time, about a thousand years," he said quietly. "The very stars have shifted since my youth. Yet it seems like no more than a long summer's day."

Aeron stared at the elven lord. A thousand years . . . if he lived to be a hundred, Fineghal would have lived his life span ten times over. "By Tchazzar," he murmured, awestruck. "A thousand years . . ."

Fineghal smiled sadly. "Time doesn't touch the elves in the way it touches humans. Although you may find, Aeron, that your elven blood is stronger than your human blood. I suspect that the years will pass lightly for you." With a fluid ease of motion, Fineghal came to his feet and stood over Aeron and Eriale. "I am afraid that I must leave now. I have responsibilities elsewhere within the forest's bounds. You are welcome to remain here, both of you, as long as you like. No humans will find you here. Come and go as you please, Eriale. Aeron, you would be wise to abide here for a time to avoid those who seek you. Perhaps matters will settle themselves in a few months."

"You're leaving us here?" Eriale asked.

The elf nodded gravely. "I ask only that you do not reveal this place to anyone else and that you treat it with care. Harm nothing that lives within this dell." He paused and then added, "I may be back in a month or two, certainly before autumn. Eriale, Baillegh can show you a hidden trail back to Maerchlin." He picked up his thin pack, slung it over one shoulder, and started down the gorge, lightly stepping from stone to stone in the white-rushing stream. Baillegh wagged her tail and followed with a yip.

Aeron and Eriale exchanged puzzled glances. "Did we say something to offend him?" Eriale asked.

"I don't know," Aeron replied. Fineghal's offer was generous. The valley would make an excellent campsite, with good water, plenty of fishing and hunting nearby, and Maerchlin only ten miles away when he chose to go home. But as he watched the noble elf striding off into the emerald shadows of the Maerchwoods, he found that he longed to know more. He could remain here, but he would be a peasant squatting in a king's castle, never understanding the many fine and beautiful things that surrounded him. A strange intuition coalesced in his mind, a certainty that his meeting with Fineghal was no accident, no fortunate coincidence, but the intangible hand of fate at work. Fineghal had said that he'd been waiting for Aeron, but Aeron realized that he had been waiting for Fineghal, too, a sign to shape him into the man he was meant to be.

Without thinking, he splashed across the cold, swift stream and scrambled down the wet gray stone after Fineghal. Desperation gripped his heart. He forgot Eriale, gaping after him. "Wait, Fineghal! Wait a moment!"

The elf turned, his face impassive. "Yes, Aeron?"

He stopped ten paces short of the elf, his breeches darkened to the knee with cold water, breathless and suddenly horrified by his own temerity. What in Faerûn was he thinking about? Fineghal waited patiently as Aeron wrestled with his fears. Closing his eyes, Aeron forced himself to speak what was in his heart. "I—I want to come with you. I want to know more . . . about the elves, about the forest. . . ." His voice trailed off as he fumbled for the words to express what he felt. "I want to know about the old magic."

Fineghal studied him. "Aeron, the power that I wield is no magician's trick to be learned and forgotten on a young man's whim. It is a road that will chain your feet from the moment you set foot upon it. Should you take this step, there will be no turning back for you."

"You were waiting for me," Aeron said. "Why? What's

special about me?"

"More than you might guess, Aeron Morieth."

"Aeron! Have you lost your mind?" Eriale stood pale as a ghost, her mouth open in shock.

Aeron ignored her, his attention fixed on Fineghal. "I can keep up. I'll do anything you ask. I need to see what you see, to learn what you know. I have nothing to lose."

The elf faced Aeron, measuring the boy with a long, serious glance. An hour ago, Aeron would have wilted beneath that searching gaze, unable to confront the scrutiny of the elf's ancient wisdom. But as he met Fineghal's face, the turmoil of emotion in his heart calmed. His destiny was bound up with the elf lord; all his life had led to this confrontation beneath the soaring spray of the cascade.

Fineghal's cool gaze softened. He recognized the unbending purity of purpose that infused Aeron at that moment. "All right, Aeron. I will let you come with me . . . if you consent to a test."

"A test?"

"Yes. Before I try to teach you, I must know whether or not you can be taught."

"Anything!" Aeron replied.

"You should think before you answer so quickly. There may be a time when you discover that your heart's desire is not what it seems." Fineghal shook his head. "I can see it would be useless to ask you to reconsider. Very well, then. Come with me." With a rueful glance at the misted dell, the elf turned and started down along the stream again, moving slower this time. Aeron and Eriale hurried after him. Baillegh skipped and bounded from rock to rock behind them, bringing up the rear.

* * * * *

Fineghal chose a nearly invisible path that wound southeast, crossing the rocky ridge and snaking through the rugged country beyond. By midday, they were deep into the spine of the forest, the great range of tree-mantled hills that ran through the heart of the Maerchwood. Fineghal led them on a steep trail that eventually climbed clear of the trees altogether, bringing them to a windswept spire of weathered stone. "This will do," he announced as Aeron and Eriale collapsed on the ground.

"What is this place?" Eriale gasped.

"The *cumarha midhe*," Fineghal said over his shoulder. "In Common, Forest's Stonemantle. It's a place of strength and purpose, a place of magic."

"This is where you'll test me?" guessed Aeron.

Fineghal turned his ancient eyes on Aeron. Despite himself, the young forester quailed. "Aeron, you will imagine that you are in another place, facing a dire threat. The test varies for every person who attempts it; the place and the peril are locked within your heart. But anything you can imagine, you can attempt."

"Is it dangerous?" Eriale asked.

"Magic is dangerous," Fineghal replied. "If Aeron succeeds, he won't be harmed. If he fails . . . many have sustained injury in tests of this kind."

The girl frowned. "Aeron, maybe you should—"

Aeron cut her off with a curt slash of his hand. "I'm ready," he told Fineghal.

"As you wish," Fineghal said. He raised his hand, pointing at Aeron, and hummed a soft melody under his breath. A strange prickling sensation danced across Aeron's entire body, and the hollow of his chest reverberated with a chordlike resonance that drew his breath away. For the second time in the span of a day, Aeron felt magic at work nearby. He gasped in astonishment, closing his eyes.

The world tumbled away in darkness, vanishing like a bird taking wing at dusk. His heart fluttered in his chest in sudden panic, and his hands scrabbled at the nothingness that embraced him. Before his panic could master him entirely, light silently flared around him. He gaped in amazement at what he saw.

He was standing in the great hall of Raedel Keep.

Every detail was perfect, down to the tiny crack in the flagstone by the door, the stale sunbeams that slanted in through the leaded-glass windows, the dancing of dust motes in the yellow light. Aeron had only been in the great hall half a dozen times, and never alone, but here he stood. A ghostlike flicker caught the corner of his eye, and he saw a pale lord hovering behind him.

I am here, Aeron, Fineghal said silently inside his mind. *This is the test you have created for yourself. Be strong.*

Aeron turned slowly. He could sense the dreamlike quality of the vision, the inordinately still air, the rhythmic beating of his heart in his ears, the impression that things wavered and vanished when he wasn't looking directly at them. Why Raedel Hall? he wondered.

Ghostly shapes began to fill the chamber, becoming darker and more substantial. Phantom guards in black mail lined the walls, holding gleaming halberds. In the empty wooden seat before him, an image of Lord Raedel materialized, a stout man with a blunt, unforgiving face. He scowled past Aeron. Turning his head, Aeron saw the tall figure of a proud, golden-haired man in chains. A cold lance of pain seared his heart. "Father?" he whispered. Behind Stiche Morieth, a young and beautiful woman stood holding the hand of a small, thin boy with a bright mass of yellow curls atop his head. Aeron realized that he was looking at himself as he appeared that day.

The wraiths ignored him. In an eerie absence of sound, Raedel stood and spoke, his eyes cold flecks of granite in his stone face. The beautiful woman sagged to her knees, her open mouth wailing in perfect silence. The boy hid his face in her skirts. The guards seized Stiche by his chains and dragged him away.

The scene faded suddenly, the ghostly figures vanishing. Aeron reeled and shifted his weight. The rough scrape of iron on iron startled him. He looked down and saw that he was chained at his wrists and ankles. The silence was gone, broken by a murmur of voices and clattering weapons and armor. His eyes leapt to the wooden seat, where Phoros Raedel, no phantom but a real and living enemy, leaned back, sneering at him. "Are you prepared to follow your father to the gallows, Morieth?" he hissed. "We should've let you swing the same day he danced on the rope."

Aeron tried to retreat, but the shackles held him fast. Rusty iron abraded his wrists. "Damn you, Phoros!"

"Silence!" Phoros gestured at the guards on either side and rose from his seat. "Take him to the gallows."

Two heavyset guardsmen in black armor caught his arms and dragged him backward, through the hall's great doors and into the bright sunlight of the castle courtyard. Phoros sauntered after him, one hand cocked on the hilt of his sword. Aeron tried to struggle, but it was no use. The guardsmen merely tightened their grip. Their boots clomped on the wooden steps of the gibbet. The weathered planks barked his shins as he tried to get his feet under him. "Let me go!" he roared in desperate fury.

You can stop this, Aeron, said the wraith of Fineghal. The elven lord watched dispassionately from the side, his arms folded. *If you have the will, you can end this or turn it to any course you desire. Defend yourself, escape, do anything you want.*

"But how?" Aeron shouted. One of the faceless guards pinned his arms, while the other slipped the coarse noose over his head. "What do I do?"

Magic begins in the heart and is shaped by the will. Decide what you want, then want it with all your being. Use your will to shape it into what you need.

Aeron gagged as the noose was drawn tight around his neck. For a moment he panicked, too stricken with terror to do anything except thrash and struggle, but then he tried to make sense of Fineghal's cryptic words. *Decide what you want.* . . . Right now, he wanted the noose off his neck and the fetters removed from his limbs. The guards stepped back, clearing the gallows for its grisly task. The structure creaked and swayed slightly in the wind. He kept his attention on the manacles, fiercely wishing them to fall open.

A faint vibration or prickling seemed to hum softly in the center of his chest.

He sharpened his desire to a white-hot fury, driven by his old grief for his parents and his simple desire to live. He became aware of a sea of discordant melodies surrounding him, a chaotic maelstrom of light and life and energy. The wind currents danced and sang in his ears. The faded life of the wood that made up the gallows smoldered dimly, a memory of water and sunlight. Multicolored auras burned around each of the men who stood by the scene, the potent fire of their life-forces burning like brands in the night. The rush he felt in his heart was the echo of his own life, the great magical power of being.

Aeron flailed out, trying to seize the strongest auras and bend them to his will. They seemed to slip through his grasp, and he felt panic rising in his throat.

Shape yourself to the Weave, Aeron. No one can bend the Weave to himself.

The executioner threw his lever, dropping the trapdoor from beneath Aeron's feet. The world wheeled slowly as he felt the aura of his body fluctuate, gaining energy as he started to fall. A fleeting resonance sounded between the wind currents in the courtyard and his own motion, and with a sudden act of will, he altered the energy in his heart, matching the wind again, imitating it, imagining it beneath his feet.

He stood on a column of air, his fall arrested.

Tentatively he reached out, feeling through the stone and earth beneath his feet until he detected a faint resonance that matched the iron chains that bound him. With care, he softened them until they glowed cherry-red and sagged from his legs and arms. He basked in Fineghal's silent approval. "I can do anything?"

A long silence stretched out for a dozen heartbeats as Aeron marveled at the sensation of magic in his grasp. *Anything*, Fineghal replied at last.

Aeron turned to confront the frozen statues of Phoros Raedel, the guards, and the ominous towers of the castle. He listened for a deep, powerful force far beneath him, heat and crushing power from miles within the earth. Fineghal's approval turned to astonishment as Aeron coaxed the incalculable energy upward, linking it to the cold and ordered stones that surrounded him. At the last moment, Fineghal raised a hand in warning, but Aeron was too caught up in his task.

From the center of the courtyard, a gigantic fist of red-hot rock smashed its way into the sky and shattered the castle like a man kicking apart an anthill. The towers almost exploded with the force of their destruction as Aeron deliberately battered Raedel Keep to pieces, allowing the hot fire of his rage to strike again and again. Phoros and the guards disappeared beneath tons of seething lava, crushed and burned past recognition. The white fury burned hotter in Aeron's breast as the world dissolved in raging chaos and incandescent destruction, until he lost himself completely in the storm of violence.

* * * * *

Aeron awoke on the Forest's Stonemantle, weak and disoriented. The sun was red and low in the west, and the air had taken on the cool damp of evening. The dark stone bluffs around the heights gleamed with ruddy light.

Fineghal gazed silently over the forest, wrapped in a cloak that fluttered softly in the wind. Aeron pushed himself upright, studying the elf's tall, weathered figure against the sunset.

"Aeron! You're awake!" Eriale scrambled to her feet beside him, rubbing her arms against the damp breeze. "Fineghal wasn't sure if you would return."

"I'm here, Eriale," Aeron said. He pressed his hand against his head and stood. "I . . . I think I'm all right now."

The elven mage turned at his words. His mouth was a thin white line across his face, and he regarded Aeron with a look of such intensity that the forester took a step back. "What do you remember of your test?" he demanded.

"I was in Raedel Keep. I watched my father hang. And then they were going to hang me. But then . . ."

"Go on."

"I touched the magic," Aeron whispered, staring at his hands with unseeing eyes. He remembered the sweet fire singing in his heart, in his blood. "I wielded magic!"

"Aye. And you used it to destroy Raedel Keep."

"Assuran's tears," he breathed. "Is it truly destroyed?"

"Why?" asked Fineghal. "Is that what you wanted? Is that the best use you can think of for the marvelous gift you possess?" The elf lord trembled with suppressed emotion. With a visible effort, he forced himself to relent. "The castle is unharmed. It was only a test, an illusion you wove for no one but yourself."

"Did . . . did I pass?"

Fineghal barked acerbic laughter. "In the sense that you demonstrated that you can grasp and wield magic, oh, yes, you passed, Aeron. You have extraordinary potential; you nearly exhausted my power in your enthusiasm to raze the castle. I never expected such strength in a stripling."

"Is Aeron going to be a mage?" asked Eriale.

The elven lord nodded. "He must be, Eriale. He will consume himself if he does not learn to wield his power."

"What power?" Aeron asked crossly, rising to face the elf lord. "I've never even thought of magic before today. What's so special about me?"

"You don't understand yet what you are," Fineghal said. His expression softened. "Whether you know it or not, most people can't do what you did; almost anyone can learn to touch the Weave, if only for a moment, but those who can truly perceive it and seize it with will alone are rare indeed. It's your elven blood, Aeron. It runs strong in your veins."

Aeron hugged his chest, pacing away in amazement. The memory of power tantalized him, and he furrowed his brow as he tried to reach out and gather the living magic again. "But I feel nothing now," he said.

"You will learn to see with new eyes, to hear with your heart. My spell of testing allowed you to borrow my strength, if you had it within you to touch the Weave."

"So you'll let me stay and study with you?"

Fineghal's expression became stern. "Yes. But you must swear to abide by my judgment of what you will learn, and when, and how you will employ your knowledge. You have great potential, Aeron, but it is potential for harm as well as good. Do you understand me?"

"I think so," Aeron said slowly. But deep within his heart a dark, triumphant voice added, *He fears me. He fears what I can do.*

"Good," said Fineghal. He held Aeron's gaze for a long moment before turning back to Eriale. "Now, Eriale, let's see you home. Your father must be worried about you." He started down from the windswept cliff.

Aeron scrambled down after him, but Eriale caught his arm as he passed her. She gazed into his face, her open features taut with concern. "Do you know what you're doing, Aeron?"

He attempted a reassuring smile. "Eriale, if you could have touched it, you'd understand. I have to go with him."

She held his eyes for a long moment more and then smiled weakly. "If you think this is right, Aeron, then I won't worry about you." She caught him around the shoulders and hugged him spontaneously. "Just promise me you'll be careful."

Three

Aeron expected Fineghal to begin by teaching him how to summon and control the magic, but he was disappointed. In the weeks that followed, the elven mage barely spoke a word about the working of spells. After they returned Eriale to Kestrel's house and retreated into the depths of the forest, they traveled from sunrise to sunset each day. Fineghal seemed absorbed by his own thoughts, leading the way with an easy, absentminded stride that Aeron found hard to match. Baillegh ranged far ahead, bounding through the green shadows like a silver phantom.

Sometimes they rested in the vine-covered ruins of elven towers, but most of the time Fineghal passed the night in clearings beneath the open sky. By starlight or moonlight, he taught Aeron the names of the creatures and the growing things of the Maerchwood as the elves knew them when the world was young. The ancient elf rarely slept; instead, he gazed at the stars as Aeron drifted off to sleep.

Slowly Aeron learned Tel'Quessir, the elven language, and Fineghal shifted his lessons to his native tongue. "Tel'Quessir is a language made for magic," he explained one night. "It will be much easier for me to teach you when you can read and write in the runes of Espruar."

"Do all mages speak their spells in Elvish?"

"All elven mages do, and some humans. But others study ancient human sorceries and use forgotten human tongues."

Aeron sat up straight, intrigued. "There's more than one way to wield magic?"

Fineghal smiled, a ghostly expression by the clear starlight. "Oh, yes," he said quietly. "When an elf creates a spell, he beckons to the magic, calling to the Weave that surrounds us. The old human ways are different. A human wizard's words force his will upon the Weave around him, demanding compliance."

"Which way is better? More powerful?"

"I know only the elven spells, Aeron; I can't teach you human magic. Since you ask, it is my opinion that human magic is easier to employ and a more dangerous weapon than elven magic. But it exacts a greater toll."

"When will you show me how to cast a spell?"

"Be patient," Fineghal said. "You have much to learn yet." He fell silent for a long time.

The long summer of the Maerchwood passed swiftly, and the short, wet fall came over the forest, drenching the land with cool rains. Aeron and Fineghal had circled the forest several times in the months that he'd journeyed with the elven mage. From one end to the other, the Maerchwood was almost one hundred miles in length. Aeron had seen the golden Maerth Hills to the west, the fiery peaks known as the Smoking Mountains, and the wild rushing waters of the untamed Winding River. He was beginning to gain a sense of the immeasurable moods of the woodland, the pace of life in different regions and in different seasons.

Hardened by his endless trek, he could now keep up with Fineghal without trying, and he moved through the trackless maze of the forest's hidden depths with the skill and silence of a full-blooded elf. On a clear, cold day late in the season, Fineghal led Aeron to a dark, rock-walled valley in the heart of the forest, a place Aeron knew as Banien's Deep. They halted by a cold, rushing stream that tumbled out of the stony heights and into the forest below. Fineghal shrugged his slim pack from his shoulders and surveyed the clearing. "This will do," he announced.

"Why are we stopping?" Aeron asked.

"I think it's time for your first lesson."

Aeron blinked. "My first lesson? What have I been doing for the past three months?"

"Well, you've learned to speak passable Elvish, and you've learned a little about the forest. Any elf would have known these things before he began his studies," Fineghal said over his shoulder. "Now we can move on to the working of magic."

Aeron remembered the intoxication in his heart when he'd touched the Weave in Fineghal's test. He'd almost forgotten the sensation of rightness, of strength, that he'd tasted before. I will do it, he thought proudly. I will shape magic with my own hands, like one of the great wizards of old. I will do it! He scrambled to his feet, shrugging his pack to the ground. "I'm ready."

Fineghal regarded Aeron with his customary detachment. The young woodsman waited, his keen eyes hungry with anticipation. "There are two things you must do in order to work magic . . . to cast a spell, as humans say," Fineghal began. "First you must summon the energy for your spell. We live in a magical world, Aeron, surrounded by unseen powers and forces. Every living creature carries a spark of magic, but the very stones, earth, wind, and waters multiply this living magic a thousandfold."

"So magic comes from the land around us?"

"Yes and no. The life of the world around us is the power that makes magic possible, but it is a force without direction, without volition—unrealized potential. In order to tap this energy, we immerse ourselves in the Weave."

Aeron frowned, thinking. "Aren't magic and the Weave the same thing?"

"Almost, but not quite. The Weave is the soul of magic, the manifestation of all the untapped energy around us. It is the surface that we can perceive and shape to our purposes."

"I don't understand."

Fineghal steepled his long, graceful fingers before him. "A fire can be used for hundreds of useful things—warming you in the winter, cooking food, heating iron that it might be worked into useful shapes, and so on. You might say that wood contains the potential for fire, just as the world around us contains the potential for magic." The elf lord smiled and picked up a small piece of deadwood near his seat by the stream. He tossed it lightly to Aelies. "Cook your dinner with this stick."

Aeron shrugged and reached into his pouch to retrieve his flint and steel. Fineghal held up his hand and laughed. "Stop. What are you doing?"

"Getting my flint," Aeron replied, mystified.

"And why do you do that?"

"To start the wood burning, of course!"

"So, in order to release the potential within that branch, you must strike a spark. The fire within that old branch sleeps until you find a way to release it. Similarly, the Weave is the means by which the potential for magic is transformed into the shape a wizard seeks."

"I think I understand," Aeron said slowly.

"Now, wielding the Weave is only part of casting a spell. The other part is shaping the spell with your will. You've seen me gesture or heard me speak words under my breath when I work magic. I was creating the pattern for the magical energy to follow."

"You've lost me again," Aeron said bitterly.

Fineghal grimaced. "Here's another analogy. Let's say that you want to make a house. Living trees represent the unshaped potential, the raw magic, of your effort. The Weave shapes the living wood into a form you can work with, finished boards and planks ready for your hand. Finally you'll need tools and skill to work the finished wood into the form you desire. This is your spell."

Aeron nodded, imagining the work he'd put into crafting the bow strapped to his back. Magic required raw material and a tool to work it. That made sense. "Is there any difference in what kind of magic you gather or the tools you use to shape it?" he asked.

"Yes and no. The Weave is the same in all spells. But there are all kinds of purposes to which this energy may be bent—the dark magic of necromancy, the fragile veils of illusion, and so on. I have always studied the magic of wind, stone, fire, and water, the elements around us. Most of my learning lies in spells of this sort."

Fineghal pointed at the dark, cool stream beside them. "Here. Observe what I do." He fell silent, furrowing his brow in concentration. With one hand, he reached toward the water, his hand turned to one side. Aeron shivered as he felt the touch of magic at work, the cool flutter in the center of his chest. Fineghal murmured a few words in Elvish.

On the surface of the stream, a knuckle of water formed and then rose into the air, taking the shape of a slender arm and silvery hand. It hung, shimmering wetly in the air, defying gravity, as Fineghal continued to guide it with gentle motions of his hand. The watery hand reached out to touch Aeron's outstretched fingers. It felt cold and damp, but left no moisture on his hand. With a wry smile, Fineghal released his spell. The watery limb lost its cohesiveness, returning to the stream with a splash. Aeron grinned in childlike delight. "Bring it back!" he pleaded.

Fineghal shook his head. "Alas, I cannot."

"Have you exhausted the magic?"

The elf laughed. "No, not by any means. I could power a spell dozens of times greater than that with the magic that surrounds us in this place!"

"Then why can't you do it again?"

"Because I do not have that spell in my mind anymore. You see, Aeron, any wizard may speak a spell only once, and then it is gone. In shaping the magic, the tool is expended, destroyed, used up in the creation. A trained wizard, like myself, may hold dozens of spells in his mind, but each time I work magic, the shape of the spell vanishes." Fineghal glanced up, taking in Aeron's bewilderment. He sat back on his heels with a sigh. "One more analogy, then. A spell is like an arrow. Once you fire it from the bow of your mind, it is gone."

"But you can retrieve an arrow," Aeron said.

"Well, these arrows you cannot. If you have three spell arrows in your quiver, you can carry them with you indefinitely, but once you speak the words and shape the magic to give it form, a spell performs its purpose and vanishes. You'll have to make a new arrow in order to work that spell again."

"How do you do that?"

Fineghal groaned and rubbed at his temples. "By the stars, I forgot how many questions lived inside a young human. Trust me, Aeron, we'll get to that when it's time. Let's return to my original intent in this lesson, which was to show you how to speak a spell. Do you recall the words I spoke when I made the hand of water appear?"

Aeron thought for a moment. "*Allagh—*"

"Wait, don't speak them! Even if you don't have the spell ready, it's not a good idea. Save the words for the casting. Now, did you see how I held my hands?"

Awkwardly Aeron tried to mimic the gesture he had seen Fineghal perform. The elf reached out and corrected his posture. "With your will, you summon the magic. With the words, you shape it. And with your hand, you hold it in the place you want." He reached into his belt pouch and produced a small, smooth stone. Engraved on the stone's upper surface was a curving sign or diagram. "Here. Examine this sigil and lock its shape in your mind."

"What's this?"

"It's the shape of a spell. I keep most of my enchantments as sigils drawn on waterworn stones. Other wizards write them out as formulae in great tomes, or record them as long pronouncements or rhymes in old tongues. It doesn't matter, really. But this symbol, with the words and the gesture, will give you the key to unlocking the magic and making the spell."

Aeron took the stone and peered at it. He glanced up at Fineghal, who nodded. He looked back down at the stone, studying the simple curve and whorl. "Okay, I've got it."

"No you don't. You'll know when it's fixed in your mind." Fineghal set his back to a tree and stretched his legs out in front of him. "Stare at it intently. Forget everything around you until nothing exists but that one simple sign."

Aeron shot another look at Fineghal, but the elf was holding up another stone, gazing at it with an absent expression on his face. He shrugged and returned his attention to his own stone. Time passed, and he almost felt that he was sinking into the one small symbol, and then finally it was *in* his mind, a curved bar of stone that lay just under his tongue like a word he hadn't given voice to yet. He yelped in surprise. "Fineghal!"

The elf looked up. "I know that look. It's in your mind?"

"I think . . . yes! Yes, it's right there."

"The spell you've just committed to memory is a simple cantrip called water hand. Now, in order to cast the spell, you'll first concentrate on the symbol in your mind. While you do that, you'll reach out to gather a tiny bit of the Weave around you. You know what that feels like already; try to borrow some from the stream, here, since that is appropriate to the spell. Once you have touched the water's energy, speak the words and make the gesture." Fineghal paused, measuring Aeron. "Are you ready?"

Aeron nodded. He summoned the stone's symbol to the forefront of his mind. Distantly he became aware of the play of the Weave around him—the rushing of the stream, the sighing of the wind, the green and rich vitality of the trees and grasses nearby, his own bright spark. He concentrated on the stream. The cold water seemed to wash over him, a chilling, vaguely frightening sensation. Alarmed, he barked out the words, remembering to lift his hand just in time.

Before him, the water stirred and surged. A crude pillar of coherent liquid rose free of the stream, groping blindly as Aeron struggled to control it. It started to sag, and he desperately reached out and caught it with all of his strength. Suddenly the pillar loomed over him like a small mountain of cold water, arching toward him as he scrambled away. "Fineghal, help!" he cried. As his concentration broke, so did the spell, and a deluge of icy water drenched him completely. He spluttered and shook his head.

"Congratulations, Aeron. You've just cast your first spell," Fineghal said, laughing. "Next time we'll work on your control. But that was well done, anyway." A wide, proud smile brightened his ancient features, and even Baillegh yelped playfully, dancing in delight.

Aeron scowled at the elf's amusement and began to wring out his shirt. "I'll get it right next time. You'll see!"

* * * * *

In the months that followed, Aeron practiced the speaking of spells over and over again under Fineghal's tutelage. The fall of that year, the one later named the Year of the Helm, was long and glorious, with bright, clear days and cold, starry nights. Aeron virtually ignored it. He drove himself to master each cantrip and enchantment that Fineghal demonstrated, refusing rest until he'd conquered anything the elven mage placed before him. A hidden flame or spark in his spirit that he'd never suspected ignited with the thirst to excel, flaring like a brilliant hunger.

Fineghal viewed magic as an art, an expression of harmony with nature, concerning himself with the why of things. Aeron's intelligence and temperament ran in a different direction. He aspired to an unfailing technical perfection, always asking *how* something could be done. Fineghal endured his apprentice's intense drive with patience and grace.

As the good weather finally came to an end and the ceaseless rains of Uktar descended over the Maerchwood, Fineghal and Aeron settled for the winter in a lonely white tower overlooking the white waters of the Winding River. It was the only one of the ancient watchtowers still standing, and it served as Fineghal's home. The wizard called it Caerhuan, the Storm Tower. The narrow windows of the tower's study looked out over the green, spray-misted gorge, and its paneled walls were carved with intricate woodland scenes by long-vanished elven craftsmen.

By the ceaseless crescendo of the river below and the rattle of cold rain against elven glass, Aeron devoured every scrap of knowledge that Fineghal shared with him. As he'd promised, he learned swiftly and gained in skill. He was blessed with an instinctive grasp of the Weave, a graceful and easy command of the flow of magic around him. He lacked only the knowledge of the spells to unlock this gift, and one by one he drove himself to learn their names, their purpose, and the details of their working.

Aeron learned that the price a wizard paid for his power lay in endless hours of studying spells, casting them briefly, and returning to the tedious process of memorization again. While he could not retain the shape of a spell once he spoke it, the record remained in Fineghal's collection of enigmatic glyphstones. "The most powerful of my spells require dozens of sigil-marked stones, each of which must be studied in exact order to lock the spell's shape in my mind. At any given time, twenty to thirty are in my memory," Fineghal explained. "So you might say that I own more arrows than I can carry. I must decide which I will take with me before I set out on a journey."

Aeron grimaced. "I have a hard time keeping more than three or four simple ones straight," he said.

"You are still a novice, Aeron. There is much you have yet to learn." Fineghal drew one of his stones from his pouch and held it between his fingers, lost in a moment of reverie. "In time, you will need to shape your own spellbooks. You cannot rely on mine forever." Absently he stared out the window, falling into a silence that lasted for the rest of the day.

As the months passed, Fineghal proved to be a patient but silent tutor. When Aeron asked questions, the ageless elf directed him to the ordered shelves of his library. It was not unusual for Aeron to pass days at a time without seeing Fineghal; sometimes the wizard ventured out of the tower to walk the forest's eastward slopes, Baillegh at his heels, while on other occasions, he fell into absent reveries that lasted for hours at a time.

While the young forester spent many hours poring over old elven histories and discussing the nature of magic, it was not in Aeron's nature—or Fineghal's, for that matter—to spend too much time indoors. From time to time, the elven lord allowed Aeron to set aside the books for a few days and accompany him on his treks through the forest. Under the early morning frosts of winter, the forest was breathtakingly beautiful, alive with the constant trickle of ice and water from every branch and rocky face.

On one occasion early in the winter, a week or so before the end of the year, Fineghal sent Aeron to the tower library to search out a text on the ancient history of the elven folk. "You've asked me enough questions about the old lands of the elves," he said. "Go read about them for yourself." With an exasperated sigh, Aeron returned to the library and began to search for the text in question.

Fineghal's library was not very well organized. The ancient elf had read every tome within, and his memory for such things was so phenomenal that he almost never needed to refer to them again. Even if he did, the elven sorcerer welcomed the excuse to ransack his bookshelves and surprise himself with what he happened across while in search of the book he really wanted. Like him, Aeron could rarely resist the urge to rummage and wander through the hundreds of tomes, plates, and scrolls.

An hour or more passed as Aeron explored the depths of Fineghal's collection, browsing through a dozen books that had nothing whatsoever to do with elven history. He'd just given up on one corner of the shelf when he spied a slender spellbook in a tooled-leather jacket. "What's this?" he asked himself. Fishing it out, Aeron moved over in front of a window and began to page through it.

The cover was marked with an unknown wizard's sigil, but the frontispiece was a thin sheet of beaten gold, stamped with arcane lettering. Aeron peered at it for a moment before he recognized the script as ancient Elvish. "*Rhymes of Magic and Wonder?*" he murmured. "A bardic spellbook . . ." His curiosity piqued, Aeron carried the book to a table and sat down to read. He skimmed over a pair of simple spells he already knew, past a dozen or more that he didn't, and then found himself hovering over a page marked, "The Changing of Form."

The changing of form, Aeron thought. He glanced out the window, where a lonely hawk wheeled and cried over the rocky cliffs. Involuntarily he glanced at the door, even though he knew Fineghal had left the tower to walk the nearby forest. So far, Aeron had spent his time working with lesser magics until he had a number of those well in hand. But this seemed a much more formidable spell, an enchantment of some potency. I wish I'd known how to do this when Raedel and his friends set after me last summer, he thought bitterly. To turn into a bird and fly away . . . or to change into a bear and tear their arms off, that would be something. I'd never need to fear him again.

"Fineghal would be angry," Aeron said aloud. He hadn't attempted to lock a spell in his mind using rhymes such as this book contained; he'd only attempted the feat with Fineghal's spell tokens. He took a deep breath and composed himself, studying the long set of lyrics, trying to impress them into his memory. After an hour, he finally rubbed his eyes and admitted defeat, leaning back. It's a rhyme, he thought. Maybe you commit it to memory by reading it aloud.

Steeling himself, Aeron began to read aloud the lilting words of the spell. Even as he spoke the first words, he sensed the gentle stirrings of the Weave at work, while the printing in the spellbook vanished as he read it. He recognized two unpleasant facts at the same time: first of all, he was actually casting the spell, not committing it to memory; second, he would have to read swiftly and certainly in order to finish it before the words vanished altogether. Trying to remain calm, Aeron picked up his pace, until the words tumbled from his mouth in a high-pitched declamation that rang throughout the tower.

A shimmering emerald glow began to play over his hands and arms. Aeron kept reading, pushing his wonder and growing fear to the back of his mind. He considered abandoning the enchantment altogether, but decided that he could carry through with it. "I can do it," he muttered aloud during a break in the lyrics. Then he plunged into the last stanza, blindly channeling all his strength into the effort before him.

He spoke the last word, and his world exploded into emerald agony. Terrible pains wracked his entire body, shooting through each joint. His skin flared with pain as if liquid fire had been poured over his body. Aeron screamed, and in midshriek, his howl changed to the raucous cry of a seabird. The pain receded almost as quickly as it had started, leaving him floundering on the floor awkwardly.

He blinked his eyes, trying to make sense of his surroundings. There was something wrong with his vision;

the colors were washed out, and there seemed to be a dark bar in the center of his view, making it difficult to look straight ahead. He turned his head to one side, and suddenly realized that his body had changed to that of a seagull. It worked! he thought exultantly. Experimentally he spread his wings, wondering how one actually took flight.

His wing tips began to glow green. He opened his mouth to protest, but nothing but a squawk came out. The horrible agony of the change came over him again, even worse than before. In a matter of moments, his feathered wings shrank and vanished as he writhed on the floor. He thrashed his legs, but a dark, scaly coil twisted through his fading eyesight. When the pain stopped, he tried to right himself but only succeeded in rolling over. What am I now? he thought miserably. As it turned out, he didn't have time to concern himself with the question, since he started to change again almost immediately.

This time the green fire left him as some kind of mouse or rat, lost in the now titanic library. He chittered in fear and ran in a small circle, uncertain of whether he wanted to remain in this shape or to chance something worse. The spell gave him no choice, and after an eternity of bone-snapping agony, he found himself encased in an armored shell, with ridiculously tiny limbs.

Something seized him and lifted him into the air. From an impossible distance, Fineghal's face peered into his. The elf spoke, but Aeron heard not a sound. He tried to reply, but he couldn't tell if he'd even opened his mouth. With a thump, he was set down on the table, and he watched the gigantic figure gesticulate with his hands. The emerald aura flickered brightly, and Aeron endured one final transformation. When he was capable of coherent speech again, Aeron looked up shakily at Fineghal and said, "Thank you. How did you end it?"

"A simple dispelling," Fineghal snapped. "May I ask how you started it, Aeron?"

Weakly Aeron pointed at the leather-covered book. "I read it out of that tome."

Fineghal's eyes widened. "Do you have any idea how foolish that was? How easily you might have been killed? Think, Aeron! What if you had changed yourself into a fish? You would have asphyxiated right here on the floor!"

"I only wanted to see if I could do it," Aeron replied.

"Then why not throw yourself off the roof of the tower to see if you've learned to fly?" Fineghal barked.

"If you didn't want me to read some of these tomes, Fineghal, you should have warned me," Aeron retorted. "How was I to know that what I did was dangerous?"

"I placed more trust in your common sense." Fineghal snorted and turned away, examining the book. He looked at the blank page in disgust. "Do you realize that you also erased a very rare and valuable copy of that spell?"

"Erased? How?"

"It's possible to cast spells of this sort by reading them out of the book. But the magical energy must come from somewhere, so if it was not locked in your mind, it consumed itself. It is gone."

"I tried to memorize it, but I couldn't," Aeron said.

"That's simple. It was beyond your skill. That should have warned you against your course of action, Aeron." Fineghal sighed and sat down. He scratched Baillegh behind the ears, staring out the window for a long time before he looked back to Aeron. "Yet this was not entirely your fault. I too share some blame for this. I should have paid more attention to ensuring that you were aware of the dangers your studies may pose."

"I did not mean to erase your spell."

The elf lord glanced up at him. "I know you did not. But perhaps it is time for you to have a spellbook of your own. You've borrowed mine for long enough."

"I'll mark stones, like yours?"

"That depends. There are dozens of methods for recording the shape of a spell, Aeron. We taught the bards of old to keep their dweomers as poems in ancient Tel'Quessir, and many human wizards have borrowed from this tradition." Fineghal nodded at the spellbook open on the library table. "You have some passing familiarity with this now, I see."

"What's the best method?" Aeron asked.

"It depends on the wizard. I chose to mark signs on stones because it worked . . . and so I carry a pouch of stones at my hip, and will do so for as long as I practice magic." Fineghal rose and moved to the door. He took down Aeron's bow from its place on the wall. "I've noticed that you are a fair hand at fletching."

"My father was a fletcher," Aeron replied. "And a bow-maker, too. Kestrel taught me some of my father's craft to help me honor his memory." He glanced at the weapon in Fineghal's hands, and the intent of the wizard's remark struck him. "Could I mark a spell on an arrow?" he wondered aloud.

"I'd use a length of wood a little shorter and stouter than an arrow's shaft, but the idea is sound," Fineghal replied. "The type of wood you choose, the way you shape it, the design you trace . . . you could represent a complicated enchantment with ease."

"Do other wizards mark their spells in this way?"

Fineghal smiled. "My master of old did, long years ago. He called them *duarran* glyphwoods." With a glance outside at the pale winter daylight, he continued. "It's an hour or two until nightfall. Why don't we see if you can find a form for the water hand in a piece of driftwood?"

* * * * *

Within a week, Aeron had carved his first three glyphwoods. As winter slowly slipped away and the rains of spring returned to the Maerchwood, he struggled to master as many of Fineghal's signs as the elf lord would allow, adding to his store of knowledge. With painstaking care, he crafted a sturdy leather pouch to hold the duarran and wove simple spells of preservation and protection over the growing collection.

Despite Aeron's progress, or perhaps because of it, Fineghal began to exercise more control over the spells that Aeron chose to study. A number of the elf lord's sigils marked spells of war, enchantments that could wreak grievous harm to the wizard's enemies by fire, lightning, ice, or subtle terrors of the mind. But Fineghal discouraged Aeron from these enchantments, giving him instead spells of learning, concealment, and evasion. Aeron ached to wrestle with more difficult topics, but Fineghal simply deflected him with more reading, more research, and quiet challenges to learn more of the forest around him.

Finally Aeron openly broached the matter as they gathered their traveling gear and prepared to leave Caerhuan for the summer. "I would like to study some new spells," he told Fineghal. "The incandescent missile, or maybe the charm of blindness."

Fineghal considered in silence as he pondered which of his books to take with him. "Those are dangerous enchantments," he said at length.

"I'm ready for them. They're within my skill."

"I do not doubt that, Aeron. I suspect you have learned your lesson about tampering with magic beyond your abilities. However, I question the wisdom of teaching you spells of that sort."

"Why? I wouldn't use them wrongly."

Fineghal gave up on the bookshelf and turned his full attention to Aeron, his face taut and serious. "Some would say that any use of those spells is wrong. Wielding magic as a weapon demonstrates shortsightedness, a weakness of the will. There is always a better way."

"But many of your spells are meant for battle," Aeron said. "No one would dare raise his hand against you."

Fineghal snorted. "I learned the greater portion of those many years ago, Aeron, when I was not so old or wise as I am now. And my skill in battle, such as it is, has provoked more fights than it's deterred."

"If I do find myself in a fight, wouldn't it be common sense to know a spell or two that can end it quickly? I don't want to be able to kill people with a word. I just want to know that I can defend myself if I have to."

"Answer me this, Aeron: If you had no spell that could serve as a weapon, would you seek out a fight or avoid it?"

Aeron snorted. "Avoid it, of course."

"That's why I'm hesitant to teach you spells that might lead you into a fight you can't win. If you know you cannot prevail, you'll make sure that you don't find yourself in a dangerous situation. In my experience, if you give a boy a sword, he starts thinking that it's the answer to any problem that comes along." Fineghal glanced away, rubbing his temple. "You're young yet, Aeron. Despite your best intentions, you're impulsive and rash. I'd rather not encourage these traits if I can help it."

"You've used your magic in battle before, haven't you?" Aeron pressed. "Were you wrong when you did that?"

"I won't be baited, Aeron," Fineghal said sharply. "The matter is closed. Now, make certain that you have packed the books you wish to study over the next few weeks."

Aeron bit off his response and stomped away. Some mage he'd be if he was beaten to a bloody pulp by the first brigand to corner him, a headful of safe and useless spells in his mind!

He resolved to change Fineghal's mind one way or another. For the next few weeks, he badgered the elven lord several times a day on the topic, until even Fineghal's elven patience began to wear thin. The unfinished argument soured Aeron's taste for elven lore, and their wanderings in the Maerchwood's golden glens and green hills became a series of tedious hikes and silent, tense evenings by the campfire. Aeron knew his limits. He was capable of mastering the enchantments in question and had the common sense not to use them unless he had to. Fineghal's suspicion and reticence abraded his nerves and challenged him to show that he was more advanced than the elf lord believed.

The festival of Midsummer approached, a time of dancing and celebration in Aeron's home. For the first time in his studies, loneliness crept into his heart. Even though his mind was fully engaged each and every day with the boundless learning Fineghal offered him, Aeron still missed Kestrel and Eriale. I'd be a dead man if I returned to Maerchlin and Phoros caught me, he decided. But what if I could ensure that I wouldn't be caught? I could come and go as I pleased.

Fineghal was still in the habit of setting off by himself for a day or two, leaving Aeron in the campsite they'd last moved to. For months now, he'd allowed Aeron to keep one or two of his spellstones at a time in order to create a glyphwood of his own based on Fineghal's token. Over the spring, Aeron had recorded a dozen spells in this way, including a minor illusion that could change the appearance of an object. This was the key element in his plan.

The green, humid heat of Flamerule found wizard and student in the cascade-misted glen where Aeron and Eriale had met Fineghal. After a few days of exploring the nearby area and discussing elven history by night, Fineghal decided to cross the forest to check on the western woodlands. "I may rest under a different tree every night for my spirit's ease, but I roam the Maerchwood to watch over it as well," he said as they rested by the stream that evening. "I have a feeling that trouble's brewing near Oslin, and I'd better go look into it."

"Can I come?" Aeron asked hopefully.

Fineghal shook his head. "No. I mean to travel fast and return within a day or two. And to be honest, I want to strike a little fear into the hearts of those bandit lords who are cutting into the forest, and it's better if I don't have to watch out for you as well. You'll be fine here."

"Hmmmph. I guess so." Aeron's heart skipped as he realized that this was the opportunity he'd waited for. Calming himself, he asked, "May I study the spider's climb while you're away? I'd like to carve another glyphwood."

Fineghal glanced up absently. "Of course. I should have no need of it. Help yourself."

Aeron stood, dusted off the seat of his breeches, and moved over to the pouch that held Fineghal's spells. The wizard had set it down near his bedroll. Deliberately suppressing the urge to steal a guilty look over his shoulder, Aeron spoke the word of passage necessary to open the pouch and reached within, feeling for the desired stone. His fingers brushed over the cool blue slate that held the spell of spider's climb . . . and moved on to grasp the stone called the fire hand. He removed both stones, concealing the fire stone in his sleeve.

From his left sleeve, he removed a red, egg-shaped rock that was a perfect duplicate for fire hand. He'd used his spell of seeming to create the fake earlier that day. Unless Fineghal actually examined that particular stone, he'd never detect Aeron's theft. Shaking like a leaf, he closed the pouch and straightened.

"Find it?"

Aeron gave Fineghal a nervous smile and showed him the blue stone marked with the climbing spell. The second spellstone was hidden in his sleeve. "Right here. I think red maple would suit it well."

"For your glyphwood? Yes, that should work." If Fineghal suspected anything, he showed no outward sign of it, and with no further words, he returned his attention to the smooth stones of the spell he readied. Aeron quickly retreated to his place by the fire, his heart pounding. He was horrified by his own audacity, but now that he had taken this step, he'd have to work fast to copy both spells before Fineghal returned.

At length, Fineghal dropped the stones he held back into his pouch, picked up his few belongings, and whistled to Baillegh. The white wolfhound shook herself and stood, tail wagging. "No time like the present, as humans are wont to say," Fineghal said. "Be careful not to stray too far from the vale, Aeron. You're near Maerchlin, and you never know when one of the lord's men might be about. I should be back in a day or two." He touched his hand to his brow in the silent farewell of the elves and vanished into the starlit night.

Aeron waited an hour, to make certain that Fineghal was well on his way. When he was sure that he wouldn't be caught, he slipped fire hand from his sleeve. The stone seemed a hot accusation in his hand. With a scowl, he silenced his reservations and began his work. If he finished the fire spell but didn't master the spider climb, he could tell Fineghal that he'd had trouble with the translation, gaining an extra few days to finish his study of the spell sigils. "I'll need a wood that burns clean and hot," he murmured, considering the spellstone. "A dry old bit of deadwood, maybe hickory. And I'll need to find a way to keep it away from the rest of my glyphwoods." He couldn't ever let Fineghal see the *duarran* he'd make from the stolen stone.

Of course, there was also the question of how he would smuggle fire hand back into Fineghal's pouch without alerting the wizard. Cold apprehension gripped Aeron's heart as he realized the depth of his duplicity. It might have been a petty theft, one that would do Fineghal no harm at all, but the elven lord trusted him. Stilling the protests of his conscience, Aeron stood and began to search for a suitable length of wood.

Four

A long week passed, and Fineghal did not return to the thunder and mist of the cascade's glen. Aeron mastered both spells with ease and then devised a hidden pouch in his bundle of glyphwoods to conceal the intricate shapes and markings of the fire spell.

On the morning of the twelfth day of Fineghal's absence, Aeron awoke to another hot, hazy day typical of high summer in the Maerchwood. It was the ninth day of Eleasias, one year to the day since he'd fled Maerchlin. A full year, he wondered. It didn't seem possible, yet his breeches and sleeves were a little too short, and his shirt felt tight across the chest. He washed in the cold, clear waters of the stream, shaking his golden mane dry and relishing the cool, damp air of the glen.

Climbing out of the swift-moving stream, he searched the green, wet walls of Fineghal's dell for some sign of the mage's return. Nothing but cool mists, water-shaped boulders, and the lowering trees above met his gaze. Aeron was usually comfortable being alone, but today the silence and solitude weighed on his spirit. On a sudden impulse, he dressed, packed his bow and pouch of glyphwoods, and set out toward Maerchlin. He wanted to see with his own eyes how the town fared.

He covered the twelve-odd miles to Maerchlin in the long, still hours of morning, trotting effortlessly. As he approached the village, Aeron slowed his pace and used all of his woodcraft to circle toward Kestrel's house without setting foot on the villagers' runs and lanes. He emerged from the forest in the broad cleared lands behind Kestrel's homestead, pausing in the warm shadows of the tree line to gaze out at the cottage and farmyard. It was silent; the barn was open and dark. Abandoning caution, he broke out of the forest's cover and trotted forward, his face taut with worry.

The house was empty.

He circled it three times to make sure, searching each

room. Broken crockery was scattered by the hearth, and every chest or cupboard in the place had been ripped open and its contents dumped on the floor. As far as Aeron could tell, nothing was missing except for Kestrel and Eriale. It was clear that the place had been searched, and there might have been a struggle, but there was nothing that could tell him what had happened.

Aeron swore and kicked angrily at the wreckage. He stepped out the front door, looking across the brown rooftops of the village at the walls of Castle Raedel. Could he risk approaching one of the neighbors to ask after Kestrel and Eriale? Finally he turned away and retreated to the safety of the forest. He didn't dare enter Maerchlin, not without a chance to plan and prepare. Raedel would have no mercy on him if he were caught, and whatever had happened to Kestrel's household had happened weeks or months ago.

By the time he returned to the cascade's glen, it was late in the afternoon, and the small dell was shadowed by the sheer tree-crowned bluffs on all sides. Aeron was tired and hot; a tight knot of concern was clenched under his breastbone, and it dragged at his steps like a physical burden. He collapsed on his bedroll unceremoniously, staring out over the darkening forest.

"Greetings, Aeron. If I'd been a goblin, I could have run you through." Fineghal stood from the shadows, a glimmer of moonlight rising from a dark, still pond. The elven lord seemed nearly ethereal in substance, as if he lacked the strength to tether himself to the world around him. Fineghal rarely showed fatigue, but Aeron could see at a glance that he was exhausted.

"Fineghal! I—I was worried about you!" Aeron scrambled to his feet. "What happened?"

The wizard sighed and moved closer, taking his customary place across from Aeron. With a brief word and a gesture, he caused a small dancing flame to appear in the stone circle they used for their campfire, when they needed one. Aeron noticed that the glen was unnaturally cool, despite the warmth and stillness of the air in the forest. Fineghal shivered visibly, chilled in some way that Aeron could not perceive. "As I feared, trouble was indeed on my doorstep," he began. "All of southern Chessenta is in chaos these days. For years now, the land's been ruled by brigands, rebel noblemen, and mercenary kings who spend their time bickering over their meager holdings like starving dogs fighting for a scrap of food. More than a few have decided to win a fortune from the Maerchwood by pillaging the ruins of Calmaercor, so every now and then I must . . . discourage them. It is usually not too difficult to do so."

"What was different this time?"

"I discovered that Baerskos of Villon had hired a wizard of his own, fearing the reputation of the Storm Walker. He set a trap for me."

"You fought Baerskos? Are you hurt?"

Fineghal shook his head. "I survived. I was forced to employ many powerful spells. Baerskos and his armsmen are no more, although I don't doubt that some other ruthless outlaw will take his place in a decade or two, with the same dream of carving out a kingdom for himself."

"What of the wizard?"

Fineghal warmed his hands by the flame, staring into the flickering light. "I was forced to deal with him as well. A dangerous conjurer, skilled in the raising of fiends and horrors from the darkest depths of the netherworld. I couldn't allow such a creature to set evils of that sort loose on the world. He was nearly a match for me."

Aeron was stunned. "I thought you were the greatest mage of them all! You know spells that I could never dream of mastering."

"I am far from the greatest of mages, Aeron. And even if I claimed that title, I should be far from the wisest. My strength is in knowledge and skill. But there are those who take an easier road to power—like the conjurer I faced in Villon—and if power is all a wizard cares to master, he can be a dangerous enemy indeed." Fineghal rubbed his hands together and sighed again. "It was a dreadful contest, one that I nearly lost. He drew me into the planes of darkness and shadow that lie alongside our own, where he was strong and I was weak. There was something wrong with his sorcery, a taint or corruption that fed on the darkness."

Otherworlds and fiends . . . Aeron shuddered at the references. He'd heard the tales, and a few of Fineghal's tomes attempted to explain the mysterious spheres and planes that lay beyond Faerûn, but he'd never thought that he might speak to someone who had been there. It unnerved him to think that a world of invisible peril surrounded him, a world that might reach out to claim him should he misspeak a spell or set foot in the wrong place at the wrong time.

Fineghal unclasped his pouch of spellstones, dropping it to the ground. "How did matters stand in Maerchlin?"

"Maerchlin?" Aeron glanced up in guilty surprise.

"You went back there while I was in Villon, did you not? I thought that was where you'd gone when I returned here and found you missing." Fineghal's eyes fastened on Aeron. "It was not a wise thing to do, Aeron. You know that Raedel's men consider you a criminal."

"If I'd known that I was going to be driven from my home, I might've done something to earn it," Aeron growled. "I could have shot Phoros dead instead of stabbing him in the shoulder." He sighed and looked up at Fineghal. "It's been a year since I've seen my home. When you vanished for days and days, I started to get restless. I knew Maerchlin was close by, and I wanted to see how Kestrel and Eriale fare."

"A year? It didn't seem so long," Fineghal mused. "But I forget that a year means so much more to one of your age than it does to me. I scarcely noticed." He returned his attention to Aeron, his piercing gaze holding the young forester's eyes. Imperceptibly the elf's detachment relaxed. "Not all was well?"

"No. Kestrel's house was empty. They weren't there."

"Ah. You fear they've come to grief?"

"I can't see why they would leave. Kestrel's not wealthy, but he's got everything he needs on his lands. Raedel must have imprisoned him or driven him away, and Eriale, too." Aeron sighed. "Probably to get back at me."

"They don't have kinfolk somewhere else?"

"No," Aeron replied. "Kestrel was the last of his family. He lost his brothers in the rebellion of thirteen years ago. And Eriale, of course, has no one but her father." The more Aeron thought about it, the more concerned he was. "There's something wrong here. I've got to find out if they're all right or not."

"If you even set foot in Maerchlin, you're likely to be clapped in irons," Fineghal pointed out.

"I don't care." Aeron had had a glimpse of his old life when he visited Kestrel's house. Now that he thought about what might have happened in his absence, he felt as if he'd left them to face his enemies by fleeing into the forest. "If Phoros has hurt Kestrel and Eriale, I'll make him answer for it. They've done nothing wrong."

"Raedel's father may not hold Kestrel and Eriale."

"Well, I have to find out, don't I?" Aeron stood and kneaded his hands together, gazing up at the narrow band of stars shining overhead. "I'll go back tomorrow, late in the day. Someone will know what's happened."

Fineghal sighed and stood. "I agree that you must find out whether your kin are in danger, but you won't help them at all if you fall into Raedel's hands. I know a spell or two that may be useful for slipping into Maerchlin without revealing yourself. You told me that Kestrel's house looked as if it had been empty for some time, right?"

"Yes, that's right. Several weeks, at least."

"Then another day won't hurt. I'll teach you the spells you need to know, and you'll be much safer."

"Would you come with me, Fineghal?"

The elf shook his head. "Aeron, I'll travel to the edge of the forest and watch for you, but I don't think I should set foot in Maerchlin. In the first place, I am still recuperating from my fight in Villon. Secondly, if it becomes necessary for me to confront and defy Lord Raedel, he'll hold all elves to blame, if not the Maerchwood itself. I might be able to topple one spoiled noble, or maybe two, but if all the lords of Chessenta were to come to Raedel's aid against the elves who remain in these lands, we wouldn't stand a chance. If my actions gave Raedel or any other Chessentan lord the excuse he needed to invade the Maerchwood, I could bring ruin to this place."

"Then this is something I must do myself," Aeron said.

"The night is still young. I will begin by showing you the charm of invisibility. If you are careful, this may be all the magic you need to enter Maerchlin and leave again unharmed." Fineghal reached into his pouch and produced a cloudy, translucent piece of quartz, marked with a complicated symbol. "Here. Examine the stone, Aeron."

* * * * *

By the time dawn grayed out the stars, Aeron was able to cast the spell of invisibility competently, if not comfortably. Despite his fierce desire to strike out for Maerchlin immediately, the need for sleep overwhelmed him, and he was forced to rest a few hours in the early morning. When he woke, he found Fineghal sitting cross-legged on a boulder overlooking the icy pool at the foot of the small cascade. The elf stared absently into space, lost in the endless halls of his ancient memory. He stirred slowly as Aeron approached. "Fineghal? Are you well?"

"Merely tired, Aeron. Let's use this afternoon to transcribe the charm of invisibility to a glyphwood, so that you will have a permanent record of your own. Then, tomorrow or the next day, you can study a new spell."

"Fineghal, I don't have time for that."

The elf looked away, watching the play of the water upon the rocks. "Another spell may be the difference between success and failure in your endeavor, Aeron. If it turns out that you needed the extra preparation, you'll regret your haste now."

Aeron forced a shrug. "We'll see."

Fineghal rose smoothly. "Your human side is too strong, Aeron. Haste will be your undoing someday. Very well, let us go. Baillegh!" With an anxious yelp, the white wolfhound appeared, prancing with eagerness. The old elf ran his fingers over her head with a sad smile, shouldered his slim satchel, and followed Aeron out of the dell.

By now, Aeron could travel nearly as swiftly and silently as Fineghal himself. Ignoring Fineghal's reservations, he loped north and west along hidden trails, approaching Maerchlin by a circuitous route. They reached the edge of the village by midafternoon. The day was hot and overcast, and the gray skies threatened a violent storm before long. Beneath the eaves of the forest, Fineghal caught Aeron's arm. "Remember, if you cast the charm of invisibility, you will be invisible to the eye only. You can still be detected by sound, smell, or touch. If you attempt to harm someone, or if you cast another spell, the charm will fail. Good luck. I will wait here for you."

"Don't worry, Fineghal. I'll be careful." Aeron gave the wizard a reassuring smile. He hopped the fence that surrounded Kestrel's homestead and gave the place a cursory search. At first he thought that nothing had changed from his last visit; the barn was still empty, and there were no chickens or goats in the farmyard. But by the house, a deerskin was strung on a frame, scraped and drying, and the small smoking shed was acrid with recent use.

With some trepidation, Aeron entered the house but found it empty. No one was home at the moment. Could Kestrel and Eriale have returned? Many of their small belongings were missing, but others remained and showed signs of use. He thought it over and decided to question the neighbors. Old Toric, down the lane, had always been a friend and had little love for Lord Raedel.

Aeron turned west and trotted across the open fields to the farmer's house. Toric's fields seemed in good shape; it had been a good summer for the crops so far, with sunshine and rain in the right proportions. He glanced around furtively, but no one was near, so he rapped on the farmer's door. "Toric? Shiela? Anybody home?"

Shiela Goldsheaf, wife to old Toric Goldsheaf, opened the door and peered out. She was a stout apron-clad woman of middle years, blessed with the ability to talk incessantly about even the most trivial matters. "Aeron? I never thought to see you again! Where in Faerûn have you been?"

"Hello, Shiela. I hoped you could tell me where Kestrel and Eriale have gone." Aeron glanced up and down the lane. "May I come inside? I'd rather not be seen here."

"Of course, of course! Come in, quickly. Why, it's been a year that you've been gone now! So much has happened. The old lord, he's fallen ill, and young Phoros is pretty much in charge at the keep. Kestrel—well, Kestrel is in the castle's dungeon. But Eriale's—"

"Aeron! You're back!" Eriale rushed up and caught Aeron in a strong embrace. "Where have you been? What have you been doing?"

"I was going to say, Eriale was released a few days ago, and she's staying here with us while she cleans up Kestrel's cabin," Shiela continued. "And I was going to add that she was here right now, but I see that you've found that out for yourself." The matron ushered both Aeron and Eriale into the cluttered interior of her home, pulling up a couple of stools by the hearth.

Aeron looked from Shiela to Eriale. It was good to see human faces again. Eriale . . . he hadn't realized how much he had missed her. Kestrel might have been a father to him, but Eriale was both his sister and his best friend. He missed her direct honesty, her wit and dry humor, even the shape of her face. "I can't stay, Shiela. Raedel's men still have a warrant for me. You're at risk as long as I stay here."

"Oh, hush!" Shiela snapped. "Answer Eriale, young man. She's been beside herself with worry."

Aeron drew in a deep breath and replied, "I'm still staying with the friend I met last year, Eriale. I'm sure you remember him. I've learned a lot in a year. I can read and write in both common and Elvish, and my . . . other studies are going well. But there's so much more for me to learn. Even if I could come home, I think I'd stay where I am." He returned his attention to Eriale. "Now tell me what's happened in Maerchlin."

Eriale glanced up at Shiela. Her face lost some of the enthusiasm she'd shown at seeing Aeron again. "Father's been imprisoned in Raedel Keep for almost three months now," she said quietly. "I was thrown in the dungeon, too, but they let me go on Midsummer."

"Why did Raedel arrest you?"

"Phoros was very angry with Father and I for helping you to escape Maerchlin, but the old lord wouldn't allow him to arrest us. After all, we didn't *know* you were wanted when you left. But over the winter, old Lord Raedel fell ill."

"They say he hasn't risen from his bed in two months or more," Shiela added.

"So Phoros is the lord of Maerchlin now?" Aeron asked.

Eriale nodded. "Not in name, but he's the heir, and he's serving as regent until his father gets better."

"If he ever does," Shiela observed.

"The very day his father agreed to relinquish his powers to Phoros, he drafted a warrant for Kestrel's arrest, and mine as well. Aiding a felon, obstructing the law, seditious speech, conspiracy to rebellion . . . I didn't know he could think of so many charges!" Eriale paled and her voice grew small. "So Father and I were thrown into the dungeons."

Aeron snorted. "Raedel's nothing but a bloodthirsty brigand! He can't use his father's laws to pursue his own vendetta against me."

Shiela frowned. "King Gereax in Oslin came down on his side thirteen years ago, Aeron. The castle's guardsmen are the only law in Maerchlin. You should know that by now."

The young mage spat a curse. "I'm sorry, Eriale. Did they . . . were they rough with you?"

She shook her head. "Some of the guards would say things to me, but no one ever touched me."

"Why did they let you go?"

Eriale shook her head. "I don't know."

Aeron thought about the news. What could he do to help Kestrel? Could he spirit the forester out of the dungeons with magic? If he did, Kestrel would be no better off than Aeron was. As an escaped prisoner, he'd have to flee Maerchlin, too. What if he turned himself in? Phoros would have no reason to hold Kestrel—well, nothing save spite, he reminded himself—but Aeron's own life would almost certainly be forfeit. Aeron even considered the possibility of circumventing both Raedel and Gereax to appeal directly to Gormantor, the Overking in Akanax, but he couldn't begin to imagine how he might do that.

Outside, he heard the clattering approach of a number of horsemen. Animals nickered and snorted, stamping the hard earth of the farmyard. Aeron frowned, puzzled. Why would so many riders be coming to see Toric at one time? Unless . . . soldiers. The lord's men! He leapt to his feet, seeking escape. "Phoros Raedel didn't let you out of prison to show his generosity. He let you out to see if you would lead him to me!"

Eriale groaned. "It makes sense. And I did exactly what Raedel wanted me to. Oh, Aeron!"

"Surround the house! The boy's inside!" Through the oil-skin windows, Aeron could see the dark shapes of guardsmen racing for the door, six or seven at least. He thought desperately. There was no place to hide, and Raedel's men already covered both doors.

"Eriale, Shiela, cooperate. Tell them anything they want to know," he hissed. Then, raising his hand and dusting himself with a pinch of pure white sand, he brought the mystic symbol of the charm of invisibility to his mind. The Weave streamed through him, electrifying his senses. With a word, the world around him seemed to become gray and mist-wreathed, as if he viewed it through a dark glass.

"Aeron! Where did you go?" Eriale cried. At that instant, mailed swordsmen kicked in both the front and back doors of Shiela's cottage, storming into the room with their blades ready. More streamed in behind them, ransacking the place, overturning furniture, tearing down every hanging or curtain that could possibly conceal a slender young man.

Aeron whirled, avoiding contact with the enraged soldiers and barely escaping a fatal collision. At the sergeant's command, two guardsmen dragged Shiela and Eriale out into the farmyard, blades at their throats. Aeron used the opportunity to slip outside just behind them, while the rest of the soldiers continued to wreck Shiela's home. Just outside, the young Lord Miroch sat atop his horse, eyes glittering with anticipation. "I thought it a waste of my time to watch the lass, but it looks like Phoros's plan has worked," he remarked. "Where's Aeron?"

"Here are the women, m'lord. There's no sign of the boy," growled the sergeant.

"What? There must be!" Miroch roared. "Search again!" The sergeant nodded and ducked back inside to supervise the efforts of his men. Aeron moved slowly to one side, holding his breath. There were soldiers all around, but none even glanced in his direction; he was safe for the moment, but Eriale and Shiela were held securely by Raedel's men.

After a long moment, the sergeant stomped back outside. "There's no sign of him, m'lord. I'm certain of it." The sergeant spread his hands. "We saw him enter and watched the house closely. I don't know how he got out."

Miroch scowled and turned his gaze to Eriale. "Where's Aeron? We know he was here!"

Eriale cried out in pain as the soldier holding her knotted one hand in her hair and twisted savagely. "I don't know!" she gasped. "He used magic to disappear!"

"What kind of nonsense is that?" Miroch roared. "Phoros will have my head if I let Aeron escape!" He glared at his prisoners and narrowed his eyes. "Fine. Burn the house!"

"No!" shrieked Shiela. "It's my home!"

With two quick steps, the leader of the guardsmen reached Shiela. He smashed her to the ground with his mailed fist. Shiela collapsed, bleeding in the dry brown earth. Aeron stood transfixed by horror, watching as the guards abandoned their search and set torches to the cottage's roof. Black smoke streamed into the sky.

"Miroch, you can't do this!" Eriale wailed. "You have no right! Shiela hasn't harmed anyone!"

The stocky lord tore his gaze from the billowing flames and locked his eyes on Eriale's face. "Where is Aeron?"

"By Assuran, I don't know! Far from here by now, I

hope!" Eriale struggled against the guard who pinned her.

"How did he escape?"

"I told you, he used magic!"

Miroch sneered. "That wretched lout has mastered sorcery? Think of a better lie than that!" The burly nobleman sneered at Eriale. "Perhaps you need more encouragement," he said, licking his lips. "Strip her."

The guard holding her shot a disapproving look at the lord, but set his jaw and seized the homespun dress, tearing it from Eriale's shoulders. Miroch swung down from his horse and swaggered forward.

Aeron understood what kind of encouragement Miroch had in mind. With a loud cry, he sprinted forward, knife in hand. Guards whirled, searching for the source of the shout. Aeron reached the man holding Eriale and slashed his face. The guard screamed and reeled away, holding his hands to his lacerated jaw.

And the strange, dim haze that cloaked Aeron's vision began to brighten as full daylight returned. His assault on the guard had broken the spell. He was becoming visible again!

"There he is!" shouted Miroch. He drew his slender sword from its sheath and charged forward. The other men of the detail drew their own blades and advanced.

Toric's house was a mass of flames now, and the heat smothered Aeron. He glanced wildly about, faced with steel on all sides, and suddenly he knew with absolute certainty what to do. He pressed his hands together and summoned the image of fire hand to his mind, reaching out through the Weave to grasp the turbulent flames that danced and leapt in the burning house behind him.

A great jet of scorching red flames exploded from his hands, engulfing Miroch from the waist up. Aeron held the jet on the lord for only a moment, then slewed it around to drive back the guardsmen. Miroch shrieked and staggered away, his puffed coat burning like oil-soaked tinder. The guards in their mail fared better, but the blast of heat singed faces and hands. Most were incapacitated for a moment. As the jet of flame played out, Aeron reached down to seize Eriale's hand and bolted for the safety of the forest. The girl stumbled in shock, trying to cover herself with her torn dress, but she found the wits to stretch out her legs and match Aeron's pace. Behind them, Lord

Miroch toppled and fell in a blazing heap.

"Aeron! Where are you going?" Eriale panted.

"I've got to get you away from here!" he answered. "You can stay with me in the forest. Come on!"

Instead, Eriale slowed and stopped, wrenching her hand back. "No, Aeron. I can't come with you."

Aeron halted, panting. The guards were mounting their horses, shouting and cursing, but they had a two-hundred-yard lead. "Come on! They'll be upon us in a moment!"

Eriale wrapped her arms around her torso and backed away from Aeron. "What have you become, Aeron? You—you killed Miroch. You've murdered a lord."

"Eriale, I did it to save you!"

The girl shuddered in horror. "Don't say that!"

Aeron threw up his arms in exasperation. "We don't have time for this, Eriale. Phoros will just throw you in prison again!"

She turned her back on him. "You'd better go."

"Eriale, I did what I had to do!" Aeron looked past her, at the horsemen coming after him. He reached forward to catch her sleeve, but she twisted away from him, tears streaming down her cheeks. Aeron cursed and retreated, watching the soldiers gallop toward them. "I'll set this right somehow, Eriale." He bolted, hurdling a stone fence and sprinting for the cover of the trees. Behind him, Eriale turned and started walking toward the count's men.

Aeron crashed into the underbrush by the forest's edge, his heart hammering in his chest. He almost ran right past Fineghal, but at the last moment, the tall elf caught him by the arm and spun him around. The look on the elven mage's face was merciless. "What have you done, Aeron?" he barked. "When did you learn that spell?"

Aeron stumbled to one knee. "Miroch was going to hurt Eriale. I had to do something!"

"So you shaped the Weave into a torrent of flame and burned him alive. Where was the justice in that?"

A spark of defiance guttered up in Aeron's heart. He glared into the elf's inscrutable face. "You were right here! If you didn't want me to defend myself, to defend the people I love, you should have acted yourself!" He surged to his feet, his anger building. "You weren't waiting for me, Fineghal. You were hiding!"

The elven mage fell silent. His eyes flicked past Aeron to

the soldiers rushing into the forest, beating the brush with their sword blades. "This discussion is not over yet. Now, come! We must get away from this place." He wheeled and sprinted into the dark verdancy of the forest, vanishing almost faster than Aeron could see.

* * * * *

Fineghal did not speak to Aeron for days after they fled into the forest. They avoided the torch-lit manhunt with a few simple tricks of woodcraft and magic, but the wizard's features blazed with fury when Aeron tried to break the silence. Cold judgment mantled the ageless elven lord, an impenetrable barrier that Aeron dared not breach. Bitterly Fineghal moved deep into the Maerchwood, seeking the shelter of Caerhuan. Aeron trailed helplessly in his wake.

The cold white walls of the elven tower brought no relief. Fineghal spent long hours each day in the forest, speaking no word to Aeron when he came or went. Two days passed as Aeron waited for the wizard to berate or punish him. He tried to distract himself with his studies, but he had no desire to grapple with unknown magics or press the foreign shapes of spells into his mind. He was dreadfully worried for Eriale, although he hoped that his flight had won her some measure of safety. But the fearsome image that banned rest from his heart was the memory of roaring flame and the screams of Miroch as he withered and died like a moth caught in a candle.

After days of staring out over the endless torrent and the chaotic waters of the Winding River, Aeron came to a decision. He rose, returned to the tower, and carried his pouch of glyphwoods to the rocky bluff. He pulled the carving for the fire spell from his collection and weighed it in his hand, looking out over the gorge. With an anguished cry, he hurled the slender rod of wood end over end into the foaming waters.

He felt Fineghal's presence behind him as the elven lord watched the spell wood vanish in the foam. "Does that ease your heart?" he asked quietly.

"No," said Aeron. "I didn't want to kill him, Fineghal. But when I think about it, I would do it again, to keep him from hurting Eriale. Or me. What does that make me?"

"Killing is a hard thing. When you kill, you murder a

small part of your own spirit. Fear the day when it does not trouble you to take a life," Fineghal said. "Taking that which you have not earned is an offense to the spirit, too."

"If I hadn't known how to cast fire hand, Miroch might have raped or killed her," Aeron rasped.

"Better that you hadn't set foot in Maerchlin. Miroch would have had no cause to trouble Eriale, no reason to fire your neighbor's house. And you would have had no reason to kill him, Aeron."

"That's easy for you to say. You don't have kinfolk in Phoros Raedel's dungeons."

Fineghal looked away, a flicker of unreadable emotion crossing his face. Emboldened, Aeron pursued him and spoke to his back. "I'm human, Fineghal. I have a heart! You may find it noble to stand watch, never interfering, but I can't do that. Not when people I care for are in danger. If that means that you've failed to teach me patience, then so be it. I wasn't meant to learn it."

"You can't deny your heritage, Aeron. You are of the Tel'Quessir." The elven lord wrapped his cloak around his shoulders against the wind and spray, his face white with anger. He measured Aeron for a long moment, and imperceptibly his gaze softened. "And yet you are human, too. Maybe you are right, Aeron. I might have found a better course for you if I had intervened. Your failure is my failure." Stretching out one arm, he breathed a few soft words and beckoned. From the white, booming rapids, a small length of wood flew, tumbling into his hand. "Take your glyphwood. The spell has been cast, and the fault does not lie here."

"I'm never casting that spell again."

"You may have need of it someday, Aeron. It is foolish to forget what you have learned." Fineghal passed one hand over the *duarran* and dried it with a simple magic. Then he handed it to Aeron.

Aeron looked at the glyphwood for a long time before returning it to his pouch. "I'm going to go back. I can't let Phoros Raedel terrorize Eriale and Kestrel any longer."

"Aeron, you can't defeat Raedel."

"You could, Fineghal," Aeron said bitterly.

"Whether or not that is true, I will not attempt it. It would be reckless and irresponsible of me."

"So you'd unseat a bandit lord in Villon, but the one in

Maerchlin is beneath your notice?"

Fineghal's eyes flashed. "I live to serve Calmaercor, Aeron. Baerskos of Villon pillaged the old places of my people, and so I acted. But I refuse to endanger the land I guard by setting my hand against Phoros Raedel, his master in Oslin, and behind him, the Overking of Akanax."

"Then I'm on my own," Aeron snorted.

"I beg you: Do not throw away your life in an attempt to end Phoros Raedel's."

The young forester shook his head. "Whatever it takes, I mean to get Kestrel out of Raedel's dungeons. If Kestrel escapes, Eriale and he can leave Maerchlin. They've no other kin there. Would you be willing to find a place for them, maybe in Saden or Rodanar? Or is that interfering?"

Fineghal's voice was frigid. "Yes. I would help them, Aeron. But be warned that I will no longer teach you if you wield your magic against Raedel. I did not share my knowledge with you so that you could spite your enemies. You have it within your grasp to do much more than that." He wheeled and strode away, raising his hand for Baillegh. The hound shot one mournful look at Aeron and then trotted after her master.

Aeron watched Fineghal leave, shaking with suppressed emotion from the confrontation. To his surprise, the elven lord halted and glanced at him one more time. "I must tend to the eastern meadows for a few days," he called. "Stay here and study what you will. I am not accustomed to being castigated by half-human striplings, but I will overlook the words you spoke in anger if you, too, put it in the past. Or, if that does not suit you, then go to Maerchlin and do what you think you must. But if I return and find that you are not here, Aeron, you will not be welcome in Caerhuan again."

Five

Aeron remained on the bluff, deep in thought, until the sun sank into the west, staining the cold waters below with a thousand brilliant colors. Fineghal's parting words troubled him greatly. The elf lord was not given to exaggeration. Never to study magic again . . . Aeron couldn't bear the thought. He'd been changed by the year he'd spent under Fineghal's tutelage. He was not the simple woodcutter's lad he'd once been. Magic engaged his mind, his heart, on a level so intimate and demanding that it had become part of him. And he'd come to understand that he was only scratching the surface of what he might someday learn.

But on the other horn of his dilemma, Aeron could not stand by and let Phoros Raedel exact his vengeance by striking at Kestrel and Eriale. As far as he was concerned, Aeron had given Regos and Phoros exactly what they deserved when he wounded them last summer, and even Miroch's death had been nothing more than self-defense. But as long as Phoros Raedel was the lord of the land, the young tyrant was free to do anything he liked in order to secure his own brand of justice. Six dozen swordsmen in Castle Raedel ensured that Raedel could interpret the law any way he cared to. What choice did Aeron really have?

He turned and headed back to the tower, thinking of what he could do to even the odds against Raedel. Fineghal had told him to study what he would; as long as he was going to defy the wizard's will, he might as well stretch the letter of Fineghal's parting words. As night fell, Aeron let himself into the tower's library, searching for *Rhymes of Magic and Wonder*. The spell of shapechanging was still far beyond his abilities, even if it hadn't been erased by his carelessness, but there were plenty of other spells that might lie within his ability in the old bardic text. I'll need every edge I can get if I hope to pull this off, he thought. I might be rash by Fineghal's standards, but that doesn't mean that I can't take the time to do this right.

He found the text where he'd left it. Lighting a lamp with a simple cantrip Fineghal had taught him almost a year ago, Aeron sat down and began to page through the spellbook, looking for the enchantments he'd need.

* * * * *

Aeron worked at a feverish pace, refusing to allow exhaustion or emotion to distract him. Now that he'd chosen his course, he intended to follow it no matter what the consequences. Although he hated to waste the time, he forced himself to sleep on the second night, readying himself for the day to follow.

In the gray hours before dawn, ten days after his confrontation with Miroch and the Raedel armsmen, Aeron rose and found himself alone in Caerhuan still, with no sign of Fineghal. He turned to the glyphwoods he'd prepared and settled down to commit the spells to memory. Within an hour, he'd mastered six spells at once, a feat he'd never managed before. The minor victory felt cold and empty.

With his spells readied, Aeron stuffed his pack with provisions, shouldered his bow, and set off for Maerchlin. The village was a good forty miles or more from Caerhuan, and he used the elven run that Fineghal had taught him to cover half the distance by the time the sun set. Now that he was on his way, he was eager to press forward and get on with it, but again he made himself lie down and rest while the moon sank beneath the horizon and the darkest part of the night went by.

Before dawn, he woke and gathered his things, setting off for the village to the north. He ran easily for hours, stripped to the waist to stay cool in the sticky warmth of the day. Sweat streamed from his brow and glistened on his back.

Late in the afternoon, he arrived at the edges of Maerchlin. The fields were tall and ripe, corn and grain higher than his head. Aeron deliberately avoided Kestrel's homestead, deciding not to risk an encounter with guardsmen or trackers watching over the place. He settled down under the shadows of the wood, a mile around the village from his old home, and rested from his travels.

Eventually the long, hot afternoon faded into a warm

dusk. By twos and threes, the townsfolk sought out their homes as the light failed. Aeron waited until the sun had been down an hour or more before he finally stirred from his hiding place. "Time to get started," he told himself. Standing in the shadows beneath the trees, he dusted himself with sand and murmured the words to the invisibility spell. As before, the dweomer seemed to immerse him in a smoky, dark glass. For a moment Aeron feared that the spell's effect might ruin his own vision, too, but slowly his eyes adjusted. Confident in his concealment, he moved into the town.

First he ventured through back lanes and empty pastures to Kestrel's house, coming up on it from the town. Lights showed through the windows, but he spotted a pair of dark-clothed guards keeping watch over the house from a short distance. Aeron frowned and slid forward silently, passing Raedel's soldiers without a sound. He crouched by the open window and peered inside.

To his surprise, Shiela Goldsheaf and her husband Toric were sharing a small crock of stew in the hearthroom. Aeron glanced around to make sure that the guards were out of earshot, then whispered, "Shiela? It's Aeron. Stay where you are and keep your voice low. The guards haven't seen me."

The stout matron looked up in amazement and returned her attention to her stew. "You shouldn't have come here, Aeron," she said. "You're to be killed on sight here."

In the darkness, he smiled. "I'll take pains not to be seen. Kestrel's still in the castle dungeons?"

"Yes." Despite herself, Shiela glanced toward the window. "Eriale, too. There was talk of burning her as a witch, but the guards swore they'd seen you kill Miroch with sorcery, so Raedel's holding her for conspiracy."

Aeron nodded. "I thought that would be the case. You're welcome to the house, Shiela. I don't suppose that we'll be needing it anymore."

"Aeron, wait! What are you going to do?"

"Farewell. Don't ever tell anyone you spoke with me here." He glided off into the night, slipping past the guards easily, and made his way by open fields and farm lanes toward the castle itself.

The fortress was an old shell keep ringed by a newer curtain wall. The lower bailey was a small, muddy courtyard surrounded by crowded stables and barracks. A second wall guarded the upper bailey, the reserve of the lords of the castle. An old ditch circled the castle, spanned by a wooden trestle at the main gate. Four soldiers stood watch by the yawning doorway, their mail gleaming in the bright lantern light by the gate. Aeron paused at the far end of the footbridge and crouched by the woodwork, despite the dark mantle that cloaked him.

They cannot see me, he told himself. I have nothing to fear as long as I move slowly and silently and don't walk into anyone. Steeling himself, Aeron stole quietly across the bridge and slipped past the guardsmen, edging within an arm's reach of the two who stood beside the door. For one perverse moment, he was struck by the insane desire to shout in the guard-sergeant's ear simply to watch him jump, but he clamped his mouth shut and moved on.

Once inside the wall, Aeron darted across the bailey. The courtyard was exactly as he remembered it from the magical test Fineghal had administered more than a year ago, and his neck itched at the memory of the hangman's noose. He almost lost his nerve, standing still and silent in the middle of the courtyard while he wrestled with his fears. After a long moment, Aeron forced himself to move on, passing the inner gatehouse that protected the keep from the outer bailey. Only one sentry stood guard here, and the fellow was leaning against a wall, dozing.

Inside the keep, Aeron turned right and slid along the wall. He knew that the keep's eastern tower served as a dungeon. He met no one within the echoing stone corridor that led from the entry hall to the tower. Shortly, Aeron came to the heavy, iron-bound door to Raedel's prisons. Lantern light and low conversation spilled out from the guardroom inside.

He set his hand to the door but stopped. What would the guards inside think if they saw the door open by itself? And even if he managed to slip past them and into the dungeons, how could he bring Kestrel by them again? Aeron scowled and scratched at his chin. He had a spell to deal with the guardsmen, but he couldn't risk alarming them by just walking straight in. He thought about it for a long moment and struck upon a plan.

Facing the door, he balled his fist and hammered on the sturdy wood with all his might, rattling the door on its hinges. "For the love of Assuran, come in already!" cried an exasperated voice from within. Aeron didn't relent; he pounded the door again, until he heard the scrape of a chair being pushed back. He stopped and stepped to one side.

An angry guard with a bristling mustache threw open the room's heavy door, glaring into the hall. "Hey, knock it off!" Seeing no one outside, the guard swore viciously and stomped into the hall, looking left and right. Aeron quickly stepped inside and out of the way.

The guardroom was small, with just two jailers on watch. The guard who had come to the door returned a moment later, shaking his head and swearing. "Someone's playing a prank on us," he muttered.

"Probably that rascal Darod," the second guard said. "I guess you didn't see anything?"

"No, the weasel must've run off. He'll be back, though. He's not bright enough to pull a trick just once."

While the men talked, Aeron circled the room, taking stock of the situation. The guardroom made up the lower floor of the tower, and a staircase spiraled down into the tower's dungeons. On one wall, a heavy ring of keys hung by a hook. The first guard eventually returned to the table, where he and the second man were engaged in a game of hop-stone with ivory tokens. No other guards, the prisoners below. Good. Aeron moved into position.

Setting his jaw, he began to work a spell of slumber he had mastered not three days ago in Fineghal's library. As he reached for the Weave to shape the enchantment, his cloak of invisibility faded, but both guardsmen were asleep before they could even draw sword against the wispy apparition that faced them. Aeron quickly locked the outer door, bound and gagged the guards securely, and retrieved the ring of keys from the wall. Then he descended into the dungeon.

At the bottom of the stairs, he found a rusty iron grate. This opened easily to the second key he tried, and he pressed on down a long, dim corridor lined by small doors on either side. "Kestrel?" he called softly. "Are you here?"

"Who's that?" A weak voice replied from a cell at the end of the corridor. Aeron hurried to the door and peered in the barred window. It was dark inside, but his elven eyesight aided him. Kestrel pushed himself to his feet, brushing matted straw from his clothes. "Aeron? Is that you?"

"It's me, Kestrel." Aeron grinned. Although he looked as if he hadn't bathed in a year, Kestrel seemed in good health. "I've got the keys. I'll have you out in a moment."

The old forester rubbed his hands together and came up to the door. "Phoros is after your blood, Aeron. You'd have been better off to stay away from Maerchlin altogether."

"I tried, Kestrel. But when I heard that Phoros had imprisoned you and Eriale, I decided I had to do something. It's not right for you to be jailed for something I did."

"Nonsense, lad. In the first place, I did do something. I went straight to old Lord Raedel after you left and tried to set things square. Phoros wasn't at all happy with the idea of someone telling his father your side of the story. He remembered that when his father fell ill and he took over the ruling of the land. Besides, you're like a son to me. I'd give up my freedom to know that you were safe." Kestrel's eyes gleamed in the dim light.

"Here, I've found the right key." With a scrape and click, the lock opened, and Aeron reached in to help Kestrel out.

The woodsman stretched and smiled. "Tchazzar's sword, it's good to be out of that cell." Then his eyes narrowed. "Wait a moment. Aeron, how'd you get in here?"

"I used magic."

"Magic! But . . . That's right. Eriale said you'd taken up with the Storm Walker. She's here, too. About three cells up, on this side."

The two quickly found Eriale's cell and quietly set her free. Aeron didn't like the way she looked at all; she was pale and shivered constantly, ill from her stay in the prison cell. She'd been so deeply asleep that she hadn't heard him enter the cell row. As the two men helped her up the stairs to the guardroom, Aeron quickly recounted his visits to Maerchlin and something of the past twelve months.

"Astounding," Kestrel muttered. "I'd never have imagined that you could wield magic, Aeron. That's for the mages and lords of the great cities, not the kind of folk who live around here."

"I've only scratched the surface of what Fineghal knows." Aeron smiled ruefully. "I don't expect he'll take me in again after this. He didn't want to defy the rightful lord of the land, even a black-hearted snake like Phoros Raedel. He wanted no part of this."

"I'm sorry, Aeron." Kestrel put his hand on his shoulder.

"I wish this had turned out differently."

Aeron nodded. In the guardroom, they paused for a moment to plan their next move. Kestrel was in good shape, considering his incarceration, but Eriale was so exhausted that she could barely support herself against the wall. "Well, Aeron?" she said weakly. "You managed to get in here. What's next?"

"First, get out of the castle without getting caught. Then . . . I don't know. We'll have to leave Maerchlin. After this, Phoros will be looking for all three of us."

"I had figured that much already," Kestrel said. He scowled. "We'll have to go far and fast. Probably safest to seek refuge in the lands of some city such as Soorenar or Mordulkin. I don't care to have Oslin's constables on my trail." He glanced around the room. Both guardsmen still slept, although Aeron had tied them up to make sure they wouldn't be going anywhere. "Here, Aeron. You and I can borrow these mail coats and helmets. Eriale . . . well, she's obviously not looking too good. It's not unreasonable that a couple of guards might be taking her to the village to have old Meara look at her, right?"

Aeron agreed and knelt by the smaller of the two men, removing his mail hauberk. The fellow woke up, but tied and gagged as he was, he couldn't do anything more than glare at Aeron. Kestrel helped himself to the other guard's gear, and within a few minutes the two foresters could pass for Raedel's swordsmen at a distance.

Supporting Eriale between them, Aeron and Kestrel cautiously left the guardroom and turned back to the keep's gate. At this hour, the hallways were deserted, and they did not encounter anyone until they reached the sentry post. The drowsy watchman was now awake and alert, pacing back and forth across the stone doorway. His attention was on the courtyard, not the hall behind him. "What do we do?" Eriale whispered.

Aeron grimaced. "I'd hoped that he would still be sleeping. I can work a spell."

"No need," Kestrel interrupted. "I remember a trick or two from my younger days." He eased his borrowed dagger from his belt and crept up behind the sentry. Reversing his grip on the weapon, he quickly knocked the sentry's helmet off his head with his left hand and brought the heavy pommel down on the crown of the fellow's head. With a groan, the sentry went limp. Aeron caught his helmet before it clattered on the stone steps, while Kestrel lowered the unconscious guard to the floor. They waited, listening for a moment, but they didn't hear anything to indicate that they had been noticed.

"The lower gatehouse is guarded by four men," Aeron whispered. "I may be able to deceive them."

"What about the postern?" Kestrel asked.

"This castle has a postern gate?"

"Most do, Aeron. It's right over there, on the other side of the courtyard. Didn't you scout it out?"

Aeron shook his head. "I didn't even think of it."

Kestrel grinned in the starlight. "A year of learning, and it never even crossed your mind? If I were Fineghal, I'd be wondering whether you had rocks in your head."

"Won't the postern be locked?" Eriale asked.

"I can do something about that," Aeron answered.

"Then it sounds better than trying to talk our way out of here," Eriale muttered weakly.

The three of them started down the keep's wide steps and veered left. Yellow light burned in the barrack rooms that ringed the lower bailey, and Aeron could hear soldiers laughing and thumping tables in the castle's taproom. Kestrel led them straight toward the lantern light, but they went past the building to a small, shadowed alcove in the curtain wall. Aeron's eyes adjusted quickly to the gloom. A small, heavy door sheathed in iron plate was embedded in the wall. "The postern?" he asked.

"That's it," Kestrel said. "Thirteen years ago, I—"

"Thirteen years ago you should have been strung up as a rebel, old man," a harsh voice grated behind them. Whirling to face the threat, Aeron gasped in shock. Phoros Raedel himself stood behind them, sword bared, with a stocky soldier in the uniform of a guard sergeant a pace behind them. "My thanks for leaving the sentry with a knot on his head, Morieth. If I hadn't noticed that he wasn't at his post, I never would have caught you here."

"Phoros," Aeron spat. He was terrified, but at the same time, an incandescent rage boiled in his heart. For years the mercenary lord's son and his friends had bullied him, finally driving him to strike back. And when he had dared to raise his hand in his own defense, Phoros had seen to it that everyone Aeron loved suffered for his defiance. "Let us go, and we'll never trouble you again. You win. I'll leave Maerchlin with Kestrel and Eriale, and you'll never have to see any of us again."

"I can make certain that you never trouble me again by having you drawn and quartered." Phoros grinned ruthlessly. "Or perhaps burned at the stake. That would only be fitting, considering what you did to Miroch."

"Aeron," Kestrel said, "can you open the gate?"

"Don't bother. It's locked." Phoros sneered. "Kestrel, if you lay down your sword this very instant, you and Eriale will live. Otherwise I'll burn you along with Aeron."

Aeron licked his lips and risked a quick glance at the postern behind them before turning to keep Raedel in his vision. They were within the postern's alcove, with Raedel and the sergeant blocking their escape to the courtyard, and stone surrounding them on all sides. There were dozens of guards only a few feet away in the taproom, but Phoros hadn't called for reinforcements yet. Carefully he said, "Yes, I can open it."

"Good." With a lightning-fast motion, Kestrel's hand dipped to his belt. Steel glinted in the darkness as his dagger, thrown underhand, sank into the throat of the guard sergeant. Raedel blinked in astonishment but recovered quickly. With an angry roar, he leapt forward and stabbed at Kestrel. The wily old forester barely freed his sword from the scabbard in time to parry the nobleman's attack. "Get started!" Kestrel grunted.

Aeron watched, mesmerized, as Phoros attacked Kestrel with a furious rain of blows, slashing and hacking with all his might. The young lord was a good swordsman, blessed with a powerful build and quick hands. Kestrel stood a foot shorter and weighed at least fifty pounds less than Raedel, and he had spent the last three months in a filthy dungeon cell. But Aeron was surprised to see that he was holding his own for a moment, displaying a surprising amount of skill and reactions even faster than Raedel's. "Time's on my side, old man," Raedel said. "Guards! Guards!"

"Aeron! The gate, before more soldiers come!" cried Eriale. She dragged at his arm, pulling him away.

"Right," he muttered. He turned his back on the duel and faced the postern gate again. Closing his eyes, he set his hand on the door and uttered a simple phrase, summoning a spell of opening to his mind. Beneath his fingertips, he felt the old, rusty lock slide and click. He set his shoulder to the door and pushed it open, a breath of cool air slipping through the widening crack. "I've got it!" he cried.

"Then get Eriale out of here," Kestrel snarled. "I can hold him a little longer." He stumbled with fatigue and bled from several small cuts, but somehow he still held Phoros Raedel at bay. The young lord tried to circle past him, only to be halted by the gleaming point of Kestrel's sword. Behind Raedel, several guardsmen had already appeared, and more were coming at a run.

"I don't think so," Raedel said. He feinted, drawing Kestrel's guard out, and smashed the forester's blade against the stone wall. On the backswing, he struck Kestrel across the scalp, sending him reeling to the ground, stunned. Phoros raised his sword, poised to run him through while his defenses were down.

"Father!" shrieked Eriale.

Without a moment's hesitation, Aeron reached out to seize the taut fabric of the Weave that surrounded him. He drew his hand over his face while pointing at Raedel, and breathed the words to a spell.

Phoros straightened with a startled cry. He reeled, stretching out to steady himself on the wall. "Curse you, Morieth! What have you done to me? I can't see!"

"Be glad I only blinded you," Aeron snapped. He reached down and helped Kestrel regain his feet. Roaring in frustration, Raedel slashed out uselessly. Even as the castle's guards pushed their way past their ranting lord, Aeron pushed Eriale through the postern, then helped Kestrel. The older man was bleeding freely from a long, shallow wound across his forehead, but he seized Eriale's arm and dragged her out into the night. Aeron slammed the postern shut and released his passage spell. Inside the heavy door, the lock clicked and reset itself. The castle's soldiers hammered on the other side, but to no avail. The postern was designed to handle any amount of pounding.

"Where now?" Kestrel asked.

"The forest," Aeron said. "They'll be on our trail in moments. We can lose them in the Maerchwood."

"Good enough for now," Kestrel replied. Helping Eriale along, they hurried away from the forbidding walls of Raedel Keep and vanished into the night.

Fleeing Maerchlin, Aeron led Kestrel and Eriale to the stream-riven gorge near the ruins where he had first met Fineghal. Aeron remembered what the elven mage had told him about the safety of the hidden vale, and it seemed as good a place as any to conceal themselves. By the time they reached the gorge, Kestrel was exhausted and Eriale was deathly ill from the sickness to which she'd fallen prey during her imprisonment.

Aeron hoped fervently that Fineghal would be waiting for them there, but the only sign he found of his teacher was a leather satchel left by their old campsite. Inside, there was a small sack of coins, a wax-sealed vial, and two letters—one addressed to him, and one to someone by the name of Telemachon of Cimbar. While Kestrel built a small fire and looked after Eriale, Aeron broke the seal on the letter with his name on it. In Espruar, it read:

Aeron,

The gold is for Kestrel to build a new home. I recommend the town of Saden, at the head of the Adder River. King Gearax of Oslin calls himself Saden's lord, but the folk there are free men who show Oslin's soldiers and constables no courtesy. They'll take Kestrel's gold with no questions asked. The potion is for Eriale; she is quite ill and should drink the entire vial immediately. Make sure she rests for two or three days before you move on.

The letter is for Telemachon, a Master of the College of Mages at the university in Cimbar. If you wish to continue your studies, go there and present the letter to him. He knows me of old and will allow you to study there. I fear that I have nothing more to teach you; perhaps you will find what you seek there.

—Fineghal

Aeron read Fineghal's letter over and over again. He knew he had defied Fineghal by returning to Maerchlin, but in his heart, he had never believed that the elven mage would end their association over the issue. Humans made mistakes and knew how to forgive the mistakes of others, but in the final test, Fineghal was inhuman and unfathomable, driven by emotions and memories that Aeron could only guess at. His journey into the ancient wisdom of the Tel'Quessir was over. Elven blood or not, Aeron's path lay somewhere else.

* * * * *

In the days that followed, Eriale recovered completely from her illness, and Kestrel regained his strength and quick smile in the sunlit glades of the forest. While his adopted father and sister hunted, fished, and made themselves comfortable in Fineghal's refuge, Aeron attempted several journeys to the places that Fineghal and he had visited. There was no sign of the elven lord, and even Caerhuan was deserted and empty. He returned to the vale of the waterfall after the last trek, weary and bitter.

Eriale tended a small fire by the rushing stream, a pair of dressed rabbits at her side, while Kestrel sat across from her, carefully straightening and paring an arrow shaft. Both looked up as Aeron splashed across the cold stream and joined them. "Any luck?" asked Kestrel, watching Aeron shrug off his pack.

"Not a sign of him," Aeron replied. "When Fineghal doesn't wish to be found, he won't be found."

Father and daughter exchanged a look. Eriale turned to face Aeron. "We've decided that it's time to move on," she said. "Fall's coming on, and we'll want to raise a house while the weather's still warm."

"Saden's a good town," added Kestrel. "I passed near there when I was a soldier in the Overking's army, maybe twenty years ago. Lots of good timber and land." Aeron nodded absently, not really paying attention. The old forester studied his face for a long moment. "You're coming?"

Aeron glanced up at him. He hadn't thought that far ahead. "I don't know," he said. Over the past two weeks, he'd lost himself in his wanderings through the forest. He knew that Fineghal could not teach him anymore, but he'd hoped to at least see him face-to-face again, to justify his actions, to persuade the elf to allow him one more chance to continue his studies. He didn't think he could go back to the simpler life he'd known before the day he'd met the elven wizard. "It would have been better if I'd never met Fineghal," he said aloud. "I'd never have known what I stood to lose."

"What have you lost, Aeron?" Eriale asked softly.

He threw his hands in the air. "You couldn't understand."

The girl's face hardened. "Try me."

Aeron bit back a sharp retort. Kestrel and Eriale did not deserve his anger . . . nor did Fineghal, to be honest. He'd made his own decisions. He'd pursued Fineghal that first day, begging the elf to show him how to work the magic. And the wizard had warned him from the beginning that Aeron lacked the patience, the temperament, to follow the Tel'Quessir path.

"Imagine that you discovered one day that you lived near the sea, and that it was your heart's desire to become a sailor. You find someone who can teach you what you need to know, and you learn enough to sail within a mile or so of the shore. You don't have the skills yet to voyage wherever your heart would take you, but you can smell the strange far lands on the wind, you can feel the waves telling you of the places they might take you, and before you is the great wide sea, with nothing but your own inexperience and limitations to keep you from great voyages. Then you find that you will not be permitted to learn the last of what you need to know. So there you sit, at the shore, the sea always in your sight to taunt you with the thoughts of what might have been."

Eriale fell silent. She weighed Aeron's words, her eyes dark with reflection.

Kestrel stopped his work and turned a long, thoughtful gaze on Aeron. "Some would say that it would be better to get up and leave the seashore, in that case," he said. "Return to wherever it was you first came from and content yourself with being the person you were born to be."

"I don't know if I can do that."

"I've told you before of my days in the Overking's army, before Morieth's Revolt. They were good days, with stout comrades and a battle or two I fought in and survived. But the time came for me to lay down my arms and go home, and I did. Yet I knew many soldiers who never really went home. Oh, they returned to their farms and towns and took up their trades again. But in their hearts, they still lived in the days of their youth. And they were sadder for it, Aeron, because they couldn't find the spirit for life they'd had before, and they spent their days trying to recall it." Kestrel returned to his knife work. "We could use your help, Aeron. I'll have land to clear, timber to cut, a house to raise. In my experience, good hard work is the cure for a lot of ailments."

Because he loved Kestrel as his father, Aeron made himself think about the forester's words, but he couldn't bring the image into focus; every cell in his body seemed to shrink away from the prospect. He reached into the pouch at his waist and removed the wax-sealed letter marked "Telemachon," weighing it in his hand.

I've got to try it, he realized. "I'm sorry, Kestrel, Eriale. My road doesn't lead to Saden."

Six

A cold, gusty wind blew across the bright waters of the Inner Sea as Aeron disembarked in the crowded dock district of the city of Cimbar. The great city was a marvel beyond Aeron's comprehension. Everywhere he looked, myriads of people seethed and swarmed, engaged in a thousand activities. The docks were cluttered with the ships of many lands, and the broad roadstead within the city's seawalls was crowded with more riding at anchor, a floating forest of masts and spars. Drifting along with the press of people, Aeron shouldered his pack and headed into the city.

Dodging through the crowd, Aeron climbed up a steep hillside. Cimbar sprawled across several low hills that met the Inner Sea between two high, proud headlands about a mile apart. Aeron soon discovered that he'd landed in the part of town known as New Cimbar, which clustered around the western headland and its apron of hills. This was the commercial district, covering almost twice the territory of Old Cimbar around the eastern headland.

From Aeron's vantage high on the flanks of the hills of the new city, he could make out several majestic monoliths rising over the Old City, great pyramids of crumbling stone that towered over the white palaces and forums of the city's center. "What are those?" he asked one passerby, a merchant's tout carrying a thick ledger crammed full of cryptic notes.

"The pyramids?" The fellow gave Aeron an odd look. "New in town, eh? The biggest one is the Great Temple of Gilgeam, deserted by the Untheri when Tchazzar drove them back to their own lands four hundred years ago. It's naught but a landmark now. The little ones surrounding it are temples and shrines built to honor Untheri gods, back when Gilgeam was master of this land."

"Are any of them still in use?" Aeron wondered.

"No, not by the Untheri," the tout laughed. "Some of the philosophers hold their schools by the minor pyramids, and many of the city folk use them as meeting places and places of debate. You can see the Sceptanar's palace there by Gilgeam's pyramid."

Even in provincial Maerchlin, Aeron had heard of the Sceptanar. The faceless ruler of Cimbar, the Sceptanar was reputed to be a mighty mage and was considered one of the few kings strong enough to claim the title of Overking of all Chessenta. Aeron studied the alabaster citadel of the city's king for a long moment. To his surprise, a great dark crowd clustered around the palace gates, roiling and clashing in a sea of discontent. "There's some kind of riot going on over there," he said with some alarm.

The merchant shook his head, disappointed but not concerned. "The Mob," he said. "The demagogues have been stirring them up, claiming that Tchazzar the god-king will return someday and depose the Sceptanar."

Even though Aeron was half a mile from the scene, he could hear the dim roar of hundreds of voices shouting, and smoke drifted skyward from unseen fires. "Why don't the Sceptanar's soldiers disperse them?"

"Cimbar balances on three legs, lad. The Sceptanar, the baseborn Mob, and the noble senators, who look after their own pockets. If the Sceptanar backs the Mob into a corner, they'll burn the whole city to spite him, and the high senators will step in to pick up the pieces. No, the Sceptanar knows that it's his task to look for enemies outside of Cimbar's walls, and until the demagogues actually try to overthrow him, he'll let them be. Our city has more pressing concerns than hooligans and rabble-rousers."

Aeron stared. The great city, overrun by rioters in the streets while its overlord watched idly—he never would have believed it if he hadn't seen it with his own eyes. He felt acutely conscious of his rural upbringing; nothing in Maerchlin had prepared him for this. He let his eye rove past the Sceptanar's palace across the old acropolis. On the seaward side of the hill from the king's palace, a jagged stump of an obelisk speared the sky like a broken sword blade, barely clearing the skyline of gleaming buildings opposite him. "What's that jagged building?" he asked.

"That's the Broken Pyramid, once the stronghold of the Untheri mages who ruled Cimbar. It's said that the Untheri shattered it themselves rather than allow it to fall into our hands when Tchazzar led us against them. Those buildings nearby are the university."

"The university? That's where I'm going."

"You don't strike me as a philosopher or sage, so you must be an artisan. What is your craft?"

"You misunderstand me. I intend to study at the College of Mages."

The merchant snorted. "If you say so. You'll want to head for that building there on the seaward point of the acropolis." The stump of the Broken Pyramid was ringed by a low wall and several bland stone buildings covered by brown vines. The elevation isolated the tower and its surroundings from the city proper; its nearest neighbors appeared to be a small number of walled palaces that shared its lofty vantage, and then the cluttered streets of the docks and merchants' homes. "I'll leave you to your studies," the merchant said, "although you shouldn't consort with wizards, lad. Magic is dangerous stuff."

More dangerous than armed bands pillaging in the streets? Aeron thought to himself, but he thanked the merchant and let the last remark pass without argument. He descended into the broad, sun-warmed thoroughfares of the city's center and made his way into Old Cimbar. Here the buildings were generally smaller and built closer together, constricted by the remnants of ancient city walls that had been pulled down and moved farther outward as the city grew over the centuries. Keeping his eye on the pyramids marking Cimbar's eastern border, Aeron circled well clear of the Sceptanar's palace and wound his way up the steep, doubled roads that climbed Old Cimbar's acropolis.

At the top, Aeron got his first good look at the college. There weren't many trees or buildings on the hilltop to block the howling north wind of late Marpenoth, and his cloak fluttered and snapped behind him as he gazed over the grounds. Cimbar's great harbor fell away behind him, with its moored ships and maze of docks and piers. The hill was only a couple of hundred yards wide, and past the college Aeron glimpsed the rough brown foothills of the coastline arcing eastward along the Inner Sea.

The wind drew tears from his eyes, but he stood motionless, absorbing every detail. Once, long ago, a fortification here commanded the entrance of Cimbar's harbor. A low stone rampart of great age edged the hilltop. Long buildings of rough stone blocks formed a wide quadrangle, with a large, impressive hall of some kind in the center. A six-foot wall of the same fieldstone ringed the buildings, broken by a couple of wrought-iron gates.

To his right, the ruins of the Broken Pyramid stood to the south of the college buildings, a tumbled mound of weed-grown rubble that divided the mages' school from the rest of the university and Old Cimbar below. He could feel the Weave that surrounded the place, the subtle demands of existing spells, the bright surges of spells being worked nearby even as he watched, and the dim remembrance of unimaginable power in the ruins of the pyramid.

After a long moment, Aeron shook himself and set off for the nearest gatehouse. Two soldiers in gleaming breast-plates stood guard, sheltering inside the small building. As Aeron approached, they barred his way. "Halt and state your business," said one.

"I'm here to study at the college," Aeron answered.

The guards laughed. "If I had a silver talent for every waif that marches up here to become an archmage, I'd be a wealthy man," one remarked. "Go away."

"I have a letter of introduction," Aeron said. "Can you tell me where to find Telemachon?"

"That would be Master or Lord Telemachon to you, pup," growled the second guard. "Let's see it."

Aeron reached into his tunic and pulled out the letter Fineghal had left for him. The parchment had a golden gleam in the afternoon light. He handed it to the guard.

The guard scrutinized the letter. "What's this chicken scratching?" he said, pointing at the name.

"It's written in Espruar. Elvish."

The guards exchanged a look. "All right," one said. "Come with me." Leaving his fellow behind to mind the gate, he led Aeron into the college grounds.

They followed a paved path to the southernmost build-ing. As they climbed the shallow steps to the hall, a lean man in robes of red brocade emerged. His face was swarthy and crooked, with beetling brows, impenetrable eyes, and a bristling halo of tightly curled, oiled locks that continued into a carefully cropped beard. A fierce yellow grin seemed to be sculpted in his saturnine features, as if the greatest challenges of power and circumstance afforded him bound-less amusement. "Ho! What have we here?" he called.

"Some serf with a letter for Master Telemachon, Lord Oriseus," the guardsman answered. "He wants to enroll."

"A new student?" Lord Oriseus turned his attention to Aeron, making a show of examining him from head to toe. With comic exaggeration, he *tsk-tsk*ed his imaginary findings. "I see that the pool of undiscovered talent in this world grows shallow indeed. What's your name, lad?"

"Aeron Morieth, sir."

"May I see the mysterious missive, good Corden?"

"Of course, Lord Oriseus." The guard handed Aeron's letter to the magician. "I was going to escort the boy to Master Telemachon's quarters, my lord."

With no hint of humor, Oriseus weighed the parchment in his hand, his brow furrowed as unknown thoughts gathered behind his features. For a moment, Aeron feared that he would impulsively break the seal and read it himself, but with a sudden flourish, Oriseus returned the letter to Aeron. "Then do so, by all means," he replied to the guard. To Aeron, he said, "It is irregular for a fish to find his way into our little pond with nothing more than an elven letter, but I suspect that there is more to you than meets the eye, Aeron Morieth." With that, he sketched an outrageous bow and capered off, bubbling with a good humor that encompassed any who passed near.

"Who was that?" Aeron asked the guard, more than a little astounded by the master's exaggerated greeting.

"Lord Oriseus, High Conjuror and a senator of the city. Remember his face. He could be one of your instructors."

"I will," Aeron promised. He followed the guard into the hall. While the drab buildings of the college seemed to be nothing more than fieldstone barracks on the outside, the interior was much more lavishly appointed. The floors were made of gleaming hardwood; rich, dark paneling and crowded bookshelves covered the walls. High, narrow windows allowed symmetrical squares of sunlight to fall across the dark corridor. A melange of dust, oil, and aromatic wood created a subtle odor that Aeron found distinctly pleasant.

Corden led him past several chambers, mostly studies and reading rooms, to a paneled door at the end of the hall. The guard knocked at the door. "Master Telemachon? I have a lad here with a letter addressed to you."

"Show the boy in, good Corden." The voice quavered with age. The guardsman gestured at Aeron and followed him in. This room was a personal study, with tall windows of leaded glass that rattled in the winter wind. A rotund, stoop-shouldered man with watery eyes and a mere wisp of white hair clinging to his wattled head sat at a small writing desk, scratching at a thick journal with a sharp quill. With a heavy sigh, he set down his pen and rose to face Aeron. Telemachon was dressed in heavy robes that resembled Oriseus's in cut and style, but his were light blue in color, and he draped a long hood of indigo around his shoulders. He eyed Aeron for a long moment and said, "Wait outside, Corden."

"Of course, m'lord." The guardsman withdrew.

The old master held out his hand. "Your letter, lad?"

"Yes, my lord," Aeron replied. He quickly stepped forward and handed the parchment to Telemachon. "It's from Fineghal Caillaen, of the Maerchwood."

"Fineghal . . ." The master frowned. Moving over to stand in the light of one of the windows, he broke the seal and perused the letter several times. When he finished, he glanced up to meet Aeron's gaze. Aeron was surprised to see that some of the weakness and uncertainty in the older man's expression had vanished. "You are Aeron Morieth?"

"Yes, m'lord."

"Do you know anything of the contents of this letter?"

"No, m'lord. Fineghal only told me that it was a letter of introduction, and that I could show it to you to gain admittance to the College of Mages."

"I knew Fineghal a long, long time ago," Telemachon mused. "My studies led me to his doorstep more than forty years ago. Is he well?"

"I haven't seen him in three months, but the last time we parted, he was in good health," Aeron said.

"Good," grunted Telemachon. He faced the door and raised his voice slightly. "Corden!"

The door cracked. "Yes, Lord Telemachon?"

"Bring Melisanda here, please." Telemachon turned back to Aeron as the guard disappeared. He paced ponderously back and forth, hands clasped behind his back. "Fineghal's taught other students before you, Aeron," he said. "I've never known him to send an apprentice on to study elsewhere. He finishes what he begins."

Aeron shifted nervously. "I wanted to learn more than he was willing to teach."

"Oh?" The master glanced at him. "Very well. I don't set

much store by what you may or may not have done before you walked through that door. That includes any learning or skill with the art you may think you already possess." He held up the parchment. "Fineghal says that you must be instructed, and he cannot do it himself. For his sake, I will allow you to remain here as a student."

Aeron let a breath of relief escape from his lips.

"Don't relax just yet, Aeron. I have no idea who you are, what you know, or what you may be capable of learning. Without Fineghal's letter, you would not be a potential student. And without his offer to compensate me for your tuition, you would not be allowed to remain."

"Tuition?"

Telemachon smiled humorlessly. "It is not insignificant. But I will sponsor you, since Fineghal asks it of me."

There was a knock at the door, and a delicate Vilhonese woman about Aeron's age entered. She was short and slight, with dark eyes and a heart-shaped face. Aeron was reminded of his woodsman's garb and lack of formal learning; the girl's graceful carriage, sophisticated features, and studious expression marked her as a lady unlike any Aeron had ever known. "Melisanda of Arrabar, Master Telemachon. You sent for me?"

"Ah, Melisanda. This is Aeron Morieth, a new student from Maerchlin. You are excused from your studies for the rest of the day; show Aeron the college grounds and get him settled in, if you please."

The girl glanced at Aeron without expression. "As you wish, Master Telemachon."

The old master inclined his head to Aeron. "I expect I shall see you in a day or two in class; I am the High Diviner, and you must begin with the basics of my art." He returned to his writing desk, sighing as he sat down. Melisanda caught Aeron's attention and nodded at the door, but before they left, Telemachon held up his hand. "One last thing, Aeron. I am your sponsor, so I shall be keeping a close eye on you. I advise you to devote yourself completely to your studies. More than a few students allow themselves to become . . . distracted here. You would be wise to avoid their example."

As Telemachon requested, Melisanda led Aeron to each of the buildings within the college walls, explaining each in a smooth voice with just a hint of a throaty Reach accent. Of course, the College of Mages was only a small portion of Cimbar's great university, but Aeron had already observed that the common scribes and artists who studied in the whitewashed acropolis below did not intrude upon the affairs of the wizards in their lofty perch overlooking the city. Slaves, serfs, and commoners of all descriptions might win a place in the university by virtue of talent and patronage, but the wizards' school was evidently reserved for the noble-born. Aeron didn't need Melisanda's wary glances to figure out that the college was a place of his betters. We'll see about that, he promised himself.

Melisanda started the tour with the Masters' Hall as soon as they left Telemachon's chambers. The northern half housed the college's council rooms, administrators, and the private studies of the masters. "You won't spend much time here until you're a student, fish," she remarked.

"I'm not a student now?" Aeron asked in surprise.

"Of course not. You're a novice—a 'fish,' as we're called. Once you've shown a command of each of the eight disciplines in the novitiate examination, you are allowed to wear the student's tabard and cap." She looked him over and smiled. "I don't suppose you have any idea of what the disciplines are, do you?"

"Abjuration, alteration, conjuration, divination, enchantment, illusion, invocation, and necromancy, Lady Melisanda," Aeron replied. "I know them better by their elven names."

Melisanda raised an eyebrow. "I see you have some learning already. And you don't have to call me 'lady.' All novices are equals in the college. You should defer to a student—they're the ones who wear the tabards and caps over their tunics. 'Lady' or 'sir' is appropriate for them. And, of course, show deference to any of the masters. They dress as Telemachon does, although in different colors depending on the discipline they favor."

"I noticed that Telemachon and another master wore hoods," Aeron said. "What does that mean?"

"The hood marks Telemachon as one of the Ruling

Council, the High Diviner. The highest master in each discipline sits on the council. I don't know who introduced you to him, but he knew who to talk to. Any one of the High Masters can sponsor new novices just by saying so." She gazed at Aeron in frank appraisal. Aeron shifted his feet nervously. After a long moment, she released him with a curt nod. "Well, come on, fish. I can't afford to spend all day leading you about."

"How many masters, students, and novices are there?"

Melisanda frowned, counting in her mind. "There are nine masters on the Ruling Council, plus another nineteen masters who don't sit on the council. Memorize their names and faces as soon as possible. There are forty-one students right now, and eighty-seven novices. Eighty-eight now, including you."

"Not every novice succeeds in becoming a student?"

"No. About half of the novices can't pass the novitiate examination." She grimaced. "My own examination is scheduled for three weeks from today. I'd hoped to spend the day studying for it. I'm still uncertain of the invocation and necromancy spells I intend to cast."

Leaving the Masters' Hall, Melisanda led Aeron into the open plaza in the center of the college. Over the next hour, she showed him the East and West Halls and the great library in the center of the square. East and West were the college's instruction buildings, filled with classrooms, lecture halls, meeting rooms, and laboratories; since it was now the middle of the afternoon, many of these rooms were in use. Melisanda didn't interrupt any classes or lectures to introduce Aeron, but she quietly pointed out any masters they encountered.

By the time they left West Hall, the blustering wind had increased to gale force, and the temperature had dropped precipitously. They hurried into the last of the college's five buildings, a plain building pitted by row after row of narrow slitlike windows. "The Students' Hall," Melisanda said. "This is your home for as long as you stay here."

The foyer resembled the entrance of the Masters' Hall, but it seemed plainer and brighter. The masters' building was steeped in an air of dignity and reserve, a weight of tradition that brooked no insolence. But the moment Aeron and Melisanda stepped inside the students' quarters, they were nearly bowled over by a pair of novices bounding through the hall, attempting to tag each other with small spheres of colored light—a magician's game of tag.

Aeron caught Melisanda by the arm and dragged her out of the path of a novice. "Is everyone this enthusiastic?"

Melisanda sniffed. "No. Baldon and Eldran appear to have suddenly lost their reason, that's all."

The taller lad was a freckle-faced boy several years younger than Aeron, with an unruly shock of red hair on top of his head. Panting, he skidded to a halt. "Hey, Eldran, look—a new fish! What's your name, fish?"

The other boy spared Aeron a passing glance while he whisked the yellow sphere into Baldon's ribs with a sweeping gesture. The glowing sphere splattered as it struck the taller boy, covering him in a golden halo. "Ha! Gotcha." Satisfied that he'd had the better of the match, he paused to assess Aeron. He was a little younger than Aeron, too, and stood half a head shorter than he.

"Baldon, Eldran, this is Aeron Morieth, from Maerchlin. Aeron, these are two of your hallmates."

"Hallmates?"

"Ha! What a new fish!" Baldon snorted. "How'd you get stuck shepherding this clod around, Melisanda?"

Melisanda shot him a dirty look and then turned her back on the boy. "All the novices and students are divided among the four halls in this building, Aeron. There's an east and west wing, and each has two floors. Hallmates look out for each other. Baldon, Eldran, and I belong to Sword Hall. The others are Crown, Ring, and Scepter."

"So that's why you showed me around. Telemachon sent for one of my hallmates to get me settled in."

Melisanda nodded. "Two of our students graduated recently, so we were due to get some new fish. Come on, we'll show you to your room."

A grand staircase of polished wood swept up from the entry hall, curving into a balcony that ringed the chamber. On one side was a doorway surmounted by a heraldic crest featuring a gilded crown; opposite it, another doorway marked by two crossed swords led into a long corridor. "Sword Hall?" Aeron asked.

Melisanda nodded. They marched about halfway down the hallway past door after door before she halted in front of one, undid the clasp, and pushed it open. The room was about five paces wide, and maybe seven deep; a narrow window looked out over the outside wall and to the barren coasts beyond the city walls. The floor was gleaming hardwood; the furnishings included a small bed, a dresser, a standing chest, a writing desk, and an empty bookshelf. "Your new home," she announced.

"This will do," Aeron said. To be honest, it was a far finer room than any he'd called his own in Maerchlin, but he was determined not to let his hallmates guess the truth. He shrugged his bedroll and pack from his shoulder onto the bed, drifting to the window in amazement. He'd seen too much in one day. Wandering through the city, meeting Telemachon, walking around the College of Mages . . . he'd never dreamed how much existed outside the small villages and wide forests of his home.

"Stand to!" barked Baldon. Aeron nearly leapt out of his boots, whirling and raising a hand to defend himself. All three of his companions faced the door, bowing.

In the doorway stood a tall, handsome youth, a red tabard and cap over his gray breeches and white shirt. He leaned against the lintel, surveying the scene, a well-pleased smirk resting on his confident face. His gaze halted on Aeron. "Please don't tell me that this dung-toting peasant is our new fish," he said languidly.

"Yes, sir, Lord Dalrioc," answered Baldon. "He's our new fish, sir."

The young wizard straightened and advanced, a scowl settling over his features. "Haven't they taught you anything yet, fish?"

Aeron noted the inferior pose the others had assumed and realized that Dalrioc expected him to copy them. Awkwardly he did so. "I only arrived today, my lord."

"From what stinking midden heap, I can only imagine," Dalrioc commented. "What idiot let you in here?"

"Master Telemachon."

"And for what possible reason would the High Diviner allow a wretch like you to soil my hall?"

With a conscious effort, Aeron bit back a sharp retort and instead answered, "I'm here to study magic, my lord."

Dalrioc laughed harshly. "By Assuran! Why not teach a pig to sing while we're at it?"

Despite the warning glance Melisanda shot at him, Aeron straightened and looked Dalrioc in the eye. "I've studied some already," he said evenly.

"What, did some hedge wizard teach you how to make potions with bat wings and mudwort?"

"No. I had the honor to study under a great elven mage. He sent me here to continue my learning."

Dalrioc stalked around Aeron, circling him. "Very well. Let us see you work some elven magic, new fish. Impress me with your powers."

Melisanda raised her eyes and spoke. "Lord Dalrioc, we haven't had a chance to explain things to Aeron. He doesn't know any better. Please allow us to correct his abominable behavior. There's no need to trouble yourself with such an insignificant creature."

Dalrioc wheeled on Melisanda with such savagery that Aeron almost expected him to strike her, but at the last moment he reined in his anger. He narrowed his eyes and said, "You are not to inform me of what I may or may not find insignificant, fish. However, you are correct in observing that you have failed miserably in preparing Aeron to become a novice of the college. In reparation, the three of you may empty every chamber pot in Sword Hall three times a day for the next week. And, Melisanda, since you are so anxious to make amends, you may make my bed in the morning and turn down my covers in the evening." Dalrioc allowed his eyes to rest on Melisanda long enough for the Vilhonese girl to flush and look at the floor.

"But it's my ignorance, and no fault of theirs!" Aeron protested, disregarding the silent warnings of his fellows.

"Make that two weeks," Dalrioc amended. "Each time this fish is disrespectful to me, I'll add another."

Aeron fell silent. He could see where this was going.

"Now, I asked you to work a spell," Dalrioc continued. "I cannot believe that you have any worthwhile command of the art, but since you seem to think so, let's see you prove it." He crossed his arms and offered an indulgent smile, but his eyes were cold and hard.

"Yes, my lord," Aeron replied. He searched through his mind for a moment, seeking something appropriate. He was fleetingly tempted to lash out with fire hand or the charm of blindness simply to see how Dalrioc would react. Instead, he chose to work the charm of invisibility. With a whisper and a quick, skillful turn of the cool currents of the Weave around him, he vanished from sight.

The novices' eyes widened in surprise, but they held

their tongues and waited motionlessly. Dalrioc, on the other hand, was visibly shocked. He mouthed a vile oath and scowled. "You know the spell of invisibility?" he said, speaking in Aeron's direction.

"Yes," Aeron answered. To illustrate the scope of his spell, he opened and closed one of the dresser's drawers. "Fineghal, my old tutor, taught me the spell months ago."

"Release it at once," Dalrioc demanded.

Aeron did so, slowly fading back into view.

The older student glared at Aeron for a long moment, and then stomped out of the room. "Remember—two weeks of chamber pots, and more if you don't get him squared away quickly!" he barked over his shoulder. He slammed the door shut behind him.

Melisanda, Baldon, and Eldran heaved sighs of relief. Aeron faced them. "I'll take care of the chamber pots."

"You'll do no such thing," Melisanda retorted. "If Dalrioc suspects that you carried out just one pot, he'd skin us alive for disobeying him. Do you understand me?"

Aeron nodded slowly. "I do."

Baldon dragged out the chair by the desk and straddled it, resignation on his face. "Well, make yourself comfortable, Aeron. We've got a lot to tell you about the rules of the hall."

"Before we start, I have a question. Why was he so surprised by the spell I chose?"

To Aeron's astonishment, all three novices laughed. "Because Dalrioc can't work it himself," Melisanda said. "Illusions are his weakest school. If you already know how to weave a spell as advanced as that, you won't be a novice for long. He'll make your life miserable for a few weeks, but you'll be recognized as a student in no time at all."

Seven

Aeron met the rest of his hallmates in the refectory that evening. Besides Melisanda, Baldon, and Eldran, there were eighteen more fish who shared his lowly status. Most were highborn Chessentans from all over the country, even a few from cities that were rivals or enemies of Cimbar, and a handful from other lands. By twos and threes, they drifted into the refectory, joining Aeron and his new friends at the table reserved for the novices of Sword Hall.

Somehow Melisanda and the two boys had found the time to quietly spread the news among the novices of Aeron's arrival and his moral victory over Dalrioc. From one end of the table to the other, he was greeted with broad smiles and easy jests. Aeron was beginning to understand that adversity builds fellowship; the twenty-one—now twenty-two—fish of Sword Hall were united against the ruthless tyranny imposed by the students.

"Well, he shouldn't have challenged me to prove myself without knowing a thing about me," Aeron replied to their congratulations. He looked around discreetly; the masters dined at the high table, and long tables just below were reserved for the students of each of the four halls. Dalrioc held court among the Sword Hall students, laughing and conversing without a care in the world. From time to time, other students, and even a master or two, came over to speak with him. Apparently Dalrioc was a student of some importance. "Why does everyone hover around him like that?" Alies asked Melisanda.

"He's a Corynian," she said with a shrug.

Aeron frowned, trying to understand the significance of that statement. Then it struck him. The Corynians ruled the wealthy city of Soorenar, one of the principal rivals of Cimbar. Born to one of the highest families in Chessenta, and he's no better than I, Aeron thought. So much for nobility. He allowed himself a moment to revel in his minor victory over Dalrioc Corynian before returning his attention to his surroundings. "I thought Soorenar fought against Cimbar and was defeated," he said slowly. "If he's a prince of a beaten city, why's he so important?"

His highborn hallmates stared long enough for Aeron's face to flush red. Melisanda eventually took pity on him. "Do you know anything of the alliances of the land, Aeron?" she asked quietly.

"I've never had cause to concern myself with such matters." In rustic Maerchlin, the great alliances and intrigues had seemed a thousand miles distant. A peasant or lowborn freeholder such as Aeron was so far removed from the affairs of lords and kings that it was useless to waste thought on the matter, but here things were far different.

"Think on it, Aeron," Melisanda said, lowering her voice. "Which cities lead Chessenta today?"

"Cimbar and Akanax, of course. Their alliance defeated Soorenar and Luthcheq. They're the only strong cities left."

"And with no foes to ally against, what is there to bind them together?"

"Nothing, I suppose. But what does this have to do with Dalrioc of Soorenar? His city was Cimbar's rival before the Time of Troubles, but it's been ruined by Akanax."

"You forget that Soorenar was always a wealthy city," Baldon interjected. "Its might is in the coffers of its merchants, not its strength of arms. The Corynians have rebuilt the city very quickly."

"The alliance between Akanax and Cimbar is a thing of the past. And the fragile truce that exists now might be blown away by a strong wind. Now do you understand?" Melisanda said.

Aeron's head swam. So Cimbar as a city-state teetered precariously between one rival—Akanax—and one enemy—Soorenar—just as the Sceptanar himself faced the opposition of the city's demagogues and the censure of the noble senate. He nodded slowly, his eyes on Dalrioc. "Akanax and Cimbar balance in the scales. A resurgent Soorenar might tip them. And so Dalrioc holds court in Cimbar's College of Mages." Aeron grimaced; he couldn't have picked a more powerful enemy if he had tried.

He methodically attacked his food for a time, mindful of his common manners. The novices ate at trestle tables at the end of refectory. The students shared smaller tables in the center of the room, and beyond the tables held by the students stood the high table of the hall, where the masters ate. Aeron counted twenty-six seats at the head of the hall, but only about half were occupied. While he watched, a master in a yellow robe paused by the table of the Sword Hall students to speak with Dalrioc. "So if Dalrioc is here to entertain offers of alliance against Akanax," Aeron said, "why isn't he guesting in the palace of the Sceptanar?"

"Because the Sceptanar wants no part of the Corynians or Soorenar," Eldran replied, a little too loudly. "As soon as Soorenar chooses a side, Akanax will be forced to find other allies like Mordulkin or Airspur, and that means war all across Chessenta. But Cimbar's senators, and even some of the demagogues, disagree with the Sceptanar's stance. There's talk that the Sceptanar won't hold his seat for long." The black looks he received from his neighbors embarassed the enthusiastic apprentice into a self-conscious silence. Flushing, he shifted in his seat and leaned closer to Aeron, lowering his voice. "Or so it's said, anyway. Some of the masters belong to parties opposed to the Sceptanar," he continued. "If they overthrow Cimbar's king, who knows what might happen?"

Factions opposed to the Sceptanar? Foreign intrigue? Wizards shifting from party to party like children picking sides for a game of hide-and-seek? Wizardry seemed simple by comparison! Aeron chewed slowly, thinking. "How does anything get done?"

"In the college, the Sceptanar's men decide the issues. The senators and the demagogues oppose each other, so Lord Telemachon and the other masters who support Cimbar's king throw their weight from one side to the other," said Melisanda. "Most of the students are noble-born, and they choose sides as well."

"Which masters belong to which factions?"

Melisanda glanced around and lowered her voice. "You don't want to speculate too openly, but here's where matters stand. The High Masters of Alteration, Conjuration, and Necromancy are from families that support the senate over the Sceptanar. Five of the lesser masters from these schools are in this camp, too. Some favor peace with Akanax, and others a new alliance with Soorenar.

"The Masters of Illusion, Invocation, and Enchantment are populists who favor the Mob. Seven lesser masters in these schools stand with them. The demagogues agitate for war with Akanax and the overthrow of the Sceptanar.

"Finally, Telemachon—he's the Master of Divination, you might recall—the Master Librarian, and the Master of Abjuration are the Sceptanar's men. They lean toward honoring our truce with King Gormantor of Akanax."

Aeron eyed the mages and archmages Melisanda had pointed out. "Where do we fit in?"

"Until we're students, we don't matter," Baldon said. "And don't worry about it, Aeron. It's all scheming and double-talk. It's not as if they're going to start slinging spells at any moment. They've been at this for a very long time."

Eldran looked up from beside him and jabbed an elbow into Baldon's arm. "Whoops! Stop talking about it. Seara's coming to join us."

The camaraderie of the novices faded as a heavyset young woman in a tabard and cap of green sat down at the head of their table. She eyed the nearby novices with contempt, ignoring Aeron, then turned her attention to her dinner. Slowly the fish resumed their subdued conversations, taking care to ensure that Seara was not disturbed.

"Are we allowed to speak freely at the table?" Aeron asked Melisanda quietly.

"Yes, although it's a good idea never to say anything about a student or a master when we're chaperoned. The students take turns supervising us."

"Why?"

"To make sure that we don't disgrace Sword Hall by doing something that draws a master's attention to our table," Melisanda replied with a tight smile. "Students never brace you up when a master's present, since it wouldn't be proper to involve a real wizard in something so insignificant as correcting a novice's behavior. But you can bet that students remember everything you do wrong and take it out on you later."

After the evening meal, Aeron and his fellows returned to the Students' Hall for a few hours' study. Both novices and students alike had dozens of thick tomes cluttering their rooms and attacked them with desperate energy until late in the evening. Melisanda retired to her studies, but Baldon and Eldran remained in Aeron's room to help him memorize the names of every master, as well as the students of Sword Hall. Afterward they talked late into the night while arranging Aeron's few belongings.

Aeron found himself yawning continuously. It had been

a long day, and he finally turned in after midnight. After Baldon and Eldran left, he extinguished the lamp and dropped onto the simple mattress. Although his limbs trembled with physical and nervous exhaustion, Aeron could not sleep; his mind raced as he grappled with everything that he'd seen and learned during the day. But eventually fatigue won, and he drifted off to sleep.

* * * * *

Over the next few days, Aeron attended his first lessons at the College of Mages. The novices of Sword Hall divided their day into a morning and an afternoon class and had formal classes and lectures eight days out of the ten-day week. Each of the disciplines of magic was discussed at least once per week by a master garbed in the colors of the school he represented. Other lectures touched on history, ancient languages, the natural world, and other arcane topics. As promised, Lord Telemachon lectured on divinations the second day of Aeron's schooling. The old master ignored Aeron throughout the entire lecture.

Aeron was surprised to see no sign of the students in these lectures, but he soon found out that students did not study alongside novices. They met with the masters in smaller groups at infrequent intervals; for the most part, they pursued their own courses of study. And now that he knew what to look for, he began to spot signs of the partisanship dividing the college. More than a few masters and students went out of their way to associate with their fellows and snub colleagues belonging to a rival party. Tension and distrust were a way of life within the ivy-covered walls.

On the afternoon of the third day of lessons, Aeron and his fellows gathered in the cold Chamber of Conjuration. Like the other halls in which they attended the masters, the chamber was lined with plain stone benches for the novices. Its walls were marked with arcane designs and intricate relief work, and the room was illuminated by anchored spheres of wizard light. Aeron gazed around in curiosity while his hallmates conversed in low whispers.

At half past the hour, Master Oriseus swept into the room with a springy stride. He grinned and waved his arms expansively. "Why, if it isn't the hungry little fish of

Sword Hall!" he announced, feigning surprise. "What little piece of wisdom shall I allow them to devour today? How can I assuage their ravenous greed for knowledge?" Without waiting for an answer, he tugged on his beard and smiled. "Today, I think we shall attempt the conjuration of ordinary animals. The techniques we practice today are indispensable components of greater and more powerful conjurations you may learn as students."

Aeron straightened and leaned forward. After days of drudgery at Dalrioc's command and dry hours of esoteric lecturing in the halls of instruction, a master was finally going to show him how to work a spell! The other novices buzzed with eagerness. On average, only three or four lectures each week actually involved the working of magic. He listened attentively.

Oriseus spent an hour describing the arcane formula that locked the spell's power in the mind, the materials that energized the summoning, the gestures and phrases that bound the conjured creature to the wizard's will. While Aeron tried to absorb Oriseus's lecture without comparison to the elven magic he already knew, he couldn't help but observe that the approach was different. Human magic was ritualized. Instead of images or symbols, spells were memorized by long, complicated phrases in ancient tongues. Elven magic was more fluid, shaped by the circumstance of location and need; human magic, on the other hand, seemed swifter and more mechanical.

Oriseus concluded his monologue by causing a string of magical writing to appear in the air before the novices with a simple turn of his hands. "Record these words in your books, my dear little fish," he announced. "They are an element common to many of the easier conjurations, a single stone in the tower of your spell, if you will. Then commit them to your memory."

While the novices busily scratched away with pen and ink to copy the magical phrase, Oriseus paced the room, observing their work. "Baldon, you clod! You've miscopied *calgius* as *colvius*! You'd conjure nothing but a head cold with that! Bram, since you seem to have mastered the spell already, you shall be the first to cast. Hurry up. I'm growing tired of keeping these letters in the air!"

Eventually the last of the novices looked up with a sheepish grin, realizing that everyone else had readied himself to work Oriseus's simple spell. Aeron had taken longer than anyone else to copy and understand the phrasing, but the actual process of memorization had been easy for him. He was ready not long after Melisanda, the fastest of the novices, had finished.

"Excellent!" Oriseus announced. "Now, watch closely while I work the cantrip." He spoke the magical phrase loudly and clearly, holding his hands in front of his chest, palms turned inward. Aeron felt the light caress of the Weave at work. To his senses, it seemed cropped or truncated, squared off by the rigorous and unyielding framework of the conjuror's words . . . but it worked. There was an odd sizzling sound, and a scrawny squirrel appeared in the center of the room. "As you can see, I chose to conjure a squirrel," Oriseus explained. "I did so by concentrating on everything I would expect of a squirrel while working this spell. Now, since this is a mere fragment of a conjuration, the effect is quite temporary, and our magical phrase included no means to control or direct the animal upon its appearance."

Alarmed by the situation, the gray rodent chittered and ran in a circle, seeking escape. Oriseus watched with a crooked smile. "My hospitality does not appeal to you, Master Rodent? Very well, then. Remove yourself from my presence at once!" He raised one hand, spoke a single sharp word, and with a flash of light, the squirrel vanished. "As you can see, my little fish, the last word of the conjuration serves as a dismissal. I advise you not to forget it, in the event you conjure up something you'd rather not spend a lot of time with."

"Master Oriseus? Where did the squirrel come from?" Aeron asked.

The master conjuror beamed and bobbed his head. "Why, I have no earthly idea, young Aeron!"

"Did your magic actually create a living squirrel?"

"Oh, that would be a powerful spell indeed, to create life out of nothingness! No, Aeron, a conjuration simply borrows what you seek from somewhere else. Sometimes it is magical energy itself that you borrow, with an advanced spell of this sort . . . but to answer your first question, somewhere in this wide world there is a rather confused squirrel wondering what just happened."

"It almost seems unethical," Melisanda mused aloud.

"What right do we have to wrench a creature from its native surroundings?"

Oriseus hopped up and down in delight. "Ah, wonderful! Master conjurors have debated this very topic for years beyond counting! Truly, my little fish, you astound me this morning. But let's set aside this thorny issue for the moment, promise ourselves that we shall not injure or misuse any creature that joins us today, and proceed with the practice of this spell. For the summoning itself is not sinister, my lords and ladies. Only the purpose to which the summoner sets his guest is for good or ill!"

One by one, the Sword Hall novices worked their way through the fragmentary conjuration. Most of the students recited the words and performed the gestures correctly, but the effort to seize and wield the magic around them brought beads of sweat to their brows and grimaces of pain. Aeron felt as if he were watching tone-deaf musicians blindly plucking at an instrument's strings, hoping by dint of repetition to find the note they sought. Even Melisanda, the most skillful of the novices, frowned and seized the power necessary for her spell with a catlike lunge.

"Novice Aeron? Show us how it is done," Oriseus directed. He wore an expression of beatific patience.

"Yes, Master Oriseus." Aeron stood and advanced to the center of the room. He carefully pronounced the unfamiliar words while imitating Oriseus's posture and gestures. He could sense the ethereal currents of the Weave that swirled in the chilly air, the dense power that waited within the stones of the room, the fiery sparks burning in every living heart. With ease, he wove the elements together, heart racing with the brilliant clarity of magic in his mind and hands. He pictured a sea gull in his mind—there were plenty in and around the harbor—and through the magic of the spell, he felt the image in his mind spring into existence before him.

Aeron opened his eyes. In the room's center a gull stood, regarding him patiently. Unlike the creatures conjured by the other novices, it didn't waver or fade; Aeron had woven well enough to hold it effortlessly.

"Well done, Aeron," Oriseus breathed. "I see now why you were sent to study with us."

Aeron accepted the praise with a scant nod. "The spell's simple enough, but the words aren't familiar to me."

"The words are paint and canvas, lad. You'll need to know how to use them sooner or later. But the way you make them work, that is the essence of the art!" Oriseus stroked his beard thoughtfully. "I shall have to keep an eye on you, Aeron Morieth. Do you recall the dismissal?"

He nodded and repeated the last word of the conjuration. With a tiny portion of his mind, he released the currents of magic that held the gull in the chamber. It ghosted out of view, taking wing as it returned to nothingness. He glanced around and realized that the other novices were looking at him with open astonishment on their faces. They don't feel the Weave as I do, Aeron realized. I may not have their learning, but I can wield magic as easily as they.

The silence stretched out for a long moment, until Oriseus suddenly burst into motion, wringing his hands melodramatically and grimacing. "Alas! Our brief time together is at an end. Next week I shall return with another conjuration for you to master. In the meantime, practice and study, practice and study!" The novices stirred and rose, shuffling to the door. Aeron turned to gather his things and join them, but Oriseus caught his arm and drew him aside. "Where did you say you'd studied, Aeron?"

"I learned from Fineghal, the Storm Walker of the Maerchwood, a lord of the Tel'Quessir."

"So that was Telemachon's secret." Oriseus nodded to himself, his eyes distant. After a moment, he looked back to Aeron. "You will not remain a novice for long. You may have to familiarize yourself with the tools of human wizardry, but you can gather and weave magic that none of your fellows can even perceive yet. It is an injustice to treat you as a novice."

"I noticed how awkward my classmates were. But until I learn the languages they've already studied, I'll only be able to use a fraction of my talent."

Oriseus dismissed his objections with a wave of his hand. "When you become a student, Aeron, you will be asked to choose a discipline. Think about the tabard and cap of conjuration. I would greatly like to work with you in more advanced studies."

"I don't know what to say, Master Oriseus."

The saturnine master grinned. "You do not have to decide yet, Aeron. Now, go and catch up to your hallmates. You'll need their fellowship for at least a little longer." He bobbed his head and retreated, leaving Aeron alone in the cold stone chamber.

* * * * *

Cimbar's weather was cooler and wetter than that of the Maerchwood, especially in the last months of winter. The great city was raked by winds howling across the Inner Sea for weeks in a row. The novices were permitted to leave the college grounds during the days of the week's end, when no formal lessons were scheduled. From time to time, Aeron explored the old city with his hallmates, although his empty purse kept him from joining them in their more expensive revels. More often he spent his free hours engaged in relentless study, holed up in a remote recess of the college library or in an unused classroom in the academic halls, hoping to escape Dalrioc Corynian's attention by making himself hard to find.

Aeron struggled to master Thorass, Old Untheric, and ancient Rauric, the forgotten tongues that most of the college's masters used for the recording of spells. However, he excelled in the working of the phrases and fragments the masters used for practical demonstrations of spellcasting. Even schools with which he had little experience, such as necromancy or conjuration, he grasped quickly. In a matter of weeks, he caught up to and surpassed the most advanced novices among his hallmates.

It wasn't in Aeron's nature to be satisfied, not as long as the vast store of knowledge held within the college walls remained unconquered. Within a month of arriving, Aeron understood just how little he knew, how far he had to go, and instead of settling down to patiently journey into the realms before him, he decided to plunge ahead with inexhaustible energy. He was here to learn as much as he could; there was no point in attacking the task ahead with anything less than his complete and obsessive attention. With challenging studies to engage him, Chessenta's greatest city to explore, wealth and comfort enough to feel guilty about his good fortune, and associates who shared his intelligence and interests, Aeron was content for the moment.

But one inescapable condition ground him down every day: the spiteful malice of Dalrioc and the circle of students who followed in his wake. The Soorenaran prince had not forgotten Aeron's defiance at their first meeting, and at every opportunity, he found some way to make Aeron miserable. His room was inspected and found wanting on a regular basis. His knowledge of Chessentan history, lineage, law, and the inane trivia pertaining to the college and its former students was examined through dogged interrogations that exposed a weak chink in his armor. Aeron had never learned the histories and heroes' names that Dalrioc and his noble friends had been taught in childhood. Aeron was required to write out the rolls of kings and nobles hundreds of times and submit them to Dalrioc for review.

Aeron's only response was to immerse himself even further in his studies. His natural talent for wielding magic quickly earned him the admiration and envy of his fellow fish. Even Melisanda frequently sought out Aeron to help her study for her upcoming novitiate examination. Aeron lived for the chance to spend a quiet hour with her. Melisanda's face haunted his dreams, and it took all of his willpower to force these thoughts to the back of his mind when she was near.

On a bitterly cold evening two days before her test, he lingered after they'd finished going over the last of her spells, unwilling to return to his own quarters. "Dalrioc's waiting for me; I can just feel it," he sighed.

"I've never seen him single out a fish the way he's watching you, Aeron," Melisanda told him. "Dalrioc even arranges for other students to keep an eye on you when he has to attend a lecture or do some research."

"It's working," Aeron said bitterly. "Sooner or later I'm going to lose my temper, and then he'll really have me."

Melisanda offered a sympathetic smile. "You're something completely antithetical to what he believes about the world: a commoner who is better than he."

"I might be a better mage, Melisanda, but I don't have his wealth or his power. Why does he resent me?"

"Because Dalrioc Corynian is accustomed to being the best at whatever he turns his hand to. It's how he was raised." She reached out and touched his shoulder. "Be patient. You're as ready for a novitiate examination as I am, and once you become a student, he can't touch you."

The door thumped loudly, and Dalrioc's clear voice rang outside. "Out in the hall, fish!"

"Guess he got bored," Aeron muttered. Melisanda rolled her eyes and stood. They filed out and found Dalrioc waiting in the dark, gleaming hallway, arms crossed over his chest. He smirked with anticipation.

"Aeron, it seems that you spend a good deal of time in Melisanda's rooms," he observed. "Don't you realize that she is quite above your station?"

Aeron flushed. Dalrioc's remark cut too close to the truth. "I was helping her study," he replied.

"Ah! Well, since you have time on your hands to help your hallmates, I am certain that you won't mind running a small errand for me." Dalrioc stepped closer and sharpened his gaze. "I require a stone from the Broken Pyramid."

The Broken Pyramid? Aeron looked up. The ruins of the Untheric obelisk were avoided by all but the masters. Many precious artifacts—and sleeping dangers—were said to be lost in the blasted rubble and the catacombs beneath, but the word among the novices was to give it a wide berth. Aeron swallowed and asked, "What manner of stone?"

"About this large," the prince said, using his hands to measure an imaginary rock about the size of his two fists together. "Any one should do."

"Lord Dalrioc, the ruins of the pyramid are dangerous," Melisanda said. "Can Aeron do this in the morning?"

Dalrioc raised an eyebrow. "I am afraid that I have an immediate need for a stone in a spell I am studying. You are not a student yet, Melisanda. Do not presume to tell me how and when I should conduct my studies." He ran his eyes up and down her body, then added, "Since you are concerned for Aeron, you may join him. I don't expect you'll need a cloak if you hurry."

Melisanda glared back at the prince but held her silence. Not daring to protest any further, the two fish hurried outside into the howling night. The air was so cold that it took Aeron's breath away; on the exposed hillside, the wind scoured them with a stinging spray of needlelike ice. "Sorry I got you into this!" Aeron gasped, shouting to be heard over the wind.

"I shouldn't have opened my mouth," the girl replied. "Let's get his damned rock and get back inside. It's freezing out here!"

The sky was overcast, and the hilltop was dark. Once they left the warm yellow circle of light spilling from the windows of the Students' Hall, they could barely see their hands in front of their faces. "You know he's going to send us back at least three or four times before he gets tired of this game," Melisanda barked.

"I know. Might as well get it over with." Aeron blundered toward the skirt of rubble that surrounded the monolith, visible only as an ebon shadow in the darkness. Even with his keen elven vision, he could scarcely make out where they were going. He stumbled over some unseen obstacle on the ground and fell to his hands and knees. "Ouch! Wait a moment, Melisanda. I'll make some light."

Her teeth chattered from somewhere nearby. "Good idea. I can't see a thing."

Stone grated on stone in the darkness. A rasping growl cut through the wind's howling from somewhere ahead. Aeron suddenly felt colder, as if a ghostly hand had brushed his heart with an icy touch. He slowly rose, peering into the night. "Melisanda? What was that sound?"

Her voice was startlingly near. "I don't know. You'd better summon your light," she whispered.

Aeron nodded. He started to weave the spell, but he heard the sound of a man's voice. Something slid in the rubble. Then the sensation of magic at work tugged at Aeron's body, the powerful and desperate jolt of a mighty spell worked in haste.

Ahead of them, a brilliant flash of ruby light speared through the night, illuminating the scene. Kneeling in the apron of debris at the tower's foot, a brown-robed master with a dun hood confronted an awful beast, a dog-like thing the size of a small horse. Its mouth gaped open with a double row of teeth, one set vertically across its nightmarish maw. The master's spell launched a lance of energy at the creature, a fiery bolt searing Aeron's eyes and charring stone, but the flame splashed from the beast's flanks harmlessly. As the brief flare of light died away, the creature crouched and leapt with impossible speed. The master's scream rang through the darkness as night cloaked the scene again.

"Aeron! Your light!" cried Melisanda.

Abandoning subtlety, Aeron barked the brief syllables of the dweomer. With his hands, he wove a bobbing sphere of wizard light and cast it into the air, to hover a few feet ahead of them. A globe of eerie blue radiance brightened the night. Aeron shuddered in horror; the dog-thing had the master in its jaws, splintering bone and rending flesh. The dying man groaned and wheezed, pushing weakly at the creature's black snout.

"By the gods," Aeron murmured. Although every bone in his body ached with the desire to flee, he forced himself forward two steps and raised his hands, considering which of the spells at his command to employ. As he watched the scene in sick horror, he noticed an odd metallic gleam on the creature's foreleg. A strange silver band graven with twisted runes was clasped to its dark flesh. He pushed the odd bracelet to the back of his mind and started to speak the words for fire hand. He had to do something, even though it was clear that nothing could aid the master.

Melisanda caught his arm and dragged him back. "No, Aeron! It's too late for him."

"We've got to help him somehow!"

The Vilhonese girl shook her head. "It wasn't even fazed by the best spell a master could throw. The only thing we could do is get killed. Come on! We'll get help!"

Numbly, he nodded assent. They backed away quickly, stumbling across the loose stones of the tower's wreckage. Aeron could not wrench his eyes away from the terrible scene before him; the creature was tearing the master to pieces. "What in Faerûn is that thing?" he stammered.

"I have no idea. But I recognize the master. That's Raemon, the High Master of Abjuration."

"Not anymore," Aeron gasped. Suddenly he tripped over an unseen stone beneath his feet and fell heavily. Rubble grated and clattered over the bitter shrieking of the wind. He scrambled to his feet, bruised and a little embarrassed, but the monster's great head swiveled from its grisly work, two small, squarish ears quivering and twitching, its nostrils flaring. It doesn't have any eyes, he noted in surprise. Then he realized that the creature could *hear* quite well. It sniffed and took a tentative step toward them.

"Aeron," Melisanda whispered. "It's got our scent."

"Be quiet. It can't see us," he said softly. The bitter wind gusted, wracking him with cold, and he realized that the howling gale was the only thing standing between the two of them and an unpleasant death. They were downwind of the creature, and even with its unnaturally acute senses, it could barely make them out. Aeron stood slowly, trying not to jostle the loose rubble any more than he already had, but small stones clicked and scraped beneath his feet.

The creature snarled into the night and bounded in their direction, leaping from spot to spot as it tried to flush them out. Melisanda started to bolt, but Aeron caught her arm in an iron grip. He pressed his mouth to her ear and whispered, "If we move, we're dead. Don't make a sound."

Sniffing and growling, the horrendous creature tracked back and forth across the rubble, swinging its great dark head from side to side as it cast about for some hint of their location. Aeron could feel Melisanda shaking like a leaf in his arms. For a long moment, the thing seemed to stare right at them, only a dozen paces distant, and then, with an angry snort, it broke away, bounding back to the place where Master Raemon lay. With deliberate care, it rooted through the splintered wreckage of the wizard's body, as if to make absolutely certain that no possible spark of life remained. Then, its work done, it bounded off into the night, vanishing like a shadow.

The supernatural chill, the cold presence, faded away like a memory of pain. Aeron gasped for air and dragged Melisanda into motion. "I think it's gone. Come on."

Staggering against the freezing winds, they headed toward the flickering yellow lights of the hall. Although Aeron couldn't feel the creature nearby, his shoulder blades itched, anticipating the pounce of black claws from the flickering shadows. "What was that thing?" Aeron asked again, muttering to himself.

"Some kind of fiend, I think," Melisanda replied. "If Dalrioc had sent us out a few minutes earlier, it might have come across us instead of Master Raemon."

They darted up the steps to the Masters' Hall and battered their way inside. In a matter of minutes, they gathered a half-dozen masters and a handful of students, including Telemachon and Oriseus. Although several of the wizards viewed the novices with extreme skepticism, their obvious fright carried their story for a moment, and the procession started out into the cold.

"There had better be something truly horrifying out here," one of the masters stated as they returned to the scene. "If I've been dragged out into a night like this for a prank, the two of you will wish you'd never been born."

Telemachon remained silent, but Oriseus spoke up. "I

suspect that even the most addlepated novice would have more sense than that. But we shall see."

Several of the masters created powerful spheres of brilliant mage light, driving away the darkness as they approached the ruins with deliberate caution. Aeron's heart sank. There was nothing there, no trace of the monstrous creature he and Melisanda had seen! He could feel the eyes of the masters turning toward him. "The two of you will have a lot of explaining to do," one said ominously.

"Wait," said Telemachon. He directed his light at the rubble. A tatter of red fluttered in the wreckage. The masters fell silent as the mangled corpse of the Master Abjurer appeared. Perversely, his face was untouched, staring sightlessly into the ebon sky.

"What of the creature that attacked him?" Oriseus said. "Melisanda? Where did you see the creature?"

"It was right here, Master Oriseus. It had already killed Master Raemon when we fled."

"You abandoned him?" one of the students asked.

"Easy, now," Oriseus said. "If a High Master could not defend himself against the creature that did this, how could two novices have made any difference? In this case, discretion was clearly the better part of valor."

"There will be questions to answer," the first master said in a low voice. "Many questions."

Telemachon knelt by the body, his face expressionless. "Indeed. First we must see if the creature still lurks nearby. Summon the rest of the masters. And get these two inside."

Eight

No sign of the creature was ever found. Melisanda's novitiate examination was delayed by the death of the Master Abjurer, the extensive interrogations that she and Aeron endured, and the chaotic maneuverings of electing a replacement to the college's Ruling Council. Classes and lectures were suspended for a week as the masters debated, schemed, formed alignments, and broke them, and finally elevated a senator's son to the council. Students and novices alike waited nervously, although Aeron noticed that Dalrioc spent much of his time conferring with the masters. Supposedly no student had any say in how the masters managed their affairs, but the prince of Soorenar could and did make his voice heard.

A few days after the ceremony of advancement, Aeron was surprised to receive a summons from Lord Telemachon. When a High Master sent for a novice, the fish dropped what he was doing and answered the call, so Aeron trotted over to the Masters' Hall with all due haste. The hall felt silent and suspicious, still simmering with the unresolved arguments and the disturbing circumstances of Master Raemon's death. He went straight to Telemachon's chambers. "Lord Telemachon? You sent for me?"

The Master Diviner sat immersed in a sea of musty tomes, crackling yellow scrolls, and old rag-paper books stitched to wooden covers. His own personal library was quite extensive, but he had doubled its size since Aeron had last been in his chambers. Telemachon was visibly fatigued; dark bags pouched under his eyes, and he wheezed with each breath. The diviner frowned and looked up from his book. "Aeron. Have a seat."

The novice carefully cleared a leather chair and sat down. "Thank you, my lord."

"As Fineghal foretold, you have demonstrated great promise as a mage," the old wizard began. "While you still need to work on your mundane lessons, particularly your command of Untheric and Old Rauric, I understand that your spellcasting skills are without equal among the novices. Therefore, you will stand for your novitiate examination at the end of the week."

Aeron glanced up, his eyes alight. "I'm ready."

"Of course you're ready. I know that you can pass the examination easily, or I wouldn't have challenged you to attempt it. We'll observe the forms, but you need to be instructed as a student, not as a novice."

"Yes, my lord."

"I didn't expect this so soon, Aeron," Telemachon said, meeting Aeron's eyes. "But several students are about to graduate, and we expect to place some new fish soon, so there's no sense in holding you back. Most of the High Masters favored accepting you as a student based on your performance so far."

Aeron assented with a nod. He knew he could learn more as a student . . . and it would incense Dalrioc Corynian if Aeron climbed from the ranks of the novices to the exalted status of student. It also meant that he could remain close to Melisanda. "I won't fail, Lord Telemachon."

The old wizard leaned back behind his desk, studying Aeron. "Are you certain you've recovered from your harrowing experience of a week ago?"

"Yes, my lord. I was not injured."

"Through auguries and divinations, we've gleaned some information about the creature that attacked Master Raemon," Telemachon said. "It was a yugoloth, a supernatural horror from black dimensions beyond the circles of the world. A powerful fiend indeed."

Aeron straightened in his seat. "How could such a creature appear in the middle of the college?"

"Obviously it was summoned here," Telemachon said, a trace of irritation in his voice. "There are a number of wizards among us capable of such a feat, which leaves us to ponder the reason of it, not the means."

"I've been told that the ruins of the pyramid are dangerous. Could Master Raemon simply have stumbled across something better left undisturbed?"

"Perhaps," Telemachon said without expression. "Yet I find it curious that a powerful mage, one of the best among us, should simply happen to be abroad in the tower's ruins on such a night, and that he should happen to disturb something, and that the thing he unleashed should happen to be a creature capable of destroying him . . . and that his death should happen to occur in front of two defenseless novices, conveniently located to observe that no one else was near to rend Raemon limb from limb."

"You suspect foul play?" Aeron asked.

"Suffice it to say that I find the circumstances of Master Raemon's demise to be suspicious," Telemachon replied.

"But who would kill him, and why?"

Telemachon shrugged. "That," he said, "is what we still need to learn. Although it does not escape my notice that Raemon was one of nine members of the Ruling Council, a supporter of the Sceptanar, and that he has been replaced by Andreseus, who is a lord and senator of the city. With one unfortunate encounter, the balance of power has shifted."

"You don't think one of the masters favoring the senate killed him, do you?"

The High Diviner turned a frigid gaze on Aeron, the weakness and fatigue of his manner sloughing away to reveal an iron will beneath. "Novice Aeron, it is unwise in the extreme to speak such accusations of a High Master. The affairs of the Ruling Council are not the concern of novice or student. Do I make myself clear?"

Aeron recoiled. "Yes, my lord," he muttered. "Lord Telemachon . . . neither Melisanda or I had any part in this."

Imperceptibly the diviner's ire softened. "I know, Aeron. I suspect you were simply moved into place as one might move a piece on a chessboard. Some of my compatriots are not so certain of that." He settled his bulk into his chair and steepled his fingers in front of him, turning his gaze out the window. "Have you considered which colors you want to wear when you become a student?" he asked suddenly.

"No, my lord. I haven't thought that far ahead. Illusion and invocation are my strongest disciplines." Aeron paused and added, "A few weeks ago, Oriseus told me that he wanted me to consider conjuration as my school of choice."

Telemachon scowled. "Oriseus wants you, eh?"

"He said my talents lent themselves to summonings."

"Do you feel that is true?"

"No other master has encouraged me to choose another school, my lord. I hadn't wielded many conjuration spells before I came here; the spells I studied under Fineghal were invocations that relied on the elements around me, or illusions crafted from my own force of will." He shrugged. "I think I could choose any school except necromancy and do well, but I'd do best in illusion or invocation."

"I believe so, too, Aeron. Master Sarim is a good man, one of the best here. Think on the yellow of invocation."

Aeron smiled thinly. Invocation, the direct manipulation of the Weave through natural forces such as wind or fire, had always been his strong suit. "I will," he promised.

Telemachon nodded and drew his hand over his face, dismissing Aeron with a wave. "You are excused from your classes for the rest of the week in order to prepare. You and Melisanda will take the examination together, along with Briet from Crown Hall. Now go study. You have no excuse for a mediocre showing."

As Telemachon advised, Aeron secluded himself for the rest of the week, throwing himself into his studies and preparing for the examination. Traditionally the test lasted three days; most novices could not hold more than two or three spells in their mind at once, and since the test consisted of demonstrating at least one spell from each of the eight disciplines, the prospective student was allowed to rest and study the next spells he would have to cast during the course of the examination. Aeron probably could have managed all eight in a single day, but it would have sorely tested his limits, so he decided to take full advantage of the examination's generous rules.

The first morning, Aeron, Melisanda, and the third novice reported to a small chamber in the college's academic halls, where they were called upon to perform extensive translations of documents in Thorass and Untheric. Aeron passed these with fair marks, although he was allowed a chance to gain some additional credit by demonstrating his familiarity with Espruar.

In the afternoon, the three novices took turns casting spells before the assembled masters of the Ruling Council in the college's council chambers. This was the first time Aeron had set foot in the room, and he found it intimidating. The chamber was floored in dark, rich hardwood, and the masters' seats were gleaming, paneled boxes carved with ornate figures. While the college masters were sometimes less than punctual about attending other duties, the novitiate examination was considered a serious matter, and all nine High Masters were present. Oriseus offered

Aeron a sly grin when his turn came, but Telemachon and the others showed no partiality.

Aeron had decided to get the more difficult spells out of the way first. He started with the only necromantic spell he'd yet mastered, a baleful spell known as the cold grasp. He performed it flawlessly. Without pause, he moved on to a basic abjuration, a barrier against evil. For his final effort of the day, he demonstrated the spell of opening, the alteration he'd used to escape Raedel Keep months ago. In all three cases, he passed with flying colors.

On the following day, his morning was consumed by an extensive oral examination on the theory, practice, and ethics of magic, administered by one of the lesser masters. Again, Aeron passed without note. That afternoon, before the Ruling Council, he cast his spells of conjuration, enchantment, and divination. Melisanda struggled with her castings that day, and the third novice, Briet, fell short in his last spell, failing the examination. He was sent back to his classes with the rest of the novices.

On the third day, Aeron suffered through an interminable grilling on the fine points of Chessentan history, geography, and lines of descent, barely passing. But he saved his best spells for that day, proving his command over illusion magics by working the charm of invisibility, and then showing his affinity for invocations by casting fire hand. When he finished, the guardsmen showed him to a small antechamber to await the council's judgment.

Fifteen minutes later, he was called back into the council chamber. Telemachon, Oriseus, and the other masters watched as Aeron bowed and announced himself. "Novice Aeron at your service, my lords," he said.

Telemachon stood slowly and glanced down at a piece of paper before him. "Novice Aeron, you have passed the novitiate examination. You no longer have any assigned classes; as a proven wizard, you may pursue your studies by arranging to study under any High Master you wish."

"Although you should keep working on your history," the sardonic Master Enchanter remarked.

Telemachon resumed. "Have you decided which discipline you will devote yourself to?"

Aeron drew a deep breath. "My lords, if the council favors it, I will study in the School of Invocation under Master Sarim." He noticed Oriseus's face darken for a moment, but the Master Conjuror quickly recovered.

The assembled masters turned to a tall, muscular Calishite in their midst. He wore yellow robes with a topaz hood draped over his shoulders. He smiled and nodded. "The Master Invoker is glad to accept Student Aeron into the School of Invocation," Sarim answered.

Telemachon waited a moment for any other remarks and rapped a small scepter against the lectern before him. "Very well. By decree of the council, Novice Aeron is raised to the standing of student, and his studies now fall under the purview of the High Master of Invocation. Congratulations."

"Thank you, my lords," Aeron said.

"Come see me first thing tomorrow, Aeron," Master Sarim added. "We will speak of your next endeavors. I look forward to working with you."

Aeron bowed once more and withdrew, a spring in his step. Look out, Dalrioc, he thought. I'm not your captive any longer. On his way out, he found Melisanda waiting in the antechamber. She looked anxiously at his face as he left the council rooms. "Did you pass?" she asked.

Aeron couldn't keep the grin from his face. "Easily. And you?"

The Vilhonese girl smiled, too. "No problem." With an impish laugh, she caught him by the arm, and they paraded back to the Students' Hall, ignoring the soft spring rain that had started to fall over the college grounds.

* * * * *

The elevation of novice to student was a cause for celebration, and the other Sword Hall novices swept the new students away from the college grounds to commemorate the occasion with an evening's revelry in the city's livelier quarter. Although he had no idea where to go or what to do, Aeron allowed the carousers to drag him along as they set out into the city.

The night was still and damp, with a fine, cool rain drifting down in gray mist gathering on every surface. It was cold, but not bitterly so, and for a short time, the silver fog concealed the grime and wear of the city in a delicate shroud. They reeled from tavern to tavern, finally ending up in a respectable taphouse called The Rampant Lion.

The college's students and novices were familiar with many of the alehouses ringing Old Cimbar's acropolis, and the Lion was one of their favorites.

Inside, a merry fire crackled in the common room's stone hearth, and dozens of merchants, officers, and ribald rakes shouted, laughed, and drank their fill. The Lion didn't cater to the laborers and longshoremen of the docks; the patrons' belts were heavy with silver and gold, and they paid well to drink in fine company. Aeron tried not to gawk as they pushed through the crowded room toward a private booth. His companions might have been accustomed to taverns such as The Rampant Lion, but the taproom in Maerchlin was the limit of his experience.

"What do you think, Aeron?" asked Baldon, nudging him with an elbow. He nodded toward a dark-haired barmaid whose dress displayed her charms to great advantage. "Isn't this a great place?"

Aeron concentrated on pints of Threskelan ale. Although the novices were about the youngest of the tavern's patrons, he did see a few noble rakes not much older than himself come and go through the course of the evening. After a few pints, he stopped caring. In an hour or so, the Sword Hall novices were roaring with laughter and pounding their mugs on the table for more.

"Congratulations, Aeron," Melisanda said. "You are no longer Dalrioc Corynian's flogging post." The other novices had turned their attention to a contest of bawdy songs. Her pale, fine-featured face was flushed with drink. She straightened, smoothed her dress, and stood with a little unsteadiness. "Well, the hour's late. I think I'm going to head back to the college."

"Not alone, you aren't," he stated. "These streets aren't safe."

"You might recall that I know some magic," she said.

"Why take chances?" Aeron rose, somewhat unevenly, and settled his tab and Melisanda's as well. Their hallmates were just getting started and had found a couple of friendly dancing girls to hoot and holler over. Baldon, Eldran, and the others hardly even noticed as the two new students said their good-nights and found their way to the street.

Aeron insisted on hiring a passing carriage. The cool air reminded him of just how much he had had to drink, and everything seemed too sharp, too well defined. When he turned his head his entire field of vision seemed to stagger and swim. "The university," he ordered in a firm voice, and burst out laughing a moment later. Melisanda joined him.

The driver rolled his eyes and flicked the reins. The carriage lurched into motion, throwing Melisanda against Aeron. That started another round of laughter as the horse's hooves clopped on the cobblestones and wet snowflakes swirled in the air. Aeron glanced over at Melisanda. She was looking up into the warm, dark clouds overhead, ruddied by the countless lights and lanterns of the city. Her dark eyes and slender features took his breath away, and his heart hammered in his chest.

Aeron reached out and pulled Melisanda close, circling her slim body with his arms as he kissed her soundly. She gasped in surprise, but leaned into him for a long, perfect moment before suddenly pushing herself away. "Oh, Aeron. Why did you do that?" she said quietly.

He gazed into her eyes until she looked away. "I love you, Melisanda. I've never known anyone like you." The wine in his head and heart emboldened him, unfettering the adoration he felt for her. He leaned forward to take her in his arms again.

Melisanda held up her hands and shied away. "No, Aeron. That's the wine talking."

"No! I love you. I've loved you since I first set eyes on you, Melisanda." Aeron caught her hands in his. "I'd feel the same, drunk or sober."

Melisanda turned her gaze to the black sweep of the harbor to their left as they climbed the steep streets leading to the college. Dim lanterns bobbed on ships at anchor, far beyond their sight. "Aeron, there's no easy way to say this, so I'll just say it. You're my friend, and I care for you . . . but I don't love you, not the way you want me to. Please, try to put it out of your mind. I couldn't stand not having you as a friend."

Aeron started to speak, trying to think of something he could say to convince her that she didn't understand, but his rational mind asserted itself through the fire in his heart. In the space of a heartbeat, the world dropped out from beneath him, leaving him with a great hollow hurt in the center of his chest and a face burning with embarrassment. "I'm sorry," he managed.

"I know. Let's just forget about it." Melisanda tried to smile, but Aeron could see the wariness in her eyes. Regardless of what she said, neither of them would simply forget what had happened.

The coach clattered to a halt. With a sigh, the driver hopped down and offered his hand to Melisanda. She stepped away quickly, distancing herself as she wrapped her arms around her chest and shivered. The driver offered Aeron a blank shrug. "That's twenty talents, m'lord."

Although it emptied his purse, Aeron didn't even notice the lordly cost of the ride. Melisanda waited for him but did not speak as she turned and headed toward the college gate. He bowed his head and followed.

* * * * *

Head pounding from an excess of strong ale, Aeron dragged himself out of bed the following morning and dressed himself. It took him a moment to get his bearings, and when he sat up and swung his feet to the cold stone floor, his head still seemed to swim a little. He buried his head in his hands and groaned as the details of his encounter with Melisanda returned to his mind. There was a hot ache in his heart that had nothing to do with the drinking he'd done the night before. *I should have known I wasn't good enough for her,* he thought angrily. *A high-born noblewoman! What was I thinking about?* Melisanda had told him once that the college made no distinctions based on race or rank, but she'd remembered her station quickly enough.

Aeron might have fumed in his room for hours, but a sharp knock sounded at the door. One of the college servants appeared, a gold-hued bundle in his arms. "Excuse me, Student Aeron. Your new garments, sir." He hung a tabard of rich yellow brocade with a matching cap in Aeron's armoire. Despite his ferocious hangover, Aeron smiled in satisfaction. The servant bowed and added, "The respects of High Master Sarim. He awaits your pleasure, sir."

Aeron groaned. Sarim had wanted to see him first thing! One glance at the window told him that half the morning was gone already. As the servant withdrew, Aeron rose, scrubbed his face in the basin of cold water he kept by the door, and dressed. He belted the tabard over his tunic and donned the cap, enjoying the moment despite his tardiness, and then hurried out of the room.

He found the Calishite master in one of the laboratories of the academic halls, engaged in an esoteric conversation with a young student of abjuration. Sarim was a tall, well-built man with a broad chest and a handsome coffee-hued face. "Good morning, Aeron. I see you've finally decided to accept my invitation."

Aeron bowed awkwardly. "I beg your pardon, Master, but—"

The Calishite laughed and waved his hand. "Do not concern yourself, Aeron. I understand perfectly. The passage from novice to student is worthy of celebration, and from what I hear, you do not indulge yourself in such activities often. Come, let us walk for a while." Aeron followed as Sarim excused himself. They stepped out into the soft, still morning, admiring the first green buds of ivy appearing on the college buildings. Sarim headed toward the open ramparts facing the sea, hands clasped behind his back. "So tell me, Aeron, why did you choose invocation?"

"I felt it was my strongest school, my lord."

"When we are alone, you may call me Sarim. I do not stand on formality." He flashed an easy grin at Aeron and continued. "I have seen that you are very skilled, Aeron. But I want to know why you think that invocations are your strong point. You could have done well in any school."

"Invocation is . . . direct," Aeron said slowly. "The spells of this school are tangible, forces you can touch with your hands and shape with your will. Fire, wind, ice, and energy are all weapons. You can measure yourself by the control and discipline you achieve in wielding them."

Sarim glanced at Aeron. "I will not measure you by those standards, Aeron."

"No, but I will."

"That is your right." The Master Invoker paused by the stair that led down to the harbor landing, looking out over the city. "As a student, Aeron, you are free to pursue any endeavor that catches your interest. Read any text you wish, seek any knowledge that appeals to you. Set your own hours. The only limits placed on your learning are those that you choose for yourself. Once a quarter, you will stand before a board of masters to explain the studies you intend and to demonstrate that you continue to progress. I consider it advisable for you to meet with me or the other masters of invocation, Lady Silna or Master Derrin, two or three times a week, but if you offer me good enough reason, I will set aside even this minimal requirement."

"What should I study?" Aeron asked.

"Whatever you like, as long as it is within your skill." Sarim turned a serious look on Aeron.

"When do I start?" Aeron asked.

"Today is as good a day as any," Sarim replied. "I will meet you in the academic hall two hours after noon to show you the basics of a few advanced wind spells I don't think you've seen yet. Between now and then, I think you should visit the library and spend some time reading up on your history. And you might also call on some of the other masters and arrange for lessons in the fields you feel you need to work on."

Aeron grimaced. That was a full week's work right there! And he understood that Sarim had offered him this schedule to help him get his feet under him. Within a month, he'd be expected to keep himself this busy. But even as the specter of long nights and days upon days in the library intimidated him, he also felt some deep part of his heart igniting to the challenge. No waiting for his slower classmates to catch up to him; no time wasted in lectures that reviewed what he already knew; the freedom to attack any topic that caught his interest. His grimace spread to a smile. "I'll be ready," he promised Sarim.

* * * * *

As the final weeks of winter passed, Aeron immersed himself in his new studies. He had few other alternatives. As a student, he was strongly discouraged from associating with those who had been his friends when he was a novice. Since he'd advanced so quickly, there weren't any students he had known as a hallmate, other than Melisanda. Given the cold rift between them, Aeron couldn't stand to be in the same room with her.

Spring came fully to Cimbar as the month of Ches passed. The city was scoured by winds even more fierce than those that had whipped over the barren rock in the depths of winter, but these winds were warm and heavy with rain, not sharp and dry. Wet snow and freezing rain gave way to endless showers, leaving the college grounds a black mire that could pull off a boot if one stepped from the cobbled paths. Aeron began to grow restless, anxious to feel the warm sun on his face again. He'd been immured within the college's dark stone halls for almost five months now.

On the first day of Mirtul, Aeron found himself studying into the late hours of the evening. He finished struggling through a recent copy of an old Mulhorandi text on the wizards of ancient Raumanthar and wandered over to the library to replace it. The musty smell of old books, the endless aisles of gleaming wooden shelves, and the unearthly silence of the chamber always soothed him. He'd come to know the place well in his months at the college, and these days he probably spent more time here than he did in his room. Absently he made his way to the shelf from which he'd taken the treatise and put it back.

Aeron had run across some interesting references in the book. Although the modern copy was only about a century old, the original manuscript had been penned a few years before the wars that destroyed Raumanthar more than fourteen centuries ago. He searched the nearby shelves for some of the texts mentioned by the ancient Mulhorandi writer, with little luck. He turned his attention to the extensive scroll racks along one wall of the library. Aeron flinched at the imposing wall full of scroll cases, but he patiently set to work.

After a long hour of examining librarians' cryptic notes, Aeron finally tracked down one of the scrolls he sought. He pulled it from its place in the rack with care; it was as long as his forearm and weighed ten pounds or more. He carried it over to a table in a dark corner and spread it out to make sure he'd got the right one. The text was in a language he'd never seen before. "What in Faerûn?" he murmured. It seemed that the wrong scroll had been placed in the case.

Aeron shrugged and started to roll up the parchment again, thinking that he would bring the matter to the attention of the Master Librarian in the morning. Then his eye fell on a cryptic set of marks at the top of the page. The runes were oddly curved and punctuated with weird whorls and dots. He frowned. Something about the writing seemed familiar, although he was certain he'd never seen any example of this language in print. Where could he have seen something like this?

His heart lurched in his chest and he gasped in shock. He remembered where he'd seen it, all right—gracing the dull silver band that circled the claw of the creature that killed Master Raemon! The ominous runes in front of his eyes returned his thoughts to the frigid night in the ruins of the pyramid. He glanced around involuntarily to see if any monstrous things lurked in the dark aisles between the bookshelves, but the library was silent and empty.

With trembling fingers, he unrolled more of the parchment. "What is this?" he whispered. The familiarity of the runes was one thing, but without any idea of the language, he had no idea what they meant. He scanned ahead, despairing of ever solving the riddle—and then he saw his key. A second column of text began, running parallel to the unreadable glyphs. A translation into Old Rauric! *I might be able to read it,* Aeron thought.

Quickly he bundled up the new scroll he'd found, stuffed it under his cloak, and hurried out of the library. Aeron returned to his room and spread out the Rauric text, rummaging for some rag paper and a quill to begin his transliteration of the document.

In less than ten minutes, he gave up, his heart sinking. The scroll was encrypted in some unknown cipher. Whatever knowledge the mysterious runes and whorls held, it was not meant to be read casually. Aeron frowned, trying to decide what to do.

Blam! A massive fist rocked Aeron's writing desk through the wall, stunning him. Angry and frightened voices replaced the laughter outside. "What in the world are they up to out there?" he wondered aloud. He rose and stuck his head out the door.

As he expected, Baldon and Eldran were at the bottom of it. The far end of the hall was smoking with an acrid reek, and the walls and floor were marked with sooty streaks. A couple of small fires burned up and down the hall, adding to the smoke and stink. Aeron looked at Baldon. "What was that?" he asked.

"Oh, sorry, Aeron. Eldran and I were trying to work a spell, and—"

"I can see that. What happened?"

"I mispronounced a word, and he tried to correct me in the middle of the invocation." Baldon grinned sheepishly. "We got a little more than we bargained for."

"I'll say you did, you goat-brained fish!" Roaring in anger, Dalrioc Avan strode out of the smoke, his fine garb smoking from several burned patches. Aeron started to laugh at the comical scene, but the guffaw died in his throat when he saw the look in Dalrioc's face. The older student was enraged beyond reason. With contempt, he raised his hands and barked a harsh syllable, sending streaks of magical energy darting at both novices. Eldran was struck in the midsection; he clutched his belly and dropped to his knees, groaning. Baldon tried to twist away, but the streaking energy curved to follow him and charred a fist-sized patch of his shoulder. He screamed, staggering against the wall.

"Dalrioc! Have you lost your mind? That spell can kill!" Aeron found himself in the middle of the hall, facing the prince, before he even realized he'd moved. "For Azuth's sake, they're just novices! They didn't mean it!"

"Out of my way, peasant!" Dalrioc bellowed. "I'm going to see that they never befoul my hall again!"

"I agree that they should be punished, Dalrioc, but not with deadly force," Aeron began.

The Corynian prince ignored him and pushed by. He seized Eldran by the shoulders, raised him from the floor, and kicked him in the belly, right where his spell had struck. Eldran coughed and crumpled, retching. Dalrioc drew his foot back to kick the novice on the ground.

Anger ignited in Aeron's heart. When Dalrioc leaned back to kick the novice again, Aeron dropped and scissored his legs through the prince's, toppling him to the cold stone floor. The older student flailed in anger, twisted quickly, and barked the words for another spell. With one hand, he grasped Aeron's ankle, and a fat blue spark of energy flashed. Aeron was hurled backward as every muscle in his body spasmed at once. He crumpled against the wall, the smell of his own burning flesh in his nose. "You dare to strike me?" Dalrioc snarled, surging to his feet. "You dare?"

Shaking his head, Aeron looked up just in time to see the prince spinning to lash a kick at his head. He held his hand up, palm outward, and spoke a single word. A circular field of gleaming force sprang from his hand, creating a lambent shield that halted Dalrioc's kick with the mass of a stone wall. The prince recoiled, staggering back a few steps, and Aeron pushed himself to his feet, his mind racing. What next? Dalrioc was almost frothing at the mouth. He'd use any spell at his command and damn the consequences. Aeron needed to either subdue him quickly or leave . . . but if he fled, the prince might take out his anger on Baldon and Eldran, neither of whom could defend himself.

Dalrioc narrowed his eyes, glaring at Aeron. Deliberately he crooked his hands and started to bark out the words of another spell. Aeron started his own enchantment, but the prince finished first. With a sulfurous stink, a small, warty thing with the jaws of a bulldog and fangs like needles appeared in the hallway. It snuffled and growled. "Kill him!" Dalrioc screamed, pointing at Aeron. The creature bunched its stringy muscles and leapt with impossible speed and precision, jaws gaping . . .

. . . right into Aeron's counterspell. He'd meant it for Dalrioc, but the summoned horror seemed a more immediate threat. Seizing the Weave's delicate currents with unconscious ease, he braided them into a roaring jet of flame that burst out from his hands. It struck directly in the creature's face, impaling it on a lance of white agony. The thing discorporated with an agonized howl. Behind the creature, Dalrioc retreated a few steps and shielded himself from the heat, but the billowing fires scorched him badly.

Aeron blinked to clear his eyes, trying to get a good look at Dalrioc. A seething green sphere of acid came hurtling from the smoke, but Aeron's shield still held, and the corrosive splashed harmlessly against the wall. It sizzled and smoked fiercely, adding to the stink. Aeron closed his eyes, hummed, and quickly grasped the chords of magic that flowed through the living hearts nearby, working a spell of sleep, but Dalrioc's force of will was too great to overcome, and the prince shrugged off his attempt. With a malevolent grin, Dalrioc spoke a few harsh words and crushed Aeron's shield with a countermagic spell. "You'll rue the day you ever crossed my path," he crowed. He began another spell.

"Believe me, I already do," Aeron replied. He was running out of options quickly. Do I dare to attack with any more deadly spells of my own? he thought. Ignoring the hot pain that burned in his injured leg, he searched desperately for the right spell. Wait . . . perfect! Aeron reached out and summoned the energy for a spell of blindness, and this time he beat Dalrioc to the punch. He danced aside and called, "You can't hit what you can't see, Dalrioc!"

The prince howled in rage as Aeron wrested his sight

away, losing the spell he was attempting to cast. He thrashed helplessly for a moment. "Damn you, Aeron! This is a coward's trick!"

"Well, you should have saved your counterspell instead of wasting it on my shield," Aeron replied. "Now can we put a stop to this?"

Dalrioc uttered a vile curse and started to speak again. Aeron realized that the prince was working another counter. *I didn't think he would commit it to his mind twice,* Aeron thought. In just a moment, the prince would dispel Aeron's charm of blindness and resume the fight.

Aeron scowled. Enough was enough. He took three strides forward as Dalrioc finished his countermagic. The prince's sight returned just as Aeron's hard-driven boot caught him in the belly. Dalrioc doubled over, and Aeron delivered the best uppercut he could throw, dropping Dalrioc to the floor. Aeron stood over his fallen foe, fists raised, ready to continue if Dalrioc had any more fight left in him. "Come on!" he shouted. "Get up!"

"That," drawled a cold voice behind him, "will be quite enough of that."

Aeron turned and found himself facing Lord Oriseus. The High Conjuror's face, normally so mobile and insincere, was fixed in an icy glare.

"My lord! I—" Aeron began.

"Explanations are neither necessary or desired, student. There is no excuse for this sort of behavior. Deadly spells are just that—deadly. Either one of you might have been hurt, maimed, or killed. We will not have our students brawling like common drunkards in a filthy taphouse!"

Aeron stepped away from Dalrioc. "Yes, my lord," he said.

Oriseus contemptuously surveyed the scene. Baldon slumped against the wall, one hand clapped to his shoulder, eyes wide as saucers. Eldran appeared to still be unconscious. *Lucky for him,* Aeron thought. Dalrioc, singed, tattered, and pummeled, was just now pushing himself to his feet. Finally Oriseus turned his eyes on Aeron. There was a large charred patch on his breeches where Dalrioc had grasped his ankle and loosed his spell. And his arm stung with smoldering drops of acid. The hall itself had suffered spectacular damage. "All of you, come with me. It is clear that you need the attention of a healer."

"Master Oriseus, I demand that Aeron and these two louts be escorted from the college grounds immediately," Dalrioc groaned as he climbed to his feet. "They are to be expelled at once."

The High Conjuror turned his gaze on the Soorenaran. "And you were blameless in this incident? I think not, my prince. I shall give your recommendation all the consideration that it deserves and act accordingly. Now, come on. I don't want to hear one more word."

The moment Oriseus's back was turned, Dalrioc turned a look of bilious venom on Aeron. "I'll get you for this," he promised darkly. "If they don't expel you, leave now. It's your best chance to stay alive."

"Dalrioc!" Oriseus didn't break stride. Aeron tried to ignore the prince's threats, but he feared that Dalrioc was right. Any discipline the Ruling Council chose to impose on him was the least of his concerns.

Nine

By the ancient laws of the college, a sorcerous duel between students meant expulsion for both parties involved. Aeron fully expected to be dismissed within a matter of hours after the incident in Sword Hall, but one day passed, then two, and then a week without any summons from the Ruling Council. Finally Aeron was ordered to move from Sword Hall to Crown Hall. He hated the idea of leaving his few friends behind, but it was clear that he and Dalrioc couldn't share a hall any longer, and it was no surprise that the prince was allowed to remain where he was comfortable.

Aeron's new hallmates offered little in the way of a welcome. The novices, of course, avoided any student like the plague, and Aeron's peers in Crown Hall were not anxious to befriend someone who had earned Dalrioc Corynian's hatred.

The week after Aeron's transfer to Crown Hall, the summons he had dreaded arrived. He hurried over to the Masters' Hall and presented himself to Lord Telemachon. The old wizard was even more haggard and worn than Aeron remembered, and he rubbed his temples constantly, as if to smooth an excess of pain from his mind. "You are satisfied with your new quarters?" he grated.

"Yes, my lord. I miss my hallmates, though."

"You might have made more of an effort to get along with Dalrioc, if that is how you feel."

"Yes, my lord."

"Do you know how close you came to expulsion, Aeron?" Telemachon turned his tired gaze on the young mage. There was no good answer to this question, so Aeron shrugged uncomfortably. "It came down to a vote of the Ruling Council. As your sponsor, I abstained. So did Sarim. Naturally Corynian's friends wanted you out."

Aeron counted the High Masters in his mind. "If you and Master Sarim abstained, my lord, Dalrioc's friends hold four of the seven remaining seats. Why wasn't I expelled?"

Telemachon sighed. "The masters who feel no friendship toward the Corynians of Soorenar defended you. And Master Oriseus chose to cast his vote in your favor. So you remain here by a single vote."

"What of Dalrioc?"

The old diviner laughed humorlessly. "He was in no danger of expulsion, not with his puppets on the council. You've chosen a powerful enemy for yourself, Aeron."

"He chose me first," Aeron replied darkly.

"Hmmmph. Be glad that one of the High Masters voted his conscience. Otherwise you'd be on a hay wagon back to Maerchlin." Telemachon leaned forward on his elbows, fixing Aeron with an unblinking stare. "Had I a vote in the council, I would have expelled you despite my old debt to Fineghal. I do not believe the rules of the college are to be so lightly dishonored, Aeron. You may go."

Aeron stood and left. He paused in the door, considering an apology. Telemachon ignored him. Aeron bit back his words and stalked out of the room.

To his surprise, he returned to his new room in Crown Hall only to find Master Oriseus waiting impatiently, rifling through Aeron's notes with nervous energy. "Ah! There you are, Aeron. May I have a word with you?"

"Of—of course, Lord Oriseus," Aeron stammered.

"Good, good! Let us take a stroll about the grounds." With a broad grin, Oriseus bounded down the hall and out into the long-shadowed afternoon. Aeron lengthened his stride to keep up with the red-robed master. The Master Conjuror led him to the wedge-shaped ramparts mantling the college grounds, whirled dramatically to survey the city below, and perched on the cold stone. "I am delighted that you are still among us, Aeron," he stated, leaning forward in a conspiratorial manner. "It was only by the narrowest of margins that I kept you in the college."

"So I'd heard," Aeron said. "Thank you, Lord Oriseus. I couldn't imagine abandoning my studies."

"Nor could I, Aeron. Your skill is truly extraordinary for one so young. Your gift must be cultivated; it would be a crime to let you slip from our grasp, so to speak." The master leaned back, his eyes glittering. "You chose the yellow of invocation upon your elevation."

"I felt that my talents were best suited for it, my lord."

"Oh, I am not jealous. You see, I hope to persuade you to

study with me yet. May I explain?"

Aeron nodded his assent. The master stood quickly and began to pace anxiously as he spoke. "The wielding of magic," he stated, "is nothing more than common craftsmanship. A potter or woodcarver takes a raw material and then shapes it into the form he desires with his skill and labor. Well, any wizard does exactly the same thing. He takes the raw stuff of magic and uses the tools of his willpower and learning to shape the spell he needs."

"The analogy isn't perfect," Aeron observed. "The materials a craftsman works with require no special gift or skill to acquire. But not everyone has the ability to manipulate the Weave."

"Indeed! And what, may I ask, is the Weave? From where do we draw the power to wield our spells? Have you ever wondered how it is that you grasp this power, Aeron?"

"My master Fineghal taught me that it is the life of the world," Aeron replied. "A spirit or potential in all things—"

"Not true, not true," Oriseus interrupted. "I did not ask you whence magic comes. I asked you, what is the Weave by which we wield it?"

Aeron acknowledged the point. "The Weave itself is the means by which we perceive and wield the magic potential all around us, Lord Oriseus. I ask your pardon. It is easy to forget that the Weave is only the surface. Fineghal once called it the soul of magic."

"And the priests teach us that the Lady Mystra is the Weave, the divine gift bringer who makes the working of magic possible. Is that not so?" Oriseus did not wait for Aeron to answer. "Yet not all mages have acknowledged her existence or stewardship. Oh, I do not question the existence of the Weave, and the relationship between the Weave and the fabric of raw magic that underlies all things. But Mystra has been known in this land of Chessenta for perhaps four or five centuries now. Before the worship of Mystra came to Cimbar, when the Untheri held this land in thrall, we were taught that Thalatos—Thoth, in the Mulhorandi lands—was the lord of magic."

"In my classes, the philosophers state that Mystra has always held power over the Weave since the very beginning of things," Aeron replied. "Whether or not she is known and worshiped is immaterial. She chooses to make the Weave available to all, and so it is. After all, you don't need to venerate a god of fire in order to strike a flame."

"Ah! An excellent point, young Aeron. So, could you make a fire if a god of fire did not exist?"

Aeron shrugged helplessly. "I suppose so. I'm afraid that my learning in philosophy and theology is not equal to my skill in other arts."

Oriseus grinned wickedly. "On the contrary, dear boy, it simply means that you are not fettered with the age-old lies and deceptions perpetrated upon generation and generation of our youth. Allow me to rephrase the question: Could you work magic if no Weave existed?"

"Of course not!" Aeron stated instantly. "I couldn't even imagine where you would begin."

"What would you say," Oriseus said quietly, "if I were to tell you that you are wrong?"

Aeron scowled at the High Conjuror, trying to gauge the master's mood. Oriseus leaned close, his grin fierce and yellow in his wide, handsome face. His dark eyes danced with an animated mischief, a formidable intellect toying effortlessly with daring, unthinkable suggestions. Whatever one might say about Oriseus and his ambitions, his cynicism, his arrogance, the man feared nothing and bent his knee to no one. "Go on," Aeron said.

"The Weave exists," Oriseus said. "It is one way to wield magic, to touch the power that sleeps in all things. Say that Mystra is the Weave, if you like to think so, or that the Weave is the soul of magic—it's all semantics, empty words for those who do not wish to accept responsibility for what they do. The Weave is, perhaps, the *easiest* way to wield magic. But there are restrictions, limitations, to what one may do." The master stood abruptly and spread his arms, changing his course. "Tell me, Aeron, what do you know of the Imaskari?"

"The Imaskari?" Taken aback, Aeron frowned, gathering his thoughts. He'd had only a few weeks of learning of this sort, but he tried to recall what he'd been told. "They were old, perhaps the first humans to raise kingdoms. Their lands lay beyond Mulhorand, in what is now the desert of Raurin. The old empires of Mulhorand and Unther are descended from the people who fled the Imaskari kingdoms thousands of years ago." He shivered in his tabard, suddenly chilled by the cold spring wind. "It's said that they were mighty sorcerers indeed, sorcerers who thought they could become gods. That is all I know, Lord Oriseus."

"Indeed. Well, the Imaskari were correct, Aeron. They wielded magic from beyond the circles of this world, magic of staggering power. And they did it without the hindrances, the limitations, of the Weave. The Imaskari spells wielded a different power, Aeron. A second theme of magic, one reserved for those with strength and will enough to command it. A completely different symbology to impose one's will upon a completely different source of power. Only the dimmest memory of this ancient way remains in the hoary texts and garbled fragments studied inside these walls. It's called shadow magic in these impoverished days."

"Shadow magic?" Aeron turned his head to study Oriseus for a long moment. "Why are you telling me this?"

Oriseus's artificial humor died, and his eyes grew dark and serious. "I mean to show you what I've told you about, Aeron. You are one of the few students here who has the strength of will, the breadth of experience, to comprehend the secrets I have to share. You'll wield power few wizards living today could hope to command, learn mysteries that only a handful of mages have explored in more than a thousand years. Now will you study under my tutelage?"

Aeron considered the wizard's offer. Power? Magic that others cannot master? Oriseus's promises intrigued him; the High Master of Conjuration radiated confidence, puissance, under his foolish caperings. Oriseus acted like a buffoon because he could afford to. He forged his own path, and Aeron found that he wanted to enjoy that same unshakable self-assurance. Aeron scratched his chin. "I'm interested, but what will become of my studies in invocation?"

"Study with Sarim as long as you like," Oriseus replied. "All I ask for is an hour or two of your attention each week. But I think you should know that you have rivals who are already delving into these secrets of which I have spoken. You showed great courage in standing against Dalrioc Corynian last week . . . but it would have been unfortunate for you if he'd known then what he knows now."

Aeron frowned. The one thing he could claim over Dalrioc Corynian was his skill with spells. He knew Oriseus was manipulating him, but he decided that he didn't care. I'll be damned if I'll let Dalrioc become a better wizard than I am, he thought. "Very well, Lord Oriseus. When do we start?"

"This very moment, if you like," Oriseus said. He stood, dusted off his robes, and turned to survey the surroundings. He hummed comically for a few moments, tugging at his beard as he thought. "Aha!" he exclaimed. He took two long steps and snatched a fist-sized rock from the ground, hefting it in his hand. Returning to the battlement, he sat down beside Aeron. "I'm going to cast a spell that will enable you to sense the magic inherent in this stone," he said.

"I can perceive it already, Lord Oriseus. I've always been able to sense the currents of the Weave."

The lean conjuror glanced at Aeron. "Really?"

"It's my elven blood, I think." Aeron closed his eyes and allowed himself to draw in the air, the cold stone under him, the distant sense of the great sea. With concentration, he felt the sleepy sense of magic imprisoned in the small stone. "Yes, I can sense it."

"So much the better, Aeron. I won't have to demonstrate the way things normally appear. Observe." Oriseus lifted the stone in his hand and muttered a few guttural words. The rock quivered and then flew out of his hand, streaking across the open courtyard to roll to rest about thirty yards distant. Oriseus smiled and twitched his hands, causing the rock to hop, frogwise, even pushing it into the air to perform great flying bounds. "What do you sense?" he asked Aeron.

The young mage frowned, extending his perception. He found nothing. He should have felt the Weave thrumming in resonance with his own mind and heart, the kindred spirit that bound all things together, but Oriseus worked his sorcery with no outward sign. "How are you doing that?" he asked.

"Doing what?" Oriseus asked innocently.

"Are you working a spell at all?"

The conjuror laughed. "Of course," he snorted. "You are simply unable to perceive the forces that I manipulate."

"Why not?"

"You are untrained in this magic," Oriseus replied. "With time, I can show you how it's done."

"This is the shadow magic you spoke of?" Aeron asked, watching in fascination. "The magic the Imaskari mastered?"

Oriseus nodded. With an exaggerated wave, he sent the stone hurling high into the air and let it plummet to the ground as he rose again. "Come see me later this week. We will begin your lessons. I think you'll be amazed at what you can do, once you learn to remove the blinders that have been placed on you." He sauntered off, whistling.

Aeron watched him go, puzzled. How did he do that? he thought. I sensed no magic at work, none at all. What does he know that I don't? He walked over to where the rock lay on the ground and picked it up. It felt strangely warm to his hand, as if it had been near a fire, and as he examined it, the edges seemed to crumble away. He hadn't realized that it was so old and worn. He studied the rock for a long moment and then let it fall to the ground.

* * * * *

Over the next few weeks, Aeron met with Oriseus only a handful of times. The High Conjuror demonstrated some complicated spells of binding and command, patterns that seemed incomplete to Aeron. It was as if the techniques allowed him to see only part of some mysterious whole, a painting that called upon every bit of willpower and knowledge as a broad palette lacking one critical color, a hue that Aeron could not yet imagine.

The cool, humid winds of Mirtul passed, giving way to Cimbar's warm, rainy summer. Cold water surging past Cimbar toward the Alamber Sea brought torrential rains every few days, and the days of sunshine between rains steamed Cimbar in sweltering humidity. Aeron retreated further into his studies, attacking every lesson with a single-minded zeal that left no room for questions of temperance or balance.

Aeron soon realized that he was not the only student Oriseus had recruited. Just as Master Sarim oversaw a half-dozen students in the school of invocation, and Oriseus also sponsored five young adepts in the red robes of conjuration, the High Conjuror had a second circle of students he tutored personally. Dalrioc Corynian was among these, but there were students who wore the green of alteration and the purple of necromancy in Oriseus's confidence. The sessions were always informal; Aeron found that Oriseus never asked him to meet him at any specific time, but waited for Aeron to come to him.

"You've told me that the Imaskari derived their magic from powers in the planes beyond this one," Aeron observed one time. "The shadow Weave is a ghost, an echo of our Weave in dark planes close to our own. Didn't the Imaskari fear the taint of evil in the sorcery they taught themselves? And aren't we treading in dangerous territory?"

"Would you be concerned if the Imaskari had learned how to make crossbows? Or catapults?" Oriseus asked.

"No. That is mundane knowledge. It isn't evil in and of itself," Aeron answered.

"Nor is magic," Oriseus answered. "It is a tool. The hand and heart that wield it define its morality."

Aeron frowned and weighed the master's words, but he could find no reply. Oriseus freely placed in his hand any knowledge he requested, and in the books and scrolls he studied, he could find no single hint that the ancient magic had ever been marked by evil. He often spent more time perusing the old tomes than the spells of invocation he was supposed to study, and his room was soon littered with scraps of yellow parchment and charcoal rubbings from unspeakably ancient tablets of stone that Oriseus kept in his private collection.

A week after Midsummer, the longest day of the year, Aeron was interrupted by a soft knock at his door. Melisanda quietly let herself in as he hurriedly straightened the tangled mess of parchment and paper that cluttered his room. "Hello, Aeron. I haven't seen you much lately."

Aeron held up his book. "I've been keeping busy. And I didn't want to make a pest of myself."

She smiled sadly and perched on the sill of the window. "Well, you haven't. You've vanished any time I've set foot within ten feet of you."

"I thought that was what you wanted."

"No, it wasn't. I wanted you to keep your distance, yes. But I didn't want you to pretend as if you'd never met me. I've missed your friendship, Aeron."

"I'm not Dalrioc Corynian. I won't force my attentions on a woman who isn't interested in me."

"Why does it come down to that, Aeron? In a college filled with arrogant men who think they deserve any woman they fancy, I thought that you'd be above that. But if that's all you see in me, you're no better than they are."

"No one here equals my skill," Aeron said coldly. "What Dalrioc Corynian and the others were given, I've had to earn. I'm proud of that, Melisanda. If you can't see—"

"Can't see what, Aeron? That I belong in your bed instead of Dalrioc's?" Melisanda hugged her knees to her chest. "I'm not a trophy for you to fight over." She fell silent for a long time.

Aeron didn't know what to say and simply waited. Finally she spoke again. "I've decided to go home."

"Home? To Arrabar?"

She nodded. "I've learned a lot, but I'm homesick, and I don't think I'm ever going to become a great mage. It's just not my heart's desire to be the best."

"You're an excellent mage!" Aeron protested.

"No. I'm competent. I don't have the gift that you do, Aeron. You know that as well as I, it seems." With a wry smile, she pushed herself to her feet. One old tome caught her eye; she picked it up, weighing it in her hand, her brow furrowed. "What's this?"

"That? Oh, that's an Untheric translation of an old Imaskari text. Pretty dry, really."

"Imaskari? I'd heard there were some Imaskari works in the library, but I didn't know students were allowed to see them. It's not for everyone." She flipped it open and skimmed through a few pages. "The letters are familiar, but I don't know the language. You can read this, Aeron?"

He shrugged. "Master Oriseus has taken an interest in my studies. He's been helping me with a lot of the older texts. The old Imaskari knew things we don't today. They did not wield the Weave the way we do. They used another source of power to fuel their spells."

Melisanda set the book down. "I've heard nothing good about the old Imaskari spells, Aeron. Be careful. Oriseus's interest in these musty old tomes is unhealthy."

"You don't trust him?"

"Not a whit. That fool's manner he wears is nothing more than a veneer. He's laughing at all of us underneath his smile, I'm certain of it."

Aeron bridled. "Abrasive or not, Oriseus is one of the few people here who seems to give a damn about me. He's extremely talented, and I've made great strides since he began tutoring me."

"I thought you studied under Master Sarim. Why should

Oriseus treat you like one of his own conjurors?"

He shrugged. "Oriseus says I have great potential. He thinks I can master spells that other students can't understand."

"Do you believe that?" she asked quietly, sinking to a hard wooden stool Aeron kept beside his desk. Her glacial eyes settled on his face, cool and distant, waiting for his answer. For the first time, Aeron noticed how tired Melisanda appeared. Her features, once lovely and perfect, now seemed to be stretched tight over an unforgiving frame, silk taut against a steel blade.

"Yes. I won't pretend to any false modesty, not where my magical skills are concerned. I've learned a lot since I was a novice, Melisanda."

She dropped her eyes. "Yes, you have, Aeron. I'll be taking ship in a couple of days for Chondath and home. It's the right time of year to find a tradesman bound for the Vilhon Reach, so I won't linger long."

Aeron stood up, scattering pages of cryptic notes, and paced nervously in the narrow space in front of his bed. He expected Melisanda's departure would wound him deeply, but instead of pain he felt only a relief. With Melisanda gone, that was one less person to whom he had to explain himself or measure his actions. A sudden thought struck him, and he stopped his pacing. "You're not leaving because of Dalrioc, are you?"

Melisanda shook her head. "No, not in that sense. He's set off in search of easier prey, I guess. I'm just tired and lonely, Aeron. That's all. Won't you wish me well?"

Aeron stared down at his feet for a moment. He was vaguely surprised by the gray and white tunic he still wore, the polished boots, the golden tabard that rustled as he moved. For a moment he wondered how the reckless young forester dressed in peasant's clothes had come to be standing in this room, surrounded by forgotten lore and ancient mysteries, heart open to the beautiful noblewoman who watched him pace. "Don't go, Melisanda. I love you, and I want you here."

"I was afraid you'd say that," she replied. "I suppose I've been wasting my breath." She stood and brushed her lips across his cheek. No warmth remained in her eyes, and she crossed her arms like iron bars between them. "I'll see you again, Aeron. Take care of yourself, and don't forget who you used to be." Then she dropped her eyes and slipped through the door.

* * * * *

Aeron emerged from his research long enough to watch Melisanda's coach clatter away through the college gates on a still and fog-shrouded summer morning. By the time the black coach disappeared in the ivy-bordered streets beyond the college walls, Aeron was already back at his studies.

For several weeks, he returned to his virtual isolation within the college walls, ignoring his fellow students and the novices who fearfully bowed any time they crossed his path. From time to time, he happened to run across Baldon or Eldran, but he tried to steer clear of his old hallmates for their own good. He knew that Dalrioc Corynian would make life hell for the fish if they were caught relaxing in the presence of a student.

Surprisingly, his lessons with Master Oriseus came to a halt in the middle of the summer. The High Conjuror left the college on several extended trips, and he wasted not a minute in the brief days between his journeys. He simply didn't have time to spend tutoring Aeron, although all of the students in his circle suffered. Aeron didn't mind; he returned his attention to his studies in the school of invocation, beneath Master Sarim, and filled his odd hours with a redoubled attack on the old double-text he'd found in the library after Master Raemon's death.

The goal of the High Conjuror's labors became clear on a muggy evening in late Eleasias. Aeron had retired to his room to delve into his books and tomes for the night, but a clamor in the hall caught his attention. He straightened and cracked the door. The corridor was filled with students and novices. "What's going on?" he asked a passing novice.

"There's going to be a Masters' Duel," the girl replied. She curtseyed. "It's Lord Oriseus and Lord Telemachon. They're going to start any minute." Aeron dismissed her with a nod.

Oriseus and Telemachon? Aeron frowned. He'd heard of Masters' Duels, of course. Novices and students were not permitted to turn their spells on each other, but the masters were allowed to settle differences in a ritualized trial by combat, testing skill against skill. By custom, the loser left the college. It was considered to be better for an irreconcilable difference to be hammered out under strict rules of conduct than for a rift or faction to form, spreading the disagreement. Aeron shook himself free of his astonishment and joined the crowd forming on the barren lawn beyond the Students' Hall.

Oriseus stood on the city side, calm and confident, his scarlet robes resplendent in the setting sun. His dark face was split in a fool's grin. Telemachon stood with his back to the bay, leaning on a tall black staff as if his legs could not support his sagging body. His blue robes were dyed ebon by the twilight. Aeron found himself standing next to Baldon and Eldran. He whispered, "What's this about?"

Eldran glanced over nervously and smiled. "Hello, Aeron. None of the masters are saying anything, but a fish I know overheard the council meeting this morning. He said that Telemachon accused Oriseus of murdering Raemon."

"That was months ago! Why wait until now?"

Eldran shrugged. "Who knows? My friend told me that Telemachon moved to have Oriseus dismissed and charged, but the senators' faction blocked his motion. Since he couldn't have him removed by a council vote, he demanded the right to face him in a Masters' Duel."

Aeron chewed his lip as he watched the two wizards prepare for their contest. Since Oriseus's supporters controlled half the council, it didn't surprise him that the conjuror feared no dismissal. Was Telemachon's charge a political move, or had the High Diviner actually learned something that incriminated Oriseus? If anyone could reconstruct the events of that night, Telemachon could. Did Oriseus do it? The Master Conjuror had never spoken about the matter to Aeron. "What does Lord Telemachon know?" he wondered aloud.

"Shhhh! They're getting ready to start," Baldon hissed.

In the center of the field, Master Sarim signaled for silence. The excited buzz of conversation died away. Telemachon and Oriseus approached, standing about ten yards apart. The conjuror pranced and grinned, unable to contain his nervous energy. Telemachon simply waited, his face pale and expressionless. "You are familiar with the rules, gentlemen?" Sarim asked in his lilting accent.

Both wizards nodded. "Very well, then," Sarim continued. "Master Oriseus, you are the challenged party. The first casting is yours."

Oriseus sketched a flamboyant bow. He wheeled once to wave to the crowd of onlookers, his teeth flashing white in his dark face. Then he raised one hand, muttering a toneless chant under his breath. Aeron felt the flow of power that snapped to the conjuror's outstretched arm as he expertly demanded power from the Weave of the muggy air around him. A crackling blue nimbus sprang into sight around Oriseus. With an odd snickering laugh, the conjuror pointed at Telemachon and sent a lashing bolt of cerulean energy dancing away from his aura. Acrid ozone reeked in the air.

The High Diviner planted his staff in the ground, took a half step back, and shouted a quick word that was too potent for Aeron's mind to grasp. The dancing bolt of energy swerved from his heart and struck the staff instead, grounding with a shower of sparks and an angry roar.

Oriseus's first thrust parried, Telemachon readied his counterstroke. With businesslike precision, the diviner barked a phrase of forgotten words that resounded with contained power. Aeron sensed the intangible tendrils of the Weave as Telemachon turned Oriseus's own life-force against him. Aeron had a sudden impression that Oriseus's skeleton was shining through his flesh and robes, scorching hot inside his body.

The conjuror grunted and staggered back, wisps of smoke escaping from his lips. "I didn't think you had the ruthlessness to wield such a spell, Telemachon," he gasped. He dropped to one knee, but through sheer effort of will, he managed to raise a field of negation that broke Telemachon's fiery grip on his bones.

The old diviner wheezed with fatigue, but Oriseus was not in much better shape. The conjuror took a long moment to catch his breath, stood up on unsteady feet, and with determination called out a summoning. A lean, powerful beast with bone-edged jaws appeared on the ground between Oriseus and his foe. Aeron recognized it from his studies—a leucrotta, a dangerous monster of the northlands. Students and novices alike retreated from the field of battle, pushing back four or five nervous steps. Oriseus raised his hand and sent the creature at Telemachon in a bounding leap, its jaws gaping wide.

The diviner started to speak a spell that would destroy the monster, but it was too swift for him. It seized him in its jaws and, with a quick twist of its head, sent him sprawling, his left arm raked to the bone. Telemachon shrieked and scrabbled backward awkwardly, his girth preventing him from escaping. The leucrotta darted in to finish him, but from some hidden reserve of strength, Telemachon managed to cough out a word of dismissal. Even as its jaws snapped at his face, the leucrotta disappeared, banished back to whatever place it had come from. In the sudden silence, Telemachon whimpered in pain and flailed to find his feet, but somehow he did so. "I cry foul! No summonings are allowed in the duel, not unless the creature is bound and controlled!"

"The creature was under my control," Oriseus retorted.

"You cast no binding spell upon it," Master Sarim observed from the side.

"Had you watched my spell carefully, you would have seen that I bound the monster as I summoned it." Oriseus grinned suddenly. "It's a refinement I worked out a long time ago. Now, have you had enough, Telemachon? You can end the duel by yielding."

Blood dripped from Telemachon's mangled arm, but defiance blazed from within the old man's heart. "No, I'm not done yet," he said. "It's my turn, I believe."

He took two steps forward to his staff, still stuck upright in the ground, and seized it in his good hand. Blue energy crackled and snapped as Telemachon summoned the first spell that Oriseus had cast back from the ground. He shouted a long spell of rolling, brittle words. The staff disintegrated in his hand, and the blue nimbus disappeared, sinking back into the ground again. But a moment later, a brilliant column of energy exploded under Oriseus's feet, ravening skyward as the spell burst free of the earth. Oriseus was bathed in white-hot power, his flesh blistering and bursting wherever the blue-white energy touched him. He reeled back and fell in a smoking heap.

Aeron blinked the afterimage from his eyes, stunned. Oriseus was dead; he had to be. No one could have survived that. But to his amazement, the sizzling wreckage stirred and slowly rose. Oriseus was badly injured, but Aeron could detect the fraying remnant of a sorcerous halo that had protected him from the worst of the blast.

Oriseus's cheerful manner was gone, replaced by deadly hate. "Again you surprise me," he croaked through blackened lips. "Let me show you how it's done, old man."

Oriseus began to weave a spell, his hands turning and flashing as he muttered a cold and inhuman invocation. Aeron strained forward, trying to see what Oriseus was doing, but he could not sense the Weave at work. The delicate web of earth, air, fire, and water remained untouched. Even Oriseus's own life-force was undimmed by his efforts. Aeron realized that the conjuror was employing the shadow magic, the power he'd shown to Aeron on that afternoon on the ruined ramparts. A clot of darkness formed in the air in front of Oriseus, growing larger as his chant continued. How does he do that? Aeron wondered.

Oriseus cried out with an inarticulate shout and released the sphere. The darkness darted forward, leaving streaming shadows in its wake as it arrowed toward Telemachon. The Master Diviner raised a barrier of gleaming light, but the dark sphere punched through it like a spearpoint through thatch. It engulfed the portly wizard, seeming to crumple the substance of his body as if he were a paper doll consumed by an unseen flame. Telemachon's screams were swallowed by the thing that destroyed him. In a matter of moments, nothing remained of the High Diviner.

The black sphere bobbed, flickered, and faded into oblivion. The assembled college was silent with horror and shock. After a long moment, Master Sarim strode into the field. "Oriseus? What has befallen Lord Telemachon? What did your spell do?"

The conjuror raised his eyes, hot and hateful. "If he failed to deflect it, he did not survive," he said. "It was a potent enchantment."

Sarim's face darkened. "You slew him?"

"He had his chance to yield," Oriseus replied. "Now, if you'll excuse me, I am injured and must seek aid." With an iron effort, the conjuror turned awkwardly and staggered toward the college grounds. Within a few steps, several lesser masters and students—the adherents of his faction—caught him and helped him off the field. Aeron watched him go, dazed. It didn't seem possible that Telemachon was dead. He drifted over to the place where Telemachon had vanished, seeking some sign of the fallen master.

"Telemachon was your sponsor, was he not?" Master Sarim stood nearby, evidently as shaken as Aeron.

"Yes," Aeron replied. "I never thought that he would meet his end this way."

"Nor I, Aeron." Sarim scowled, glancing around. No one else was near. The novices and students wandered away from the field in a daze. "Listen, Aeron. I know that you have been spending some of your time studying under Oriseus's tutelage. Do you know how he worked the spell that doomed Telemachon?"

"He is capable of drawing on a source of magic that I can't yet perceive," Aeron replied. "He's been showing me some of his lore, but I don't yet understand how he does it."

"Be careful of him. There is more to Oriseus than meets the eye," Sarim said. He paused, watching Aeron closely. "Where are your allegiances, Aeron?"

Aeron considered the question carefully. "I'm not ready to abandon my studies, not yet. I want to know what power he wields and master it if I can."

Sarim nodded. "It occurs to me that with Telemachon's death, Oriseus and his allies in the senators' faction control a majority of the council. They'll pick whomever they like as his successor."

"Who do you think it will be?"

"Anyone who will swear fealty to Oriseus against the Sceptanar. I think the High Conjuror is getting ready to make a move on the throne, and that Dalrioc Corynian of Soorenar is out to make a friend of the next king of Cimbar."

"Won't the Sceptanar destroy him?" Aeron asked, surprised.

"Perhaps, perhaps not. It is the way of things in Cimbar, Aeron. The Sceptanar is the most powerful mage who wants the throne. From time to time, a new mage rises who has the skill and the ambition to overthrow the old king." The Calishite watched the crowd of students and novices excitedly following Oriseus back into the college. "I've always known that man possessed the ambition. Now I begin to believe he possesses the skill as well."

"You're going to oppose him?"

Sarim met his eyes with a haunted look. "I wouldn't be surprised if Master Raemon's murderer strikes again. Those who stand for the populists or the Sceptanar are going to be removed from positions of authority . . . one way or another."

"Telemachon was my sponsor. Without his support, I'll be forced to leave anyway." Aeron paced away, examining the place where Telemachon had stood before he died. "Sarim? I know it's not a matter for students, but why did Telemachon think Oriseus had killed Raemon? What evidence did he have to make that accusation?"

"I do not know. Lord Telemachon was not allowed to argue his point before Oriseus's allies passed a motion absolving Oriseus of suspicion. That was what provoked the argument; Telemachon felt that he was denied the opportunity to present his case."

"I'd like to know what he found out," Aeron said quietly, speaking his mind aloud.

Sarim measured the wiry student with a long, thoughtful look. "So would I. Keep me advised of how your studies with Oriseus proceed, Aeron. I want to know what he teaches you. And in the meantime, you are not without a sponsor. I'll see to it that you can stay here as long as you like. You've been a good student, and you have amazing potential. But watch yourself, Aeron. Knowledge is power . . . and risk."

Ten

Within a week of Lord Telemachon's passing, the Ruling Council named a young master Aeron barely knew as the new High Diviner. It was no surprise that the new ruling master was a minor senator and Soorenaran advocate who openly deferred to Oriseus in council meetings and conversations. Although Aeron had little contact with any of his fellow students, and even less with the masters now that Telemachon was gone, he slowly became aware of a growing tension in the air. After years of maneuvering, a challenge to the remote Sceptanar was growing within the halls of the college.

Oriseus spent days at a time attending to private business in his estates and lands surrounding Cimbar, and the students of the college whispered that he was building support among Cimbar's lords and generals for a move against the city's faceless king. It struck Aeron as senseless and negligent that the Sceptanar should sit idly by, watching his foe grow in strength, but the Cimbarans among the college thought nothing of it. The city's rules of succession decreed that the Sceptanar must answer any personal challenge brought against him. The king was free to crush any coup or rebellion with whatever forces he deemed appropriate, but as long as his challenger did not rise in arms against him, he could not use Cimbar's soldiers and heroes to defend his own position. Of course, Oriseus ensured that the Sceptanar abided by his own laws by building his support among the generals, the lords, and the people.

Oriseus grinned and jested when bold or contentious lords and mages demanded to know his intentions, deflecting any suggestion that he prepared to challenge the city's overlord. But the city's demagogues proclaimed his virtues and cried out for Oriseus to sieze the throne and lead Cimbar to war against Akanax. It was widely known that the Sceptanar did not desire war, but the mood of the city was shifting away from its faceless overlord. Aeron fumed as the college ground to a halt, students and masters alike wasting their days in shameless rumormongering. Annoyed by the distraction, he wondered what would happen if the storm hanging over the college broke.

Lord Oriseus, as energetic and capricious as ever, resumed his duties a few days after defeating Lord Telemachon. A week after his return, he sent for Aeron. The young student found Oriseus in his spartan chambers in the Masters' Hall. He'd never seen the High Conjuror's quarters, and he was surprised by the barren walls and utilitarian furniture. Oriseus's flamboyance was carried in his face and his manner, leaving no exaggeration for his belongings. "You sent for me, Lord Oriseus?" he asked.

"Ah, Aeron! Yes, of course I did." The lean sorcerer grinned and bobbed like a servant, pulling out a chair by the narrow window for Aeron. "How are your studies proceeding? I haven't spoken to you in a couple of weeks."

"Very well, my lord," Aeron replied. "Master Sarim has been helping me with some difficult invocations."

"Indeed." A fleeting grimace crossed Oriseus's bearded features. "I was surprised to learn that Sarim had assumed Telemachon's place as your sponsor."

"I could not remain here if he hadn't."

"I would have been glad to sponsor you, Aeron. Your potential is extraordinary, extraordinary! We cannot allow you to leave." Oriseus glanced from side to side, even though they were completely alone, and leaned close. "Besides, I think things will change here soon. The college has grown too . . . conservative. Too hidebound by the artificial distinctions of class and wealth, instead of the real potential of the students. You are perhaps our finest example of a student whose talents far exceed the abilities of those who call themselves his betters. I see a college where the only measure of a student's standing is his power and skill, Aeron. A change for the better, I believe."

Aeron did not know how to reply to that. "I wish it were so," he laughed nervously. "I'm in favor of any arrangement that sets me level with Dalrioc Corynian."

"Yes, I suppose you would be," Oriseus said thoughtfully. "Do you recall the details of our first conversation after your novitiate examination? We talked of the Weave and the old Imaskari shadow magics."

"I remember. You hinted that the Imaskari had mastered another method for working their spells, a power that freed them of the Weave." Aeron met Oriseus's gaze. "The same power that you used against Lord Telemachon."

Oriseus smirked and rocked back on his seat. "Ah, Aeron, you cannot understand how delighted I am that someone perceived the skill of my final spell! I wondered if everyone had missed it."

"It was plain as day. You touched no Weave that I could see. Do you mean no one else noticed?"

"Aeron, your gift is unique. You are the only one with elven blood among us, and I suspect that you are the only wizard within these walls blessed with mage sight." Oriseus nodded eagerly. "Yes, I used the old magic against Telemachon. He was stronger than I expected."

There was something almost unhealthy in Oriseus's fevered eyes, the anxious intensity that kept him dancing from foot to foot, trembling and shaking like a man on the verge of a seizure. Aeron sensed danger, risk; a cold hand of caution settled over his heart. But despite himself, he was intrigued. He'd thought he understood where all the pieces fit, but now he realized that at least one part of the puzzle had eluded him. "How did you do it?" he asked quietly.

Oriseus sighed and spread his hands. "Alas, I cannot explain. How could you describe what you see of the Weave to one of your blind fellows? How could you tell a deaf man what the song of a nightingale is like?" He paced away, hands clasped behind his back. "You are brilliant, Aeron, but you lack the sense you need to wield the power."

Aeron straightened, glaring at Oriseus. "I don't understand. In our lessons, you've shown me several powerful spells that demand this shadow magic, this source of power beyond the Weave that I can reach and shape. But if I can't perceive this source of magic, you've only been wasting our time by demonstrating spells I cannot work." He snorted. "For that matter, how did you master this ancient magic in the first place?"

"I did not say that no one can perceive it, Aeron. I merely observed that at the moment you cannot. That can be rectified, if you are strong of will and do not lack courage. As far as my own expertise goes, allow me a few professional secrets for the moment. It would be easier to show you than to explain."

Fuming with impatience, Aeron scowled. "What must I do?"

Oriseus grinned and leaned close to Aeron, his dark eyes glittering like jet. "Meet me by the ruins of the Untheric pyramid tonight, an hour before midnight. You won't need any of your books, but you should prepare as many spells of protection and defense as you can manage. We may encounter some frightful dangers in our journey. Oh, and you should ready a spell of night seeing if you know of any. Wizard light may fail us."

"I have little need of seeing spells," Aeron said. He raised his hand to his almond-shaped eyes. "I've always had a knack for seeing where others cannot. Where are we going, Master Oriseus? And when will we return?"

Oriseus smiled. "Not far, my boy, not far. Only a few steps, really, but they're some of the hardest steps you'll ever take. We'll be back by morning—if we come back."

* * * * *

Oriseus's cryptic offer occupied Aeron's thoughts as he absently found his way from the High Conjuror's chambers. Aeron hadn't forgotten that Master Raemon had met his death in the ruins of the obelisk. Had Oriseus extended a similar offer to the Master Abjurer months ago? No trace had been found of the spell that summoned the beast to the college . . . and Aeron had seen how Oriseus could work spells that no one else perceived. The High Conjuror's melodramatic admonitions did nothing to ease Aeron's mind.

He found himself standing in the mouth of the redolent paneled hall leading to Telemachon's chambers. On a sudden impulse, he turned aside, with a furtive glance, and strode over to the door. He was not yet ready to return to his quarters to await nightfall, and the disquiet in his mind demanded some action. If Telemachon knew something about Oriseus, he might have left some record among his books and notes, Aeron thought. It didn't seem wise to walk into Oriseus's circle with his eyes closed.

The door was sealed with a rune to deter casual trespassers; Aeron concentrated, sought the knot of magical energy that formed the barrier, and slipped it aside with a thought. Telemachon's chambers had been rifled but not ransacked. The disorderly mass of paper and uneven stacks of tomes had been straightened, evidence that someone other than the High Diviner had been here since his death. Aeron carefully circled the room, cataloging its contents in his mind. Nothing seemed to be missing since his last conversation with Lord Telemachon. The longer he looked, the more certain he became that something important was in this room.

He sat in the heavy carved chair behind the desk, thinking. Telemachon had believed Oriseus killed Master Raemon. Not only had he believed it, he was so certain of it that he made his accusation public and challenged the conjuror when the Ruling Council failed to act.

"What does that mean to me?" Aeron breathed aloud, steepling his fingers. Oriseus seemed to be one of the few friends he had in Cimbar—after all, he was the first mentor who'd seen fit to treat Aeron as an adult, to encourage him to exceed the bounds of tradition and experience. But Aeron didn't believe for a moment that the High Conjuror's patronage was completely altruistic.

Someone tried the door. Aeron froze, holding his breath. The latch fell still, and he breathed a sigh of relief—until he sensed a simple magic at work. The latch suddenly lifted itself, and the door opened. "Who's in here?" demanded the tall wizard outside. "Aeron? Is that you?"

"Yes, Sarim." Aeron slumped in the chair as the Calishite master entered and shut the door behind him.

He expected the master to be incensed by his act of breaking and entering, but Sarim showed no anger. "I detected someone tampering with my sealing mark, but I didn't expect you. What are you doing here, Aeron?"

Aeron started to answer and realized he didn't have a reason he could easily explain. "I'm not sure. I just wanted to think, I guess," he said.

"There are more accessible places for that," Sarim remarked. He cleared one of Telemachon's sitting chairs of its debris and joined Aeron, gazing around the room. "What is on your mind?"

Aeron studied Sarim for a long moment, thinking. He wanted to test himself against the ancient mysteries that Oriseus offered . . . but he wasn't certain that he trusted the High Conjuror. Sarim, on the other hand, he did trust. "Oriseus has offered to show me how he worked the magic that destroyed Telemachon. He's asked me to meet him before midnight at the Broken Pyramid."

Sarim's eyes widened, and he leaned forward alertly. "Do you intend to keep your appointment?"

"Yes," Aeron said. "Oriseus says I'm one of the few students here who can understand his sorcery. I want to know how he does what he does." He offered a confident smile. "After all, I'm here to learn, aren't I?"

"Not everyone feels the same, Aeron." Sarim shook his head. "You should be wary of Oriseus's generosity."

"Why do you say that?"

The Calishite fixed his dark eyes on the young mage's face. "Aeron, you and I both know that Oriseus is the most likely suspect for Master Raemon's murder. He stood to gain from Raemon's death; Raemon was a staunch defender of the Sceptanar. Thanks to Telemachon's demise, we've all seen that Oriseus has the capability to work lethal magics that we can't understand or unravel. So let's assume that Telemachon was right, and Oriseus murdered Raemon. Why would he wish to help you understand how that might have been accomplished?"

Aeron frowned and thought for a moment. "You believe he wants to silence me? With Melisanda gone, I'm the only remaining witness to Master Raemon's death."

"Doesn't it strike you as a possibility?"

"If that's the case, why bother to show me anything at all?" Aeron replied. "We've been working for weeks on some of his conjurations and enchantments. He wouldn't have gone to all that trouble if he meant to kill me."

"Unless he deemed it necessary to gain your trust," Sarim said blackly. "What better way?"

"No, I don't believe it," Aeron answered. "I'm different, Sarim. I can become something greater than any other student here. And I mean to. Regardless of what you think of Oriseus's ethics, he can teach me lore that no other master can."

"That's your arrogance speaking, Aeron," Sarim said.

"Is it arrogance if I can back it up with ability?" Aeron said. "Sarim, I don't trust Oriseus. I'll exercise all due caution. But, if he shows me the power that slew Raemon and Telemachon, I'll have the answers to their deaths."

Sarim's eyes flashed, and he stood abruptly. "As you wish," he said. "Your studies are your own; that's the principle we live by here at the college. But they're my business, as well, since I am your sponsor and share responsibility for you. I will join you this evening to see how your lessons with Oriseus go."

"But—"

"Enough, Student Aeron!" Sarim held his gaze until Aeron reluctantly acceded. The tall mage paused a moment, then added, "Aeron, I am only interested in your safety. I do not intend to intrude more than I have to in order to be sure of Oriseus's intentions." He glanced at the window outside. "It's getting late. I'll leave you to your reflections."

Aeron watched Sarim leave, deep in thought. *I never should have mentioned the tower,* he grumbled in his mind. *Sarim didn't need to know about my lessons with Oriseus. Then again, the High Invoker may have been right.*

He stood, pushing himself up from the desk. Halfheartedly he began to rummage through the stacks of paper and flip idly through the tomes. Many were incomprehensible to him; Master Telemachon had had a full lifetime of learning, and Aeron couldn't even begin to make sense out of most of his research. One book, marked by a twisted serpent sigil, caught his eye. He picked it up, skimmed a few pages, and found a slip of yellowed parchment caught between two leaves, covered in Telemachon's crabbed handwriting. It was a column of letters beside strange, curving marks and dots.

He struggled to place it for a moment, chewing his tongue. *Wait! The Rauric scroll, the yugoloth's bracelet! It's the same lettering!* Aeron dropped the book and clutched the scrap of paper in his hands, peering at it. The letters were in ancient Rauric, arrayed in a single row. One mark or whorl stood under each. He realized that he was looking at a letter-for-letter conversion—the key he needed to understand what was in the mysterious scroll he'd taken from the library months ago.

Should I take this to Sarim? he thought. He hardly even considered the notion before dismissing it out of hand. He'd see what he could make of it first. If Sarim confiscated it or demanded the old Rauric scroll, Aeron would never know what was hidden within. He folded the parchment, slipped it into his sleeve, and hurried back to his own chambers, sealing Telemachon's room as he left. The shadows were growing long as he crossed the quadrangle; the afternoon was fading to dusk.

In his chamber, he bolted the door and sat down with the old scroll. The Rauric text was a circuitous, meandering narrative by an old scholar named Derschius. Aeron had assumed that it was a straight translation of the mysterious second column of writing, but now he suspected something else entirely. In fact, now he thought that it might not have anything to do with Derschius's work. Ancient scribes had often scraped or written over older texts, especially if they didn't seem useful. Derschius had probably had no better idea than Aeron what the other column of text said.

Ignoring the scribe's scratchings, Aeron looked carefully at the first lines of the odd text. On a piece of blank paper, he carefully copied the symbols in the exact sequence, leaving plenty of space between each line. Then, using the key he'd found in Telemachon's office, he searched for each symbol's corresponding letter. When he had finished the first line, it read, "The Chants of Arcainasyr, as declaimed by Macchius the Ebon Flame."

"It's an artificial alphabet," he breathed in amazement. The words themselves were in ancient Rauric, but each letter had been replaced by an arbitrary symbol. Macchius, or whoever had dared transcribe the chants, had invented the cipher to mask its contents. Aeron frowned, wondering what in Faerûn he was looking at. Nothing in the title meant anything to him.

And it can't be completely artificial, he realized. The markings on the yugoloth's bracelet matched these symbols. They have power, significance. It's not a mundane fabrication to hide this text only. Aeron set his pen to the tip of his tongue, thinking. Deciphering the old scroll might be dangerous. If the symbols could bind a yugoloth, they could certainly carry curses as well. "Well, I won't know until I start," he said aloud. He pulled out a sheet of common parchment and set to work by the yellow light of the late afternoon, his pen scratching in the stillness of his chambers.

* * * * *

At the appointed hour, Aeron set down his pen. Pale and shaken, he rolled up the chants and, after a moment's thought, stuffed them into an unmarked scroll tube, stashing a simple text on alchemy over it to conceal its presence.

It didn't seem like a good thing to leave lying around. Absently, he dressed and stepped out into the cool night. The late summer heat had finally broken, and the night was cool, windy, and damp, with scudding clouds concealing a crescent moon.

He hadn't had a chance to make a complete translation of the scroll, and he doubted he would ever finish the work. The chants deserved to be left in obscurity. Aeron understood exactly where the ancient Imaskari had found their power, and it sickened him. Each chant was a litany of destruction, a hateful incantation of decay and foulness. Many were framed as prayers to nameless deities who had poisoned the ancient world with lies, shadows, and war.

Oriseus had once asked him how humans wielded magic through the Weave and dared him to imagine a way in which a sorcerer could wield magic without touching the Weave. Now Aeron knew. Creatures such as the yugoloths—and even fouler things—came from beyond the circles of the world. The sorcerer-lords of the Imaskari had won their power by binding dark spirits of the planes beyond in their own bodies, gaining unspeakable power at the cost of their souls. Just as the Weave was tied to the life of the world, shadow magic was intertwined with forces of chaos and decay that fed on the world.

Aeron hoped that there was a chance that he had misunderstood Oriseus, that in the forgotten lore of the old Imaskari mages he'd found something clean, a redeemable power, but he didn't think it likely. He had to go through with his appointment to make sure that what he suspected was true. If it was not, then he had no reason to fear Oriseus. But if it was, the scroll of Macchius and Oriseus's own words would damn him.

He circled the ruins slowly until he spied a faint light bobbing in the darkness ahead. "Hello? Lord Oriseus?" he called, advancing slowly.

"Here, Aeron," the conjuror replied. He emerged from the tumbled heap of cold stones, holding a blue-glowing staff in front of him. The eerie light shadowed his features in a macabre fashion. Oriseus grinned fiercely, stalking forward. "Are you ready?"

Aeron closed his eyes, hoping that he could conceal his true fears from the High Conjuror. "I am," he answered. Behind Oriseus, Aeron noticed several other cloaked shapes waiting, students and some of the younger masters. Dalrioc Corynian glared at him with ill-disguised contempt, but held his peace. Aeron took an involuntary pace backward, glancing at Oriseus. "What are the others doing here?"

Oriseus shrugged. "You are not my only student, Aeron. Here we all are equals. Now, let us be about our night's work."

"And what exactly is that, Lord Oriseus?" From the shadows of the tower's ruins stepped Master Sarim, dressed in his yellow robes. "You won't mind if I attend, will you?"

"Master Sarim. This is an unexpected surprise." Oriseus's face was inscrutable in the darkness, but Aeron could sense the irritation in his voice. The conjuror glanced at the ring of students and sorcerers behind him as if to ferret out the individual who'd informed Sarim of their meeting time.

"I won't interfere with your lesson, Oriseus," Sarim continued. "Go on. Pretend I'm not here."

To Aeron's surprise, Oriseus's face split into an ingratiating grin. "Of course, Master Sarim. We are honored by your presence. I shall proceed." He turned away and took a few steps into the cracked rubble that mantled the pyramid. Exchanging silent looks, Aeron and the others followed in a rough semicircle. The lean sorcerer halted suddenly, stooped, and brushed dirt and overgrowth from a red-black slab gleaming among the stones. "Help me clear this," he instructed, and two of the nearest students knelt to assist. In a few moments, they'd uncovered a man-sized stone that didn't match any of the rubble or foundation stones nearby.

"What's that?" demanded Dalrioc Corynian. He hadn't bothered to get his hands dirty with the work.

"Our portal," Oriseus answered. "Tonight we will walk in the plane of shadow. This is one of those rare places where the walls between the worlds are thin enough to part with nothing more than an act of will."

Sarim raised an eyebrow. "A dangerous place to visit, Oriseus. Is this wise?"

"My lesson lies within," Oriseus retorted. "Do you object?" The Calishite fell silent, although Aeron could sense his concern and agitation. Oriseus turned to the other mages present. "Any of you who wish to depart now may go. This is the time to leave if you have second thoughts."

Satisfied that no one was leaving, Oriseus returned his attention to the slab of cold stone, speaking over his shoulder. "Stay close to me when we enter, and do not stray from the path I choose. Master Sarim is correct in observing that the shadow plane is dangerous, and you must be very careful."

No one required any more clarification. Dalrioc cleared his throat and asked, "When does the portal open?"

"When the light of the waning moon falls on this stone. That is why I left it covered with dirt." Oriseus stared up into the sky, watching the passing clouds. "Ah, here we go. The moon will emerge in a minute. When it does, I shall go first. The rest of you follow one by one, waiting two or three heartbeats each."

Aeron looked up at the sky. Overhead, the dark cloud glowed silver along its trailing edge, and through wisps of dark mist, the luminous crescent appeared. He glanced back at the stone. Silver light rippled and flowed as if the rock had suddenly become a liquid mirror. Oriseus waited a moment to let the shimmering settle, then stepped onto the stone. It was as if he stepped into a puddle of shining water, slowly sinking to his knees, his waist, his chest, and then vanishing silently as the silvery moonstuff closed over his head. Although each man there was a mage, no one was untouched by Oriseus's feat. After a brief hesitation, Dalrioc Corynian pushed himself forward and plunged into the shadow pool, flailing for his footing but sinking out of sight. One by one, they all followed, leaving Aeron and Sarim to the end.

They paused at the brink of the portal and exchanged a glance. "Do you still wish to do this, Aeron?" Sarim asked.

The fear he'd suppressed all night threatened to overwhelm Aeron; all his instincts railed against following Oriseus into the stone. His feet were rooted to the ground, and cold sweat trickled down his back. This is a fine time to come to my senses, he thought. "We're here," he answered. "I have to see this through."

"Very well," Sarim said. He stepped onto the stone and glided through it, a luminescent ghost in the moonlight.

With a determined grimace, Aeron set his foot on the silvery surface of the stone and stepped into it, sinking slowly into the cold light as if the stone were bottomless. As he slid into the portal, a chill, sharp as a razor, climbed his body, so intense that his feet ached with cold by the time he had sunk to his chest. His heart surged with panic, and he desperately gulped for air as his head sank under the moon mirror, leaving nothing but a ripple in his wake.

When Aeron opened his eyes again, he was standing beneath a starless sky, far hills on the horizon limned by an eldritch glow. Bitter air seared his nose and throat, drying the tears in his eyes. He still stood on the acropolis, but the hill was different. Below him, crowded Cimbar had vanished, leaving only a handful of spare lights glimmering faintly along a sluggish, leaden bay. The topography was not quite correct; there was less water, and the hills seemed steeper and more forbidding. Overhead, the cold skies were empty of all but a few dim and hateful stars.

"Come, Aeron. This is no place to dawdle."

Aeron turned at the sound of Oriseus's voice. It took him a moment to understand what he saw. The High Conjuror beckoned from within a tall shadow, silhouetted against a looming shape that towered into the night sky. Oriseus was shrouded in a violet aura, a faint flickering light that stemmed from the power of his will and the skill of his magic. Marching toward the great dark shape, each of the other mages was similarly marked, although the color and strength of their auras varied. Aeron glanced down at his bone-white hands and found a delicate blue faerie light dancing over his skin. The sight fascinated him, and he stared in frozen wonder, the unnaturally still and frigid air slicing through his chest with each breath.

The conjuror frowned with impatience and repeated his summons, holding out his hand. "Aeron, the others have gone ahead to the temple. Come on."

"The temple?" Aeron asked, puzzled. He took two steps toward Oriseus, the cold, hard ground crunching beneath his boots. He looked past the red-robed master, and his heart stopped. Behind Oriseus, the Broken Pyramid stood intact, looking as it must have centuries ago. No other building of the college, or even the city, was mirrored within the shadow, but the pyramid stood, a stark and inescapable monolith beneath the eternal dark. His jaw fell open. "It stands again!"

"It never fell here. That is the way of the shadow. It remembers things lost to the daylight, places long gone, people long dead. In some places, it even holds the memory of what might have been. The city below is ephemeral, a vanity of no importance. But the pyramid is quite real here, Aeron." Oriseus stepped forward and took Aeron's arm in a firm hand, steering him into line. "This is the least of the wonders I have to show you today, lad. Now follow me."

Nodding mutely, Aeron fell behind the others, trudging to a dark and narrow door in the pyramid's flank while his mind reeled numbly. Oriseus moved on to shepherd them all within, watching vigilantly. Aeron spared one more look for the sere hilltop, stretching out with his senses, searching for something more than the empty cold that surrounded him. His unease was growing by the moment, a hopeless panic that frightened him all the more because he could not pinpoint its source. Something was terribly wrong here.

The Weave, he realized. It's gone. The stony earth was cold and dead, the air still and lifeless. The spark, the flame of the living world was missing here. No magic, no life, existed for him to perceive. Yet as he adjusted to his surroundings, he sensed the barest trickle of magic. The shadow held the merest whisper of the Weave, but it was not entirely desiccated.

As Aeron turned his attention to the pyramid, he became aware of a dark, hot energy suffusing the structure, a tangible emanation of potency that he could sense as surely as if he turned his face to the sun during the day. It streamed and coiled away from the obelisk like a leaping flame, invisible and silent, yet fraught with unearthly power. The thick, ancient stones could barely contain the raging conflagration within. The sensation terrified Aeron, yet he hungered to feel the black warmth on his face, to stand unharmed in the dark pyre and tame the power.

Aeron scrabbled forward after the others, eagerly moving to view with his own eyes the wonder hidden within the stone tomb. He didn't even spare Oriseus a glance as he passed between the blank door and felt himself pulled down the long, silent corridor of worked stone that led within. He trailed Dalrioc Corynian as the circle of sorcerers wound through the lightless labyrinth of the pyramid's innards, spiraling downward through winding stairs and echoing chambers until they reached a chamber set beneath the center of the structure. Midnight power thrummed in the stones under his feet.

Oriseus pushed the door open, leading the way into a wide, low vault of dark stone and squat columns. Arched galleries circled the room, and intricate bas-reliefs defaced the walls, but Aeron had no eye for these. The stone in the center of the room seized his attention.

It was a simple thing, an uneven shard of smooth, glossy black rock about the size and shape of a horse's skull. A weird lambent light danced in its ebon depths. It was bound in rune-carved iron bands, suspended in a rude circular stand of black metal. The mages surrounded it in an even circle five paces wide. For a long moment they gazed on it in silence, unable or unwilling to speak. Finally Master Sarim wrenched his gaze away. "Oriseus? What is it?"

The High Conjuror did not reply immediately. He stepped close and laid a hand on the cool rock, his face absent. Finally he answered. "Thousands of years ago, the Imaskari arose, first of all men to walk in this world. Unfettered by the powers and restrictions of gods, they had nothing to defy their understanding, their comprehension. The glories of Netheril and fallen Raumanthar were mere reflections of the first mages, the sorcerer lords who mastered magic in that forgotten age.

"And so the Imaskari ruled vast lands thousands of years before the rise of Mulhorand, of Unther, of Netheril and the other ancient kingdoms of man. They roamed the planes, building portals to a thousand times and worlds. And so they aroused the ire of the petty gods who rule over this sphere. These powers sought to bring down the Imaskari by withholding the Weave from them. The lords of the Imaskari thus turned to a source of magic from beyond this world, a source of magic that they could wield without answering to the rude demipowers of this sphere. They brought the Shadow Stone into this world, establishing a link or conduit through which they could draw on an energy that exists outside all time and space."

Oriseus circled the stone, studying the mages one by one. "This stone represents that which existed before anything else existed. It is a symbol, a link to the blind and voiceless power that was displaced from our sphere in the very beginning of things. It did not save the Imaskari, but with this they slew gods when the world was young."

Oriseus looked up at them, his eyes glinting. "Here, my fellows, is the strength that even gods fear. Set your hand on it and it is yours. You need only ask."

Aeron closed his eyes, his face flushed with the energy that danced before him. Oriseus had once told him that the Weave was the spirit, the soul of the world. The stone was something else, a void or vacuum that injured the world by its very existence. It was potential without purpose, eager for the hand and mind to guide it. With nothing more than his intuition, Aeron understood that once he touched the stone with his will and sight, he would be able to call upon its power anywhere, anytime, joined by an ethereal link to something that defied distance and hesitation. He shuffled closer a half-step, drawn by the power.

Ahead of him, Dalrioc Corynian broke the ranks of their circle and boldly stepped forward, an arrogant sneer on his face. "Very well, Oriseus. I ask." He moved to stand beside the stone, studying it without a hint of hesitation. Dalrioc reached out and set his hand on the glossy rock and stood petrified, enraptured, his face twisted in a rictus of astonishment as the black energy coursed over him, freezing him in his grasp.

Aeron paused, waiting and watching while, one by one, the other students and masters stepped forward to join Dalrioc beside the stone. As each touched the gleaming black surface, he ceased to move, straining to contain and master the power that exceeded him.

Oriseus's face contorted with unholy glee. His eyes flashed living darkness. With the light touch of his hand on the stone, he directed the fearsome black energy as it coiled and smothered each mage who approached. His expression appalled Aeron, and for the first time, he allowed himself to sense what he'd known from the moment he felt the stone's influence.

It reeked of evil.

It was powerful and majestic, a conflagration of energy that defied his senses. But it stained him to stand so close to it. There was a conscious malevolence behind its splendor, an ancient, aching hunger that shrieked for Aeron's willing soul. He knew that if he set his hand on the dark stone, he would be lost forever, consumed and filled with something older than time and unspeakably, irredeemably evil.

As if waking from a dream, Aeron gasped and threw a

panicked glance around the cold stone chamber. Cold and hateful light seared his eyes, leaving painful afterimages that blinded him. Across the room, Master Sarim—the last who had not touched the stone besides Aeron himself—staggered forward, his teeth bared and eyes staring vacantly, fighting with every ounce of his dying will to resist the stone's greedy pull. It was not enough. Marching like a broken doll, he was jerked to his knees and thrown prostrate before the black talisman, betrayed by his own muscle and bone. He whimpered in terror as the energy surged forward to devour him.

Aeron had thought the room silent, but now he became aware of a crackling, snapping sound as violet energy whirled and darted in a sickly aura around the rune-marked ring. The roaring deafened him, but now he heard clearly the mindless yammering, the moans and shrieks, the insane howls of the mages who stood transfixed by Oriseus's will and the sinister font of energy. How could I not have sensed this? he thought. How could I have been so blind?

"Again you are last, Aeron," Oriseus called, voice clear and strong above the din. "Join us. You are part of our circle now."

Stark terror jolted Aeron into action at Oriseus's words. He took two steps back, not in defiance, but in weakness. "No," he whispered, horrified. "No."

Oriseus smirked, confident of his victory. "You wanted power, Aeron. You left your home behind to come to the college. You desired the strength to shield yourself from harm, to strike down your enemies. Well, here it is. Stand with me and you will carve your name on the heart of the world. None will stand against you. None!"

"This isn't what I wanted," Aeron said in a small voice.

Oriseus snorted. "You've wanted this all your life, boy. More than anything, you want to be the one people fear. Come . . . you are damned already." The conjuror raised his hand, and Aeron felt his feet slog forward, dragging him toward the stone's fatal embrace. In horror, he tried to will his feet to stop, but his body refused to obey.

In blind panic, Aeron reached into the recesses of his memory and seized a spell of translocation, a spell he'd barely grasped just a few short days ago. In the daylight world, under perfect conditions, it strained his abilities to the utmost to work the enchantment. Here, it was completely beyond his skill. But desperation lent him the strength to gasp out the words that keyed the spell, and in his mind, he unfettered the complex sigil that defined its form.

His own life-force was the merest fraction of the power the dimension leap required. Yet there was no Weave to work the spell. The stones were cold and lifeless, the air still and dead. The only power Aeron could tap was the dark inferno before him, and in his terror, he seized it and channeled it before he realized what he was doing. The dark energy seared him with a cold taint; he gagged in revulsion, as if grave dirt had been shoved beneath his skin. It sank frigid fingers into his belly and knotted under his ribs, drowning him in madness even as the chamber whirled away in shadow and mist.

Aeron caught one last glimpse of Master Oriseus's startled face as his spell wrenched him out of the Shadow Stone's chamber and hurled him through the vast, lightless void between the worlds. The darkness wormed its way through his veins, creeping into his heart with tendrils of cold fire. Unable to withstand another moment of the venomous assault, Aeron's mind slipped into the shadows and reeled away into the night.

Eleven

Cold, wet dirt fouled his mouth.

Aeron gagged and coughed, weakly scraping the back of one sleeve across his face. He was lying with his face pressed into mist-wreathed earth. The lightless dusk of the shadow plane surrounded him still, and he shuddered uncontrollably as his body reminded him of the numbing cold. When he'd first stepped through the silver door, the chill air had sapped the heat from his feet and hands, searing his nose with each breath. Now the center of his chest ached with a dull leaden pain, as if the blood in his heart was starting to freeze. Aeron groaned and tried to push himself upright, his limbs shaking with fatigue.

He was at the bottom of a steep hill, lying in a patch of soft ground where a noisome trickle of dark water carved a bitter rill at the foot of the slope. Dead gray grass grew in wiry tufts, broken by forbidding thickets of black briars and stands of sere, leafless trees. At first his mind was as blank as slate, devoid of any thought except a cognition of his surroundings, but like a candle guttering in the wind, his faculties began to return. Where am I? he wondered. How did I get here? Awkwardly Aeron gained his feet and staggered a few steps, struggling to wring motion from his hollow frame.

I'm still in the shadow land, but the pyramid isn't in sight, he thought. He'd been standing in the chamber of the stone, the last of Oriseus's circle to resist its influence . . . and then he'd worked a spell to escape. He felt he'd traveled a very long way indeed. Apparently his spell had worked, only not in the way he'd intended.

That led to the next obvious question: Where was he now? Aeron frowned, thinking. He was not anywhere near Cimbar's harbor or the place in the shadow plane that corresponded to the city's location. The lay of the land was wrong. But he could be a few miles inland, or hundreds of miles away. Or it might not make any difference, since he stood in the shadow plane. He'd heard that time and distance were distorted here.

"Of course," he muttered to himself. He knew a minor divination that would pinpoint his location. Absently he unlocked the spell's symbol in his mind, reaching for the spark of power within his own heart to give it life. The land and air around him were cold and dead, devoid of the Weave. He touched the merest flicker of his own life and spoke the spell.

A dark, coiling veil seemed to shift and slither in his heart. It was as if a black, hungry worm crawled through his thoughts, rasping against the inside of his skull, pulling at the substance of his mind like a piece of bone dragged through mud. Aeron clapped his hands to his head, reeled, and fell, gabbling in animal terror as the cold, slimy form extended thousands of needlelike bores throughout his body. Light and sanity fled as he shrieked in revulsion.

From a tiny island in the inchoate confusion of his shattered mind, Aeron realized that he'd felt the stone's influence again. In the tower, he'd touched the stone, drawn upon its power, and like a serpent, it had embedded its venom in his heart. Reaching for the Weave to work his divination had awakened the poison.

He became aware of a distant arrhythmic thumping sound and realized that he was listening to his heels drumming on the ground while the dispassionate stars wheeled over his head. After a time, the trembling seizure released him from its grip, but an icy fist remained clenched in the center of his chest.

In blank horror, Aeron stood and moved away with clumsy, jerking steps, a marionette driven by nothing more than a weak desire to flee. No strength or volition remained to him, but after a time, the dark rill and the bracken-covered hill faded into the gloom behind him, and he found himself following a worn and ancient track that cut through the brooding hills.

He walked until his legs gave out. After a time, his strength returned and he walked again. The road wandered, tunneling through dark woods filled with whispers and rustling sounds, though no wind blew. From time to time, he crossed ivy-grown bridges of cracked stone that spanned sluggish dark brooks, or passed watchful old ruins that slumbered on barren hilltops. The twilight never brightened or faded; it was impossible to say whether it was day or night.

He walked for a long time, determined to find something familiar, some sign of shelter or a way back to his own world, but the road wound through mile after mile of gray, barren hills and black thickets. The chill slowly permeated every portion of his body, knifing into his chest with each breath, deadening his face and limbs with the cold. He staggered and fell, picked himself up, then collapsed again. The dim twilight sapped his will with each step.

Can't give up, he told himself. There must be other doors, another way back. Aeron fixed his eyes on the distant hills, limned by the cold glimmer that served as the only source of illumination in this gray land. I'll find something there if I can just push on a little farther, he thought.

After an endless struggle, he looked up and saw that the hills were no closer. But there was something peculiar in the way the light danced and brightened in front of him. Streaks of rose and orange were appearing over the hilltops. His breath caught in his throat as a sliver of crimson sunlight slid over the hill. The fields, the trees, the road, shone with a faint red blush as they caught the sunrise and sparked to life.

As the sun appeared, the shadows fled. The cold grip on Aeron's heart wavered and dissipated as the daylight drove back the borders of gloom. The racing edge of dawn swept over him, and the dead gray hills and twisted black forests seemed to come alive, the gloom fading away to reveal fresh green slopes and lush young buds gracing the trees and shrubs. The sunrise brought me back, Aeron realized. I must have been right on the borderline between the shadow and the real world.

But where am I?

Groaning, Aeron pushed himself to his hands and knees, then tried to stand. His legs wouldn't bear his weight. He collapsed and surrendered to a deathlike sleep.

* * * * *

"Hey, there! You dead or alive?"

A harsh voice dragged Aeron back to consciousness, accompanied by an ungentle toe in his ribs. He blinked, stirred, and found himself staring up at a large, dark-skinned man who towered over him. The fellow was dressed in a colorful dyed jacket and pantaloons, and he scowled as he looked down at Aeron. "Oh, you're alive," he muttered. "Well, you shouldn't be. It was bitter cold last night. You're damned lucky you didn't freeze to death, lying out in the road like that."

Aeron shook his head and climbed to his feet. He was weak, trembling with cold, completely disoriented, but the supernatural chill that had nearly extinguished the fires of his life was gone. He turned slowly, studying his surroundings. The long, low valley and crossroads matched the last place he'd seen in the plane of shadow, but the empty fields now seemed to be furrowed with an early spring planting. "Where am I?" he said to himself.

The big man beside him took Aeron's question literally. "You're near Markelmen, lad. It's maybe five miles down that road there." He looked at Aeron's dress and added, "You certainly don't look like you're from around here."

Now that Aeron was standing, the man didn't seem quite so tall, although he topped six feet. He was a heavyset fellow with a round gut and thick, powerful arms. A draft horse and a cart full of small barrels waited a few yards away. The mage considered the carter's words and shook his head again. "Markelmen doesn't mean anything to me. Where's that?"

"Did some highwayman give you a knock on the head, lad?" the carter asked. Aeron met his eyes with a clear and level look, and the fellow shrugged. "Well, this is the county of Orsraun. The Ors Valley is just over that rise; the river empties into the Reach about twenty miles farther south."

Orsraun? Reach? They still didn't make much sense. Aeron struggled to fit the names into his mind. Finally he made some sense of it. "You mean we're in Turmish?"

"Tyr's blind eyes, lad! Of course we're in Turmish! Where in Faerûn did you think you were?"

I wasn't certain I was in Faerûn at all, Aeron thought, but he chose not to give voice to that remark. He'd read about Turmish and seen its shape on a map during his studies of the lands about Chessenta. It lay west of Cimbar, on the other side of the Akanapeaks, along the northern shore of the Vilhon Reach. He was hundreds of miles from the college. "What day is it?" he asked the westerner.

"Today? It's the eighth day of Ches. Are you certain you haven't been rapped on the skull?"

Ches? But last night was the fifteenth of Marpenoth. Could I have been in the shadow plane for five *months?* Aeron stared at the man in amazement until the fellow shifted his feet nervously and took a half-step back. "Well, you seem to be up and about. I'll be on my way, then."

Aeron shook himself out of his astonishment. "Wait! Which way is it to Hlondeth?" If his memory served him right, that was the major port in this part of Turmish.

"Take the western way from the crossroads," the trader said, pointing. "The road leads straight to Hlondeth, but it's forty miles or more."

"Thanks," Aeron said. He left the Turmishite shaking his head as the fellow drove his cart off in the other direction. He began walking north, slowly warming up as the morning sun brightened and his exertions worked some of the ice out of his limbs.

At first he kept his mind on the road and the wind-scoured hillsides, deliberately avoiding any serious thought. As the morning wore on, he eventually found himself considering his situation. He had nothing more than the clothes on his back, a handful of coins in his pouch, and a dozen or so spells locked in his mind, ready to use . . . if he dared. Each spell he expended would be gone, and without his spellbook—presumably resting on his desk in the college, five hundred miles away—he could not refresh his memory of any spells he cast. More to the point, what would happen if I did work a spell? he thought. Will the stone's influence reach me, now that I've left the plane of shadow? Or am I safe now?

There was one certain way to find out, but Aeron was hesitant to experiment. In the first place, he would waste an irreplaceable spell, and secondly, what if the experiment demonstrated that he was still within the stone's grasp? He shuddered, recalling the abominable sensation of cold foulness boring through his body, mind, and spirit. He quickly turned his thoughts elsewhere. "Well, where to now?" he asked of the empty road. "Back to the college?"

He frowned, weighing his words. Oriseus waited back at the college. And the stone was much closer there, even if it lay across the threshold of night. The Shadow Stone's power would certainly not be diminished the closer Aeron came, and it might even increase. That thought frightened him. His spellbooks, his studies, everything he needed remained in Cimbar, but Aeron did not dare return. Well, where then? he asked himself irritably.

From a still place deep in his aching heart, the answer welled up into his mind: home. It had been more than a year—no, almost a year and a half now, if Ches was already upon the land—since Aeron had left Kestrel and Eriale to study at the college. Suddenly he missed them terribly, longing for the shelter and simplicity of his former life with a fierce pain that brought tears to his eyes.

He gazed east for a long time, until his homesickness faded into a quiet despair. It would take weeks, maybe months, to round the Vilhon Reach, cross Chondath on the southern shore, and then find his way across Chessenta. "It won't get done until I begin," he said softly, and he started on his way again.

* * * * *

Late in the afternoon, Aeron began to flag. He'd been walking all day after a harrowing ordeal, and his strength was giving out. The biting wind and dropping temperatures served as an additional discouragement to pressing on. He looked for an inhabited house or a roadside tavern, but the land nearby was desolate, and he eventually settled for a ruined cottage, its roof open to the sky.

To his surprise, he was neither hungry nor thirsty. He felt only a leaden exhaustion and a bone-deep chill that ached in his limbs, although he was too tired to shiver. One of the spells in his mind would serve to revitalize him somewhat, restoring some of his energy and dispelling his fatigue, and Aeron thought long and hard about attempting it. Another cold night could leave him a very bad way, and he desperately wanted to feel warm again.

Should I try it? he thought over and over. Sooner or later he would have to know what the Shadow Stone had done to his magical abilities. For better or worse, Aeron was a wizard. He'd wielded magic for years now; it was his life. He did not think he could ever go back to being the simple forester he was once, and that meant that he would have to learn whether or not he could still work magic. And there was only one way to do that.

"I'd better try this with a spell I don't mind wasting," he muttered, staring into the fire. He considered the spells that lay ready in his head, eventually settling on mage light. It was useful, but Aeron could see better in the dark than most, and he could always light a torch or lantern if he really needed to see.

He steeled himself with a grimace and whispered the words to the spell. He brought the symbol to his mind and unlocked it, shaping the magic. And he reached for the living energy to power his spell, grasping at the dancing fire in front of him.

He couldn't feel anything. His rational mind told him that the bright currents of the Weave had to be dancing in the fire, ready for his touch, but he could not perceive the magic with any of his senses. He floundered, grasping desperately.

His outstretched senses brushed against something cold and dark. The campfire guttered, died, and blazed back to life in sick, black flame. Aeron jolted backward, sealing himself from the power he'd found, but it was too late. A streamer of darkness burst from his chest, and he screamed as vile black corruption oozed from his skin, cloaking him in a mantle of shadow. The floating sphere of light took form, but it was pale and sickly, casting a greenish glow through the room. Flailing his arms in disgust, Aeron slashed the spell to pieces.

The darkness retreated, leaving the stone walls slick with black frost. Aeron scrambled to his feet, digging his nails into his flesh as if to drag the ordure from his veins. He tripped over a low stone in the floor and stumbled into the wall. There was a moment of cold, dark pressure as he slid *through* the old rock, and then Aeron tumbled to the ground outside. He retched weakly on the grass until finally his thought and reason returned. He rose on unsteady feet and wiped his hand across his mouth.

He could see the ground through his arm.

In dull amazement, Aeron held up his hands. His clothes and flesh seemed translucent, indistinct. He could see the umber hillside and the rich red glow of the sunset right through his arms. He whirled, looking around, only to see a second landscape shimmering into view, overlying the world around him. It was a landscape of dead brown grass and leafless trees, roofed by a lightless sky.

To the west, the last sliver of the sun's orb was vanishing behind the gray hilltops. A cold wind began to blow contrary to the brisk salt breeze from the sea, making his cloak flutter and twist against the wind as bit by bit he discorporated on the border of night. "Help me!" he screamed, his thin voice wailing on the shadow wind. No one answered.

I'm being dragged through the veil, he thought, trying to master his panic. With each moment, his hold on the real world grew more tenuous, and he could feel tendrils of ebon substance reaching out to seize him, to hold him within the darkness. Mustering all his willpower, he concentrated on restoring his tattered frame, anchoring himself to the wet grass and clean rock of the hillside in Turmish.

Somehow it worked. The sky brightened, the winds failed, and he grew heavier and more substantial until he felt his heart lurch into motion again, moving blood that had begun to freeze. The darkness retreated, and with a weary sigh, he collapsed outside the cottage, staring up into the twilight.

* * * * *

Aeron walked from dawn to dusk for the next month or more, turning his footsteps toward home. He traveled south and west along the coast until he reached the bustling port of Hlondeth, but he had no money for passage to Cimbar. He also feared what would happen if the wind between the worlds came upon him while he was dozens or hundreds of miles out to sea. He resigned himself to a long walk and resolved to endure it as best he could.

He followed the shore of the Vilhon Reach west from Hlondeth, passing through the rugged hill lands of the Cloven Mountains and then into the green eaves of the Winterwood. From the old city of Ormpetarr, he followed the river Arran into the mighty Chondalwood, striking southeast through the forests mantling the western flanks of the Akanapeaks. The great greenwood reminded him of the Maerchwood and home, although it was darker and wilder than the golden glades of his youth. On several occasions, he fell in with fellow travelers, pilgrims and merchants who shared his road for a time, but Aeron learned that he could not keep the same company night after night; when the sun set, he began to fade, wraithlike, into the shadows until the bitter winds of the crossing buried their icy talons in his bones and the deathly cold covered him in sparkling frost. Nothing he could do prevented form and substance from slipping away, and more than one erstwhile companion fled, screaming, at Aeron's unnatural disappearance.

As Ches gave way to Tarsakh, he joined a party of pilgrims braving the old road through the Chondal Gap and climbed into the high vales of the Adder Peaks before winding back down into the sheer foothills in the southwestern corner of Chessenta. In the dense pine forests south of Oslin, he picked up the headwaters of the Winding River and followed it east as it wound through the wild and deserted lands in the southern marches of Chessenta. The land grew gentler and more open as he wandered into the old heartland of Chessenta, checkered with prosperous farmlands and crisscrossed by well-traveled roads.

As the miles passed behind him, Aeron gained a stronger command of his mind and spirit, healing from the foul touch of the Shadow Stone. The chaos and corruption that had nearly driven him mad faded, and he discovered an amazing clarity of thought, a pure and lucid apprehension that illuminated every recess of his mind. But even as his spirit strengthened in the face of the journey, his body weakened. Each night a little less of his substance returned from the shadow crossing. He was slowly starving, not from want of food, but from want of solidity.

Two nights before Midsummer, he crossed completely over, despite every effort to keep a tenuous hold on the world around him. For long hours, he pushed himself along a dark road beneath a barren sky, convinced in his heart that if he gave up and stopped moving, he would never see the dawn again. Finally, near morning, the shadow dissipated, leaving him standing alone on an empty road, hollow as a piece of weathered bone. Somehow he found the strength to continue.

In the rugged hill country of Villon, only six or seven days from his home, Aeron lost the struggle. He had already walked most of the afternoon in the same tireless pace he'd used for weeks, his feet barely seeming to touch the ground. He came to an empty crossroads beside a burned-out, abandoned inn, and paused to consider his way. It was raining steadily, and the road was churned into thick black mud. To his left, an old signpost stood, its markings blurred. Aeron stepped closer and brushed his hand over the wood, trying to make it out.

Something struck him low in his back, a handspan left of his spine, driving a red-hot wedge of pain into his torso. He clapped his hand to the source of the pain, twisting about, and felt something hard sticking into his back. Wincing, he glanced over his shoulder and saw the dark fletchings of an arrow quivering in the air. He drew his hand back and was surprised to see bright red blood running through his fingers.

"Damn, Rolf, what're you waitin' for? Shoot him again!" a coarse voice hissed in the middle distance, behind him.

"The damned bowstring broke. Besides, I got him. He ain't going anywhere." A second voice, deeper and slower.

Aeron felt his legs beginning to give out and leaned against the wooden post for support. In dull shock, he turned to look back at the ruined inn. Several men were rising from the wreckage, tattered ruffians with hollow cheeks and burning, feverish eyes. One of them, a big stoop-shouldered man with long, strong arms, held a longbow in his hand. He scowled at the weapon and then looked at Aeron. "Horse dung. He's just a small fellow. I didn't need to break my string for him."

"He's still standin', Rolf," one of the men in the back observed. "You can't have got him too square."

"It was the bowstring," Rolf complained. "If it hadn't broke, I'd have put the arrow clean through the bastard." He tossed the bow to the ground and sauntered toward Aeron, drawing a heavy knife from his belt.

Aeron could feel warm, wet blood trickling down his back, and the arrowhead burned with a white-hot fire just under the last rib. He could feel metal scraping on bone when he gasped for breath. He pushed himself away from the signpost and staggered away down the road, one hand holding the arrow in his lower back.

"Hey, don't you run off with my arrow, you sorry bastard!" Rolf called, to the harsh laughter of his fellows. Aeron ignored them, trying to get away, but when he looked up again, he saw that the highwaymen were easily pacing him, moving up to surround him.

He reeled to a halt, turning to watch them move closer. "I don't want any trouble," he gasped. "Just let me go."

"Doesn't matter what you want," the first highwayman

said. "Trouble's what you got." He leaned closer, scrutinizing Aeron. "Say, what kind of man are you? You don't look right to me."

"Those're elf ears," Rolf announced. "We've found a half-breed, lads. Now, what'll we do with him?"

"Whatever it is, better make it quick," the last bandit observed. "This fellow's bleeding like a stuck pig, Rolf. You might've got him after all."

Aeron felt his knees buckle and he sagged to all fours, fighting to remain conscious. He felt nauseous, and his vision swam drunkenly. I'm going to die, he realized. It made him sick and sad, but he didn't feel any real fear yet, just surprise.

"Ahh, you're right, I guess. Besides, the king's men might come along. No sense wasting time." Rolf advanced on Aeron, knife held casually in one hand.

Aeron forced himself to look up at the burly brigand. "Stay back," he warned in a weak voice. "I'm a wizard."

"Is that so?" Rolf said. "You'd better use any magic you've got, boy, 'cause you're going to be a dead wizard in just a moment." He leered wickedly at Aeron and seized a handful of Aeron's hair, jerking his face up to the sky to bare his throat.

One last spark of resistance flared in Aeron's heart. Closing his eyes, he banished his pain for one moment, long enough to unlock a spell from his mind. He stretched out his senses to work the magic, knowing what would happen. Dark, potent force rushed to fill him, springing out of the quiescent blackness in the marrow of his bones, filling him with remorseless strength. Aeron locked his eyes on the bandit's and spoke the words for the fire hand spell.

With nothing more than his force of will, he directed the jet of raging flame against the highwayman Rolf, charring his arms and face to brittle cinders. Aeron allowed the searing heat to play against the toppling bandit until he vanished in a pillar of fire, then swept the jet around to scorch Rolf's companions. With a distant fragment of his mind, he noted that the flames were a shade of black or purple that made his eyes ache.

One of the highwaymen nearly escaped, but Aeron greedily drew power enough to beat the ruffian into the ground and blacken his flesh until it sizzled and smoked. When all four had stopped moving, he allowed the dark flames to gutter and fade, leaving a roaring, buzzing sound in his ears and bitter ice clinging to his bones. The world began to grow ghostly, and he looked down to see his body fading into insubstantiality. But dusk isn't near, he thought irrationally. The unearthly chill of the crossing blasted him, freezing the flow of blood down his back to a dark trickle. Aeron howled in pain as the shadow claimed him.

He opened his eyes and found himself standing in the phantasmal gloom of the twilight plane, looking at the hills and the burned-out tavern as if through dark, smoked glass. Aeron realized that he felt neither the cold nor the pain of his wound. He reached behind him and set his hand on the arrow shaft. As if he'd done it for years, he willed himself to intangibility and watched the arrow clatter to the ground, passing through the dark wisps of his body. He was part of the shadow plane now. There was no going back.

He turned in a slow circle, his thoughts sluggish and indistinct. He wasn't hungry, he wasn't thirsty, he wasn't cold. There was no pain, no urgency. He remembered that he'd been walking east, but it was hard to recall why he'd chosen that path. Closing his eyes, Aeron tried to decide what to do.

He could dimly sense a brilliant hint of power somewhere to the north. He turned his thoughts that way, trying to discern what it was that he felt, and suddenly in his mind's eye he saw the Shadow Stone, pulsing in its vaulted chamber beneath the ruined monolith. Its energies were intertwined with his, and it responded to his silent call, flaring into life and reaching out with an inarticulate demand that dragged Aeron ten paces to the north before he opened his eyes and realized that he was marching mindlessly in that direction.

From the cold ashes of his razed soul, the first stirrings of fear arose. "I'm not dead," he said, willing his feet to stop moving. "I'm not dead. Not yet. I don't know if I'm alive, but I know what that damned stone will do to me if I let it."

But that's the price you paid for your knowledge, Aeron, a voice inside his mind mocked. *You wanted power, and you found it. Now you try to flee your fate?*

"What fate? Oriseus deceived me. I didn't choose this."

You knew exactly what Oriseus offered, and you didn't

shy away. He didn't deceive you. You deceived yourself.

"How can you say that? Who would want this?" Aeron deliberately turned his back on the insidious pull from the north and willed himself over the road. He hardly felt his feet strike the ground, and with every few steps, the gloom around him seemed to shimmer and he found that he'd covered hundreds of yards with a step. He decided that it didn't matter and continued to argue with the cynical voice. "He won't fool me again," he stated.

He'll have no need to. You're a slave of the stone. Where's your life, your substance? You're nothing more than a wraith, hollow, empty. The voice seemed to relish this thought. *As long as you struggle against the darkness, you are a mere phantom, a ghost caught between the worlds.*

Aeron stopped, unwilling to confront the bitter thought. "You're lying. I'll leave any time now. Dawn can't be far off." He realized that he was speaking to himself, yet the argument seemed to have a fearsome weight to it, as if his very soul depended upon the outcome. The stars danced and burned in frozen glory overhead, but Aeron ignored his surroundings. The internal battle was much more significant; anything that he saw or thought he saw around him was a mere manifestation of the contentious struggle within.

You begin to understand.

Aeron thought carefully for a long time, holding his mind to the task with iron discipline. "I touched the stone with my magic, and so it is my magic that is tainted."

Had you set your hand on the stone, as the others did, you would have been lost without hope of redemption.

"And it is my magic that keeps me here. I don't belong in the shadow land; no living man does. And so by daylight I've been free to walk the waking world. At night, the Shadow Stone grows strong enough to drag me into its own plane. And each day that passes, each night I walk in the realm of the shadow, my reality fades."

You are almost spent. You lack the strength now to return to the daylight against the stone's influence.

"I must expunge any magical power that I have left to me in order to eliminate the stone's hold." Aeron mulled that over. He still had a half-dozen spells remaining in his mind, spells he'd managed to preserve throughout his travels. The only way he could imagine to rid himself of magic would be to speak each spell, cast it here in the shadow, and dissipate its energies. When all the spells were gone, he'd have no magic for the stone to retain its hold on him. And he might escape the shadow prison that sought to claim him.

You will be left powerless. Your spellbooks remain in the college. And there is only one source of magic here for you. Each spell you speak must be powered by the stone, and therefore, with each casting, its influence over you will grow stronger. You will fall completely under its power long before you escape the plane of shadow.

"That," said Aeron, "will depend on me."

He weighed the options, thinking it through, but there was really no choice. The plane of shadow was devouring him slowly, dissipating his life in its endless gloom. He was certain to perish if he remained. The stone might or might not overpower him. His only hope lay in the course of madness.

He turned and looked around him. He stood on a long, open ridge, a dark line of woods off to his right, a dim ruined castle a mile or so across untended fields to his left. It was as good a place as any. Deliberately he closed his eyes and forced the knotted symbol for the spell of shielding to the forefront of his mind and set it free.

Streaming up from the barren ground, icy tendrils of blackness poured into Aeron's body, filling him with something hateful and cold. His mind reeled and his heart ached with revulsion, but he worked through the spell and discarded it uselessly into the night. He immediately selected the charm of blindness and stammered it out while his body convulsed and his blood ran as sluggishly as a filthy, choked sewer. His mind already reeled on the brink of oblivion.

You can't do it. The stone's overwhelming you.

"Not until I let it," Aeron hissed in response. He reached deep into his reserves of will, finding strength even beyond the limits of what he'd thought he possessed, and barked out the next two spells, enduring the cold, black rottenness that surged and seethed in his soul, forcing his mind above the rising tide of insanity. If he failed, his life was the least of the things he would forfeit.

Phantasms of terror and mist swirled around him under the lightless sky, drawn by the sorcery he unleashed. He was burning like a beacon on the hilltop, shrouded in a cold white fire that danced like will-o'-the-wisps in the marshes. He hammered his way through the next, a spell of disenchantment, and botched it badly . . . but it was spent, and now one last spell remained, a spell of illusion. With the last of his strength and sanity, Aeron gibbered the words, and the raging power of the Shadow Stone gave it form and then destroyed it.

And a silence as final as death fell on the sere hillside.

Aeron lay on the cold road, exhausted, starving, his gut aching with violent nausea. But he did not feel the stone's touch in him anymore.

He looked down at his hands and noticed that an odd rose-and-orange glow was staining his flesh, his robes. It puzzled him for a moment, and then he realized that he was seeing the first light of morning shining on him, although it touched nothing else yet in the gloom of the shadow land. He glanced to the east, watching as the sunrise dispelled the preternatural darkness.

The sunlight touched him, but it brought no warmth. Weakness assailed him, and he collapsed to his hands and knees, every last reserve of his strength suddenly depleted beyond hope of restoration.

He found himself kneeling in a broad farm field sown with young corn. A long line of dark trees sketched the horizon, rising and falling in gentle hills and deep dells that Aeron knew like the back of his hand—Maerchlin. With the last of his strength, he snorted in amazement. "I'm home," he whispered. Then he collapsed into the rich, wet earth.

Raedel's soldiers found Aeron before the sun had risen an hour into the sky.

Twelve

Aeron was dragged through the village and into the castle's gaping mouth by a squad of mailed soldiers. They spared him no discomfort, manhandling him with angry shoves and cuffs to his head as if he'd been a struggling berserker. At first Aeron almost welcomed their attention; each blow confirmed his escape from the plane of shadow and reminded him of his reality.

The guards wasted no time in bringing him before Phoros Raedel, in the musty, oak-paneled great hall. The room was crowded with the men-at-arms and retainers of the Raedels and a handful of village leaders who had business with the count this morning. The conversation died away as Aeron was led into the room.

Phoros Raedel rose from the high seat, openly amazed. "Morieth!" he stated, his face slack. The young lord had filled out in the two years since Aeron had last seen him; some of his hard-won muscle was settling around his waist, and his face, once chiseled and clean, seemed more florid now. But the strength of his arms and the cruelty in his eyes remained, and a wide smile of satisfaction spread across his features as he slowly approached. "Oh, how I've dreamed of this moment. My sight was gone for a month before my father found a priest who could undo your spell."

Aeron drew himself up and met the count's glare with a calm gaze. "I did what I had to do. You'd have killed Kestrel if I hadn't acted." He hesitated, then added, "I didn't want you for an enemy, Phoros."

"You didn't want me for an enemy?" Raedel brayed harsh laughter. "Regos still carries the scar you left when you laid open his arm. Miroch you burned alive. You bewitched my guardsmen, and you blinded me! And now you're sorry for it?"

Aeron waited until Raedel had stopped laughing. Familiar or not, Phoros still meant him no good. He bit back an angry retort, the old scar across the top of his left ear aching as if to remind him of how his feud with the young lord had begun. "I only sought to protect myself and those I love. I don't regret saving Eriale from Miroch's attentions or helping Kestrel to escape from your dungeons, but I wish it had never been necessary."

Raedel blinked. He studied Aeron for a long moment, eyes narrowed. "You've changed," he said at last.

"I've little fight left in me," Aeron replied.

The young count held his gaze for a long time before looking away to the guards. "Take him away," he said. "He's guilty of raising his hand against a lord, sedition, sorcery, and a dozen other charges. He'll hang tomorrow morning."

"One favor, Raedel?" Aeron said.

Phoros wheeled on him, astonished. "You want to ask a favor of me? Are you insane?"

"Pardon Kestrel and Eriale. You only arrested them to catch me."

"Pardon them? Why? They're rebels and traitors, fugitives from my dungeons!"

"Now that you have me, let them go," Aeron said.

Phoros scowled. "What does it matter if I pardon them or not? They fled Maerchlin two years ago."

"They never did anything wrong, Phoros. It's not right for them to be outlaws on my account."

The count weighed Aeron's words and abruptly agreed. "Very well. Kestrel and Eriale are pardoned, for what it's worth." He waved his hand at Aeron's guards, dismissing them. "Be careful with Morieth. He is a skillful sorcerer. Keep his hands bound, and keep a hood over his head. And I want him guarded around the clock by two swordsmen in his cell. He will not walk out of my dungeons again."

The guards dragged him away to the castle's cells. They grudgingly spared him some food, so before the hood went over his head, Aeron gnawed at a piece of tough black bread and washed it down with cold water. He felt much better for it, and by the time he finished, he felt simply tired instead of exhausted beyond his limits.

Aeron didn't even consider escape. With all of his magic expended, he did not stand a chance against the guards whom Raedel had posted over him. And even if he still had some magic left, he wasn't sure that he would have been able to wield the Weave without drawing on the power of the Shadow Stone; even to save his own life, he was unwilling to do that. So Aeron closed his eyes and slept dreamlessly, still trying to rest from his ordeal.

He was awakened late in the day by a guard poking his foot into his ribs. "You've got visitors," he said.

Aeron shook his head, wondering why he couldn't see, and then he remembered the hood. "Who is it?" he asked.

"Aeron? Is it really you?" Eriale knelt down beside him and held him tight, her voice cracking with emotion. "We feared we'd never see you again!"

"Aye, lad. Where have you been? We've sent a dozen letters to the college, but they knew nothing of your whereabouts." Kestrel's strong hands clasped his shoulders.

"Step away from the prisoner," said one of the guards. "The count ordered no contact." Steel rasped on leather as the fellow drew his blade to emphasize his point.

Reluctantly Eriale released him, and Kestrel's hands fell away. Aeron sensed them shuffling back a few steps. He shook his head again, trying to clear the cobwebs. "What time of day is it? I've been asleep."

"It's about an hour before midnight. We came as quickly as we could," Kestrel said.

Aeron thought for a moment. "It's a half-day's ride from your new home. How did you know I was here?"

"You remember Toric and Shiela Goldsheaf," Eriale said. "When Toric heard of your return, and the count's pardon for Father and me, he borrowed the fastest horse in the village and set out for my homestead. I've never ridden so fast in my life."

"I didn't think you'd risk setting foot in Maerchlin again," Aeron said quietly. "The count might revoke his pardon." He heard a soft, choked sob. "Eriale? Are you all right?"

There was a long pause before she answered, and her voice was taut. "Yes, I'm fine. It just doesn't seem fair that we've finally seen you again, but you're to hang tomorrow."

For the first time, the weight of Phoros's sentence crashed down on Aeron. It might have been a mundane death compared to what would have happened to him in the shadow, but it was still death, now only a few hours away. Aeron had forgotten what it was like to be powerless and blind. With his magic, he could have escaped from his bonds in a dozen different ways. "It's better than what might have happened to me," he said softly.

"What do you mean, Aeron?" asked Kestrel.

Aeron sighed. "It doesn't matter now, I guess." He wanted to tell them something about his experiences in the college, to explain how he'd come to be in Raedel's dungeons, but he couldn't bring himself to speak of it. "I learned a lot at the college, and I threw myself into my studies. But patience was never my strong suit, and I became involved in dangerous lore. One of my spells went wrong, and here I am. I'm lucky to have survived the experience, I think."

"Lucky enough to land in the dungeons of your worst enemy," Kestrel remarked wryly. "Aeron, what do—"

"All right, that's enough," barked the guard. "Ten minutes was all I was supposed to allow you, and you've had a fair piece more. Now, let's go. You might be allowed to say your farewells tomorrow morning."

Aeron heard scuffling footsteps as the guard escorted Kestrel and Eriale to the door. Suddenly he felt very small and alone.

"Aeron, is there anything we can do?" Eriale called from the door of the cell. "Someone we can talk to, a way to delay the execution?" She sobbed. "We've got to do something!"

"I said that's enough!" the guard snarled.

Aeron thought quickly. There was only one hope that came to his mind. "Tell Fineghal!" he called.

"Where can we find him?" Kestrel asked.

"Eriale can show you. Try the ruined tower, or the vale with the waterfall—" Something heavy crashed into the side of his head and spun him to the floor. Even with his eyes covered, he saw twisting shapes of colored light, and he tasted blood in his mouth. He realized that the guard had hit him.

"That's all from you!" the guard snapped. "Keep running your mouth and we'll hold your friends here just to make sure they don't cause any mischief. So go ahead, keep talking if you want to. Got anything more to say?"

Aeron held his tongue. He could hear clanging doors, Eriale's voice as she argued with the guardsmen escorting her away, harsh replies from the other jailers. He hoped that the soldiers would let them leave. Of course, they could walk the Maerchwood for weeks and see no sign of Fineghal, he thought. The elf lord might be anywhere. Or he might not want to be found. And even if they did find him, he might not be willing to help, not if it meant inter-

fering in human affairs. Aeron tried to stifle the rising
ache of despair in his heart and failed. He let himself fall
back against the ground, bowing his head in silence.

"Good. I thought you might hold your tongue, wizard."
The guardsman laughed, and he fell to trading colorful
tales with the other fellow on watch.

* * * * *

"Get up, you piece of filth. You're not going to be late to
your hanging on my watch." Two or three men dragged
Aeron to his feet, shaking him awake with a start. He
coughed and groaned. "By Assuran, I fell asleep again!" he
muttered. He'd worked furiously against his bonds for an
hour or more after Kestrel and Eriale left, only to find his
hands too well secured. He remembered giving up in frustration, thinking of what to try next . . . and then nothing.
He'd missed his chance.

"Wait," he said, trying to dig his feet into the ground.
"Don't I get a last meal? An appeal? A chance to speak to
my friends?"

"Count's orders. You're to swing at sunrise, no visitors,
no discussion. Now stop wriggling. The count will have my
hide if you're not swinging by the neck at first light." The
guard snorted. "Your day's not looking too good, but there's
no reason that my day should be miserable, too."

Aeron kicked and stomped, wrenching himself from side
to side, but the guards only laughed and tightened their
grip. He managed to get one arm free, but someone behind
him struck him in the back of the skull with a weighted
truncheon. He found himself lying on the ground, his foot
tapping the wall, with hot agony burning in his head. He
didn't struggle anymore when the guards dragged him to
his feet and through the castle's halls.

They hauled him out into the courtyard and removed the
leather hood. Aeron shook his head and looked around; the
early morning air was cool and damp, and it felt clean on
his face after wearing the hood for nearly a day. The light
was dim and rose-hued, long shadows slanting across the
open bailey. A small crowd had gathered to watch; in a
quick glance, Aeron saw a score of faces he recognized. The
guards hustled him across the yard to a wooden platform
with a bowed crossbeam and a single noose. Stunned by

the swiftness of events, he offered no resistance as they pulled him up the short flight of steps and positioned him beneath the noose, standing on a simple board over a square hole in the wooden decking. A black-hooded executioner stood by with a large mattock to knock the board from under his feet.

While the guards worked on his bindings, retying them for the hanging, Aeron glanced around the courtyard. Most of the people watching were Raedel's housemen and soldiers, but a few villagers shifted nervously, watching the preparations. "No tricks now," growled one of the men beside him as he positioned the noose around Aeron's neck.

Aeron grimaced but did not resist. The rope scraped at his neck. He glanced around the courtyard again, hoping for some miraculous reprieve, and his eyes fell on Kestrel and Eriale, watching from the back. Eriale's face was streaked with tears, and Kestrel glowered as if he could burn Aeron's guards with nothing more than the heat of his anger. Two guardsmen stood right behind them, detailed to watch over his kinfolk and make sure that they did not interfere.

The men readying the gallows finished their work and stepped back, waiting. The brief pause stretched into a maddening wait for Aeron as he shifted and tested his bonds. A disturbance in the crowd caught his attention, and he looked up to see Phoros Raedel and his closest retainers sauntering into the courtyard. The young count stopped a few feet in front of the gallows, looking up at Aeron. "If he starts to speak a spell, silence him," he said to the guards nearby. To Aeron, he said, "Any last words?"

Aeron considered an impassioned plea, but one look into Phoros's eyes told him all that he needed to know. Raedel would not be moved. "No," he answered.

"Very well, then." Phoros started to gesture to the sledge man, when a piercing shriek shattered the morning stillness.

Eriale screamed and clawed her way through the small crowd. "No, my lord! I beg you, don't kill him! He never meant to do you any harm." Two of Raedel's guards caught her five paces before she reached the count and restrained her, although she struggled with the fury of a wildcat. "No!"

Phoros jerked his head at the guards, and they dragged her back. "Do it," he ordered.

In the corner of his eye, Aeron saw the sledge wielder raise the heavy maul and bring it down. The impact jolted his feet, and the board beneath him flew away, spinning.

He managed nothing more than a grunt of surprise before the rope snapped tight, cutting off his air. Something popped in his neck, and then he landed heavily on the ground, stunned and breathless. He was lying on his side on the cold ground, his arms still bound behind him, and in his sideways view of the courtyard, Raedel's guardsmen suddenly appeared, shouting at each other. "You damn fool! The rope parted!"

"I checked it twice. It was fine!"

"Well, get another rope and do it right this time."

Aeron wanted to roll back and look behind him, but he seemed to have forgotten how. His eyes smarted from staring, but he could not close them, and he couldn't work the dirt out of his mouth. With a cold, sick shock, he realized that he wasn't breathing. No need to do it again, he thought. The rope must have snapped my neck clean.

Two guards seized him by the arms and dragged him upright, but he was left staring down at the ground. The voices in the courtyard were growing fainter, and it seemed that a cloud had passed before the sun, since it was growing very dark.

". . . think he's dead."

". . . here, look. He's dead."

". . . guess the fall broke his neck."

"Here's the physician. Is he . . ."

". . . no doubt. Take him away."

A heavy white wrap of linen was laid over his face, and he was distantly aware that he was being shrouded where he lay. He wanted to protest, but he had no voice and could not move at all. He mustered every ounce of willpower remaining and tried to move, but he couldn't tell if he succeeded or not.

". . . Assuran's eyes! His hand moved!"

". . . seen a corpse, you idiot? They do that."

He was lifted and dumped against creaking wood, his limbs straightened and arranged, and then another blanket was thrown over him. In his mind, he ripped the cloth away from his face, hammered his way free of the cart, shouted for help. Despite his panic, his body refused to move. A new voice nearby caught his attention—Eriale.

He could hear the grief in her words. "Can we take him home now?"

"We'll bury him in the castle's graveyard if you want."

Kestrel now: "No. We'll lay him beside his parents."

"Get him out of here, then. It's your business now."

The cart moved and creaked, trundling along a rutted road. Aeron gave up on trying to escape his condition and waited in blank hopelessness. Was this death, then? Consciousness trapped in an inert shell? How long would thought remain, how long would it take before whatever dim spark that still burned inside was mad beyond all reason? He prayed for oblivion before that happened.

". . . far enough yet?"

"Keep going. They may follow just to be certain."

He was moved again, strapped to a narrow board, and then dragged for quite some distance. He wasn't sure, but he thought he was in the forest, for he felt roots and twigs catching at the sledge, and it seemed cooler and darker here. Careful hands stretched him on a cold stone surface, and he felt the shrouds and wraps being removed from his body. Finally the band of cloth over his eyes was peeled away.

He was looking up at the forest canopy. It was still early morning, for the treetops were gold and orange with the light. Eriale and Kestrel knelt over him, rubbing his limbs, their faces tight with concern. A silver wolfhound began to lick his face, whining softly. A voice of inhuman perfection laughed, and the hound drew away. Fineghal knelt over Aeron, smiled, and spoke a brief word that Aeron once knew. "Rise, my friend. The paralysis should be fading from your body."

With all his effort, Aeron managed to blink and shiver. He tried to speak but only groaned instead.

"Will he be all right?" Eriale asked anxiously.

"Give him a moment," Fineghal replied. "The spell that feigns death wears off slowly, but he should be with us soon." He leaned forward and set his hand on Aeron's brow. "Come back, Aeron. You are not as dead as you think."

This time, Aeron managed a word. "How . . . ?"

The elf lord grinned. "I made certain that the rope would not support your weight, but of course they would have found another and hanged you a second time. So, while you lay stunned on the ground, I worked a spell for which I'd never had a use before today—the death glamour."

Aeron licked his lips and found that he had strength enough to prop himself up on his elbows. "They . . . they thought I was dead?"

Kestrel snorted. "Aeron, I knew what to expect, and *I* thought you were dead. Raedel and his henchmen are celebrating even as we speak, certain that they've rid the world of the last of the Morieths."

Aeron heaved a sigh of relief and fell back against the ground. He recognized the place now; it was the same elven tower where he and Eriale had first encountered Fineghal. "I take it you managed to reach Fineghal, then?"

Eriale smiled. "We found him here, in fact. Or I should say he found us. It seems he was expecting your return." She reached out for his hands and dragged him to his feet.

Aeron embraced her, and then Kestrel as well. Finally he turned and took Fineghal's hand in the elven welcome. "Thank you. I'd be dead if you hadn't helped."

"We may have parted in anger, Aeron, but I have no desire to see harm befall you." The elven mage nodded to Kestrel and Eriale. "Thank your kinfolk, too. If they hadn't sought me out, I might not have arrived in time to help."

Aeron stretched and rubbed his shoulders. "I wish you could have let me know what to expect. I was certain that I was dead."

"There wasn't much time, Aeron, and I could not risk revealing my presence. They'd have cut you down in your cell if they'd suspected that I might show up."

"Where did you hide?" Kestrel asked the elf. "I saw no sign of you, none at all."

Fineghal smiled. "I stood right beside you the whole time. I was the miller."

Kestrel gaped. "That fat old miser?"

The elf shrugged. "Any stranger in the courtyard would have been watched closely."

Aeron was silent a long time, registering the tide of events in his mind, coming to grips with where he stood and what had happened. "Listen," he said slowly, "I've made some grave mistakes, some very bad decisions. I was caught up in dangerous intrigues in the college. And when I left, I was stranded in dark and strange planes for a long time. I was nearly killed, several times. I . . . I don't know whether or not I've really escaped from what waited for me there."

Eriale paled in horror, and Kestrel grunted and shifted nervously. Fineghal simply gazed at Aeron, his face inscrutable.

Aeron continued. "I touched a stone of darkness, something strong and evil beyond belief. It left its mark in the part of me that once wielded magic. In order to escape, I had to expunge what power I had. I . . . I can't wield magic anymore." As he spoke the words, his voice broke.

"If that was the price you paid for your life, count yourself lucky," Kestrel said at length. "You're here and alive. That's something to be thankful for."

"What will you do now, Aeron?" Eriale asked. "Will you go back to the college?"

Aeron shuddered. "No. I don't know if I can learn to wield magic again, and even if I was certain that I could, I don't want to go back there." He thought of Oriseus and his followers, standing in the black glare of the Shadow Stone. The city of Cimbar was too close to the shard. "No, I don't want to go back. What's done is done." He looked over to Kestrel. "Can you use another set of hands in Saden?"

"You're welcome to come with us, Aeron," Kestrel said. "There's always a place under my roof for Stiche Morieth's son. We've land to clear and trapping to look to."

"Kestrel's suggestion bears merit, Aeron," Fineghal said. Aeron had almost forgotten that the elven lord stood watching until he spoke. "However, I must remind you of the deception we enacted for Phoros Raedel's benefit. Saden is not so far from Maerchlin that he wouldn't hear of your return sooner or later. And I doubt that he would be glad to learn how he was fooled."

Aeron's heart fell. "So I can't go home."

Fineghal shook his head. "Not yet, I think. Give it a few months, perhaps a year or two. That's enough time for those who knew you in Saden to forget about you. Your appearance has changed since you left Maerchlin, and if I remember anything about growing up, it seems to me that a couple of years more should help you to vanish altogether."

"What do you suggest? That he sets out on his own again for years?" Eriale asked, an edge in her voice. "Where would he go? What would he do?"

"He could come with me." The elven mage shrugged and

looked at Aeron. "I walk the Maerchwood still, and few humans mark my path. You are welcome to remain here, Aeron. You know the forest well, and I would enjoy your company."

"But my magic's gone," Aeron protested.

"The time of your apprenticeship's long past, I think. I ask you as a friend, not as your master." Fineghal swept his arm out to indicate the green and golden wood, alive with the early spring. "And if your heart is heavy, I know no better cure than the Maerchwood in spring."

Aeron glanced from Kestrel and Eriale to Fineghal, and back again. "If you'll stand my company, I'll come with you," he said. "I'll be able to visit my family?"

"Of course. Just take pains to avoid being seen in Kestrel's house for a while."

He weighed the elf's words for a short time and then agreed with a nod. "Thank you, Fineghal."

The elf lord rose and summoned Baillegh with a gesture. "Then let us be on our way. We're still too close to Maerchlin for my taste, and we have an empty grave to dig before we leave."

Thirteen

For the rest of the summer, Fineghal and Aeron returned to their old life of walking the forest from one end to the other, sleeping under the stars in a different place every night. At first Aeron had a hard time keeping up; his long months at Cimbar's university hadn't involved daily marches with the fleet-footed elf, and his ordeal in the plane of shadow had not improved his constitution. But as the weeks passed, he regained and then surpassed his old conditioning; he was now in his twentieth year, a wiry and athletic man, not a rail-thin boy.

Aeron did not speak of what had passed at the college or during the months of his trek through the western lands and the shadow realm, and Fineghal did not press him. Nor did Aeron attempt to wield magic. He was unwilling to face the consequences of attempting to shape the Weave into the form of a spell; the Shadow Stone's influence might still be present, and he did not want to risk allowing its malign power into his heart and mind again. He had survived it once, just barely, but he did not believe he would be so lucky again.

If Fineghal was puzzled by Aeron's new reluctance to pursue the magical power he had craved before they parted, he did not speak of it. Aeron was content to let matters stand. Sensing Aeron's reluctance to discuss his experiences in the college, Fineghal turned to an exhaustive study of the beautiful woodlands and glades of the Maerchwood, filling Aeron's mind with the elven knowledge of the forest and all that lived and grew within it. Aeron sated his insatiable hunger for knowledge with the mundane lore of the woodlands, avoiding his old studies and interests.

As Fineghal had promised, they visited Saden frequently, guesting with Kestrel and Eriale for the night before slipping away under the cover of the predawn mists. Kestrel had done well for himself in the freehold, and Eriale was the belle of the village. She was now eighteen, tall enough to look Aeron level in the eye and blessed with the wide, brown eyes of her mother and long, flowing chestnut hair she wore in a braid. At first Aeron was a little amused to watch the young men of Saden competing for Eriale's affections, since she was thoroughly independent and had no real desire to find a husband. She was the best archer in Saden, with the possible exception of her father. Aeron realized his foster sister could marry any time she wanted to, and it made him very conscious of his own solitude. Other than Fineghal and his family, he had no one to speak to and no friends of his own.

One day, when he and Fineghal hiked along a steep trail that looked toward the Smoking Mountains east of the woods, Aeron found himself thinking of Melisanda again. He tried to imagine where she was and what she was doing, and he couldn't seem to get her face out of his mind. After a time, he asked, "Fineghal, do you ever become lonely?"

The elf halted and turned to face him. "I've become quite comfortable with my own company." He shrugged. "I have friends. You, Baillegh, even Kestrel and Eriale, though I do not know them as well."

"You didn't answer my question."

The elf looked out over the distant peaks. It was a warm day, and the faint sounds of the forest rose lazily over the sunny hillsides. "I miss my people," he said slowly. "Once the Maerchwood was filled with the Tel'Quessir. The wood itself was much greater then, of course, reaching to the Chondalwood in the west and the Methwood in the east. The great court moved every day to a new place, and the fair ladies and gallant princes were countless as the stars in the summer sky. Everywhere I turn, I see their ghosts and I hear the echoes of their laughter. But they are gone."

Aeron looked down, a little embarrassed. Besides Fineghal's loss, his own loneliness seemed trivial. "You've told me before that many still live today, in other lands."

Fineghal nodded. "I visited with my kinfolk in the distant forest of Evereska for a time while you were away at the college. It reminded me of times long gone." He paused, thinking. "I believe I will join them someday."

Aeron glanced up at him. "And leave the Maerchwood?"

"Perhaps, although that day is not yet here." He turned Aeron's question back on him. "I take it that you wish for more company?"

"I had several good friends at the college. One was a beautiful girl called Melisanda. She came from Arrabar, in

Chondath. I fell in love with her, although she didn't feel the same way about me." Aeron smiled ruefully. "She's back in Arrabar, I guess." He went on to relate the story of his infatuation with Melisanda, and after a long time, he realized that his tale was growing to encompass the sum of his experiences in the college. Fineghal was a patient listener, and from time to time he prompted Aeron into explaining things that Aeron would rather have omitted. Before he knew it, the sun was low on the horizon, and he had finished by telling how he returned to Castle Raedel. He felt better than he had in a long time, at peace with himself. Telling his story had lifted a heavy weight from his spirit.

"Your loneliness is very understandable," Fineghal said after a time. "You walk between two worlds, Aeron. I've taught you the Tel'Quessir ways, but I am the only elf you have ever spoken with. And in Chessenta, the blood of your elven ancestors marks you as different, unusual."

"I don't know if this is what I truly wanted."

The elf lord reached out to grasp Aeron's shoulder. "Home, hearth, family, and friends are not to be your lot in life, Aeron. Your human side will never be satisfied with the lonely road you will follow. And if you denied the elven magic in your blood, you would be just as unhappy."

"So I must accept the fact that I will be alone for the rest of my life? That I won't fit in anywhere?"

"That is the price of wisdom, Aeron. And you are quickly becoming wise beyond your years." Fineghal stood, gazing up into the night sky. The first stars were beginning to flicker into view. "The stars, the waters, and the wind will be your friends in years to come. And the wood is your home. There is comfort in that, if not the comfort you yearned for."

Aeron considered the wizard's words for a long time. "You think I should resume the study of magic?"

"It's in your nature, Aeron. Almost anyone can learn a cantrip or two of the magician's art if they put their mind to it, but only a handful in a generation can become mages, and you have the potential to be a great mage. Magic comes naturally to you. Resist the call if you want to, but I don't think you will ever be truly happy if you do."

"I'm content now, and I haven't cast a spell in months."

"Are you? Are you truly content? Or do you feel lonely,

out of place?" Fineghal smiled sadly.

"Even if you are right, you know that I cannot risk casting a spell. I told you about the Shadow Stone and its effect on me. Anything I touch, I might destroy."

Fineghal returned his gaze to Aeron. "Let's consider that for a moment. Tell me, what is 'elven' magic?"

Aeron looked up. "The Weave," he answered automatically. "The forces of nature. The power of the elements—wind, earth, fire, and water—and also the intangible spark or spirit that lies within every living thing."

"This is the essence of our magic, although many humans can also touch the Weave. But the Weave is not the only source of power in the world." Fineghal frowned and pressed his hands together, considering his words. "The Weave is a positive force, an energy that is creative and necessary to the order of things. Even events we view in a negative light—death, for instance, or the elements raging out of control in a forest fire or a great storm—are natural. The magic of the Tel'Quessir is bound by the circles of the world around us.

"Yet there are forces from beyond the circles of the world, forces that seek to insinuate themselves into our own world and poison it. The Shadow Stone, I suspect, is a manifestation of one of these forces."

Aeron shook his head. "I don't see what that has to do with me, other than to reaffirm my fears of trying to use magic. If the shadow magic is all I can reach, then it would be better if I did not cast spells at all."

"Listen to me, Aeron. When I was young, long before the fall of Calmaercor, my instructors told me of creatures their own masters had fought in the very beginning of things. Many of the old elves possessed the gift of mage sight, as you do, and they reported that the fiends and sendings they battled used no magic that we could perceive or comprehend. We often wondered where these forgotten sorcerers and monsters had found their magical power. This is how I know that the Weave is not the only way in which a spell may be crafted."

"I wonder if they knew the Imaskari," Aeron said quietly. "I learned that a few of the ancient human wizards gained the power to shape shadow magic by binding themselves to powers from the planes beyond their own. They sold their souls to master a sorcery no other beings of this world dared to touch."

"I believe it could be so," Fineghal replied. "You have touched this, Aeron, but I cannot perceive it. It is beyond me. You, however, with your human blood and your human determination, may be capable of wielding this magic."

"The shadow magic is evil," Aeron said emphatically. "Believe me, Fineghal, I know."

The elven wizard fell silent for a long time. They listened to thunder booming in the distance as a storm gathered about the mountain peaks miles away and began to descend toward the Maerchwood.

"Here is my thought," Fineghal said at last. "Magic is not 'good' or 'evil,' although some forms of magic clearly lend themselves more easily to noble purposes or sinister ones. As an elven mage, I can only perceive the Weave, the natural energy of the world around me. And since this is natural to me, it is hard to pervert into something innately evil. Similarly, magic derived from a darker source, such as the Shadow Stone, lends itself to fell purposes, and if that were the only magic one knew how to use, then eventually it would corrupt. But what if the truth lies somewhere in between?"

"You believe that I may be able to find some balance between the two?" Aeron said. "I think you're mistaken. I don't have the strength to resist the taint of magic drawn from darkness."

"Very few things are wholly good or wholly evil, Aeron. The dark Weave does not even exist for me. I cannot sense it or shape it to my hand. But you might be able to. And if this is the price you must pay for your magic, then so be it."

"What if I fail? What if it masters me instead?" Aeron whispered. "I saw what the Shadow Stone did to those who set their hands on it."

"You must decide if you are willing to take the risk." Fineghal sat down on a boulder across the path from Aeron and drew out his pouch of spellstones. "I see that you have lost your glyphwoods," he observed. "If you wish to, you may borrow my spell tokens again and begin to rebuild your collection of enchantments. I suspect there are few spells in my repertoire that would be beyond your skill now."

Aeron wavered. He could sense that Fineghal's words had an elemental truth to them. The elven magics were not enough for him, but he feared the black, seething malice of the Shadow Stone. The road to wisdom and power lay somewhere in between. With a grimace, he reached out for a spell token. "We'll see how it goes," he said. He looked down at the pebble. It was marked with the sign for the charm of invisibility. It took only a few moments to commit the symbol to his mind, locking its potential like a line of poetry held ready behind his tongue.

"You have the spell memorized?" Fineghal asked.

"I'd forgotten what it feels like," Aeron replied. He hadn't had a spell readied in months. "Now what do I do?"

Fineghal shrugged. "Cast it," he said. "With this spell, you normally weave from the spirit and the air. I do not know what other sources you may be able to tap."

"Should I try to use the shadow magic?"

The elf shrugged. "See what forces answer your call."

Aeron licked his lips, closed his eyes, and muttered the syllable that unlocked the spell's power. He stretched out his senses, seeking the delicate threads and forces that he needed to weave the spell. Instantly he realized his perceptions had changed from his earlier days. Before he'd seen the life, the light, the energy of everything around him. He'd drawn on the motion of the wind, the strength of the earth, the life-force blazing within his own breast. But now, in his mind's eye, he perceived a black echo of each of these threads. The rock beneath him was old and fissured. The wind held the telltale imbalances of the storm brewing over the mountains. Even the vital flame of his own spirit guttered with uncertainty and the frailty of his flesh.

Carefully he tried to avoid plucking the dark strings of energy, grasping only for the bright threads he'd used with impunity before. But as he seized the wind's sighing breath in his mind, he also gathered the anger of the coming storm. When he used the living energy of his mind to shape the spell, the darkness and doubt followed. Aeron struggled to disentangle them, but it was useless; light and shadow were intertwined, and the effort to part them was exhausting him. His heart thundered in his chest, and he gasped for breath, caught on the cusp of a spell that was indiscriminately drawing its power from his own body.

"Aeron! Finish it!" Fineghal shouted from a great distance. "You cannot power the spell without the Weave!"

In desperation, Aeron seized the dark with the light.

Shivering with fear at the power he touched, he wove the invisibility spell and vanished from view. Shaking with fright, he held his head in his hands, trying to understand what had happened.

"Aeron? Are you well?" Fineghal asked the night.

"I . . . I think so," he answered. "Did it work?"

"You wove the spell well. I cannot see you."

"This is not so pleasant an experience as weaving a spell from nothing but the Weave," he said carefully. "It's like . . . grasping a rose that cuts with its thorns."

"Did you feel the stone's influence?"

"In a sense, yes, but I suspect the Shadow Stone merely opened my eyes to something present all along. Maybe under the stone's influence a wizard is forced to accept only the dark forces of decay and corruption." Aeron felt his voice shaking. He was maintaining the spell, but it was not an unconscious effort.

"So you did not tap any power directly from the Shadow Stone," Fineghal observed. "You simply used magical energy, both dark and bright, that exists all around us. I never suspected I stood so close to the shadow."

Aeron ended the spell and took stock of himself. He seemed unhurt, although his hands ached with cold and his muscles were weak and watery. "So the stone is not the sole source of shadow magic. It serves as a magnet, a lens of some kind, blinding you to the living Weave of our world." He leaned back, staring up into the sky. "I can't imagine what I would have seen in the world around me if I'd been fully caught by the stone's curse. All the world would have been an open grave in my eyes."

"What will you do?" asked Fineghal.

"I think I will resume my studies," Aeron said. "But more carefully this time."

* * * * *

The summer passed, lazy and golden, as Aeron worked out the forms and rules of the magic he now wielded. Fineghal helped where he could, but the noble elf was blind to half of what Aeron wrought. Aeron had to devise a new method for recording his spells, a new symbology and logic for casting them, and he had to learn how to use his power all over again.

Two summers came and went. Aeron painstakingly defined the structure of his sorcery, the medium by which he could record and speak his spells, the techniques with which he could wield both the Weave and the shadow magic from the endless dusk. He moved carefully, setting aside his studies for weeks at a time to roam the forest with Fineghal or to visit with Kestrel and Eriale, spending days helping Kestrel with his woodcutting, trapping, and hunting.

In his third summer with Fineghal, war swept through Chessenta. Cimbar and Akanax spent months battling in the rugged lands along the Akanamere, while their allies and supporters fought to a standstill elsewhere. Soorenar stood neutral, still husbanding its strength for the future. But the tide of conflict never ran as far south as Oslin, and the Maerchwood was undisturbed. Aeron wondered if Oriseus or Dalrioc had anything to do with the strife, but there was no way he could find out without returning to Cimbar, and he was not ready for that. He doubted if he ever would be.

In the winter that followed the temporary waning of the war in the north, Aeron translated all the old spells he had once known by heart, rephrasing them so that they made sense to his symbology. He spent long, lonely weeks in the paneled libraries of the Storm Tower, transcribing his old notes. He'd been forced to abandon the glyphwoods; the old elven spell tokens could not encompass the magic he worked to master. Instead, he used written spellbooks after the style of the college, but he phrased the spells in his own cipher.

Within the year, he mastered all the spells he had formerly learned from Fineghal and even worked out transcriptions of several spells he'd been taught at the college. Fineghal studied his writings intensely but could not make the leap to Aeron's unique symbology. "Your cipher seems meaningless to me," he told Aeron on one occasion. "Yet the structure seems familiar."

"Elven magic accounts for the Weave, and so the glyphs and runes you've taught me work for recording part of my spells," Aeron explained. "But it does not account for the shadow magic, the powers of darkness and entropy that exist in the planes alongside our own."

"You've found an answer, I trust."

"That's what I've been trying to work out," Aeron said. "I've found that the notations and the logic behind magic as it's taught at the college are useful. The forms of human magic work, regardless of which powers are manipulated."

"That is why your work seems familiar," Fineghal said. "It is derived from human magic. But if human sorcery is capable of wielding power from beyond our world, how do human wizards resist the corrupting influence of shadow magic and similar forces?"

"Many do not," Aeron replied. "I believe a great portion of the magical lore that has become rite and rote for human wizards is shielding, protection against the darker influences that might otherwise swallow a mage. Sorcerers who are unwilling or unable to take these steps are devoured by their work. That is a road I don't want to walk."

"You seem to have survived so far."

"I don't think I'm the same person I used to be." Aeron closed his book and rose, pacing over to the window. "Everything is ambivalent now. I used to be able to tell the difference between strength and decay, between growth and sickness, but now I can't sense one without sensing the other. I can't find beauty anymore, Fineghal. There's always a flaw, a cancer in the rose."

The elf lord was silent for a long time. "I had no idea you'd have to pay such a price," he said quietly. He set his hand on Aeron's shoulder and left him to his work.

Late in the following spring, Aeron visited Saden for several weeks, helping Kestrel to clear some land and raise a sturdy new house to replace the simple cabin the forester had first built when he settled in the freehold. It cheered him to see how happy Kestrel and Eriale were, although it saddened him, too. He was reminded again of the loneliness of his chosen life. Aeron made up for it by throwing himself into the work, chasing the cobwebs and unsettled fears from his mind with hard physical labor.

On the last night of his stay, they all enjoyed a fine dinner in the newly finished cabin with a handful of their neighbors. After the cider and ale were passed around, Aeron went outside and sat on the porch, gazing out into the woods. The door creaked open behind him, and he glanced up as Eriale joined him. "You don't care for company?"

"I've become used to my own," he said with a smile. They

shared a long silence, gazing up at the clear stars that glittered above the rustling trees. "You've done well," he said after a time.

"I didn't know I needed your approval," Eriale laughed. "But thank you. I think so." She reached out and pinched his arm. "Do you have any thoughts of settling down?"

Aeron frowned. "I am settled down."

"All you ever do is study, locked up in that tower. What are you going to do when you finish your studies? What's the point of it all?"

"I can't finish, Eriale. That's the nature of magic, of being a mage." He thought for a moment, seeking the words to express what he'd come to recognize over the last few years under Fineghal's tutelage. "I'm not an apprentice, learning a craft to earn my keep for the rest of my days. Magic isn't what I do; it's what I am, and what I'll always be." He laughed quietly. "You might as well ask me what I'll do with myself once I learn how to be human."

"No one's meant to be alone, Aeron," Eriale said. "What did you do to deserve such a lonely existence?"

"Even if I lived in a house in the middle of Maerchlin, I'd still be on the outside," he replied. "People fear what they don't understand."

Eriale shook her head and looked away. "Do you ever wonder how things would have turned out if you hadn't met Phoros, Regos, and Miroch on the path that day? What you'd be doing now, what your life would be like?"

Aeron glanced at her. "It never occurred to me."

"Not once? With a mind as sharp as yours?"

He closed his eyes and tried to picture it. He'd have stayed in Maerchlin, working Kestrel's land on the outskirts of the village. Maybe he would have finally escaped Phoros Raedel's notice when the young nobleman inherited his father's seat. He thought of the girls he remembered from Maerchlin, but he couldn't imagine being married to any of them. "I don't think I was ever meant to be anything but a wizard," he said at last.

* * * * *

Fineghal and Baillegh were not at the Storm Tower when he returned, so Aeron returned to his studies. He was engaged in devising a new spell, and it quickly absorbed his full attention, so that he didn't notice for three more weeks that Fineghal had still not returned. This wasn't unusual; over the years he spent more and more time pursuing his own studies, while the elven wizard went his own way, but as each day passed, a vague unease settled over him.

Finally, a month after his visit with Kestrel and Eriale, Aeron set out to some of the places he knew Fineghal often lingered. At first he followed a methodical pattern, moving from place to place to cover the most ground, but within a day, he felt he was being guided to one particular spot. At sunset of the second day of his search, he found himself standing on the ancient hilltop of Forest's Stonemantle, the same place where he'd withstood Fineghal's test seven years before. Patiently he settled down to wait.

His intuition did not disappoint him. As the dusk deepened and the stars emerged, Fineghal appeared, leaping gracefully from stone to stone as he ran up the path in his effortless stride. Baillegh bounded behind him, dancing with delight. "Greetings, Aeron. I see you received my summons," he called.

Aeron scrambled to his feet just in time to meet Baillegh's playful rush. He scratched the hound's ears while she rubbed her head against him. "I didn't realize you wanted me," he said. "I'm afraid I delayed a day or two."

"No matter." Fineghal settled himself on a boulder, a smile flickering across his face. He almost seemed to shine with the starlight, radiant under the night sky. The night was warm, with a steady breeze out of the east that carried the sounds and scents of the woods up to the rocky heights. The elf lord's gaze settled on Aeron. "Tell me, Aeron, are you content in this existence?"

"Content?" Aeron blinked. "Magic challenges me in a way that I never could have imagined. It's a dark and silent path we walk, but I had no choice but to follow it."

"What would you have done differently?" Fineghal asked. "Would you have stayed in Maerchlin to face Count Raedel's justice for wounding his son? Would you have allowed Kestrel to die in Raedel's dungeons, or remained in Saden instead of going to the college?"

Aeron weighed Fineghal's words. "No," he said. "I don't think I would have made any of those decisions differently."

"Then what does it matter if you had any choices or not?

You would not have availed yourself of them. You would not be the man you are today if your life had followed a different road, so why waste time on regrets?"

With a rueful smile, Aeron shook his head and sat down by the edge of the precipice. "I guess that in a thousand years you learn to accept the decisions you made in the past. If you had to bear the weight of every mistake you'd made over such a long time, you'd be useless."

Fineghal laughed in the dusk. "If anyone ever asks you, Aeron, that's the secret to happiness. Forgive yourself and learn from your mistakes." He turned his head into the breeze, inhaling deeply. It occurred to Aeron that he'd never seen Fineghal so lighthearted. The elf's mantle of dignity was softened by a childlike delight in his surroundings, despite the gravity of their conversation. After a time, he returned his attention to Aeron. "You said that you wondered if you'd ever made any choices in your life. I have another decision to offer you."

A faint apprehension narrowed Aeron's eyes. "You called me here. What is it?"

"I have lived in this land for a thousand years. For the past three centuries, I have lived here mostly alone, the keeper of this land of golden glens and emerald groves. I have guarded its borders against dragon and man. But I weary of this burden, Aeron. The time has come to set it down."

Aeron was speechless. He started to protest but fell silent. Instead, he waited for Fineghal to continue.

The elf lord fixed his bright gaze on Aeron's face. "I want you to take up my watch, Aeron. You know this land nearly as well as I, and you have a wisdom far beyond your years. The Maerchwood needs a guardian."

"I don't know what to say," Aeron stammered. "What are you going to do?"

"I want to rejoin my kinfolk. To wander, free of care. To know that, should I be slain tomorrow, someone else stands over this land and guards it."

"Fineghal, I don't know how I can replace you." Aeron stood and paced away, dusting off his pants. "You taught me the elven magic when I first began my studies, but my sorcery is something different now. It's . . . darker, tainted by the forces you've fought against all your life."

"That is the human conflict, Aeron. To be Tel'Quessir is

to be immortal and unchanging, one with the land, one with yourself. Humans must struggle every day to lead the life we live of our own accord." Fineghal closed his eyes, picking his words. "I sometimes believe the elves cannot know virtue, since we do not have to fight for it. Perhaps this is why it is so easy for the elves to misjudge men.

"Aeron, the world has grown old since my youth. The Tel'Quessir are long gone from Calmaercor. The time has come for a human heart to love and guard it."

"Fineghal, I don't know what to say," Aeron replied.

"You need a purpose, Aeron. And the forest needs a guardian. Think on it." Fineghal watched him for a moment, and then retreated from the cliff top, leaving Aeron to consider the question in solitude.

Aeron stared out over the dark blanket of trees that lay spread out below, broken here and there by gleaming streams of water or the gray, shaggy stone hilltops. On the Forest's Stonemantle, he could feel the living forest all around him, from the bright stands of cedar facing east toward Unther to the low, mist-cloaked marshes in the southern reaches of the woodland. It was his anchor, the one place in which he had no pretensions, no delusions, no fears.

He thought for more than an hour, until he heard Fineghal returning to the hilltop. The elf trotted up and sat across from him, waiting for his answer.

"I'll do it," Aeron said. "When do we begin?"

Fineghal grinned. "Begin? Six years ago, when you came to me and begged me to show you how to work magic."

"Wait, that's not fair. What do I do? Where do I go? How do I protect the Maerchwood?"

"Do what you think is right," Fineghal replied. "Your heart will not lead you astray." He suddenly laughed in delight. "There is one more thing I must do." Fineghal spoke a string of liquid syllables, an elven tongue so ancient that Aeron could barely understand it, and passed his hand over his chest. As he extended his arm toward Aeron and unfurled his palm, a tiny dancing flame appeared, a jewel-like point of light that stole Aeron's breath. Fineghal pressed the flickering light to Aeron's shoulder. "May you hold this honor with courage, compassion, and wisdom."

Aeron shivered as an electric sensation ran through his body. He sat back, blinking at his chest, but there was no light to be seen. His skin tingled beneath his shirt, and he pushed his shirt aside to see what was there. A strange mark in the shape of a lightning stroke marked his right shoulder, just under his collarbone. "What is this, Fineghal?"

"It's the mark of the Storm Walker, Aeron. I've carried it for centuries. Now I pass it to you." The elf's features seemed youthful, illuminated by some light from within. The elf released him and rose, seeming to shimmer before him. "Turn your sight inward for a moment, Aeron. You'll understand what I have just given you."

Aeron looked down, his face taut with concentration as he tried to describe to himself the strange sensations that electrified him. He had to grasp the earth with both hands to keep from falling. He felt the land as if it were an extension of his own body. The weathered gray hills were his bones, the rich earth and magnificent groves his flesh, and the running waters his blood. All the countless animals and birds and fish that lived within the forest's borders burned like brilliant myriad points of light and life, bathing him in a boundless sea. He rose to his feet, feeling the faint stirrings of warmth and dawn in the east, sensing the rustling motion of the animals of the night seeking their lairs, the restless sleep of other creatures anticipating the new day.

A slight motion by his side disturbed him, and he opened his eyes as Fineghal stood. "One more thing, Aeron. I leave Baillegh in your care as well. You'll find that a hound can be a wizard's best friend." The silver wolfhound gazed up at Fineghal with her dark, intelligent eyes, and then trotted across the clearing to Aeron's side.

"You're not going right now!" Aeron exclaimed. "There's so much you have to teach me about this. And what about all your belongings in the Storm Tower?"

Fineghal tapped his chest. "Everything I need I have here. As for the gift, it's best that you learn for yourself." He drew a deep breath and clasped Aeron's hand. "It's a fine morning for a parting. Good-bye, Aeron. You will do well." He turned quickly and bounded down the path, vanishing into the woods.

Fourteen

For the rest of the summer, Aeron tried to convince himself that Fineghal was not really gone, that the elf had simply entrusted him with the guardianship of the wood for a short time. But his preternatural perception of the forest and its countless webs of living and elemental energy did not fade, and in fact grew stronger as the weeks passed. By closing his eyes and conjuring the image of a place he knew within the forest, Aeron could see what transpired there, hear the sounds, smell the air, taste the waters.

Fineghal's gift immersed him in a world that had existed beyond his senses, and for the first time, Aeron began to understand what had kept the elven mage at his watch for years beyond number. He understood that he saw the forest differently than Fineghal had; the undercurrents of shadow and horror existed here, too, and he could not open himself to the forest's life without seeing also its rot and decay. But the Maerchwood was a beautiful place, and the dark threads only served to remind Aeron of his responsibility to it.

As the first cool winds of autumn shifted and began to sigh out of the north, Aeron returned to the Storm Tower and found that only a few of Fineghal's personal effects were gone. The elf had left a great storehouse of lore and magic to Aeron, including a slender staff marked with the liquid writing of the elves. Around the lustrous wood was wound a small sliver of paper that read: *Aeron—I enchanted this staff long ago to serve the next Storm Walker. May you never have need of its powers.*

Aeron lifted the weapon. It hummed in his hands, seeming to recognize him. He glanced at the runes marked along its length; a dozen potent spells were woven into the staff, ready to respond to his demand. "I'll wield it well," he promised the empty tower. Then, setting it aside for the time, he continued his examination of the Caerhuan. He discovered that Fineghal had even set the tower's magical defenses to recognize Aeron as its master.

One morning, soon after Aeron and Baillegh had finished exploring the last recesses of the Caerhuan, Aeron woke from his sleep with a strong sense of something amiss. He couldn't put his finger on it, not at first, and worked through the morning, Baillegh drowsing at his feet, while his sense of unease grew stronger.

Finally Aeron was jarred from his work by Baillegh's nose battering his knee. He looked down and saw the silver hound gazing up at him expectantly. "So you feel it, too?" he asked.

The hound barked once in reply. "I know," Aeron replied. He shut the book in front of him, trotted down the circling stairs and out into the warm autumn afternoon. The trees were arrayed in a thousand shades of red and gold, and he grimaced at the thought that he'd wasted the day indoors. He turned in a slow circle, letting his mind scroll through the countless trails, clearings, and glens of the forest.

There! Along the forest's northern borders, Aeron sensed fear in the forest. He could taste the scent of iron-shod men, horses hobbled in a clearing, smoking meat over campfires. Fineghal had never felt it necessary to drive off all human incursions into the Maerchwood; hunters, trappers, even loggers were welcome so long as they reaped the forest's bounty with respect and moderation. Aeron was inclined to agree. But there were a number of humans in the Maerchwood this day, and whether they meant to or not, they were hunting a large region into desolation.

"What am I supposed to do?" he wondered aloud. Fineghal had said that he wouldn't go wrong to follow his heart, but Aeron didn't know exactly what that meant.

Baillegh barked from the tower's gate. She had carried Aeron's pack to the door and held it in her mouth, watching him. He shook his head. "You're right. I won't do anything standing here. Let's go."

They set off toward the north and east, following Aeron's uncanny intuition. By nightfall, they had covered more than thirty miles. Aeron and Baillegh both rested for a few hours in the darkest hours of the night. They could have pressed on, since neither needed much light to see by, but it seemed wise to make sure he didn't show up on the intruders' doorstep staggering with fatigue. Aeron ate a light breakfast of waybread and dried apples, and resumed his journey an hour before first light. Two hours after noon, Aeron slowed his pace to a walk and kept his eyes open for signs of the intrusion he'd sensed.

He found the camp within an hour. A dozen pavilions were spread out in a wide forest glade, with servants moving about, engaged in a variety of chores. On one side, a crude timber frame held the carcasses of dozens of deer, five or six bears, and hundreds of smaller creatures. A hunting party, Aeron realized. He halted in the shadows of the trees, considering his options. He begrudged no man the right to hunt in the forest, but the nobles of King Gereax claimed the Maerchwood as their own, from the northernmost edge of the forest all the way to the borderlands of Unther. From time to time, Raedel or one of his peers would invite his fellows to visit for a few weeks and hunt to their heart's content. It was the waste that angered Aeron; they'd eat only one out of ten animals they cut down. "What would Fineghal do now?" he asked Baillegh in a whisper.

The hound growled softly, showing her teeth.

"I know. They've been here too long. We need to make them shift their camp and reduce their take. Now, how can I do that?" Aeron thought for a time. As he thought about it, he realized that he wanted the people nearby to know that the forest was watched, that someone would hold them accountable for their actions. The myth of the Storm Walker needed reinforcement from time to time, and today was as good a day as any.

A little before sunset, the noble hunting party returned. Phoros Raedel led the way, beaming with pride, Regos following behind. Six or seven high lords whom Aeron did not recognize laughed and jested coarsely as they rode back into camp, guests of the Count of Maerchlin. Nearly two dozen drivers, trackers, and porters followed, burdened with the day's game. Aeron waited for more than an hour, judging his moment; when the nobles were deep into their cups, he wove the charm of invisibility around himself and crossed the camp, slipping unseen into their pavilion.

Phoros Raedel sat at the head of a stout table, a flagon of wine in his hand as he recounted the day's hunting to a pretty blonde-haired girl. Aeron quietly sealed the door to ensure that he would not be disturbed, leaving a single servant inside with the nobles and their ladies. He briefly considered using a minor glamour to change his appearance into something truly impressive, but decided against it. He hoped to reason with these people, and if they were frightened, they might react violently. *The Storm Walker deserves a name and a face,* Aeron thought. *And I've spent enough of my life running from Phoros Raedel.*

When he was ready, he allowed the spell of invisibility to fade and appeared at the foot of the table. "Good evening, my lords," he stated in a clear voice. "I am Aeron Morieth, the Storm Walker. I wish to have a word with you."

The nobles blinked in astonishment. They'd seen Aeron materialize out of nowhere. Others who hadn't been looking in his direction simply spluttered in outrage or scowled in annoyance at the intrusion. Phoros Raedel paled in astonishment, dropping his flagon from nerveless fingers. "I hanged you four years ago!" he gasped. "Guards! Guards!"

Aeron held up his hand. "They will not hear you," he said. "We will not be interrupted."

Regos was sitting with his back to Aeron. He rose suddenly, spinning as he reached for his sword. Three other noblemen near him followed suit. Aeron spoke a brief word and plucked at the bright threads within each man. Before Regos even cleared his seat, he collapsed back into the chair, dropping into a sorcerous sleep. The other swordsmen sank down and clattered to the floor, unconscious. Raedel's eyes flashed in anger. "You half-breed bastard!" he grated. "What have you done?"

"They only sleep," Aeron said. "Phoros, I have no desire to resume our feud by killing your guests."

"Raedel! Who is this man?" barked one of the other nobles, a short, stocky man wearing the emblem of a golden stag on his tunic. It took Aeron a moment to place the heraldry. The man was the lord of Villon, the southwestern county of Chessenta. Phoros Raedel was entertaining some high-ranking nobles indeed. Aeron glanced to Phoros to see how his old enemy would answer.

"This is Aeron Morieth, the last of a long line of rebels who have plagued this land for years," Phoros snarled. "I thought I'd seen the last of him on my gallows, but it seems he's used his sorcerer's tricks to cheat death."

"A sorcerer?" Villon flicked his gaze at Aeron and back to Raedel. "The spell he just spoke was nothing more than an apprentice's trick, one of the simplest of enchantments."

"That does not mean that I am not capable of more powerful spells, Lord Villon," Aeron said. "It simply means that I do not kill lightly."

"I see," said the nobleman. He straightened up and fixed his eyes on Aeron. A mocking smile settled over his face. "Well, you seem to have us in your power for the moment. Perhaps you should speak your piece."

"You have hunted in this place long enough," Aeron said. "Move your camp at least ten miles tomorrow, and reduce your take to no more than one bear, two boars, or five stags in a day. Your slaughter's done harm enough, and I will intervene if I must." He paused and then added, "You should see the sense in moderation. If you kill everything in the forest this season, what will you hunt next year?"

Phoros spluttered in rage. "By what right do you tell me how I may hunt in my own forest?"

"The Maerchwood belongs to no man, commoner or king," Aeron answered. "I am the Storm Walker. It is my task to preserve this forest against any who would do it harm—brigands, settlers, loggers, or hunters. You would raise your hand to defend the lives and the homes of the people of Maerchlin. I will do the same for the Maerchwood."

"Are you calling yourself the lord of the forest?" Raedel demanded. "King Aeron, whom we shall all fear and obey?"

Aeron took a half step forward, angered by the lord's mocking manner. Why did I even bother trying to reason with Raedel? he thought. He's still the same boorish robber lord he always was, nothing but a thug whose father seized these lands at the head of a war band. He started to consider the spells at his disposal, seeking an enchantment that might erase Raedel's confident swagger and, perhaps, finally teach the count to respect him.

Or to fear him.

While the nobles watched scornfully, waiting for his answer, Aeron frowned and lowered his staff. I won't make myself any better a man by proving to these wolves what I already know, he thought. I'll do what I have to do in order to make them understand my point, and no more. I don't care if he hates me, fears me, or thinks I'm Assuran descended from the higher planes. I only want him to stay his hand against the Maerchwood. Choosing his words carefully, Aeron forced himself to ignore Raedel's provocation and continued. "I require no man's fealty. I won't bar anyone from entering the wood or tell him what to do while he's here. But I will be watching, and when someone harms the Maerchwood, I will act."

"And what is your definition of harm?" asked Villon. "It hardly seems fair to hold us to your standard without telling us what it is."

"I ask you not take more game than you can eat. You may cut one acre in twenty within five miles of the forest's edge, and you can take dead or dying trees anywhere you find them. If someone wishes to settle more of the forest, don't clear more than one mile in ten of woodland."

"I refuse to listen to this rubbish!" Phoros said. He advanced on Aeron, drawing his blade. "You cheated me once, Morieth, but this time I'll make sure you are dead."

Aeron stared him in the eye, raising one hand. "Is this what you want, Raedel?"

Phoros halted in midstride, caution momentarily gaining the upper hand over anger. He'd seen what Aeron was capable of and remembered the last time Aeron had put a spell on him. "Strike me down with your sorcery and you won't live a week," he said.

"Then agree to abide by my conditions. Honor my requests within the bounds of the Maerchwood. In turn, I will render you the honor that you deserve as the lord of Maerchlin when I pass through your lands."

"Don't even set foot outside your forest," Raedel growled. "In my land, you're marked for death."

Aeron shrugged. "So be it."

The count of Villon stood slowly. "What if we refuse to heed your warning? I've only seen you work two minor magics. Why should I fear your wrath?" He gestured oddly with his hand, and Aeron suddenly felt the ripple in the Weave as the count wove a spell. From his fingertips, a brilliant arc of light snapped forward, striking Aeron full in the chest with a thunderous crack! "I, too, know something of the wizard's art," Villon gloated.

Aeron staggered back two steps in blank surprise before he managed to blink the glare from his eyes. Unconsciously, he clasped his chest, and he slowly smiled as he realized he was unhurt. In his hand, Fineghal's staff hummed brightly with the power of the trapped lightning; Aeron silently thanked the elven mage for the day he'd enchanted the staff. Count Villon's face fell open in shock as he realized his spell had failed.

Aeron regained his composure first. "It's not for nothing that I call myself the Storm Walker," he said. He gestured and worked a powerful spell, one of the most formidable he knew, that immobilized Raedel, Villon, and the other remaining noblemen. Clasped in an invisible grip of iron, they watched him with terror in their eyes. "I will return tomorrow. I expect your camp to be gone. I have the means to compel you if you do not care to listen to reason. Now I bid you good night. You should regain the ability to move in an hour or two."

Mustering all the dignity he could, Aeron turned his back on Raedel and strode to the door. Over his shoulder, he added, "Remember, I had you all in my power and chose not to harm any of you. Don't make me regret that decision." With that, he sketched a shallow bow and left.

* * * * *

The following day Aeron took the shape of a small falcon and soared over the campsite, expecting the noblemen to resist his directions. To his surprise, the camp was gone. He easily found their trail and followed it north. They'd left the forest by the most direct route possible. He arrowed out over the terraced hills and green fields of Maerchlin, reveling in the rush of the wind past his face and the intoxicating freedom of flight, and even circled the gray towers of Castle Raedel three times before heading back to the forest. None of Phoros's guests remained.

Aeron returned to the small campsite he'd made for himself, resumed his own shape, and greeted Baillegh with a good scratch behind the ears. "I suppose Lord Raedel's guests didn't care for my hospitality," he said. He exulted in the first successful defense of his domain.

Baillegh turned a heavy, measuring gaze on him, as if the hound were asking if he'd really done the right thing. "Of course I did," Aeron answered. "I protected the forest without harming even a single soul." But a small, dark seed of doubt grew in his heart. But for the lightning ward Fineghal had placed in the staff, Aeron would have been killed by Villon's spell, and if the count had happened to strike with other deadly spells, Aeron would have been defeated in his first confrontation. And he'd enjoyed the sensation of bending others to his will with the strength of his magic, and that disturbed him greatly.

I used my power to defend the Maerchwood, a noble purpose, so my shielding against the corruption of shadow magic held that time. But what happens if I lash out in anger or work a spell for a less altruistic purpose? he wondered. The taint of the shadow in his magic might have already twisted his judgment, giving him pleasure in the fear of others. "Perhaps I shouldn't be so quick to compel their cooperation," he said after a time.

Baillegh barked once in affirmation. Aeron looked up, frowning. "Did Fineghal leave you in my care, or the other way around?" he asked. The hound poked her nose into his stomach and bounded away down the path, yipping impatiently. Aeron sighed and followed.

Autumn passed, then winter, ending the Year of the Shield and marking the arrival of the Year of the Banner. From time to time, Aeron detected intrusions against the Maerchwood, and he responded to the forest's call. Several times he had to rein in timber seekers or miners who were pushing too far into the wooded hills. Some were amenable to his suggestions and curtailed their efforts voluntarily; others refused to heed him, and he compelled them to listen to his words. On other occasions, Aeron found bands of brigands or raiders lairing in the recesses of the woods, preying on the honest folk who lived along the forest's verge. Fineghal had never moved against these vermin, preferring to leave human affairs to human law, but Aeron saw no reason to allow the Maerchwood to serve as their refuge. He drove them out when he encountered them, or quietly helped the constables or rangers of the neighboring towns to locate the bandits' dens.

As the seasons passed, Aeron maintained his watch on Maerchlin, taking the form of a falcon by day, or an owl by night, and flying over the castle. Aeron had no intention of interfering with Phoros Raedel's rule of Maerchlin, but it seemed wise to make sure he'd know beforehand if the count ever meant to raise his hand against him. Perching on the battlements, he noted who entered and who departed, and sometimes he even listened in on a conversation by clinging to a window ledge.

One overcast summer day, almost a year since his last

encounter with Phoros, Aeron approached the castle and sensed something wrong. He circled it carefully, searching for the source of his unease, but everything appeared normal. He drifted in toward the courtyard and suddenly felt an invisible hand shoving him aside, forcing him to flare his wings and wheel awkwardly to one side. What in Faerûn was that? he thought.

He circled outward, gliding past the castle. He concentrated on the emanations of the Weave that surrounded the castle and discovered a subtle weave of light and dark doming the entire fortress. At each cardinal point, an intricate rune had been drawn on the battlements, scrawled in rough circles of red paint the size of a small shield. Wards against magic, he realized. But who made them? Since Aeron kept his falcon shape by means of a spell, the wards were sufficient to bar his physical passage. If he released the spell, he could walk right past them . . . but he'd lose his disguise in the process. He orbited the gray tower, thinking.

As he wheeled over the keep itself, he spied a dark figure standing in an open window. It was a thin man, his features obscured by a loose cowl over his head. Aeron slipped a little closer, drawn to the man by an intangible mantle of power that streamed around him. This was the maker of the runes, an adept of no small skill. Aeron peered at him with first one eye and then the other, trying to discern the robed man's features.

Without warning, the dark hood swung his way. He caught a glimpse of a dark, bone-thin face with long teeth bared in a snarl of challenge. At the same time, an electric jolt arrested his heart, seizing him in a fierce contest of will. Aeron reeled and fluttered, trying to break free, the wind howling in his ears as the ground and sky tumbled crazily. He sensed the man below him knotting his fists in the stuff of the castle, gathering magical strength for a fearsome onslaught.

Screeching shrilly, Aeron broke free of the sorcerer's will and arrowed away, regaining his strength and determination as he widened the distance between them. But he could still feel the hateful eyes of the wizard on his back, waiting for him to resume his presumptuous reconnaissance of the castle. Aeron declined the fight, although he didn't feel that the encounter was done until long after the gray towers of Castle Raedel had slipped beneath the horizon behind him.

When he returned to the Storm Tower, Aeron resumed his own shape, stretching his arms and legs. He turned to let himself into the tower's door, but suddenly an odd wind shifted and blew at his back, clutching his cloak. Aeron tensed and whirled, scenting sorcery in the air, a manifestation of the shadow weave that deadened the breeze with a cold, clammy odor. He searched the dark forests nearby for any sign of a foe, but nothing appeared until a small yellow slip of paper blew into sight, scuttling across the ground until it came to a rest right at his feet. With that, the eerie breeze failed.

Aeron stooped down and carefully looked over the paper without touching it. Many deadly spells could be triggered by the simple act of reading the cursed signs. After a moment, he decided that he sensed no magic on the parchment, so he cautiously picked it up and broke the seal. It was a letter, written in a thin and spidery hand:

To my esteemed colleague, the Storm Walker:

Greetings. I have been retained by Lord Phoros Raedel, Count of Maerchlin, to advise him on matters magical and to defend him against the assault or scrutiny of any hostile sorcerers. I should greatly like to meet with you in person and discuss affairs of mutual interest. In the meantime, I must ask you to desist in your surveillance over my lord's lands. He feels that they are adequately looked after.

Your humble servant,
Edias Crow

Aeron shuddered. The parchment felt cold and somehow sinister, as if it had been written with ink made of blood. He destroyed it with a simple cantrip of fire and let the breeze carry the ashes from his fingers. " 'Affairs of mutual interest'?" he muttered, thinking. What was that supposed to mean? This Master Crow had already secured Castle Raedel quite thoroughly against his intrusions. Well, I can't be surprised if I've taught Phoros Raedel to fear wizards, he thought. Of course he'd take steps to defend himself against me.

Absently he let himself into the tower, still considering the day's events. He'd only held his watch over the forest for a little more than a year, but already he sensed that he was falling into the same routine, the same patterns, that had held Fineghal for a thousand years. He was a sentry on a long watch, unconsciously choosing a predictable path. Now something had happened that finally broke the routine, demanding his attention, and he didn't know what to make of it. He started a small fire and settled down in an old wooden chair, listening to the distant roar of the Winding River's rock-strewn rapids and the wind rattling the windowpanes.

Aeron didn't like the feel of Crow's sorcery. Like his own, it was woven of both bright and dark strands, but it seemed out of balance, misproportioned. He wondered if this were normal for a human sorcerer, or if Master Crow had been tainted in some manner similar to Aeron's own battle against the Shadow Stone. "Fineghal, I could use your counsel now," Aeron muttered. The empty tower did not respond.

* * * * *

Aeron weighed Master Crow's request for over a week before responding with a message of his own, naming a time and a place for a meeting more than sixty miles east of Maerchlin. Aeron didn't think Phoros Raedel could lay an ambush capable of snaring him so far from his own lands, and it gave him a chance to prepare the site.

The weather had become still and sweltering in the hot doldrums that fell over the Maerchwood late in the summer. It had never bothered Aeron before, but as he labored to scribe runes and circles around the barren clearing he'd chosen, he became light-headed and queasy, as if a faint odor of death had risen with the heat. The magic he wove felt muddy, indistinct, the Weave of the air, the earth, the living forest slipping through his fingers as if he were a clumsy apprentice all over again. At the same time, the shadow magic that he summoned and shaped seemed almost eager to meet his command, coiling and surging like a restless serpent that tested the bonds of his will.

Through sheer determination, Aeron finally finished the tasks he'd set for himself and he settled down to wait. The heat of the day faded rapidly as dusk fell over the stony hilltop, and Aeron found himself shivering with cold within an hour of sunset. Something isn't right here, he thought. He stood and circled the hilltop, testing the wind with all of his senses, but as far as he could tell, the hill was just another part of the forest. "I'm jumping at phantoms," he muttered aloud, trying to reassure himself.

He waited several more hours. He'd invited Master Crow to meet him on this night, deciding that it would be difficult for any of Raedel's men to approach under the cover of darkness without revealing themselves, but Aeron began to doubt the wisdom of this request. The gibbous moon rose, casting an unhealthy yellow glow over the forest. In the shadows beneath the trees, faint fox fire flickered, dancing in the corner of Aeron's vision but vanishing when he looked right at it. The air was cool and clammy, without a breath of wind; the forest was unnaturally still. Aeron found himself straining to hear the faintest of sounds.

A black-winged shape flitted in front of the pale moon. It dropped toward him, gliding silently on leathery wings. Aeron picked up the staff Fineghal had left him and waited, watching. Just outside his circle of defenses the thing settled to the ground, croaking. It seemed to shimmer for a moment, and Aeron sensed the unbinding of magic. From the pool of darkness a tall man rose, stretching and settling his robes into place. He grinned widely at Aeron. "Greetings, brother. May I enter your circle?"

Aeron nodded once. "I see you know the spell of shape-taking too, Master Crow."

"You seemed fond of it. It was . . . appropriate." Now that they stood facing each other, Aeron realized that Master Crow was tall but startlingly thin, an emaciated rail of a man shrouded in a tattered black robe. All he could see of the wizard were his bony hands, twisting together in front of his chest, and the gleaming teeth in his open-mouthed grin. The sorcerer bowed and spread his hands, advancing into the rune-marked circle Aeron had laid out during the day. He glanced at the diagram and shook his head. "You needn't have bothered."

"Why take chances?" Aeron replied.

"Why, indeed?" The man seemed to lean forward and rasped heavily. It took Aeron a moment to realize that he was laughing. "Why indeed? It surprises me to see that you have become a man of caution, Aeron."

Aeron peered at the dark hood. "We have met before?"

"Oh, yes, though it's been five years or more. Don't you remember me, Aeron?" The gaunt sorcerer straightened and raised his hands, drawing back his hood. Aeron recoiled involuntarily, suddenly terrified of what he might see. The sorcerer looked up again to meet Aeron's eyes. His face was lean and sharp, and his hair was slashed back to a brutal stubble, but his eyes danced with animation.

"Master Sarim!" Aeron was astonished at the transformation of the Calishite mage. When he'd known Sarim at the college, the Master Invoker had been a wide-shouldered, athletic man with a handsome face and a calm, collected manner. Now Sarim's clean frame, his serenity, and his alert intelligence were all gone, replaced by endless nervous motion and a fanatic's brilliant imbalance. The sight of Sarim shrieking as the Shadow Stone devoured him in the cold stone vault under the ruined obelisk flashed before Aeron's eyes.

"I am flattered that you remember me, Aeron. We parted under trying circumstances, you and I." The sorcerer laughed again at his little jest. "I had thought that you might have chosen to forget about the college. After all, you are the great Storm Walker now. Why mire yourself in the difficulties of the past?"

"That was a long time ago," Aeron said flatly. "You requested this meeting. What business do you have with me?"

"It is not too late for you to stand with us, Aeron. We have not forgotten you. So much has happened, and yet you hide here in the Maerchwood, your head in the sand. A mage of your potential is wasted in this backwater." Sarim reached out and pawed at Aeron's sleeve. "Come back to the college. Finish the studies that you started."

Aeron pulled his arm back. "I saw enough of that road. It doesn't seem to have done you much good, Sarim. Or should I call you Crow?"

For a moment the tall sorcerer's grin faded, and his eyes sparked with cold fire. But slowly he forced the smile back to his face, and bobbed his head. "They know me as Master Crow here. That will suffice. A new name for a new man, you might say."

"What are you doing here?"

"An interrogation! Excellent, Aeron. You're not the peasant you used to be, to challenge me with such a tone." The

Master turned his back on Aeron, pacing away to measure the bounds of the circle, making a show of gazing out over the forest. Aeron waited, keeping his eyes on him. With a sigh, the sorcerer continued. "Well, someone had to answer Phoros Raedel's most generous offer of employment. Lord Oriseus thought that the post would suit me. After all, the count is in need of some supervision, wouldn't you say? If we keep young Phoros on the path, well, then, Oslin's southern lands are as good as ours."

Aeron didn't like the sound of that. "Whose?"

"Ours, Aeron. Yours and mine. We are to be Lord Oriseus's satraps over this land. He has become the Sceptanar, you know, lord over Cimbar and soon all of Chessenta. The new Emperor will need viceroys, loyal men of great ability to oversee his lands and ensure a proper order to things." Master Crow suddenly wheeled on Aeron and marched up to clutch at Aeron's tunic. "We'll let the petty lordlings, the Phoros Raedels, play at their games, Aeron. But you and I both know what the real power in this world is. With a word, we slay. With a gesture, we rule. None will dare to gainsay us, and Chessenta will be united under our command."

Aeron maintained a stony and suspicious expression, but his heart fluttered. Oriseus as Sceptanar! The Master Conjuror's ambitions had extended as far as Aeron had thought, and then some. It made sense; what wizard of Cimbar would have dared to stand against him? Aeron thought of the rumors he'd heard in the last year or so, war and fire in the great cities of the north, and wondered how much Oriseus had had to do with these dire events. He frowned and returned his attention to Master Crow. "Oriseus sent you to find me for this?"

"That, and to see to Raedel."

Aeron studied the sorcerer for a long moment. He could sense the dark taint of the Shadow Stone in Crow's heart, a black font of corruption where the bright spark of his life should have been. "I want no part of it," he said firmly.

Crow recoiled a pace, anger twisting his features. "You'll just mind the borders of your forest, then? That is all the ambition you hold in your heart, Aeron? I cannot believe that."

"Believe what you will. I want nothing to do with you, or Oriseus, or Dalrioc, or any of them. Don't set foot in this forest again, Master Crow. There is nothing for you here."

"If we did not stand inside your circles of protection, Aeron, I might teach you not to threaten me so lightly," Crow hissed. "You forget that I had the strength to tame the power that you were afraid to attempt."

Aeron spread his hands in invitation. "I'm willing to match my strength against yours. And I will, if you don't leave this place."

Crow wheeled and stormed away, black cloak fluttering like the threadbare wings of some great, dark moth. Outside the protective runes, he stopped and turned to face Aeron again. "Oriseus said you would not cooperate. But I know something you don't, O mighty Storm Walker. You'll be forced to serve us sooner or later. Oriseus means to set wizards to rule over the blundering brutes who are the lords of this land. And the Shadow Stone will set Oriseus to rule over the wizards. You defy us at your peril. With every spell you cast, you'll only make us stronger."

Aeron stepped forward, raising his staff to strike, but Crow whirled in place and vanished in a dark pyre of smoke. Aeron waited a long moment to see if he'd really gone and then sat down heavily on a rock, laying his staff across his knees. "Sarim," he said bleakly into the night. "What has Oriseus done to you?"

Fifteen

Aeron returned to Caerhuan and prepared for a magical siege. He attempted several powerful defensive spells, but each enchantment he worked seemed to go awry; the Weave seemed to slip through his fingers, while the burgeoning strength of the shadow-magic, the power of death and darkness, refused to obey his command, writhing in his grasp like a venomous serpent seeking something to poison. It took all of Aeron's effort to keep the seething magic under his control and form it into the shapes he desired.

Finally, he was satisfied with his defenses, although a task that should have taken days had consumed several weeks. Despite the fact that the Maerchwood had been vulnerable during the time it took Aeron to weave the spell of watchfulness, Master Crow had not struck at Aeron, nor had any more of his former associates from the college appeared on his doorstep. Their absence only served to reinforce Aeron's fears.

The summer failed quickly, giving way to an unusually cold and damp autumn. Day after day, the forest was cloaked in dense, still mists that left the ground-carpet black and soggy, damp with a sweet, sick odor of rot. Aeron shivered in revulsion as he went abroad; the air beaded his cloak and tunic with heavy drops of cold water, and any time he brushed past a leaf or tree it left a dark, foul smear across his skin or clothes. The animals of the forest cowered in their lairs, reluctant to go abroad in the unnatural mists.

Aeron searched for some sign that the Maerchwood was under attack, but he found nothing to indicate that the weather was anything other than natural. No spell held the gloom over the forest. Every time Aeron wielded magic, he was conscious of the growing difficulty of commanding even a glimmer of the Weave. Nothing could relieve the bleak and dismal gloom.

He set out to survey the forest, hoping to find some indication of a place where the foulness originated, but from one eave of the forest to the other, everything was the same. A month into autumn, he found himself near the western edge of the forest, and with hopeless resignation he turned his steps toward Saden and home.

Kestrel greeted him warmly, but his eyes showed fatigue. "Aeron! It's been months, lad. Where have you been?"

"I've been walking the forest, Kestrel," Aeron replied. He undid his cloak and hung it by the fire, grimacing as oily water ran over his hands. "Have you any ale?"

"Of course," Kestrel said. "But you'll want last winter's brew. The stuff they made this year isn't fit for a goblin." The old forester ventured back to the tap he kept in his cellar and returned with two leather jacks. He drew up a chair by the fire and handed one to Aeron. "So what is new in the Maerchwood?"

"I wish I knew," Aeron said with a scowl. "Phoros Raedel's retained the services of a dangerous sorcerer. I believe he's responsible for some insidious blight over the forest, but I can't fathom the magic that's at work." He described the evil change in the wind that had fallen over the forest in the weeks since he'd met Sarim in his incarnation as Master Crow. Would he have fallen if I hadn't set him against Oriseus? he wondered briefly. He sighed and stared into the dark ale in his mug.

Kestrel frowned. "I've heard tales of Raedel's mage, too, but I don't think he is responsible for this weather. It's not just the Maerchwood, Aeron. It's everywhere. You don't talk to many people, but travelers pass through Saden every now and then—herdsmen from the Akanul, teamsters carrying cargo to Mordulkin, and boatmen on the Adder River. They say it's like this all across Chessenta, maybe even all of Faerûn. People are frightened."

Aeron was stunned. "I have a hard time believing that Master Crow could work such a dire enchantment."

"From what I hear, Phoros's pet mage has been too busy to work this sort of mischief, anyway," Kestrel said.

"Why? What's happened?"

"They say that Phoros Raedel's not the master of his own castle anymore. Crow is the real lord of Maerchlin these days. I've spoken to merchants who have arranged audiences with Phoros, only to find that Master Crow did all the talking. They said the count stared into space, nodding whenever Crow asked him a question." Kestrel scratched his chin. "Phoros Raedel might be a bastard at times, but at least he's a bastard you can count on."

"Crow told me that he came to Maerchlin to take power here," Aeron said. "He said that Oriseus—the leader of the college—meant for his followers to hold high places in every land." The young mage paused, thinking hard. If Crow was telling the truth, Oriseus was not just the master of the college anymore—he was the lord of all Cimbar. "Kestrel, have you heard anything of the Sceptanar?"

"The king of Cimbar?" Kestrel shrugged. "They say there's a new one, although it's hard to be sure of a story from so far away. Cimbar's broken its old truce with Akanax, and Soorenar has sided with Cimbar. Most travelers are of the opinion that it's only a matter of time until Akanax falls, and that will leave Cimbar as the only power of consequence left." The woodsman swallowed some musty ale. "I can't see the other cities standing by while the Sceptanar crowns himself Overking of Chessenta, but who's going to stop him?"

"It seems I don't hear anything in the Maerchwood."

Kestrel chuckled. "It's just gossip, Aeron."

"Have you heard any other tales from abroad?"

"Oh, the usual tales of blights and plagues, vanishings and hauntings. They say there's an evil loose in the land, a sickness in the ground. It's been a bad harvest, with all the rain lately." The forester smiled and shook his head, his gray whiskers twitching like an otter's. "People love to tell a tale of woe. There's no substance to rumors of sorcery and witch-weather."

"I'm not so sure." Aeron shivered by the fire. "Something is wrong in the Maerchwood; that much I know." He sat back, thinking. "Kestrel, I have to go. This is much worse than I thought it was."

"That's not very reassuring. What can you do?"

"I don't know," said Aeron. "But I might know someone who does know. Give Eriale my greetings. And, Kestrel . . . if things become any worse, get Eriale and come to the Maerchwood. I've been able to counter some of this illness, and you're welcome to stay at the Storm Tower as long as you like."

"The old ruins by the gorge of the Winding River?"

Aeron smiled. "It's not as ruined as you might think. You might be safer there than you are here."

Kestrel studied Aeron for a long moment. "It's that bad?"

Aeron simply stood and took his hand. "I'll let you know if I find any answers." He drained the last of the ale, shouldered his cloak, and set out into the weak daylight again. It was surprisingly cold and clammy. Aeron wondered if a frost was near, weeks or even months before the season turned. He didn't like the idea of the land suffering through a long winter under these conditions.

On his way back to the Storm Tower, Aeron actually became lost for a few hours as the trail he followed petered out in a muddy morass of thickets, briars, and fens. He could not remember any such place in the bounds of the Maerchwood. When he finally picked up his path again he redoubled his speed, Baillegh bounding behind him like a silver streak in the gloom.

It was late in the night when he reached the tower. He rested, ate a light meal, then set to work rummaging through Fineghal's storehouse of arcane lore and enchanted devices until he found a small orb of crystal. Aeron carried the orb to a small table before one of the tower's high windows and sat down, staring into the milky glass.

In his mind's eye, he formed a picture of Fineghal's face and called out with his will. "Fineghal! Where are you?"

To his surprise, the response was immediate. The orb swirled and cleared, and he gazed upon a forest-city of slender trees and leaping pathways high over the ground. Fineghal stood in the foreground on a wide flet of gleaming wood, glancing up into the sky. "I see you have found my seeing-glass, Aeron," he replied.

"Where are you?" Aeron asked, peering at the scene.

Fineghal gestured at his surroundings. Although Aeron heard his words plainly in his mind, the orb conveyed no sound; Fineghal spoke silently. "I have kinfolk who tarry still in the great forest of the Chondalwood," he replied. "I've passed the last few seasons among them. Tell me, do you know what is going wrong with the magic?"

"You have sensed it too?" Aeron asked.

"For the last month or so, my spells have failed for no reason I can determine. And there are other wizards here who have encountered the same result. There seems to be less magic in the world, as if the Weave is dying away." The elf lord's fear and concern were evident, even through the magical link of the crystal ball. "Never in my days have I seen something like this."

"I think I know what is happening," Aeron said. "Magic is not fading. It is . . . changing its character. While the Weave you know is weakening, the shadow-magic is growing stronger."

Fineghal grimaced. "I can't perceive it. I only see the weakening of the magic that I command."

"Have you noticed anything else unusual? Strange weather, a failure of the harvest, rumors of hauntings?"

"We've heard many tales of such things from the lands to the north and east of the Chondalwood. In the past few weeks, the tide of sickness has reached us here. The failure of magic is tied to these occurrences?"

"I believe that everything—the strange weather, the failure of crops, the plagues and the wars—is tied to this. The Weave permeates everything that exists, after all. If it becomes darker, more sinister, the world will grow dark as well."

The elf seemed to turn away for a moment, as if he were speaking to someone else whom Aeron could not see. "Your explanation makes sense, Aeron. It would account for the events we've witnessed here."

"The longer we allow this to continue, the worse it will get," Aeron said. He described his meeting with Master Crow and related the rumors he'd heard of war in Cimbar.

"Could this have something to do with the Shadow Stone, Aeron? You once told me that you thought that it acted as a conduit that enabled a mage to bypass the Weave. Master Crow's appearance on your doorstep can't be entirely coincidental."

"I think you're right," Aeron said. "But that still doesn't give me any idea of how to counter the effects."

Fineghal seemed to waver in indecision. "I'll set out at once for the Storm Tower," he finally said.

Aeron smiled, his spirits climbing. "There's room for two Storm Walkers in this forest, Fineghal. I can really use your help. When will you be here?"

The elf laughed bitterly. "Before this started, I knew three or four spells that would have whisked me to your side in the blink of an eye. But I cannot wield enough of the Weave to power any of them now. I'll have to travel by more mundane means. Six or seven days, at a minimum."

"I'll be waiting for you. Go with care—I don't like the look of this at all."

"Nor do I," Fineghal said. He raised his hand, and the contact faded, leaving the orb empty and colorless again.

* * * * *

Two more watchful days passed, as Aeron used every divination at his command to study the situation with little success. On the third day, he was roused from his futile efforts by the subtle warning of one of his warding spells. Someone was approaching the Storm Tower. He rose and moved over to one of the windows, peering out into the gloom. On the path leading from the wood, three figures blundered through the mist. He quickly recognized Kestrel and Eriale, both carrying light packs, but the third person wore a large hood. Aeron scrutinized the last one for a long moment, then gave up and trotted downstairs to let them in to the tower.

"Kestrel, Eriale! What happened? Why are you here so soon?" Aeron ushered them into the tower's entry hall.

Kestrel stepped inside, his face blank. "We had to talk to you, Aeron." He glanced back at the third member of their party—a large, broad-shouldered man—and waved him forward. "I've brought Phoros Raedel to see you."

Aeron started in surprise as the nobleman took off his dripping hood and fixed an angry glare on him. After a long moment, Aeron managed to say, "I never thought I'd find you on my doorstep."

"I would have avoided this if there were any other alternative, Morieth." Phoros shifted uncomfortably, his face set in an uncompromising scowl.

"Alternative to what?" Aeron demanded.

Eriale stepped forward and laid her hand on Aeron's arm. "Aeron, listen. He's come to ask your help."

The mage snorted in anger. "You're joking."

"It's true, Aeron," said Kestrel. "Hear him out."

Raedel glowered until his face shone red. He said, "That black-hearted scoundrel Crow has turned me out of my own castle. I want your help in getting rid of him."

Aeron folded his arms and turned a flat stare on the nobleman. "You sought his services to put me in my place. If you don't want Master Crow under your roof anymore, get rid of him yourself."

Raedel bridled. "I knew this was a bad idea," he rasped.

He spun on his heel and strode toward the door, fuming.

Eriale glared at Aeron. "You're better than that, Aeron," she snapped. She started after Raedel and caught him as he opened the door. "Wait, my lord. You need his help."

"I'll be damned if I'm going to beg for it!" the count roared, wheeling on her. "If he can't be bothered with driving a black-hearted necromancer out of the town he grew up in, then so be it! I'll find a way to do it myself."

Kestrel stepped in front of Aeron and pointed out the open door. "Aeron, this is foul sorcery. The land suffers under a curse of some kind. You're the only person we know with knowledge of these things. You might not care a whit about Phoros Raedel's troubles, but the count's woes are the woes of all Maerchlin. The villagers and forest-folk don't deserve this." He fixed his keen eyes on Aeron's face, refusing to allow the mage to look away. Eriale and Phoros paused by the door.

Aeron glanced at Phoros and back to Kestrel. He sighed and waved his hand to indicate the midday gloom and the filthy, clinging damp. "This isn't Crow's doing. They're both symptoms of the same disease. I don't have any idea of how to break the spell that's poisoning the land."

Phoros weighed Aeron for a long moment. "You say that Crow's just a part of this. Fine. But if you don't have any other place to start, it can't hurt to treat a symptom. He's using sorcery to eat the minds of my people, Morieth. My people, the people who look to me to defend them! I've never sought to rule by holding a man's will in my fingers. If you let Crow stay in Maerchlin, he's going to turn this entire province into a charnel house."

Aeron grimaced. "All right. Master Crow is the least of our worries, but there's no sense in allowing him a free hand to ruin Maerchlin. We'll see what we can do." And it might be that I can get some answers from him, he thought to himself. He looked at Kestrel and Eriale. "Do you want to rest here tonight and set out tomorrow morning?"

Phoros shook his head. "I don't want to give him any more time to consolidate his position."

Kestrel nodded in agreement. "We've still got a few hours of daylight. Let's make use of them."

Aeron acquiesced. He took his cloak and satchel from the pegs by the door, and summoned his gleaming staff to his hand from its place in the library. "Baillegh!" he called. The silver hound appeared in the door, tail wagging. Aeron shrugged. "I'm ready," he said.

They set out through the mist-shrouded forest. Aeron guided them along a series of hidden tracks that he used whenever he was in a hurry; the paths were enchanted with an old elf spell, ancient when Chessenta was young, arrowing straight through the Maerchwood but ghosting through another realm, winding and twisting in and out of a world of silver mists and dark, silent trees. They camped a few miles south of Maerchlin, enduring a cold meal and the damp chill of the night without the comfort of a fire— no suitable wood could be found. As they ate, Raedel bitterly described how Crow had worked his wiles against the knights and officers of his court, slowly turning them against their rightful lord until every command Raedel issued was referred to Crow before it was carried out.

"Did you try to make him leave?" Aeron asked.

Phoros nodded with a savage jerk of his head. "The bastard laughed at me. He laughed! I went after him, of course. I had my hands around his scrawny neck before he could even mutter the first word of a spell. But my own guardsmen pulled me away from him and locked me in my chambers."

Aeron watched the count for a long moment. He had little liking for Phoros Raedel, but he still felt a fleeting sympathy for the noble. For a man born and bred to lordship, it must have been humiliating in the extreme. He chewed his lip, thinking. "To break Crow's influence over your captains and officers, we'll have to force him to release his spell. Or slay him."

Phoros grinned ruthlessly. "I don't think I'll bother to ask him if he wants to cooperate."

* * * * *

The next morning, they rose early and returned to the trail. The clinging mists lifted somewhat, revealing a motionless gray overcast that brooded with the threat of rain, and the temperature plummeted. At first Aeron thought that the change in the weather might be a sign of improvement, but as the day grew colder and grayer each hour, he realized that they were seeing nothing more than a change in the face of the ubiquitous gloom that had fallen over the land. The seasons were out of order, and he could only perceive the dimmest threads of the Weave flickering dully in the sodden landscape.

"Where is everyone?" Eriale asked, studying the village and the outlying farms. "At this time of day, there should be people out and about."

Phoros Raedel spat and knelt down to seize a handful of water-logged earth. Fat white worms squirmed through his fingers as he straightened up and showed it to the girl. "What's the point in reaping these fields?" he snarled in disgust. "It's all like this. Come on."

"How are we going to do this?" asked Aeron. "If we're careful, we can get right up to the castle without being seen, but how are we going to get in? The postern gate?"

"Don't you have some magic to whisk us into my hall from right here?" Raedel asked over his shoulder.

"I'd rather save my magic until I'm certain we need it," Aeron replied. "The last time I was here, Crow had a warding set around the castle to counter spells of that sort."

Raedel snorted. "Wonderful. Well, I've got another idea."

Aeron nodded, understanding. "You must have had a secret way out. You said Crow had had you locked in your chambers, but you never told us how you got away."

The count scowled at Aeron. After a long moment he said, "The tunnel emerges in the underbrush by the mill pond. He'll know that's how I got out, though." Raedel led them through the back streets of the town, staying out of sight of the castle's gate, until they'd circled around to the pond a hundred yards or so behind the angular keep. A stout wooden hatch was tucked away out of sight, covered with years of dirt and undergrowth that had recently been brushed aside.

A large rune was drawn over the door with fresh red paint. "What in Tchazzar's hells is this?" Phoros demanded. He stepped forward to jerk the door out of the way.

Aeron darted forward and caught his arm. "No! It's a sign of sealing. You'd better let me deal with it."

Raedel pulled his arm away resentfully, but fell back a few steps. Aeron knelt over the hatch, examining the rune carefully. When he'd studied at the college, he'd learned a little of the marking of runes and seals, but as he examined Master Crow's handiwork Aeron realized that the sorcerer had derived an entirely new system of magical markings, one designed specifically to channel and contain shadow-magic. The rune matched the ancient cipher he'd found in the Chants of Arcainasyr, the twisted Imaskari invocations Aeron had found hidden in the library years ago.

"Is it trouble, Aeron?" Eriale asked, watching him study the rune. She'd used their brief pause to string her bow and move her quiver to ride low on her hip.

Aeron rocked back on his heels. "Crow's more knowledgeable than I expected," he said. "I think I can neutralize this rune, though. Stand back." He carefully wove an enchantment of erasure, deftly drawing the mark from the wood and dissipating the magical energy stored within until nothing remained but a faded outline on the weathered wood. "There, that should do it."

Phoros Raedel nodded at the trap door. "You first."

Aeron set his hand on the iron ring, waited a moment to catch any signs that the rune was still present while his companions shifted nervously, and then pulled the door open. Stale, musty air gusted out from a narrow earthen tunnel. He reached into his pouch and produced a slim wand of ash-wood that shone with a bright yellow radiance, a simple spell that gave strong light without heat or fuel. The tunnel stretched into the darkness as far as they could see. "I'll lead if you like, Raedel, but you know the way," he said.

"Fine," the nobleman snapped. He drew his heavy longsword and pushed past Aeron, turning his shoulders to fit into the narrow passage. Aeron dropped in behind him, Baillegh at his heel, and Eriale and Kestrel brought up the rear, pulling the trapdoor closed behind them. Old timbers framed the passageway at intervals of six or seven feet, and the air was surprisingly warm and dry. Raedel wasted no time waiting for them, but set off at once for the castle, trailing one hand on the wall.

"Where will this emerge?" Aeron asked quietly.

"In the back of a linen closet adjacent to my chambers."

"Do you expect anyone there?"

Phoros shrugged. "Unless Master Crow's decided to commandeer my quarters, no one should be there. But you'll have to douse that light before we open the door."

The tunnel ran a little farther and took a sharp right turn into an arch of dressed fieldstone. From that point on, a steep, narrow stairwell of dressed stone spiraled up into blackness. Aeron counted almost a hundred steps before the passage ended in a small landing. Raedel turned back and motioned to him; the wizard returned his light-wand to the pouch, leaving them in total darkness. Ahead, he heard a small click, and a narrow wedge of brightness appeared. Phoros moved in front, peered out, and opened the door enough to slip into the chamber beyond. Aeron quickly followed, Kestrel and Eriale a step behind.

They stood in a spartan chamber of dressed stone, illuminated by a double-arched window. A few pieces of utilitarian furniture, a sword-and-shield display, and a cold hearth were the sum of its decoration. Raedel looked around, a fierce grin on his face. "Good. Nothing's been disturbed."

"He must know you're gone," Eriale said. "It's been more than three days now."

"Indeed, the count's absence did not escape my attention," drawled a voice from the chamber's doorway. Aeron and his companions whirled to face the entrance to the room. Master Crow stepped out into the open as if emerging from a solid shadow. His sallow features seemed as dead and malleable as wax in the dim light of the empty royal quarters. "I had hoped you would rejoin us, my lord Raedel. But I must admit I did not think that you would actually bring Aeron as well. Fortune smiles on me."

Phoros snarled and started forward, but Aeron quickly caught his arm. "Wait," he said. "He's not stupid. He wouldn't confront you without being certain that you were no threat."

"Listen to Aeron, Raedel. He possesses no small amount of wisdom," Crow said with a feral grin. He made a casual gesture with his left hand. Beside Aeron, Baillegh bared her teeth and growled, crouching for a spring. In each corner of the room, a dark pillar seemed to coalesce from the air, gradually condensing into tattered shapes of skeletal soldiers in mail. Their faces were blank and awful, with cold yellow light glimmering in their unseeing eyes, and they stank of death. On each warrior's stained surcoat the emblem of House Raedel was embroidered. "I've taken the liberty of improving on your guardsmen, my lord," Crow said.

Phoros shook off Aeron's hand and took another half-step forward, but the two skeletal warriors standing nearest to Master Crow straightened and advanced to bar his path, cold gleaming swords in their yellowed hands. The count ground his teeth in frustration, but his common sense won out over his anger. He halted just out of reach of the skeletons' weapons. "Damn you, Crow! Assuran curse the day I let you into my keep."

Master Crow waved his hand in a gesture of dismissal. "My lord count, I am truly sorry to hear you say that. After all, you brought me here to defend you against Aeron, and have I not done that? The Storm Walker has not troubled you once since I've become your advisor." He looked past Raedel to take in Aeron, Kestrel, and Eriale. "Now, I'll ask you to lay down your arms. Aeron, you are to keep your hands in plain sight. I'll order my warriors to attack at the first sign you're casting a spell."

No one moved. Aeron glanced around the room, weighing the enchantments that bound spirit to the armor-clad corpses that surrounded them. These were not mindless husks called back to a semblance of animation through Crow's sorcery. These creatures were far more formidable, each driven by a malicious spirit bound to Crow's will.

"Aeron, what do we do?" hissed Eriale.

Aeron hesitated, unwilling to take the first move. He was afraid of what Crow might be capable of, given Sarim's knowledge and strength. He stalled for time. "What do you want with us, Crow?"

The sorcerer shrugged. "Your friends I could care less about, Aeron. Raedel I'll keep at my side to rule this land . . . although I'm inclined to work a spell or two to render him more amenable to my advice, you might say. As for those two—" he nodded at Kestrel and Eriale, who waited with their weapons ready— "they may prove valuable in ensuring your cooperation."

"Why am I so important to you?" Aeron demanded.

Crow stepped closer, ignoring the others to direct his fevered gaze directly at the mage. "You started something five years ago that you never finished. I came here to conclude your pact with the Shadow Stone. I know you've sensed the changes in magic we've wrought over the last month or so, Aeron. This is only the first step. If you join us, if you finish the road you started down, you will become more powerful than you can ever imagine. You will be a king among wizards, a lord whose least wish can be fulfilled with the power at your command."

Aeron narrowed his eyes. "And you'll destroy me if I refuse?"

Crow laughed loudly, a brash and abrasive sound. "No, of course not. You are a mage of power, Aeron. You are far too valuable to destroy. If we cannot rally you to our cause, then there is another purpose you can serve. We can use your magic to fuel our spells." He stopped laughing and his voice grew cold. "But I'll offer you this advice, Aeron. You would be much better off as a lord among wizards than you would as our slave."

"Your only purpose here is to bring Aeron into your circle again? Maerchlin itself is nothing to you?" Eriale demanded from behind Aeron.

Crow shrugged. "All of Chessenta will be my prize someday, young lady. Maerchlin is important to us because that's where Aeron resides." He raised his hands, and Aeron felt shadow-magic swirl and gather around his fingertips. "Time enough for talk later. Lay down your weapons."

Phoros Raedel snarled, "Rot in Tchazzar's hells!" He launched himself forward in a blinding rush that carried him past the two skeletons, somehow dodging the deadly cuts they leveled at him as he rushed by. Master Crow barked out a spell against the burly young lord that blasted stabbing fingers of black fire at him. Raedel roared in pain and pressed ahead through the agonizing flame, swinging blindly until Crow was forced to dance backward a few steps to stay out of his reach.

Aeron immediately raised his staff and began an old abjuration to discorporate the evil spirits from the bodies of Raedel's soldiers, hoping to even the odds. It was a long and complex spell, and his high, clear voice echoed in the chamber as he recited the incantation while weaving threads of magic to each of the skeletal warriors. But the undead soldiers surged forward, weapons raised to strike. Baillegh leaped forward in a silver streak, knocking down the first warrior that charged Aeron while he was engaged in working the spell.

Behind him, Eriale whirled and sank an arrow into the breastbone of one skeleton, staggering it in its tracks. The creature seemed to shake it off and surged at her again, but she laid another arrow across her bow and fired again with uncanny speed and precision, burying the second arrow in the skeleton's left eye socket. The impact shattered the back of its skull, and it collapsed to the ground in a clatter of bone and steel.

Beside her, Kestrel ducked under the first swing of another skeleton and knocked its legs from under it, spilling it to the ground. He yelled a wordless challenge and leaped across the body to defend Eriale from another skeleton rushing her from the flank, driving it back with a flurry of blows. But the first creature he'd felled clawed at him, pinning his legs in place, while another moved forward, a heavy axe in its talons. It flew at Kestrel with a fierce bloodthirst, pounding at the slight woodsman's guard until Kestrel buckled beneath the attack. The axe fell one more time and came up dripping red.

Eriale turned back from the skeleton she'd just shot and cried out, "Father!" She dropped Kestrel's attacker with a single arrow in its eye, but Kestrel lay crumpled on the ground, a spreading pool of blood growing under his motionless body.

Aeron nearly lost the spell as he saw Kestrel fall, but with iron discipline he forced himself to finish it. The chamber rocked with the power of the last word he spoke, stone cracking and wood splintering with the weight of the magic. The remaining skeletal warriors dropped as if their strings had been cut, the animating force behind them suddenly barred from the room. By the door, Phoros Raedel pushed his way to his feet as his assailants collapsed, but Eriale fell to her knees by her father, cradling his head. Aeron whirled to face Master Crow. "Damn you, Crow!" he howled.

The dark sorcerer snapped out a quick spell that conjured bolts of magical energy and hurled them at Aeron and Raedel. The count grunted and staggered as the bursts hammered his torso, leaving the stink of charred flesh in the air, but Aeron managed to raise a short-lived shield to block the assault. He sought a spell in response, but the uncertainty of his hybrid sorcery halted him. Do I dare retaliate? he thought, frozen in one long agonizing moment of indecision. What if I end up like him?

"Morieth, do something!" Phoros screeched from the floor, writhing under Crow's magical attack.

"I can't!" Aeron responded. He took several steps back, trying to think. The shadow-magic boiled in his heart, surging through his limbs and flickering like black witch-fire about his fingertips. Before his eyes he saw the horrible scene in the crypt of the Shadow Stone, Oriseus gloating as he invited Aeron to seize the power he craved. *You want to be the one people fear,* the saturnine conjuror whispered in his ears.

Beside him, Eriale turned an anguished gaze up to Aeron. "Please, Aeron. Help us!"

Crow laughed out loud as he scorched Phoros with his sorcerous powers. "Considering my offer, Aeron? I'd hoped you would come around, sooner or later. Let's put an end to this, shall we?" His hands flashed and sparked as he tortured the nobleman with snapping arcs of black fire.

It doesn't matter what it costs me, Aeron realized. That's not Sarim anymore, and I can't let him win. He shouted out the words for the storm's stroke, pushing to the back of his mind the black tide from which he drew his power. A great bolt of lightning leaped forward from his fingertips, blasting Crow off his feet and smashing the door behind him into flying flinders. Aeron narrowed his eyes, surprised that Crow had not countered the spell.

In the scorched wreckage of the entrance to the room, Crow suddenly sat up. His robe was burned and shredded, but he seemed otherwise unhurt. "You'll have to do better than that, Aeron," he called.

Crow snapped out a word that sent Aeron and Phoros hurling toward the ceiling. Aeron flailed in the air for a moment before crashing into the hard stone with bone-jarring force. Bright light spun over his eyes, and suddenly he fell to the floor again, landing heavily on his left arm and side. Something crunched in Aeron's forearm and an electric jolt of pain raced up his arm. Raedel grunted as he landed flat on his back.

"What? No counterspell to that one?" Crow gloated. He gestured and sent both men slamming into the ceiling and then dropped them to the ground again.

Aeron's vision reeled, and he could hardly tell which way was up, but Baillegh bounded into his field of vision, worrying at Crow's arm. The sorcerer managed to gasp out a quick spell that repelled the silver hound, sending her skittering into a corner. In the momentary respite that Baillegh's attack earned him, Aeron raised himself to his knees and unleashed a spell of transformation, striking Crow full in the chest with a flickering green ray. "Let's see how you look as a mouse," Aeron muttered, concentrating on the transformation from human to rodent. Crow seemed startled for a moment as the shimmering emerald aura washed over his body, but again the spell did not affect him, vanishing like water draining into a sinkhole.

"A noble effort, Aeron," the sorcerer smirked. "But your spells are useless against me. Any enchantment you work, I will absorb and add to my own strength."

"Absorb this," said Eriale from somewhere behind Aeron. Her bow thrummed, and a white-feathered arrow suddenly appeared low in Master Crow's throat, just above the notch where his collarbones met. The sorcerer's eyes bulged in astonishment and he flailed his arms, trying to keep his balance. Crow opened his mouth as if to say something, but a dark rush of blood streamed over his chin. His eyes rolled up and he collapsed in a heap.

The chamber fell eerily silent. Aeron could hear the blood pounding in his ears, and he slowly pushed himself to his feet, watching Crow for some sign of movement. The sorcerer's body lay still. He turned slowly, and saw Eriale kneeling by Kestrel, her bow in her hands. "Thanks," he said. He moved over and dropped down beside her, hoping to help Kestrel.

The woodsman lay on his back, staring sightlessly at the ceiling. The rough homespun shirt was soaked with blood where the skeletal warrior's axe had split Kestrel's breastbone. "Kestrel," Aeron whispered, bowing his head.

Eriale's voice trembled. "Aeron, can your magic—"

"No," he answered. "He's far beyond my skill." He reached down and closed Kestrel's eyes, a hot ache growing in his chest. "Eriale, I'm sorry. I shouldn't have—"

"Why didn't you act, Aeron? What hold did he have on you?" Tears streamed down Eriale's face. "What were you waiting for?"

Aeron sagged back, unable to answer her. "I didn't want to face him," he said quietly. "I should have known that it would come to this."

"My father's dead, Aeron. Raedel and I would have been next. Wasn't that reason enough for you?" She looked over at the doorway to the chamber, where Crow lay with the white-feathered arrow protruding from his throat. Close by the sorcerer's body, Phoros Raedel wheezed heavily, one arm clamped over his wounds. "You'd better check on

Raedel. We'll need him to explain why we're here."

Aeron reached out and caught Eriale's arm, turning her to face him. "You're right, Eriale. I wasn't ready for this. I didn't want to confront Crow, and my hesitation might have cost Kestrel his life. But I won't make that mistake again—I swear it."

He held her eyes for a tense moment, until she relented and looked away. Then he stood, picked up his staff, and faced the door. "Look after the count. I have work to do if we're going to put this castle back in his hands."

Sixteen

Aeron and Eriale spent several days in Maerchlin, helping to set things right as Raedel reclaimed his castle. Crow had left a tangled web of dangerous enchantments, wardings, curses, and magical coercions over the places and people of Maerchlin. Aeron worked for days expunging every rune and warding, dispelling charms and curses, and undoing as much of Crow's influence as he could. Kestrel's death demanded no less of him.

Phoros Raedel made no objection when Aeron and Eriale reopened Kestrel's old house at the edge of Maerchlin. The count had been badly wounded and burned during the fight against Crow and his undead minions, but through raw force of will he was on his feet again within a day, making certain that no one in Maerchlin had any doubt as to who was the lord of the county. He relayed no words of thanks to Aeron or Eriale for their service, instead ignoring their presence in his lands. If it had been anyone else, Aeron might have felt slighted by the lack of gratitude, but he knew that it must have angered Phoros beyond reason to be indebted to him. He intended to remove himself from the count's domain as soon as he was satisfied that Crow's magic would work no more mischief.

Three days after their confrontation with Master Crow, Aeron and Eriale burned Kestrel. Aeron used his sorcery to create a clean, pure pyre; he could not stand the idea of burning Kestrel with the sodden, sickly firewood at hand. A somber handful of their old friends and neighbors turned out for the ceremony.

Eriale and Aeron lingered for a long time by the pyre, watching the funereal flames dance and crackle. Eriale was silent and worn, with dark circles under her eyes, and Aeron was exhausted as well.

He was shaken out of his reflection by Eriale's voice. "Aeron? Why did this happen?"

"What?" He turned toward her with a startled look.

"What did we do to earn Master Crow's hate? Why did he

come to Maerchlin, and why did he do what he did?"

Aeron tried to think of an answer and failed. Eriale looked up at him, the cold damp air plastering her hair to her cheeks like a dark hood. "He said that he came here because of me," he said at length. "I don't know whether I believe him, though."

"I remember what he said, but what I want to know is why. What did you ever do to him?"

"I knew him back at the college, Eriale. His name then was Sarim, and he was one of my mentors. A terrible wrong was done to him by Lord Oriseus after I left." He repressed a shudder as a cold tendril of water pierced his hood and ran down his back. "I'd thought that I was no longer of interest to Oriseus and his followers. Out of sight, out of mind. After all, they never tried to contact me or hunt me down after I left. I guess I was wrong."

"So you think that Oriseus made Sarim into Crow and sent him after you?"

Aeron thought it over. "Yes. I think he did."

"Do you think that Oriseus told Crow to use his magic to enslave the people of Maerchlin? Or do you think that was Crow's idea?"

"I don't know, Eriale. I just don't know what he's capable of."

Eriale stepped closer and fixed her gaze on his eyes. "Do you think Oriseus might try again?"

Aeron fell silent. He didn't have an answer.

Eriale turned and paced away. The mists and rain shrouded them in a world of gray, bleached of color. The dark line of trees that started beyond Kestrel's homestead might as well have been a wall of wet stone. "Didn't Crow say that he and his friends were responsible for this?" She waved her arm in a gesture that included the earth, the forest, and the gray sky overhead. "That this was all a spell they were working on?"

"What are you getting at?" Aeron asked.

"We can't let this go on," Eriale said, speaking into the shadows under the trees. "This is killing the land. Whoever is behind this must be stopped. Whoever—" her voice broke for a moment— "Whoever sent Master Crow to Maerchlin and forced us to confront him must be stopped."

"They're dangerous, Eriale. Ruthless, arrogant. We're beneath their notice. Do you understand? They have no fear of me." Aeron clenched his fists, his shoulders taut. "You don't know how close I came to sharing Sarim's fate. There are powers in the world that no one was meant to tamper with, and they almost destroyed me.

"I'll set myself against Oriseus. I'll try to make him stop what he's doing. But I don't know if I'm strong enough to resist Oriseus and the Shadow Stone." He faced Eriale, iron fighting despair in his voice. "I might become the next Master Crow."

The archer's face softened as she studied Aeron for a long moment. "Aeron, someday you're going to have to confront what happened at the college in Cimbar."

"Easier said than done," Aeron observed with a wry smile. He dropped his gaze and saw Baillegh scramble to her feet. She barked twice and bounded away, back to the forest. Aeron watched, puzzled, before seizing his staff and spinning to see what had alarmed the hound.

Baillegh barked somewhere in the distance, obscured by the mists and the trees, but after a moment she reappeared, trotting happily by the heel of a tall, gray-cloaked figure. Aeron recognized the stride at once. "Fineghal!"

The elf lord looked up, pushing his hood back over his shoulders and shaking out his pale golden hair. He was dressed for traveling, in a seamless tunic of pearl gray and green that seemed to melt into invisibility in front of the dark trees. He carried a long, thin staff, and there was a short, straight-bladed sword belted at his hip. He grinned, ruffling the top of Baillegh's head, and raised his hand. "Well met, Aeron! I am glad that I found you."

Aeron rushed up to him and caught his forearm in a warm clasp. "I thought you'd be a week or more yet!"

"I found an old gate to take me from the Chondalwood to Calmaercor without resorting to my own magic," the elf replied. "From the Storm Tower, it's not much of a walk." He nodded at Eriale. "Hello, Eriale. It's good to see you again. How is your father?"

Aeron and Eriale exchanged a silent look. Aeron moved aside and pointed at the raised bier, smoking in the damp morning. "He fell, fighting Master Crow, the sorcerer I told you of," he said.

Fineghal bowed his head. "I am sorry, Eriale. He was a good man, one of the best I have had the honor to know. How did it happen?"

Aeron related the events of the past few days while they stood by Kestrel's pyre, and then adjourned to the warm sitting room of the forester's old house. Eriale prepared some hot tea, while Fineghal shook the rainwater from his traveling cloak and settled by the fire. Aeron could not recall a time that he'd ever seen the elf lord glad to be indoors and out of the weather, but the hard pace he'd set for himself had apparently sapped even his elven reserves of strength.

"I heard some strange tales as I traveled here, Aeron," the elf said. "The folk of the countryside whisper that the dead are walking, that the ground has soured, that evil is abroad in the land."

"Any word of other sorcerers at work?" Aeron asked. "Crow seemed to imply that those who served Oriseus might be abroad, working to further his purposes."

Fineghal frowned. "No, I heard no such stories. But I did encounter tales of a different sort, of mages and magicians who had suddenly disappeared. Wizards are uncommon folk to begin with, so I didn't pay it any attention, but now I wonder if it might be important."

"Disappeared? How?"

"In some cases, the mage vanished years ago, but in Villon people were speaking of their lord's magician, who had deserted his master's court only a few days ago."

Aeron scowled in thought, trying to make sense of it. "I suspect that these are all symptoms of one illness," he said. "Do you remember what I told you of my journey through the plane of shadow? It seems to me that all of this is familiar. I've experienced this before. There's no Weave in the Shadow, only the magic of the dark powers."

"That sounds like what we have witnessed in our own world over the past few weeks," Fineghal said slowly. "Do you think that the borders between the worlds are growing weak for some reason? That we are seeing the planes of shadow in the living land around us?"

"I'm certain of it," Aeron replied.

"Assuran preserve us," Eriale breathed.

"Such events have happened from time to time over the years," Fineghal said thoughtfully. "Yet these conjunctions have rarely lasted for more than a few nights. By day, the shadow-realm's power cannot exist in our world. How can this continue week after week? When will it end?"

"I don't think it will," Aeron said. "I think Oriseus has mastered the Shadow Stone. This is his doing."

"That," said Fineghal, "is a dire thought indeed."

"Can you do anything to set things right?" Eriale asked.

Aeron turned to look at her. "You told me that I'd have to confront my failure at the college again. I think you're right. I cannot conceive of any magic that would undo Oriseus's enchantment. But if I go to Cimbar I might be able to find out what he's doing and how I can stop it."

"Do you really think you can defeat Oriseus and his allies?" Eriale asked quietly.

"I'll have to try. I might be able to find help at the college. Master Telemachon is long dead, and Sarim's fallen now too, but a few other masters opposed Oriseus's rise to power. And I had other friends there, too."

"I'll help in any way I can," Fineghal said.

"And I as well," Eriale added.

Aeron shook his head. "Eriale, you can't help me if it comes down to a confrontation with Oriseus and his allies."

"Why don't you ask Master Crow if I was any help to you or not?" Eriale replied. She leaned forward, her face intense with emotion. "You've told me Oriseus was responsible for Crow and the evil he worked here. I want to make him pay for what Crow did to my father. Don't try to protect me from this, Aeron. It's my right."

"We may not be able to count on our magic for much longer," Fineghal added. "Your sister may be right, Aeron. Let's not discount the possibility that we'll need an archer of her caliber to defeat your old master."

Aeron grimaced in distaste. He didn't like the idea of deliberately leading Eriale into danger, but she was right. "All right," he surrendered. "But I'll ask that you try to stay out of harm's way."

Eriale only smiled. "When do we leave?" she asked.

* * * * *

Early the following morning, Aeron, Fineghal, and Eriale commandeered horses from Phoros Raedel's stables for their journey. To his surprise, the stableman let them have three sturdy coursers without a word of protest. The soldiers and servants of Castle Raedel knew the part Aeron and Eriale had played in freeing them of Master Crow's lordship and were grateful. Aeron secured some provisions as well, and they rode west out of the castle within an hour of sunrise, Baillegh trotting at Aeron's heel.

By all rights, it should have been mid-fall, a beautiful time of year for a ride. The Maerchwood should have been ablaze with a thousand hues of flame and gold, and the nearby fields of Maerchlin should have been head-high with ripe wheat and corn. But the ground was sodden and damp with thick, black mud. The fields were strewn with pale, sickly crops ruined by a plague of rot-causing worms. Even the trees had sloughed off their black leaves, standing naked to the skies with soft, rotten bark.

After a long day's ride, they reached the wide fields and scattered farmhouses of Saden. The outpost was in no better shape than Maerchlin, with large pools of black standing water fouling its fields and a stink of rotten grain permeating the air. Eriale wrinkled her nose in disgust. "This is even worse than it was a week ago."

"I wonder if the Shadow Stone's influence is still increasing," Fineghal said. "Its effects may grow even more pronounced with time."

They stopped for the night at Kestrel and Eriale's house in Saden. After a supper of black bread and stew, Aeron and Fineghal stayed up late, talking of Aeron's time in the college and his final days there. Fineghal hoped to find some insight into the nature of the Shadow Stone's power, but they had little success.

The next morning, the three travelers restocked their provisions and resumed their journey. The first time Aeron had made this trip, he'd gone north from Saden to Oslin on the Akanamere, taking passage on a keelboat to Soorenar before switching to a coastal dromond for the last leg of his journey to the great city. This time, Eriale's neighbors warned them against that path. Between Akanax and Soorenar the armies dueled like blind, dumb beasts, lurching from village to village as they grappled for advantage. Few ships on the Akanamere were safe, and Akanax itself was virtually under siege. Aeron and Fineghal agreed that it seemed wiser not to ride into a war if they could avoid it, and set out northeast, following the Adder River and riding across the empty lands of eastern Chessenta.

They managed several days without any serious incidents, setting their course westward along old cattle trails and cart tracks. The lands they rode through had once been heavily populated, with prosperous towns and crowded fields nestling close together in the gentle hills, but in the chaos surrounding the fall of Unther's empire four centuries before, Chessenta's eastern provinces had been ravaged by plague and war. "All this land," murmured Eriale. "It's so desolate, so lonely."

"It will be full of people again someday," Fineghal told her. "In a lifetime or two, folk will come to take up the land that has fallen into disuse. They'll make a good life for themselves, and kings will rise to defend them against those who want to take it from them. It's only a matter of time."

"I hope you're right," Aeron said. "For the past two days, I've been wondering if this is how things will go if we can't undo the Shadow Stone's spell. Each year another house falls empty, another field grows wild, a stone wall falls and is not rebuilt. The circle of light and life around every hearth shrinking closer and closer, until all who are left wait shivering for the darkness to fall. It won't be a quick end, or a noble one."

* * * * *

That night, they came to a small crossroads with a battered old inn sitting beside it. A worn sign creaked from above the door, and warm yellow light seeped out from shuttered windows. Horses stamped and shuffled in the large stable yard beside the building. Aeron was tired and sore from riding, and he did not look forward to another night of camping underneath the cold, clammy mists. He reined in his horse and regarded the innhouse with a thoughtful look.

"Should we stop here for the night?" he asked.

Eriale nodded emphatically. "A warm bed would be worth a handful of gold."

Fineghal hesitated. "I've never been comfortable in such places, but we need the rest, and it would be good to stable the horses someplace warm for a night." He sat up straight in the saddle and muttered a few words in Elvish, drawing his hand over his face. When his hand fell again, Fineghal's elven features were gone, replaced by the careworn, blunt features of a human mercenary nearing his fiftieth year. His elven tunic had become a shirt of sweat-stained ring mail, and he'd even added a slight paunch to disguise his rail-thin build. He turned to Aeron. "You'd be wise to conceal your own features, too," he said. "In my experience, the elves are sometimes not welcome in a house such as this."

Aeron shrugged and worked the same spell. He could not help noticing that he was able to master it with much less effort than it had taken Fineghal; his ability to draw on magic from a source beyond the diminished Weave was a significant advantage as the magic of life and light ebbed away from the world. He settled for masking himself as a plain forester, although his own traveling garb was fairly close to that anyway. "I'm ready," he said. "Let's go in."

They led their mounts into the innyard and stabled the horses themselves, since no servants appeared to help them. After watering the animals and rubbing them down with what little dry straw they could find, they gathered up their saddlebags and headed into the inn's common room, leaving Baillegh outside to watch over their mounts.

It was a dirty room of unfinished wood, rendered almost uninhabitable by a badly made fire that put out more smoke than heat or light. A dozen or so men, farmers and teamsters by the look of them, sat around the room's low tables. In one corner, five mailed swordsmen wearing the insignia of the King of Oslin kept to themselves. Aeron selected an unoccupied table at random and dropped onto one rickety stool, his saddlebags by his knee. He tried to ignore the hard stares the other patrons subjected them to. "Friendly crowd," he muttered to his companions.

"Hard times," said Fineghal. "Strangers always come under suspicion when things aren't right."

They waited a long time before an overworked tavern-maid appeared at their table. She might have been a pretty girl once, but her eyes were dull and glazed and her frame was too lean, as if the life had been wrung out of her drop by drop. "What d'ya care for, gentlemen?" she asked in a mechanical voice.

"Ale," Aeron replied. "The best of what you've got. And we'll need rooms for the night, and feed for our horses."

"That'll be ten gold drakes, in advance," she said.

"Ten drakes!" Eriale recoiled in surprise. "That's a prince's ransom. You must be joking!"

The tired barmaid merely looked at her. "Pay or not, it's your choice. But that's what it will cost you."

"Five drakes should buy us lodging for the week," Fineghal said to the barmaid. "But I've no wish to sleep outside tonight, so I'll give you three now and two tomorrow morning for a place to sleep and a meal."

The woman narrowed her eyes, studying Fineghal for a long moment before agreeing. She turned away to fetch their ale. While she was gone, one of the soldiers rose from his table, sauntered over, and kicked a chair into place beside Eriale. He was a pock-faced man with dense black hair on his arms and a gap-toothed, yellow smile. The soldier offered Eriale a leering wink and said to Fineghal, "I see you're a fellow swordsman. Where're you bound?"

"Mordulkin," Fineghal replied.

"A long way," said the soldier. He leaned back in his chair, folding his hairy arms. "Taking service there?"

Fineghal replied with a shrug. "There's always work to be found in the city."

"Especially with war in the air," the soldier observed. He studied Fineghal, his eyes narrowed. Despite his affable manner, he was not nearly so drunk as he wanted them to think he was. "Who do you intend to sell your sword to?"

"Doesn't matter."

"Stay out of Akanax's service," the soldier said, "unless you want to fight against wizardry." He made a sour face, leaning over to spit on the floor.

Aeron and Fineghal exchanged guarded looks. "Wizardry?" asked Aeron.

"No right man would take up such foul habits," the soldier declared. "It's a sign of the times, I suppose. Dead walking, fields rotting, people forgetting who they are and what they do. It's all the work of wizards, I tell you. We'd be better off without 'em."

"What do wizards have to do with Akanax?" Eriale asked.

The fellow leaned close, whispering in a conspiratorial fashion. "See, the high-and-mighty Sceptanar, he's no fool. He knows that Gormantor of Akanax would beat him in any kind of stand-up fight. So he's looking for a way to break the deadlock. I've heard that he has a coven of sorcerers working for him, silencing the few wizards Gormantor employs, razing Akanax's castles and firing its towns. He's had the Akanaxans on the run all summer."

"Doesn't seem right," Fineghal grunted.

"Well, that's what the king of Mordulkin thought, so he jumped in on Akanax's side. Airspur, too. Forced Cimbar and Soorenar to split their armies, one to march south against Akanax, one to march west along the coast to deal with Airspur, and the third landed by Cimbar's fleets on the shores under Mordulkin's walls." Satisfied with his answer, the soldier moved closer to Eriale as the barmaid returned with their ale.

"Oslin sends her soldiers to fight for Gormantor of Akanax?" Eriale asked. Gereax of Oslin had been Akanax's vassal for decades.

"Of course. If we don't help Gormantor beat Cimbar and Soorenar, we'll all be singing the praises of the Sceptanar by the end of the year," the soldier said. "I'll be damned if I'll call some wizard my king."

Aeron weighed the soldier's words. He had to get to the college to see for himself what was going on. Dalrioc Corynian must have secured Soorenar for Oriseus after all; it seemed likely, based on the course of the war the Oslinite described. Did Oriseus openly flaunt his command of shadow-magic, or did he conceal his role in the sorcerous winter that had fallen over Chessenta? The soldier was only reporting rumors and speculation, but he didn't doubt that there was truth in the fellow's words.

The soldier leaned forward, making a show of pouring Eriale a mug of ale. "Enough politics. What business sets your feet on the road on a cold, lonely night?" he asked her.

Eriale set her face in a stony expression. "I travel with these gentlemen to Mordulkin."

"You mean to find work there, too?" The soldier's coarse laugh indicated the type of work he thought she might be looking for. "Where the armies go, there's always a place for an enterprising woman to earn some gold. Me and my fellows—" he jerked his head over at the other soldiers-"have been riding back and forth across this country for a week now with not a night to relax. Why don't you join our table for a bit?"

Eriale shook her head. "No, thank you. These gentlemen have offered to escort me to Mordulkin. I'll stay with them."

The soldier turned a hard stare at Aeron and Fineghal. "You fellows don't mind, do you?" Behind him, the other soldiers pushed back their chairs, slowly standing. The taproom fell silent as the other patrons felt the tension in the air. Aeron sensed an ugly black flicker in the weak currents of the Weave that flowed through the room. Why would the corruption of magic limit itself to the forces of nature? he realized. Every living creature carries a spark of the Weave in its heart. Could a person's spirit be poisoned just as the fields and the waters have been tainted?

Playing his part as an old mercenary, Fineghal scraped his chair back a half-pace, clearing his sword arm for action. "I think that the lady has made her preference clear," Fineghal said quietly, smiling without humor. "If she wants to stay with us, she'll stay with us. But we'd be more than glad to buy you and your fellows a round or two of drinks to show our appreciation for the good king of Oslin and the fine men who serve him."

The soldier's face darkened. "I don't want your lousy ale. I want the woman. There's two of you and five of us, old man. If you're smart, you'll just get up and walk out that door."

"All right," Aeron said. He stood and reached down to help Eriale to her feet. "We'll leave. All three of us."

The soldier twisted his face into a vicious sneer. "The two of you must be hard of hearing. I said, the woman stays here!" He lunged forward and caught Eriale's free arm.

"Take your hands off me!" Eriale barked. "I don't want your company, or your fellows either. Leave me be!" She yelped in pain as the soldier twisted her arm and pulled her away from Aeron. The fellow turned back to grin at his friends and took one step back across the taproom before Eriale's hard-driven heel came down on his instep with bone-cracking force. The swordsman cursed and drew up his foot, while Eriale leaned back and swept his remaining leg out from under him, throwing him to the floor. She took two steps back, fire flashing in her eyes. "I am not a piece of property," she said in a clear voice.

The hairy soldier rolled quickly and stood, wincing and favoring his foot. He drew the broadsword from his belt with a long, rasping hiss. "You'll be sorry for that," he snarled. The other soldiers bared their blades as well, advancing with menace in their eyes.

The soldier yelled and threw himself at Aeron, who stood closest to him, leveling a furious high cut that Aeron barely ducked under. The other soldiers followed in a rush of steel and leather. Aeron caught a glimpse of Fineghal's sword flashing as the elven lord parried two attacks and riposted, stemming the tide for a moment. Another man tried to seize Eriale, but the archer danced back, vaulting over a table.

The soldier attacking Aeron recovered from his swing and brought the sword back in an overhand cut that would have split him in two if it had landed, but Aeron rolled aside. He found his staff and brought it up to deflect the next blow. Steel rang on steel as Fineghal duelled with two of the soldiers. Chairs and tables clattered to the floor as Eriale dodged away from her pursuer. That's four, Aeron thought. Where's the last one?

Behind Fineghal steel glinted, catching Aeron's eye. The last man had circled around to position himself behind the elf, and he was preparing to strike. "Fineghal! Look out!" Aeron yelled, just as he barely managed to twist away from a vicious thrust by his opponent. He dropped one end of the staff squarely on the injured foot of the black-haired swordsman, and was rewarded by a howl of pain and a momentary stumble. He started to speak a spell, but the swordsman unleashed a flurry of blows that drove Aeron back, unable to find the opening he needed.

Fineghal leaped and whirled, running the last soldier through as the fellow rushed him. But his sword caught in the man's mailed ribcage for a long moment. The two men who had first engaged him pressed forward, scenting an easy kill. The elven mage released his sword, backed away two steps, and barked an incantation, extending his hand to unleash a dazzling spray of brilliant sparks. The shower blinded his attackers and drove them back, although the spell left Fineghal staggering with fatigue. The glamour that hid his features shimmered and vanished.

"Sorcery!" spat Aeron's attacker. "I should have known!" "Wizard! He's a wizard!" The other patrons cried out in fear or anger, suddenly scrambling aside to give Fineghal a wide berth. From one dark corner a dagger glinted in the air, thrown by a beefy teamster. It turned once and struck Fineghal high in the shoulder, lodging just above his collarbone. The elf reeled and went to one knee, his hand reaching up for the knife.

This is getting worse, Aeron realized. He ducked away

from another slash and countered with a jab that the soldier stepped into, clamping one hand over the end of Aeron's staff and trapping it against his body. The soldier grinned ruthlessly and raised his sword to cut Aeron down.

Without even thinking about it, Aeron barked a word that triggered the staff's magical powers. Blue light flashed and a wave of arctic cold raised patterns of white hoarfrost all over the room. The hairy soldier stood frozen to the spot, covered in a cloudy rime of ice a handspan thick. Shouts of dismay and rage echoed around him. Aeron wrenched his staff away from the frozen soldier, ignoring the sick crack and crunch of icy fingers snapping away with the dark wood. "Stop this!" he roared.

Across the room, the spark-burned soldiers stood over Fineghal, their swords red. They looked up in surprise, just as Aeron spoke another word that hammered them like the strike of a sledge, blasting their broken forms against the opposite wall and splintering the wooden floor. He whirled to search for Eriale, and found her struggling on top of one of the tables as the lout who had been chasing her tore her shirt open.

Aeron shouted in rage and charged him, striking the soldier across the shoulders with a staff empowered by a smiting-spell. The mercenary's mail shirt literally disintegrated with the blow, and he collapsed in a nerveless heap. As Aeron reached down to help Eriale to her feet, something heavy struck the back of his head, knocking him to his knees. Cold wetness ran down the back of his shirt. Blinking in astonishment, he focused on a large wooden mug rolling on the floor.

"He's a wizard too!"

"He killed Jonos!"

"Get him before he casts any more spells!"

Eriale hauled him to his feet. Everywhere he looked, the tavern's denizens were charging forward, armed with knives, clubs, or just their bare hands. "Aeron, do something!" Eriale cried.

Aeron thought for a split second, and mumbled the words to a spell he'd crafted only a few months ago. He exerted his will to seize the tangled threads of the Weave that burned just out of reach, building a cage or barrier. As he spoke the last word, the room suddenly became smoky and dim, as if viewed through thick, dark glass, and the sounds faded to mere whispers.

"Aeron? What did you do?" Eriale's voice was clear and close to him; she was within the barrier. She flinched away as a heavy stool hurled through the air at them, but it seemed to strike something in midair a few feet from her face and clattered to the ground. Around them weapons rose and fell, but nothing could seem to reach them.

"It's a magical barrier," Aeron explained. "Unless someone in here is a wizard with the right spells at hand, nothing can harm us. We'd better get Fineghal and leave while it lasts." With Eriale clinging to his side, Aeron walked ahead slowly, the furious blows of sword and club no more tangible than the flutter of a moth's wings. He moved over to where Fineghal had fallen, and knelt by the elf, gently turning him over.

Fineghal's white tunic was scarlet with his blood. He'd been stabbed several times. His face was white as ice, and his skin was cold. "A skillful barrier, Aeron," he gasped. "Yet . . . it is a little . . . too late for me, I fear."

Aeron's heart seemed to shudder and stop. "We'll have you out of here in a moment, Fineghal," he said. He reached down to pick up the elven wizard, uncertain of what he could do to help, but determined not to leave him lying in the wreckage of the tavern. He'd never imagined that Fineghal could be hurt, let alone wounded to the point of death.

The elf lord grasped his hand, stopping him. "It won't matter, Aeron." He gazed into Aeron's face. "I had hoped . . . that I could aid you . . . against your enemies, but this quest will be yours alone. You must succeed, Aeron. My death—and Kestrel's—will be but two . . . of a countless number . . . if you cannot break the stone's spell."

Aeron leaned over the fallen elf, openly weeping. "Fineghal, I don't know what to do."

"Nor do I, Aeron. This sorcery is . . . beyond my comprehension. But you have learned both . . . the elven and the human ways of magic. I think that you have it within you to understand . . . and destroy this evil." Fineghal coughed raggedly, drawing a deep gasp that bubbled in the back of his throat. "Telemachon would have known . . . what to do," he whispered. "He was a great diviner. I believe . . . he saw this day coming."

"Telemachon is dead," Aeron said.

"His work may not be," Fineghal said. "Go now . . . before your barrier fails. You cannot fall . . . ."

"I won't leave you!"

"My spirit . . . is passing, Aeron. If you perish . . . my death will have been for nothing. Please . . . flee while you can."

"You're not going to die," Aeron stated, determination in his voice. He bent down and tenderly cradled Fineghal in his arms, struggling to his feet. "You've taught me something of the old healing songs. All I need is a little time to ready them—"

"After a thousand springs . . . it seems ironic . . . that I cannot spare you that," Fineghal said with a faint smile. "Farewell, Aeron." The light faded from the elven lord's eyes and his fingers slipped from Aeron's grasp.

Aeron dropped to his knees in shock. Outside his gray wall, the angry peasants and laborers waited in silence, watching for some break in his impervious defenses.

Beside him, Eriale knelt and reached down to disentangle his arms. "Come on, Aeron. We've got to get out of here."

Dully, he nodded. He reached down and took Fineghal's pouch of spell-tokens, and then stood again. "Oriseus is going to pay for this," he said. Then he led her out into the night.

Seventeen

For the rest of that night and most of the next day, Aeron and Eriale pressed on, stopping only when exhaustion forced them to. Aeron's spirit was empty, and his heart ached as if it had been filled with cold ashes. Kestrel's death still seemed unreal to him, an awful mistake of some kind. Now Fineghal was gone as well, a noble spirit whose death seemed senseless. One by one, every person he'd ever learned from had been taken from him, with the sole exception of Oriseus, and Aeron didn't like to think of what the High Conjuror might intend for him. He could only keep his horse's feet on the road leading north, and lose himself in the dull rhythm of the ride.

Eriale matched Aeron's own silence. Grief set her face in a forlorn stare, and the endless mist and rain beat her hair into a dark, wet hood, so that she looked like a lost child. Aeron knew that he should send her back to Saden before evil befell her too, but he didn't have the strength. Lost in her own sorrow as she was, it still comforted him to know that she rode beside him. If he needed any reason to continue on, any incentive to confront the failures of his past, Eriale provided it. For her sake he had to carry on.

Late in the afternoon after their flight, they came to the road that sliced northwest from the ruins of Luthcheq to Soorenar and the great city of Cimbar beyond. They turned west, riding more carefully—they were traveling into the heartlands of Chessenta, the broad belt of townlands and terraced hills that ran from Akanax to Cimbar, and the relative safety of the desolate hinterlands was gone.

Near sunset, they left the road and camped in a dense copse a few hundred yards to one side, building a small fire and drying out their traveling clothes as best they could. "How much farther is it to Cimbar?" Eriale asked over a cold and cheerless meal of trail rations.

"I'm not sure. I traveled by sea when I was here before," Aeron replied. It raised his spirits a little to break the silence. "I think we'll reach Soorenar by late in the afternoon. After that, it's another two days to Cimbar."

Eriale nodded. "Have you thought about what you'll do when we get there?"

He closed his eyes, shaking his head. "No. I haven't even thought about it, with—"

"I know. I haven't been myself lately, either. I didn't know Fineghal as well as you, but he was one of the noblest souls I've ever met." She smiled softly. "The world's a sadder place without him."

"And Kestrel."

"And Father, too." She set a tin cup on a stone by the fire, dropping a handful of coffee grounds into the water. Aeron was struck by the severe lines of her face, the weariness in her gestures. Eriale was too young to have so many cares. "So? What will we do?" she asked.

"I don't know," Aeron replied. "I'll need to get to the chamber of the Shadow Stone, examine it closely, see how the spell works. Maybe I can determine how to stop it."

"Won't that be dangerous? Could it be guarded?"

Aeron shrugged. "It might be. Then again, the stone seemed capable of protecting itself."

"That's not what I meant. Wouldn't Oriseus be careful to protect the stone, to make sure that no one tampered with what he was doing?" Eriale stirred the coffee with a stick. "If Oriseus's got any sense at all, he'll guard his work to make sure no one interferes."

"He might not need to, Eriale," Aeron said. "Oriseus's spell may be unbreakable. Even if he knew I was coming back to Cimbar to stop him, he might not care."

Eriale's eyes flashed. "Listen, Aeron. If you can't undo Oriseus's work, then there's no hope for any of us, and there's no sense making any plans at all. We might as well go home and wait to see what the world's like when he's finished with it.

"Since we both know that we're not going to turn around and go back to Maerchlin, let's assume that you'll be able to find some way to reverse the spell. And if we assume that's true, we'd better also assume that Oriseus knows it, and that he'll take steps to make sure that no one can upset his work." She held his eyes, cold determination in her face. "I am not going to let you give up on this before we see what we're up against, Aeron."

He flinched, but refused to look away. "All right. I don't

think we'll have anything to worry about until we reach the college grounds. The city's far too big, with thousands upon thousands of people and places to hide. But the college sits on the acropolis, surrounded by the university and the Sceptanar's palace, and everyone inside knows who is supposed to be there. That's where we have to worry."

"Why can't you walk right in? There's no law against it. You have every right to be there if you wish," Eriale said.

Aeron shook his head. "That might be true, but why ask for trouble? Oriseus is Sceptanar now; he'll command hundreds of soldiers in the immediate vicinity. If he is inclined to make sure that I can't undo his design, there's no one in Cimbar who can defy his authority."

"Do you know a spell that would let us creep in without detection?" Eriale asked.

He thought for a long moment before shaking his head. "There are wards around the college to defeat magic like that," Aeron said, "and I'm certain Oriseus would have added to them."

He warmed his hands, watching his coffee beginning to boil. There was just too much he didn't know. Did any factions oppose Oriseus's rule? The demagogues of Cimbar's Mob had railed against the reign of the previous Sceptanar, albeit to little effect. Were there any masters within the college who still opposed Oriseus? How many of Oriseus's disciples were at the college, and how many had been sent out into Chessenta, like Crow? Any scrying spell he cast might be noticed and investigated. Suddenly Aeron laughed at himself with a sharp and bitter bark.

"What? What is it?" Eriale asked, sitting up straight.

"The problem with being a mage," Aeron said, "is that you try to figure out how to do everything with magic." He gingerly retrieved his cup from its place by the fire, blowing on the hot coffee. "I know four or five spells that could have warmed this coffee or conjured it up out of nothing. But this campfire and a few old grounds will do just as well."

"You have an idea?"

Aeron smiled at her, a long-hidden lightness in his heart surfacing after months of care. He reached down and scratched Baillegh behind the ears. "I think I do," he said.

They reached Cimbar two days later.

From the busy street end that faced the main gate, the college seemed unchanged from Aeron's days as a student. The weathered brick buildings still stood in the same quadrangle, wreathed by ivy and watching over the city below with blank, dark windows. Aeron and Eriale strolled down the center of the street, two passers-by in the crowd, turning left toward the harbor to skirt the college walls.

Aeron glanced over at Eriale and repressed a smile. "You're staring again."

"I've never seen anything like Cimbar. I'd heard that this was a great city, but I never understood what that meant until I saw it for myself. It's wonderful and terrible at the same time." Eriale's face fell. "What a tragedy that the capital is so full of hate and feuding these days."

Aeron snorted. "I wonder if the Shadow Stone's presence had anything to do with it all. The fall of Unther's empire, the shattering of Chessenta, the rise of the Mob, the ambitions of lords like Oriseus . . . " His voice trailed away as they came to the place he'd been looking for, a steep escarpment where the street dropped the last fifty feet to the wharves while the rocky mass of the acropolis began its climb up to the point on which the broken pyramid sat. Briars and tough, coarse-barked whitelock trees clung to the slope, masking the college wall behind a band of untended foliage. Aeron glanced up and down the street— no one seemed to be looking their way. He grasped Eriale's arm and pulled her into the undergrowth. They burrowed into the thicket, scrambling up out of sight of the street and pausing just under the crumbling brick wall. Baillegh followed, her silver tail high.

"Did you do this often when you were a student here?" Eriale asked with a note of disapproval.

"No. I didn't get out much, but all the students knew about it." Aeron cocked his ear, listening. "I don't hear anyone nearby. Go ahead and change."

From his satchel, he pulled out a simple black skirt and blouse with black piping and passed it over to Eriale, then studiously turned away and watched the wall while she wriggled out of her tunic and into the servant's garb.

After a moment, she tossed the satchel back. "Your

turn." Aeron listened again, then peeled off his own breeches and shirt in order to don a matching outfit. It had taken a couple of hours of shopping in the trade districts of New Cimbar to find clothes close to what they wanted, and another hour to have a few minor modifications made to make them match the college livery exactly, but Aeron thought it worth the wait. When he finished, he stuffed his own clothes back into the satchel and concealed it under a pile of dead leaves.

"You really think this will work?" Eriale asked as she watched him conceal the sack.

"The masters, students, and novices all know each other by sight. We'd be spotted in an instant. But no one pays attention to the servants."

"Except the other servants," Eriale noted.

"We'll just have to avoid them. Where we're going, there shouldn't be many around anyway." Aeron took a moment to whisper a minor glamour over his staff, reducing it to a slender wand that he slid into his sleeve. Eriale concealed her bow in her ankle-length skirts. Aeron watched her arm herself, then reached into a pouch at his side. From it he pulled six slender arrows, their shafts emerging straight and true from the impossibly small pouch. "Wait," he told her. "I have got a gift for you." He handed her the arrows.

"Where'd these come from?" Eriale asked.

"I brought them from Fineghal's collection in the Caerhuan. They're enchanted to strike through magical defenses. I thought we might need them against Master Crow, but they might prove useful here. Ready?"

Eriale took a deep breath and nodded, hiding the arrows in the folds of her skirt. Aeron stood up, caught the wall, and quickly slid over into the dense brush on the opposite side. He glanced around, but no one was in sight, so he reached down and helped Eriale scramble over.

"Which way?" she whispered.

"The Students' Hall. I want to see if my old rooms have been disturbed. I left some valuable notes and materials there," Aeron said.

"Do you really think that no one would have bothered to clean out your chambers in five years?" Eriale asked.

Aeron shrugged. "It's worth a look." He turned and knelt to face Baillegh. "Stay here, and keep out of sight. We'll come back for you after we've scouted things out." The hound whined softly and licked his face, but she sat down and worked her way into the heavy undergrowth.

No one was in sight, so Aeron stepped out of the shrubs and dusted himself off, straightening his servant's tunic. Eriale followed, adjusting her skirt. The path by the wall skirted the quadrangle, circling the perimeter of the college grounds. "This way," he said quietly. Eriale fell in a half-step behind him, trying not to shiver in the eerie chill.

They didn't even see anyone else until they reached the Students' Hall. As they hurried past the open end of the quadrangle, Aeron stole a surreptitious look at the heart of the college—the great library, the halls of learning, and the two long fieldstone halls facing each other. Across the wide space, a small handful of forlorn figures criss-crossed the area. The bright red robes of a Master of Conjuration caught Aeron's eye, but it didn't seem to be anyone he knew, and he didn't want to be caught staring if it was. He also noticed a handful of workmen in common clothes hustling back and forth across the open court. Eriale tapped his arm discreetly, and Aeron picked up his pace and turned his head forward to maintain the charade.

They skirted the main entrance to the Students' Hall and slipped in the smaller servants' door at one end of the building. This led into a large linen room, with laundry tubs and shelves stacked with white sheets and heavy blankets. One stout maid was at work scrubbing out some clothes, but she didn't even look up as Aeron and Eriale entered, so Aeron scooped up an armful of folded sheets from the shelf. With a nervous wink, Eriale helped herself to a bucket and rags at the same time.

Aeron found the servants' stair leading to the second floor, a dark and cramped passage with smooth-worn steps. At the top, he opened a narrow door and stepped out into Crown Hall, his home for almost a year of his life. Despite the urgency of his mission, he stopped, caught by the powerful memories. It looked much the same as it had when he'd left. Yet he was also struck by the differences, too. At first he thought that he'd come to the college during a break of some kind, since the hall was empty, echoing and silent. In his days, there'd always been a handful of novices gossiping by someone's door, a student striding grimly to or from his studies, some indication of life and energy. But the hall felt barren and cold to him.

"You stayed here for a year?" Eriale whispered.

Aeron shook his head. "It was different then. Things have changed for the worse. Come on, my room was over here."

He turned right and followed the corridor, halting at the sixth door on the right. To his relief, the facade still bore the complicated sigil he'd marked as his own. To be certain, he leaned close and put his ear to the door, straining to listen for any sound within.

Voices rang out sharply from the end of the hall. Aeron straightened and looked before he could help himself. A pair of students in their tabards and caps stood outside a door, talking in low voices. They seemed older than the students Aeron had remembered—these weren't teenagers, but a pair of grown men.

"Aeron!" hissed Eriale. "Don't stare!"

He nodded abruptly and set his hand to the door, trying it. Naturally, it was locked. He turned his shoulder to conceal his actions from the two students down the hall, and quietly spoke the spell of opening he'd used to enter his room. To his surprise, it worked flawlessly, and he let himself into his room. Eriale stepped in on his heels, sliding out of the hallway and out of sight.

The room was very close to the way he'd left it; his personal effects were still in the same places, and no one had bothered to remove the furniture or even to strip the bed. A few mundane books remained on his shelves, but Aeron could tell at a glance that most of the important ones had been removed, including his old spellbooks and the scroll tube in which he'd hidden the Chants of Madryoch the Ebon Flame. "Damn," he muttered.

"I wonder why they never cleaned out your room?" Eriale said.

"Well, they did in their way. Most of my spellbooks and some scrolls and texts aren't here anymore." Aeron sat down at his old desk, his chin in his hand. "No one knew where I'd gone when I first fled. It must have been months before they decided I wasn't coming back."

"The books were your only important belongings?"

Aeron nodded. "Yes. I suppose that Oriseus or one of his masters probably searched this room personally. They wouldn't bother to remove anything except materials they thought they might have a use for."

"The servants wouldn't have come in to check on you?"

"They might have been instructed not to, on the chance that I might return."

Eriale strolled over to the window and gazed out at the muddy apron of ground beyond the dormitory. She leaned forward to study something outside. "Aeron, what's this?"

"What?" Aeron stood and moved over to gaze out the window over her shoulder.

Outside, the ruins of the Broken Pyramid were not just ruins anymore. The rubble had been cleared away from the stone foundation of the ancient monument, and an effort was underway to rebuild it just as it had stood hundreds of years ago. Aeron gaped in shock; he'd never imagined that it could be rebuilt. But the smooth dark stone rose forty feet into the air, ending in a jagged course of stone blocks. The whole edifice was ringed by rickety scaffolding, and sheds for stonecutters and carpenters had been raised at the foot of the structure. A handful of masons were at work on the ground, cutting the blocks for the next course.

"What are they building here?" Eriale asked.

"It looks like they're raising the Broken Pyramid again," Aeron said. "The ruins of an old Untheric obelisk used to stand there. It was nothing more than a heap of rubble, with a few old walls still standing. Oriseus must have decided to rebuild it." He frowned, watching one mason patiently chisel away an uneven corner. "Where are all the workmen? This looks like a place where dozens of men could work without getting in each other's way."

"It's the end of the week."

Aeron grimaced. Not everything had to have a sinister purpose behind it, he reminded himself. But he did not like the look of the pyramid. He could feel the magical power imprisoned in the heavy stone blocks, as if each stone that had been laid down completed one small part of a vast and potent whole. The ebon sheen of the smooth rock drew his eye, refusing to allow him to look away. When complete, the spire would be a focus for the Shadow Stone, a magnifier of some kind.

"Aeron?" Eriale glanced at him with concern.

"I'm fine," he admitted after a moment. "The implications of this frighten me, that's all."

"Do you sense the stone?"

Aeron met her eyes and returned his gaze to the rising

pyramid. With the trepidation of a man reaching out to touch an angry snake, he allowed his vision to blur and shift, trying to sense the eddy and flow of the Weave around the tower. He could feel the stone nearby, but its chill emanations seemed muted, like sunlight passing through a thin cloth. The monument would change that when complete; it would offer a conduit from the realms of shadow into the waking world, a breach through which the stone's corrupting influence could stream undiminished.

"It's there, but it's in the plane of shadow," Aeron said after a long moment. "Close at hand, but a world away."

Eriale reached out to clasp his hand. She could tell that he was frightened by what he saw, even if she did not perceive the threat that was visible to him. "So what can we do about it?" she asked.

"I won't know for certain until I take a closer look."

The archer grew pale. "You mean, from the shadow-plane?"

Aeron nodded. "We'll try at dusk. But first I want to see Master Telemachon's chambers." He turned away from the window and glided across the room, picking up his bundle of sheets again. With Eriale trailing behind him, he opened the door and peeked out.

They were lucky—the two students were gone. He quickly crossed the hall and ducked into the servant's passage again, trotting back down to the laundry room. The laundress had left as well, so Aeron returned his sheets to the shelf and led Eriale outside into the cold, clinging fog.

"It doesn't seem like many people are here today," Eriale said quietly as they circled the quadrangle. "How many masters and students are there?"

"There used to be about thirty masters, forty students, and eighty to ninety novices in the college when I was here. But as you pointed out, it's the week's end. They might be elsewhere." Aeron chewed on his tongue. "Or maybe there aren't as many here now. A number of masters left after Oriseus became lord of the ruling council. And a lot of students and novices washed out then, too."

They found the servants' entrance to the Masters' Hall and entered carefully. A wing of the building was devoted to servant's quarters and the refectory, so a maid and chamberboy weren't at all out of place here-but their odds of encountering another servant were much higher. Aeron immediately turned to the servants' stair to circumvent the crowded scullery and kitchens, descending to the cluttered cellars and storerooms beneath the Masters' Hall.

Here the warm wood paneling and elegant furnishings of the college were conspicuously absent. The barrel-vaulted ceiling was low and dank, illuminated by guttering oil lamps at irregular intervals. Great tuns of wine and ale were crowded under each stone arch, dusty and worn. Aeron had only been down in the cellars once or twice, but he turned left and led Eriale along the dark passageway.

Someone coughed ahead. From one of the storerooms a lean old manservant appeared, carrying a small cask of brandy. Aeron kept the surprise from his face and managed a friendly nod of greeting, hoping his nervousness wouldn't show.

"Good day," he said cheerily.

"Hmmph. Good day, indeed." The valet passed Aeron with a long look. Aeron breathed a sigh of relief—the fellow hadn't seemed to notice their strange faces. His hopes were dashed a moment later. "Hey, wait a minute. Who are you?"

Aeron glanced at Eriale. Her face was carefully neutral, and she took two steps to flank the servant without being obvious about it. He turned to face the fellow and offered a smile and a shrug. "We're both new. Who are you?"

"I'm Kerrick. Did Olmad bring you on?"

Aeron just nodded. "Care for a hand with that brandy?"

The servant frowned. "No, I'll get it. What are you supposed to be doing?"

"They wanted a half-bushel of potatoes in the kitchens," Eriale replied. "Which way is the root cellar?"

Kerrick shook his head. "You'd think they'd take some time to show the new hands around. The root cellar you want is the second door, over there." He stooped and shouldered the cask, heading off for the stairs. "I'd step it up, if I were you," he called. "Nurchen'll have you scrubbing pots until your hands bleed if he thinks you dawdled down here."

"Thanks, we'll get right to it," Aeron replied. He watched until Kerrick trudged out of sight and blew out his breath in relief. "Come on, let's get out of here before we meet anyone else," he said to Eriale. He trotted down the length of the vaulted undercroft, counting the archways until he found another small door and steps leading up. "This goes up into the masters' quarters."

They emerged in the long, light-paneled hallway that ran on the lower floor of the hall. As soon as Aeron stepped out of the door, he found himself standing right in the path of a Master of Necromancy, a cadaverous old man striding along with long, shanky steps. The sorcerer glared at him with cold, dead eyes. Aeron froze in horror—he confronted none other than High Master Eidos, one of Oriseus's old allies. The vulpine eyes narrowed as Eidos scrutinized Aeron.

"What are you gawking at?" he snapped in a harsh voice.

Hurriedly, Aeron sketched a bow. "Pardon me, my lord."

He turned and slunk away, while Eriale silently closed the servant's door and followed. He could feel the weight of Master Eidos's stare between his shoulder blades, but with an angry snort the necromancer dismissed them and returned to his business. When Aeron risked a glance over his shoulder, he saw purple robes rippling like oily water in the wizard's wake, until he turned a corner and vanished.

Eriale set her hand on Aeron's arm. "By Assuran's grace, that was close," she whispered.

"I don't know how he didn't recognize me."

"When he last saw you, you were a student, five years younger." Eriale shrugged. "You've grown and filled out."

They reached the end of the corridor. The glyph marking Telemachon's chambers still guarded the door; Aeron suppressed a smile. Lord Telemachon's chambers had been among the more impressive any Master possessed, and he'd thought that out of nothing more than a desire for extra space someone might have commandeered them. Carefully, he worked a minor magic to pass Telemachon's sigil, remembering the time he'd done the same thing on the eve of Oriseus's initiation to the Shadow Stone. The mark seemed to hum as if alive, then faded as Aeron finished his spell. He frowned in puzzlement.

"What's wrong?" Eriale asked, watching him.

"Telemachon's sign. It vanished when I disarmed it."

"That's not supposed to happen?"

"No, I was only trying to counter it for a moment," Aeron said.

"It's been five years. Maybe the spell's worn away."

He shook his head. "It shouldn't have. But maybe this close to the Shadow Stone, the workings of magic aren't as predictable as they should be."

He set aside his reservations and pushed the door open, drawing Eriale in behind him. To his surprise, Telemachon's room seemed as if it had been left alone as well. From the thick coat of dust that covered the furniture and shelves, Aeron guessed that he might have been the last person to enter.

"No one straightened up in here, either," Eriale observed.

Aeron examined the leaning stacks of books and the cluttered mess of the old High Diviner's desk. "We've been lucky twice in one day. It's too good to be true."

"Why would the Masters leave this room undisturbed?"

"Who knows? Maybe no one wanted to clean up this mess. Or perhaps Oriseus and his allies feared the defensive spells Telemachon wove."

Eriale straightened up from a casual search of the shelves. "You mean this room might be trapped?"

Aeron grimaced. "I should have warned you to move carefully. Telemachon wouldn't use deadly spells unless he really meant to do someone harm, but there are quite a number of nasty surprises that might remain here."

"Greetings, Aeron."

Aeron spun at the sound of the voice. Eriale turned quickly, too, kneeling and stringing her bow in an impossibly fast motion. Behind them, sitting in the chair behind the desk, was Master Telemachon. The wizard looked old and tired, as he always had, with dark bags under his eyes and heavy jowls that quivered as he spoke.

"Telemachon!" gasped Aeron.

The wizard shook his head, holding up his hand. "No. A mere shadow of Telemachon. A message to you from beyond the grave, if you will."

Eriale stood slowly, keeping her arrow trained on the wizard's heart. "Aeron told me you were dead," she said. "What are you? An imposter? A restless ghost?" The gleaming steel arrowpoint never wavered. "Or is this all a deception of some kind?"

Telemachon dismissed her with a weary gesture. "Shoot me if it will make you feel better. But please take care not to damage this fine chair. You see, I am somewhat insubstantial." To illustrate the point, he reached out and passed one hand through a stack of books resting on the corner of his desk.

"You're an illusion," Aeron realized. "A programmed spell,

designed to appear under the right conditions. But how are you able to converse with us? I always thought that such phantasms could only be crafted at the time of the casting."

The spectral mage offered a weak smile. "I developed a certain refinement to that spell, young Aeron. Great mages are fond of doing such things, you know. But you are essentially correct. I was to appear when you entered this room in the company of someone named Eriale."

"Five years ago, you saw that this moment would come to pass?" Aeron asked in disbelief.

"Unless I made a very lucky guess, that would seem to be the case," the phantasm replied. "Remember, I was an archmage and an accomplished diviner."

Now that he'd had a chance to study it, Aeron could see that it was indeed a spectral image, shimmering with a faint light and somewhat translucent. No sounds accompanied its movements or gestures, just the tired voice of Telemachon responding to his statements and questions.

"You knew that Oriseus was going to kill you," Aeron said slowly.

The specter nodded. "That, too, I saw."

In the corner of his eye, he saw Eriale relax her stance and lower her bow. "Then why didn't you flee or decline to face him?" she asked. "How could you walk into your own death with your eyes open?"

"I had to," the image replied. "You see, if I hadn't confronted Oriseus when I did and in just the fashion I chose, Aeron would have been lost."

"Lost? What do you mean?" Aeron asked.

"You would have touched the Shadow Stone only to be consumed by it, as were the others," the specter stated bluntly. "And there would be no one today who might have a chance to undo the evil that Oriseus has wrought."

"So why didn't you warn me yourself, before your death? And then avoid the confrontation with Oriseus?" Aeron glanced at Eriale, but she only returned a blank look.

The illusionary wizard shrugged. "It was necessary to keep you in ignorance in order for you to continue your studies under Oriseus's tutelage. As events developed, you were cautious, suspicious of Oriseus's intentions. But you were not too cautious. It was necessary for you to stand before the Shadow Stone, and that you would never have done if you feared Oriseus too much." The specter seemed to sigh and offered a wry smile, an amazingly lifelike expression. "It was a fine line to walk, indeed."

Aeron sat down heavily on an empty stool, still stunned by the illusion's revelations. "I cannot believe it," he said. "You sacrificed your life merely to ensure that I would escape the Shadow Stone's influence?"

The eyes of the spectral Telemachon hardened. "No. I gave up my life because it was necessary in order to preserve all of Chessenta from a blight, a curse, of unspeakable evil. You, Aeron Morieth, are the only instrument by which that curse may be undone."

"How? What can I do?" Aeron asked.

"Destroy the stone," the image replied. "It's the source of power for Oriseus's spell. You do not have the strength or the skill to interfere with the great magic that Oriseus has worked—no one does—but the weak link in the chain is the stone. For all its mystical might, it is nothing more than a common rock, altered in appearance by the unthinkable power it contains."

"I know a few spells that might suffice," Aeron said. "The lightning-spell might do it. Or a spell of breaking."

"Neither will be of use to you. Any magic that you cast at the Shadow Stone will be absorbed by it, tainted. You can't drown a river, Aeron."

"Then how am I supposed to destroy this thing? With a sledgehammer?"

"Nor can you risk touching it, Aeron. If you come into contact with the Stone, it will absorb and corrupt your very spirit, just as it affected the others who fell to its influence five years ago."

Eriale spoke. "That doesn't leave many options."

"I could contrive some kind of physical blow," Aeron mused. "Drop a heavy rock on the stone from a great height, something like that, perhaps. It seems like a crude answer to the challenge, though."

"My time is running short," the phantasm said. Already it was growing fainter as the magical energy that had been stored for years depleted itself. "Aeron, I suspect that the stone would survive any common attempt to break it through physical force. Put it to the test, but I feel this to be true. Perhaps there is a way to turn its own power against it . . . "

The phantasm continued to fade. "Wait!" cried Aeron. "How could I do that, if I can't use my magic against it?

What do I do next?"

"I saw that you would have a chance," the image whispered, now nothing more than a white blur of light.

"Did you see if Aeron succeeds?" Eriale asked. "Or what steps he takes?"

"No," the voice said. "I could not see the Shadow Stone itself. It defeats divinations . . ." With a last glimmer of light, the image faded away completely, leaving nothing but an empty chair. The room felt empty and abandoned now, as if some watchful presence had left forever.

Eriale relaxed her guard, looking to Aeron. "He's gone."

Aeron nodded, his mind racing with possibilities. "What could he mean by turning its own power against it? How could you do that?" Scowling, he sank down into the dusty chair behind the desk.

* * * * *

They waited until well after dusk before leaving Telemachon's old chambers. Again, they slipped through the Masters' Hall without any trouble; Aeron had come to the conclusion that many of the wizards and students were not present in the college halls. Some might have been away on missions similar to the one that had sent Master Crow to Maerchlin, while others might have been on the march with Cimbar's armies. Aeron didn't think it wise to attempt to find out, not for the sake of assuaging his curiosity.

They circled back to the wall they'd scaled to get inside the college, where Baillegh was waiting faithfully. After a hurried change into their traveling clothes, Aeron led Eriale to the edge of the grounds, staying away from the buildings. As night fell, the cloying mists and rain grew heavier, precipitated by the cold waters of the harbor and the nearby sea. It made for a cloak of dense fog that restricted visibility to a dozen yards or less and deadened all sound. Aeron could have marched a company of troops around the college without being spotted under the current conditions.

Ahead of them, the dark shape of the new pyramid loomed up through the mists, disappearing into the blank vapors overhead. Aeron circled the site once, picking his way through worksheds and tumbled piles of stones to be shaped and cut. He kept a close eye on Baillegh; the hound's senses were far keener than his own, and she'd smell danger before he saw anything. The few workmen who'd been here earlier in the day were long gone, and Aeron was surprised by how lonely the place felt even at the same time that it threatened him.

"Something feels wrong here," Eriale said quietly.

"You're right," said Aeron. "The Weave, the magic that exists in all things, is wrong here. Poisoned."

"Let's do what we have to and get out of here."

"I hope it's that easy," Aeron said. He paced the ground where the stone slab he'd first entered the shadow-plane through had stood. It was not there anymore, which he did not find too surprising. With the amount of work Oriseus was doing here, the stone marker was only in the way. "I'm going to have to cast a spell to carry us into the shadow-realm. The door we used before isn't here anymore."

"Will that be difficult?"

He snorted. "The barrier between the worlds is so thin here you could stumble and fall into the plane of shadow. Ready your bow, and keep those special arrows I gave you close at hand. You may need them."

Turning away from the tower, Aeron closed his eyes and paced forward, guessing at the best place to work his spell. The next world was very close here, seeming to strain at the shape and substance of the reality around him, a cancer waiting to be unleashed. If he wanted to, he could blast a rift open that would catapult everything within hundreds of yards into the demiplane of shadow . . . but that was not likely to do anything more than annoy Oriseus and his cronies. Clearly, they were quite experienced with the twilight world. With a deep breath, he unlocked the spell-symbol that parted the veil between worlds. It was an enchantment that required the strength of shadow-magic, and there was no shortage of that nearby. In fact, it took all of Aeron's concentration not to allow the spell to slip away from him.

A rippling wave appeared in the mist, much like the heat-shimmer that rose from a hot stone in the summertime, except that it felt cold, wrong. Aeron bared his teeth in revulsion at the chill touch of the shadow-Weave but endured until he'd forced the tear into something the size and shape of a door.

"Follow me," he said, and he stepped through to the other side.

Physically, the ethereal mists of the shadow-plane were much the same as the last time he'd been here. Everything seems the same, he thought. The pyramid still stands whole and intact, as before, the city isn't here, the cold and the darkness are what I expected. Above the great jagged silhouette of the obelisk, the stars flickered weakly, dim and faint, with great wide gaps of utter blackness between them.

Magically, things had changed. As Aeron turned slowly to ascertain his exact location, he was conscious of a buzzing in his ears, a crawling sensation in his flesh, a shimmering or rippling in his vision. He blinked his eyes and shivered, wondering if this was some aftereffect of the transition from the real to the unreal world. Then, slowly, the truth dawned on him. The pyramid is the only thing that is real here, he realized. Viewed from the other side, the structure was filled with menace and purpose, a dark potential locked in stone. Here, that menace was conscious and active. Streamers of bright, sparkling magic danced in the air or flowed over the ground, drawn to the tower and spiraling around its black walls like a maelstrom. Everything—not just the dead grass or the rolling landscape, the physical fabric upon which they existed—was bending toward the Shadow Stone. Yet as Aeron staggered under the draw of the nearby locus, he had the curious sensation that something was close to pulling his very soul out by the roots.

Beside him, the ripples intensified as Eriale and Baillegh bounded through. The hound crouched and whined, hiding her head as she splayed her feet, trying to keep her balance. Eriale reeled awkwardly to one knee, her mouth gaping open in horror as she grappled with her surroundings.

"Aeron!" she cried. "What is happening? What is this?"

He staggered over to her and caught her arm. "It's worse than I thought!" he shouted, barely able to make himself heard. "I shouldn't have brought you here!"

Eriale looked up into his face, her eyes wide with fear. "Where's the stone?"

"In the center of the pyramid's foundation. Come on." He turned and led her to the dark, gaping arch that marked the only entrance to the structure.

"Surely, Aeron, you can't be in that much of a hurry to rush to your doom." Before them, stepping out of the doorway, stood Dalrioc Corynian. Unlike Sarim, he hadn't changed much. There was a feral gleam in his eyes, but his noble features and proud bearing still marked him as a man of power and influence. He wore the red robes of a Master of Conjuration over the exquisitely tailored finery he'd always preferred. "You should have been more careful in making your entrance to Telemachon's chambers. I've had a mark on that door of my own for years now, just in case someone decided to poke around in there."

"Dalrioc," spat Aeron. "I'm surprised you're still here. I would have thought that your city had need of you."

"And I'm surprised you came back. Master Sarim was to see to it that you remained in your forest fastness." Dalrioc stepped out of the doorway, an arrogant smile on his face. "What brings you back to our college, Aeron? Still thirsty for knowledge after all these years?"

"What do we do, Aeron?" Eriale asked quietly. She had an arrow aimed at Dalrioc's heart. By her side, Baillegh bared her teeth, growling.

"We have to get by him," he replied softly. To the prince he said, "Dalrioc, stand aside. I mean to bring this to an end. You have no idea what harm you are wreaking."

"On the contrary, I know exactly what our work entails." The Soorenaran halted two paces from Aeron and extended an arm toward the pyramid, a gesture of invitation. "Come and see. I'll not gainsay the Storm Walker."

Aeron was certain that the prince harbored no good intentions toward him. Everything was wrong—the confidence, the mocking refusal to confront him, the revelation that he'd been watched. Dalrioc Corynian was not this subtle . . . but Lord Oriseus was. He would have to assume that events were orchestrated to suit the new Sceptanar's desires.

"Walk ahead of me, then," Aeron said, scowling. "I don't trust you at my back. And do not attempt any spell, or we'll see whether your sarcasm is justified or not."

Dalrioc laughed. "Fine. Where am I taking you?"

"Where do you think?" Aeron retorted. "To the Shadow Stone."

Eighteen

All around Aeron, the stones of the pyramid reverberated with power, mere chords responding to the presence of something beyond his knowledge or experience. As he followed Dalrioc Corynian through the labyrinthine corridors of dark, featureless masonry, he realized that in five years the Shadow Stone's dire potency had been sharpened, honed into a weapon of unearthly capacity, imbued with purpose and malice. At even intervals, the coursing energy caused everything around him to ripple and slide like the coarse fabric of a shirt wrapped around the torso of a giant, stretching and slacking to the titanic heartbeat. It took all of his determination to ignore the sickening sensation and drive himself to follow.

Eriale stayed an arm's length behind him, watching the blank passageways behind them. Beads of sweat trickled down her face despite the clammy chill in the air; she too had to steel herself against the structure's influence.

"Aeron," she said quietly, "What are we doing?"

Ahead of them, Dalrioc strode along, oblivious to the enemies at his back. Either he was supremely foolish, or utterly confident, and Aeron was fairly certain that Dalrioc, while arrogant and overbearing, was not a complete fool. "Let's see how this plays out," he decided.

Dalrioc led them down one last corridor and stopped at a large, heavy door. Aeron had the curious impression that he'd burn his hand if he touched the bare iron plating. The Soorenaran prince turned, leaning against the wall, his arms folded. "Well? Here we are," he said. "What now?"

"Open it," Aeron instructed.

The prince's eyes flashed, but he forced a wry grin onto his features. "And so I am reduced to holding doors for peasants." As if they weren't there, he caught the latch and pushed the door wide, leading them inside.

The chamber was much as Aeron remembered it, a room of stone with a groined ceiling and gallery surrounding a crucible-like floor. The Shadow Stone stood girdled by its iron frame, a sliver of living darkness that made his eyes ache. Fierce black radiance pulsated in the gem's gleaming jet facets, illuminating the room with a hellish glow. Instantly Aeron was embroiled in a struggle to maintain his distance as the sinister artifact seemed to focus his energy on him, demanding that he approach and abase himself. His hand stretched forward, almost of its own accord.

Aeron swore silently and wrenched his gaze away from the thing. He'd forgotten the sheer allure of the power, the half-imagined whispering and beckoning, urging him to become a part of it. It was stronger now than it ever had been, but he found the will to resist. He'd tasted its power once, just for an instant, and it had poisoned him. Now it could not possess him, not unless he allowed it to.

He was distracted by a motion at his side. Eriale drifted forward, her face blank. "Don't look right at it, Eriale," he snapped, pulling her arm sharply to break her stupor. The archer blinked and shook her head.

Ahead of him, Dalrioc moved forward and stood over the tripod, reaching out to caress the smooth surface like the face of a lover. The stone acknowledged him, a trail of phosphorescence following the path of his hand. "I brought him, as you asked," he said over his shoulder.

"Excellent." The flickering shadows of the gallery roiled like silk, and a tall man stepped through. He wore archaic black robes and a drape or chasuble of rune-marked cloth of gold, and he carried a long rod of jet and silver only a foot shorter than his own considerable height. The garments seemed familiar to Aeron, and after a moment he placed them—the ceremonial dress of the ancient Imaskari sorcerers. He shifted his attention to the man's face, but it was hidden by the ornate cowl he wore. "You may leave us, Dalrioc," the man said evenly, his voice flat and reasonable.

The Soorenaran prince spread his hands in a shallow bow and withdrew, stepping into the impenetrable shadows that waited in the arched gallery. Again Aeron sensed some rippling motion in the darkness, a disturbance. "You have changed, Aeron," said the robed man. "When last I saw you, the fire for knowledge burned fiercely in your heart, and nothing could deter you from the pursuit of power."

"I've learned patience, Oriseus," Aeron said. "That's a lesson you taught me, whether you meant to or not."

The sorcerer raised his hands and pushed back his hood. If Aeron had not already known whom he was dealing with, he never would have mistaken him for Oriseus. The trimmed beard and oiled locks were shaved down to gleaming scalp and a bare, angular jaw. Even more startling than Oriseus's change in grooming was the severity of his bearing, the way he carried himself. The capering, self-deprecating exaggeration was gone, replaced by a regal aura. The old Oriseus had disarmed his foes with insincerity and biting humor; this man radiated confidence and capability.

"Timidity is not wisdom, Aeron. And indolence is not patience. While you have slept in your forest retreat, the world has passed you by."

"I see you haven't wasted the past five years," Aeron remarked. "What is the point, Oriseus? Do you know what you are doing to the world outside the college walls?"

The sorcerer's mouth twisted in a slight smile. "I should think the point of this is obvious. Through the Shadow Stone, I shall soon control magic."

"Your own command of the arts is insufficient?"

"You misunderstand me, Aeron. I shall control all magic. I am forging a conduit, a reservoir, into which the Weave of all Chessenta—indeed, of this entire world someday—shall flow. My power will be limitless, Aeron. And those who stand by my side shall share in it. We will be gods."

"How long have you worked on this?" Aeron asked quietly. "You must have studied the Shadow Stone for years to master the use of shadow-magic, to wield its power with impunity. When did this begin, and why?"

Oriseus smiled falsely. "I have sought the stone for years beyond your imagination, Aeron. This day is merely the culmination of a hundred lifetimes of work. I've dreamed of this since my people battled the gods of the Untheri on the Plains of Purple Dust, four thousand years ago."

Eriale could not contain her shock. "You are that old?"

"This body? No, not at all. But my mind, my spirit, has remained undiminished since five centuries before the death of Imaskar." Oriseus raised his hands, almost in benediction. "You have the good fortune to witness the culmination of this work, to see history unfold. I will finish what my brothers could not, all those years ago. And I will reclaim the place that was taken from us."

Aeron considered the master's words, fighting to remain

calm. Reconstructing lessons and conversations from years before, his mind reeled in recognition. "You were one of the Imaskari archmages, the first sorcerers," he breathed. "Who are you, really?"

Oriseus laughed aloud. "In the land of my birth, I was once called Madryoch. They named me the Ebon Flame."

"And you've survived all this time."

"My essence did, trapped in the existence you know as the plane of shadow. I spent centuries wandering this barren place, a formless wraith, powerless and empty. Only through the force of my will did my intellect survive.

"Over the years, I occasionally encountered living travelers, drawn to them by their life, their vitality. Some I destroyed, ignorant of my new powers. Others I learned from, slowly mastering the art of claiming a life for my own by forcing my spirit, my will, into the body of another. The sorcerer known as Oriseus came to the Shadow seeking power almost ten years ago now. Instead, he found me." The ancient wizard smiled severely. "This is the key to immortality, Aeron. I shall teach you how to live forever, if you will join me."

"I don't want that," Aeron said. There'd been a time when he was willing to pay any price for knowledge, for the power to defeat those who threatened him, to teach them fear. That time was long past. "No, I'll take the life that's dealt to me."

"Consider carefully, Aeron," Oriseus said, a hint of warning in his voice. "Despite your failure five years ago, despite the fact that you came here to upset a design I have worked on for four millennia, I bear you no malice. You are intelligent and insightful, quick to grasp and wield power. It is your nature. I can use someone of your talents by my side. Wizards of your potential are hard to find."

Sarim had been intelligent, confident, and strong of will, Aeron thought. But the stone devoured him anyway. He paced around the perimeter of the room, keeping his gaze on Oriseus and the stone before him. The rune-marked iron that banded the relic's waist seemed important, as if it contained or focused the artifact's power. Telemachon had said that he could not direct any magic at the stone, since it would be absorbed, but maybe the frame was a vulnerability?

Oriseus watched him as he took the measure of the chamber and its enchantments, an amused smile on his face. "Admiring my handiwork?" he asked in a sharp tone.

"Every object, every creature in this world creates magic," Aeron remarked. "The Weave is a great river, fed by innumerable streams and tributaries. But this stone seems to consume magic instead of create it. It absorbs magic, twists it into something else. Has it always been like this?"

It didn't seem likely that he could get Oriseus to show him how the spell might be undone, but it couldn't hurt to keep him talking. The longer Aeron studied the Shadow Stone and the complex enchantments that buffered the chamber, the more likely it was that he'd see something he could use.

"That was the secret of the Imaskari strength," Oriseus said. "In the beginning of things, the world was made from nothingness, an act of will and purpose. Magic, as you call it, is the echo of this purpose. But this purpose is not unopposed, Aeron. It is, in a sense, an abrogation of something older than creation, an accident of sorts. We live in a single bright flicker of existence, framed by oblivion before and after. That oblivion presses in on us. To put it another way, in the absence of a conscious purpose to exist, the world begins to not exist. This can be harnessed by an adept of strength and skill."

Aeron realized that Oriseus believed that he posed no threat at all. Some vestige of the intellectual conjuror remained in this hollow shell of a man, a master architect who greatly desired his work to be appreciated. "When I encountered this five years ago, I called it shadow-magic. I found that it existed in everything, just as the Weave itself flowed through the natural world and the living hearts of animals and men." Aeron turned a hard stare at Oriseus. "I read how you and your peers found a way to transcend the human limitation against making use of this power, binding evil spirits to your very souls in order to perceive and wield shadow-magic. Is that what you've done to Dalrioc, Sarim, and the others?"

"Not quite. The Shadow Stone changed that. It opened their eyes to the existence of the shadow-magic, just as it opened yours." Oriseus made a dismissive gesture with one hand. "They're fortunate. The compact with which I gained the ability to wield magic came at a much higher price."

Aeron finished his circuit of the room. He glanced at Eriale, who watched him with a pale face. She held an

arrow across her bow, but pointed it at the ground—
although Aeron knew she could aim and release the missile
in the blink of an eye. He could read the unspoken question
in her eyes as she flicked her glance toward the tall sorcerer standing before him. He offered the slightest shake of his
head as he turned back to Oriseus; he was certain that the
sorcerer would have taken steps to defend himself. Then, to
Aeron's surprise, Eriale stepped forward.

"So you intend to rule the world by ruining it," she said.
"Don't you realize that the world you're making won't be
worth ruling? It's pointless, insane. What will be left?"

"What will be left?" Oriseus repeated. "Why, my dear girl,
whatever that I decree shall be left. I shall hold the magic
of the world in my right fist, and with my left I shall mold
the world into whatever shape I fancy."

"What gives you the right?" she demanded.

Oriseus's eyes flashed. "Nothing *gives* me the right,
woman. I claim it. I was the First of the Imaskari, the Ebon
Flame. My name struck terror in the hearts of our enemies.
At my brothers' side I drove all before me and dragged your
barbaric forebears to this world to be our slaves. For forty
centuries I have been denied the prize I sought. Now I take
it with my own hand!" He raised his hand to cast a spell,
and even as Aeron reacted with a counterspell to protect
Eriale, Oriseus spat out a word of magical power.

Overhead, a great lambent cyclone of magical energy
became visible, trapped and altered by the Shadow Stone's
power. "All the Weave for hundreds of miles around flows to
this point," Oriseus said. "With each heartbeat, the Shadow
Stone takes an ever-growing portion of the world's magic
and makes it mine to command!" He batted away Aeron's
barrier as if it did not exist.

Aeron gambled on distracting the conjuror. "So why did
you seek the Sceptanar's throne and involve yourself in the
conflict between Cimbar and Akanax? Those are secondary
goals. This is the only matter of importance."

Oriseus halted, allowing the magical energy he'd gathered
in his hands to dissipate unused. "As you might imagine,
there are those who would not wish to see me complete my
work here. The Sceptanar was one of them, an old and weak
fool who commanded the misguided allegiance of this powerful city. I needed to make sure that he would not interfere.
As for the war with Akanax . . . it is a shield for me, a cloak

to distract any who would oppose me." He allowed a sly smile to spread across his face. "To be perfectly honest, it doesn't matter to me who calls himself the Over-king of Chessenta. Within a day, perhaps two, this spell will be complete. And all of the Old Empires will be mine to rule as I please. I may even allow petty kings such as Dalrioc's father to govern their cities and launch the great wars of conquest and expansion they dream of. It will be of no more consequence than the affairs of insects at my feet."

"And Prince Dalrioc accepts this?"

"He knows where the true power is," Oriseus replied. "As do you, Aeron. Will you stand by my side? You have come to master both the bright and the dark magic, guided by nothing more than your own skill and strength of will—quite a rare feat. You have nothing to fear in accepting my offer, and the world to gain."

"Master Crow made the same offer," Aeron observed. "He tried to kill me when I refused his bargain. Why do you need my help? It seems that you're satisfied with events."

"I don't need your help, Aeron. I merely extend you the opportunity to join the winning side. You could be very useful to me, and I have not forgotten our friendship."

"Crow also hinted that there was a far less pleasant way for me to be of use to you."

"That is true, Aeron. I won't bore you with the details." Oriseus stepped closer, his benevolence vanishing. "You really have only one alternative. Swear you'll serve me. You and your friend shall weather the coming storm unscathed, and stand at my right hand in the world to come."

Is there any way to play along, to deceive him? Aeron wondered. Then his eye fell on the Shadow Stone, its radiance forming a black halo behind Oriseus's form. No, he decided. I barely survived the last time I was here. Acceding to Oriseus's demand might preserve my life, but I'd be dead and lost. Steeling himself, he readied his staff. "I can't do that, Oriseus. If it lies within my power, I mean to put a stop to this."

"Trust me, Aeron. It doesn't." Oriseus made a small gesture, and Dalrioc Corynian emerged from the shadows that flickered in the chamber's periphery, followed by other masters: Eidos, the Lord Necromancer; a stout woman Aeron recognized as a former student of illusions; a stooped, sickly Mulhorandi who was once a Master of

Abjuration. Aeron realized that the shadows that danced and undulated under each stone arch were portals, doorways back to the real world. "Join us. You have no choice."

Aeron glanced at Eriale. "Get out of here," he said.

The archer shook her head. "Not without you."

"Well, Aeron? I won't repeat my offer," Oriseus said. His smile faded. "You'll help me, one way or another."

With a roar of defiance, Aeron dashed forward and swung his staff at the iron stand supporting the Shadow Stone, invoking its power. The spell failed with a flash of blue light and a stink of ozone, but the impact toppled the tripod and sent the stone crashing to the floor. "No!" shrieked Oriseus. "Dalrioc! Eidos! Subdue him!"

Aeron danced back, half expecting the gem to shatter like glass, but it struck the ground and rattled away, unharmed. Several of the mages hesitated. He used the reprieve to hurl a battery of glowing missiles at each wizard in Oriseus's circle. Dalrioc and the illusionist failed to parry the missiles; with booming thunderclaps they detonated, hammering them with brutal force. The illusionist's outstretched hand was incinerated by Aeron's spell, and she collapsed screaming. Dalrioc grunted and somehow kept his feet.

In the center of the room, Oriseus ignored Aeron's attack. It seemed to almost splash against an unseen shield, vanishing with nothing more than a brief sparkle of light. "You fool," he hissed. Crouching, the ancient warlock shouted a word of power that blasted Aeron to his knees, leaving him deaf and stunned, blood flowing from his ears and nose.

Behind him, Eriale whirled and loosed an arrow at the old High Necromancer as Eidos worked at a spell of holding. With a curse, the vulpine sorcerer abandoned his enchantment and raised a defensive ward. His wattled hands flickered in a spell of defense that would have deflected any mundane threat, but Eriale's arrow carried a powerful elven enchantment. The shaft sank into Master Eidos's heart, crumpling him like brittle paper.

Eriale nocked a second arrow, but a green ray sizzled across the chamber as the Mulhorandi abjurer whispered a spell of fatigue. The archer's muscles turned to water and she sank to the floor. With all her effort, she drew her bow to half its length and managed to stick an arrow two inches into the abjurer's knee before the spell overcame her. The emaciated sorcerer howled and hopped back, one hand clamped over the arrow.

Aeron staggered to his feet and started to work a spell, but Oriseus brushed his effort aside and lashed out with a crackling black ray that shattered Fineghal's staff in his hands, scorching him badly. With a gasp of shock, Aeron reeled backward. Relentlessly, Oriseus declaimed another spell, this one a binding that created a gossamer web of razor-sharp strands. The bone-white threads sprayed from his fingertips, winding around Aeron and sinking into his flesh until blood flowed freely from a dozen wounds. With one last word, Oriseus jerked his hand back, dropping Aeron heavily to the stone floor.

"A valiant effort, Aeron. How I wish you'd reconsidered my offer; mages of your caliber are hard to find." The sorcerer straightened and snapped his fingers. Several gray-faced soldiers in the livery of the Sceptanar's Guard appeared from another of the dark archways, moving with a blank, mechanical torpor. "Take him to his place," Oriseus ordered them.

"What of the girl?" Dalrioc asked. He cradled one damaged arm, and a wide trickle of blood marked one side of his head.

Oriseus turned and looked her over with a cold smile. "We can always use another archer," he remarked. "Leave her here with me."

* * * * *

Dalrioc Corynian and the silent soldiers dragged Aeron into one of the shadow portals framing the room, emerging in a cold maze of stone walls. To his surprise, it was open to the sky, and a lurid red overcast seemed to twist and churn sluggishly above him. We're not in the tower anymore, Aeron realized. After a moment, he amended that thought. We're not even in Cimbar anymore! Despite the change in his surroundings, he was still conscious of the ever-present chill of the shadow-plane and the jarring sense of wrongness that grated on his nerves until his head ached and nausea rose in his stomach.

"You can't imagine how long I've dreamed about this moment, Aeron," Dalrioc said smugly as he led the way. "I don't know what Oriseus ever saw in you, but I've known for years that this day would come."

They passed an alcove, where Dalrioc instructed the soldiers to halt and turn Aeron to see inside. In the shallow depression, a strange statue or relief seemed graven on the stone wall. It was the size and shape of a man, a carving of immaculate detail. Its wrists and ankles were encircled with old iron chains that were anchored in the flanking walls and sunk into the stone. Aeron peered closer, detecting something familiar in the statue's face and stance. It seemed an excellent likeness of Baldon, his former hallmate. The cold eyes stared sightlessly into the sky, and a grimace of inhuman pain was captured on the carving's face.

"This will be your fate, Aeron," Dalrioc hissed into his ear, relishing Aeron's helplessness. "Baldon is still alive, of course. We need his power, his will, to channel magic to the pyramid. But I wouldn't care to trade places with him." He indicated the dark passageway ahead. "Bring him this way."

The soldiers complied. They turned a corner and carried Aeron to a blank alcove, with iron chains waiting.

"Bind him," Dalrioc commanded.

Although Aeron attempted to struggle, he only cut his hands and face with his effort. The dead soldiers made no sound or protest as the gauzy strands covering Aeron slashed their hands and arms as well . . . nor did they bleed. When they finished, Aeron was suspended on the wall by the chains, unable to move.

Aeron noticed that the stone behind him felt unusually cold, like a great block of ice. In moments he began to shiver, feeling the warmth draining out of his body. He glanced down and saw that the tough strands of razor-gauze that held him were dissipating, vanishing like water as they were absorbed by the wall behind him. In a few heartbeats he was free, but his arms and legs were pinioned by the chains.

"What is this, Dalrioc?" he grunted, struggling against his bonds.

"You should have listened to Oriseus," the prince said. "You might have been a ruler, a lord. Now you are nothing more than a slave, to be wrung dry and thrown away."

"What do you mean?"

Dalrioc laughed, a particularly unpleasant sound. "You're clever. You'll figure it out." Still chuckling, he turned and walked away, trailed by the gray soldiers. "I'll be back in a while to see how your new accommodations suit you."

Aeron squirmed away from the pervasive chill of the wall behind him, panic welling in his heart. Every time he slumped against the stone, he could feel the heat, the warmth, draining from his body, a diabolically slow process. It's taking more than my warmth, he realized after a time. It's absorbing the magical spark of my life-force. He shuddered in fear.

In the silence, he could hear faint sounds, some distant, some near. Chains clanking on stone, voices whispering and moaning, so soft that he could almost mistake it for the sound of the wind. But there was no wind in this place, no light, only a ruddy red glow that colored the blank walls of stone the hue of old blood. He groaned in despair.

"Who's there?"

Aeron looked up. It was a woman's voice, tired and faint. He wondered if he'd imagined it. "Hello?" he called.

"Hello," the woman answered. She was somewhere to his right, down the stone hallway. "Did they shackle you to the wall?"

"Yes. I can't move."

"Are you certain?" she replied. "Your life depends on it."

Aeron craned his neck out to examine his fetters. He tested them against the wall, but he couldn't budge them at all; he'd never been strong of limb. Frowning, he tried to narrow his hands and pull them free, but after a valiant effort he gave up.

"No, I'm chained," he said. "What happens now?"

"You'll die," the woman replied, her voice heavy with resignation. "It may take weeks, even months, but this place will slowly kill you, just like the rest of us."

Aeron listened closely. Beneath the exhaustion, there was a familiarity to her voice, a hint of a burring Reach accent. "Melisanda? Is that you?"

"Who wants to know?"

"It's Aeron, Aeron Morieth."

"Aeron?" It was Melisanda's voice, sadder and somehow more distant than Aeron remembered. He could read a long tale of sorrow and hopelessness in the way her voice cracked and rasped. There was a long silence then, and Aeron strained to hear what she might say. Finally she spoke again. "It's good to hear your voice."

"And yours. Although I wish it were under better circumstances."

Melisanda laughed bitterly. "Indeed. A year or two ago I heard that you'd returned to the Maerchwood. What are you doing here?"

"I tried to put a stop to Oriseus's work. I'm afraid I did not succeed."

"We're all part of his spell, Aeron," Melisanda said. "We hold the pyramid together, and that draws the magic to this place."

"I don't understand."

"Rebuilding the monument is insignificant. It looks impressive, but it means nothing. Magic is drawn to this place because he's enslaved the souls of wizards here."

Aeron leaned back, ignoring the cold. "But we're not in the tower," he replied. "What is this place?"

She hesitated a moment before replying. "It's one point of a ritual diagram, I think. I don't know if you noticed, but this structure is nothing more than an open corridor or hallway. It takes seven turns around its circumference, so there's seven walls. Each of us is chained to one wall."

"I saw Baldon," Aeron said quietly. He thought on Melisanda's words for a time. Seven wizards, chained in a seven-sided figure . . . but they weren't near the tower. "I wager there's six other places like this, all spaced at an equal distance around the Shadow Stone," Aeron said. "Seven times seven wizards, all dying to power Oriseus's spell, focused by the structure he raised at the College of Sorcery. That's the centerpiece."

"How far apart are they?" she wondered aloud.

"Who knows? The shadow doors in the chamber of the stone might be portals to each of these places. A hundred miles? A thousand? We have no way of knowing."

"I think you may be right," Melisanda replied. "Dalrioc told me there were other places like this." She fell silent again for a long time. Aeron made another attempt to extract his wrists from the shackles that held him, giving up in exhaustion. "Aeron? Why is Oriseus doing this? What is this all about?"

"Oriseus is not our concern," Aeron told her. "It's Madryoch." He went on to tell her what Oriseus—or Madryoch—had told him, and what he'd observed of the effects of the ancient sorcerer's spell. He ended up backtracking all the way to the awful night when he'd fled into the Shadow, out of his mind with the loathing and fear engendered by his first encounter with the stone, and recounting the years that had passed since that day.

When he finished, Melisanda described what had befallen her after she'd left the college. She had returned to her home in Arrabar, choosing to study in private, away from the intrigues of Cimbar's college. Just as Aeron had become a formidable mage with years of practice and study, Melisanda had become competent too. She used her talents to help her family defend their lands and keep peace in their home, gaining a reputation as a sorceress not to be crossed.

"How did you end up here?" Aeron asked.

"Dalrioc and a handful of his allies," Melisanda spat. "They lured me into an ambush, sending me an urgent plea for help from one of the merchant lords who lives near my home. He'd always been an ally of our house, so I went to his aid and found them waiting for me instead. Dalrioc tried to convince me to join him in his work, but I wanted no part of it. So they brought me here." Aeron heard her chains clinking as she struggled with them. "Damn it!"

"We'll think of something," he told her.

"I hope so." Melisanda's struggles subsided. There was a soft sob. "Aeron, it's cold."

"I know," he said. He closed his eyes, wishing he could at least see her from where he was trapped. "I know." They waited together in silence for a long time, until he lapsed into a restless, tortured sleep.

* * * * *

Something breathed warm, damp air into his face, rooting at his loose collar with an animal cough. Padded claws pressed into his shoulders as the creature leaned close, its heavy breathing filling his ears, the smell of wet fur cloying in his nostrils. Aeron awoke with an inarticulate moan of panic, struggling wildly, his hands and feet anchored in the stone.

A wet tongue licked his face, and the animal whined softly. Aeron opened his eyes, and caught a glimpse of silver-gray fur and dark, intelligent eyes. "Baillegh!" he cried. The elven hound barked once and nuzzled his face, her tail wagging in delight. "Assuran's shield! Where did you come from?"

"Aeron? What's happening?" Worry strained Melisanda's voice. "Are you all right?"

"Yes, I'm fine," he called back. "I've just been surprised by a friend, though." He looked back to the dog. She seemed thin and weak, as if she'd been lost a long time. Frowning, he tried to recall what had happened to her. *She was with us outside the tower . . . but I don't recall that she followed us inside. Could she have tracked us through the shadow doors? Or did she come cross-country all the way from Cimbar?*

"Aeron?" Melisanda called. "What's going on?"

"Wait a moment," he answered. "I hope I'll be able to show you." He glanced up at the iron band that clasped his right wrist. Dalrioc hadn't welded the band shut; instead, it was a crude ratchetlike device that was secured by a short pin. He couldn't bend his hand back far enough to reach the pin; it was too close to the manacle.

"All right, Baillegh. Let's see if you're as smart as I think you are," he breathed. Staring into the hound's dark eyes, he bent his will to creating a clear image of the hound pulling the locking pin free. She barked once and turned to the shackle, stretching to her full length to reach it. Aeron grimaced as the hound's mouth closed over his wrist, but in a moment Baillegh dropped back with a sharp grunt.

The pin was clenched in her teeth.

Aeron pulled on the manacle, twisting it open and jerking his hand free. Ignoring the stinging abrasion on his wrist, he turned and undid the other manacle, lowering himself to the ground. The shackle that held his left ankle was jammed shut, but with his hands free and his body away from the dark stone wall, he was able to cast a minor alteration that caused the rusty iron to snap open, falling away from his legs. Impulsively, he reached over and hugged Baillegh, ruffling the hound's coat, and then stood and stretched.

"Come on. Let's see if we can help the others," he said to her. The hound licked his hand and followed behind him.

He stepped out of the alcove, turned right, and rounded the odd angle in the corridor. About thirty feet down the wall, Melisanda was pinned in another alcove. She'd been dressed in the layered skirts and blouse of a Chondathan noblewoman, but her dress was in tatters, revealing her white shift beneath. She was pale and thin, a cold and frightened waif, but the old light in her face returned with her smile, as she looked up and saw Aeron standing before her. "I knew they wouldn't keep you chained," she said.

Aeron reached up and undid her bonds, helping her down. He was shocked at how cold her skin felt when his hand brushed hers; she must have waited in this place for a long time. Her knees buckled when she stepped free of the wall, and Aeron barely managed to catch her before she fell. He half-carried her a few feet away, supporting her with his shoulder.

"Careful, now. You're not at your best."

Melisanda nodded and let him help her down the hallway. As she'd told him, it turned right at a sharp angle every fifty feet or so. The first alcove they passed was nothing but blank stone, with the manacles disappearing into the rock as if the hapless soul trapped there had sunk beyond recovery. Despite their best efforts, neither Aeron nor Melisanda could manage to free the wizard entombed within. They found that the rest imprisoned there were in little better shape. Even Baldon was beyond their aid.

"I think the only way to free them is to break or reverse Oriseus's spell," Aeron finally said. "We can't help them now."

"I'm afraid you may be right," Melisanda replied. "Well, what's next?"

"We've got to undo what Oriseus's done," he said slowly. "We have to go back."

"Overland, or do we risk the shadow door?"

"The shadow door's the only way. We might be able to scramble over that wall easily enough, but that leaves us stranded in some unknown place in the demiplane of shadow, without any idea of which way Cimbar might lie." Aeron scratched at his chin. "Yes, I think we have to risk the door that Dalrioc and Oriseus use to come and go."

Melisanda gave him a long look but did not argue. "We'll be walking right into their nest," she said. "Are you ready for a fight?"

He turned his attention inward, mentally cataloging the spells held in his memory. The touch of the wall had drained several spells from his mind, devouring the patterns of word and rune, but most remained intact. "I have enough spells to get us past one or two of Oriseus's minions, but I wouldn't want to take them all on."

"I've a few spells, but I'm struggling to remember them. I think it might take me longer to recover from being chained here." They turned the last corner and stood facing the dark doorway. It was framed against the outer wall by an arch of polished obsidian. "Do you have any idea what we can do if we do go back?"

"No. But I think I know where we might find out."

"The library?"

"If there's any help to be had, we'll find it there," Aeron said. He was going to continue, when suddenly Baillegh barked in warning. He wheeled, facing the shadow door.

It seemed to ripple and flow, like oil on water, and then Dalrioc Corynian stepped into the hallway. The prince halted in mid-stride, open amazement on his face. "How did you get free?" he snarled, raising his hands to hurl a spell.

"Dalrioc!" cried Aeron.

He shouted a dire word, unleashing one of the swiftest spells he knew. The force of his cry was amplified a hundredfold by the magic of the spell, striking Dalrioc like a physical blow and cracking the stone archway behind him. Caught in the middle of his spell, the prince fell heavily to the stone, ruining his enchantment. Aeron slumped against the wall, gasping for breath; the word of power was a taxing spell, and he'd been forced to draw upon his own life-force to power it.

Dalrioc shook his head groggily, blood trickling from his ears. Instead of rising, the prince rolled to his knees, snatched a short iron scepter from his belt, and shouted a trigger word. A white ray of intense cold sprang from the scepter, grazing Aeron's hip and burning like fire. Dalrioc swung the beam at Melisanda and caught her across the knees, sending her to the ground with a cry of pain, and then pointed it directly at Baillegh as the hound sprung at him. She crumpled in mid-spring without a sound, crashing to the ground.

"You'll wish you'd stayed where I left you," Dalrioc snapped.

Aeron replied by slapping one hand on the frozen stone and creating a thunderous crack that raced toward Dalrioc and dropped the floor from under him. With a grinding of torn rock, the prince slid feet-first into the crevasse, disappearing from sight. Quick as he could, Aeron released the spell, allowing the wound in the stone to grind shut—but Dalrioc suddenly leaped free, soaring into the air with a simple jumping spell and alighting on the wall top. His fine tunic was torn and bloody, but he seemed unhurt.

"You'll have to do better than that," he shouted, raising the iron scepter again. Its tip gleamed white with frost.

Melisanda pronounced a liquid string of words and gestured, pulling the iron scepter from Dalrioc's hand with a sharp wrench. The magical weapon arced high into the air and clattered to the ground a short way down the hall. Dalrioc cursed and started another spell, a dire enchantment that sent chills down Aeron's spine. Aeron began a spell of his own, but Dalrioc finished first this time, reaching out with his hand as if to crush Aeron's heart. Cold, strong fingers sank into his chest, ripping away his breath.

"Do you like my new spell, Aeron?" Dalrioc called. "You're not the only one who learned a few tricks over the past five years."

Melisanda started to call out another enchantment, but her voice faltered—she hadn't yet recovered from her long bondage, and the magic she sought was too difficult for her.

Aeron choked back a scream as he struggled, impaled on the intangible talons of Dalrioc's spell. He couldn't begin to develop any kind of counterspell, not while his mind was filled with the icy pain that shredded his chest. With a fierce effort of will, he pushed the pain to a distant part of his awareness and spoke a simple fetching spell. Down the hall, Dalrioc's iron scepter clattered across the floor and then flew up to Aeron's hand. In one smooth motion, he raised the weapon and barked out the word he'd heard Dalrioc use to trigger its powers.

The white beam of frost erupted from the rod's end, striking Dalrioc full in the torso. The Soorenaran wizard doubled over as his skin paled and gleaming ice coated his body. He teetered for a moment on the wall top before he lost his balance and fell awkwardly to the ground. Aeron sobbed in relief as the icy claw released his heart and faded, leaving a deep, cold ache in the center of his body.

Melisanda approached Dalrioc cautiously, ready to strike with a spell if necessary. The prince lay motionless on the ground. She turned him over carefully and stood a moment later, a fierce look on her face. "The frost or the fall killed him," she said.

Aeron nodded in acknowledgment and knelt by Baillegh. The hound stirred slowly. In a moment she shook herself and scrambled to her feet, moving gingerly. Aeron reached out to stroke her fur, ignoring the frost that covered her.

"Thanks, Baillegh. I'm sorry he hurt you." He looked to where Dalrioc sprawled on the ground. "He was never that strong back at the college," he said.

"It must be the Shadow Stone," Melisanda replied.

Aeron thought of Oriseus, waiting somewhere on the other side of the shadow door. "What do you suppose it can do for an archmage?" he asked bitterly. The effort of speaking brought a coarse, bloody cough to his tortured chest. He pushed himself to his feet. "Come on. We have to settle this."

Melisanda closed her eyes and nodded. "You're right. Lead the way, Aeron."

He studied the shadow door for a long moment, wondering if there was any way to find out what lay beyond. Well, there's always one way, he thought. Steeling himself, he squared his shoulders and stepped into the darkness.

Nineteen

Aeron emerged from the shadow door with Dalrioc's scepter held at the ready, but to his relief the chamber of the Shadow Stone was empty. The hateful artifact flickered and pulsated, illuminating the room with its eerie lambent glow. Keeping a wary eye on the umber archways ringing the vault, Aeron advanced to confront the stone.

Behind him, the shadows rippled once more, and Melisanda and Baillegh entered. The Vilhonese wizardess stood beside Aeron, gazing at the Stone. "I hate that thing," she whispered. "Can't you feel the way it pulls at you?"

"I came very close to succumbing to it the first time Oriseus led me to this room," Aeron said. "I had to draw on some of its power, its shadow-magic, to escape, and I've been marked by it ever since. It frightens me, too."

"Can you think of a way to destroy it?"

"I tried to attack the iron bands that frame it, but my spell failed. The stone absorbs magic, and even my most destructive enchantment simply drained away." Aeron crouched down, studying the inscription on the metal frame. "Telemachon told me that physical destruction was unlikely to prove effective, either. The moment I touch the stone, it will have me."

"So we can't destroy it by magic, and we can't destroy it by physical means," Melisanda said. "What does that leave?"

"I may have an idea," Aeron said. "Keep watch for a moment while I make a copy of this inscription." From a pouch at his side he produced a sheet of parchment and a quill pen. Carefully, he recorded the pattern of runes. It was not a lengthy inscription, probably no more than thirty or so words. "I'm done," he announced.

"What do you hope to do with that?" Melisanda asked.

"I think that the frame is the stone's vulnerability. If I can figure out what the inscription says, I'll have an idea of the purpose of the iron bands. And that might suggest a means to attack them."

The Vilhonese sorceress studied the dark archways lining

the chamber. "Which of these leads back to the college, I wonder?" She turned in a slow circle, examining each. "I count ten portals, including the one we just stepped out of."

"I'd guess that six of the nine that are left would transport us to other shrines," Aeron mused. "I suppose we'll have to take our chances. It stands to reason that Oriseus would build at least one portal from the college to this place, for convenience if nothing else." Rooting through the pouch at his hip, he found a small piece of chalk and stepped over to the umber archway they'd emerged from. He made a small mark on the floor to identify it, and moved to face the next portal to the left. "Ready?"

Holding Dalrioc's scepter at the ready, Aeron stepped through. His stomach dropped away alarmingly, and he found himself standing in a stone shrine much like the one he'd just left. At first he thought that he'd made a mistake and returned to the place where he'd been imprisoned, but this one was subtly different; there was a reddish hue to the rock, and as he glanced above the walls at the horizon beyond, Aeron thought he could see dark treetops.

"Same arrangement, different place," Melisanda observed. "Should we try to help the mages caught here?"

Aeron hesitated. "Time may be crucial, but it wouldn't hurt to have an ally. Let's see if anyone here is able to help us." They circled the seven-sided structure, but all the mages there were trapped in the stone.

"Maybe we'll have better luck on the next one." Aeron plunged into the darkness again, and found himself back in the chamber of the Shadow Stone. The sinister light hurt his eyes, and he could almost hear a high-pitched whining or vibration that seemed to resonate in his bones. Gritting his teeth against the sound, he marked that door too and moved on to the next. "Let's try it again," he said, pushing into the dense web of gloom.

This time, Aeron found himself standing on a windswept hilltop by a vast white-frothed lake. The waves thundered and crashed below him, and he could taste rain in the air. "Where in Faerûn—?" he began, quickly turning about to see what else was near.

The hill overlooked a great city about a mile away, barely visible through the fog and murk. Fires burned here and there within its walls, and a powerful fortress watched over the city like a brooding giant. They weren't in the

Shadow any longer; the unnatural chill and sense of wrongness that pervaded the other plane were absent.

Melisanda stepped out of thin air behind him, followed by Baillegh. A large slab of stone marked with a string of Madryoch's old runes served as the base for the portal, and Aeron recognized it as the same stone through which he'd first entered the plane of shadow. Apparently, Oriseus had moved it and modified it to create its portal as needed.

"What is this place, Aeron?" Melisanda asked.

"I'm not sure." As he studied his surroundings, he realized that the city below them was under siege by a huge army. Angled trenches encircled its walls in ring after ring, and crude war engines sat in revetments beyond the siege lines. The army's camp lay in between the hilltop and the city, a sprawling sea of dirty tents and muddy lanes. One large pavilion caught Aeron's eye; it was marked by a crimson dragon standard, the banner of House Corynian. "Wait, I think I know. This is where Soorenar's army must be. That's the standard of Dalrioc's father."

"I've seen the city," Melisanda added. "That's Akanax itself."

"So Oriseus has a way to keep an eye on his ally's war." Aeron glanced around in concern. "We'd better not linger here. Some of Oriseus's followers must be nearby, using their magical talents to help Soorenar with this siege."

He started to turn away, leading Melisanda back to the rune-marked slab, but Baillegh suddenly whined and tugged at his tunic. "What? What is it, Baillegh?" Aeron said, kneeling by the hound. The dog turned and looked down toward the camp, prancing anxiously.

"What's troubling the hound?" Melisanda asked.

"I think she's found Eriale's scent," Aeron said, standing slowly. "She's the archer I told you about, my foster-sister. When Oriseus and his servants overwhelmed us, they took her away."

"Do we go after her?"

"We have to return to the college," Aeron said. "Damn! I don't want to leave her in their hands, but we have to deal with the Shadow Stone first."

"Agreed," said Melisanda. She put her hand on Aeron's arm. "Come on. The best way to help your sister is to kick Oriseus's legs out from under him." She offered her hand to Aeron, who joined her on the stone slab. Together they braved the dark veil again, returning to the chamber of the Shadow Stone.

They found two more shrine sites after that, each with seven wizards trapped beyond hope of release. The sixth door they tried was different. Aeron stepped through and found himself standing in the center of the Council Room, the great chamber within the Masters' Hall where the ruling masters had once met. It served as the seat of authority within the college walls; Aeron was not surprised that Oriseus had chosen to forge a portal between the Shadow Stone's chamber and the Council Room. The only thing that marked the portal from this side was a circle of magical symbols on the floor, painted with faded red-brown pigment.

"We're back in the college," Melisanda breathed as she appeared. "Where to—Aeron, look out!"

Aeron started to turn, just as a crackling sphere of magical energy slammed into his side and detonated. He doubled over in pain and surprise, catching a glimpse of someone in a gray tunic rising from the row of oaken seats and bolting for the door. Melisanda barked out a spell that slammed the chamber door shut before the novice reached it, while Aeron clapped one hand over his injured side and raised the iron scepter. He barked the weapon's command word; the freezing ray caught the mage in mid-stride and crumpled him to the floor.

"Aeron! Are you hurt?" Melisanda knelt by his side and pried his fingers away from the injury.

"It's not that bad," he grimaced. "It was a novice's spell. Thank Assuran he wasn't a more skilled mage, or he could have surprised me with much worse."

Melisanda looked up at him. "You're bleeding, but not badly, and you're burned, too. Let me see if I can bind it." She tore a long strip from her ruined cloak and wrapped it around his side. Aeron tried not to wince.

When she finished, they checked on the novice who'd attacked them. He was a swarthy Untheri. The ray from Dalrioc's scepter had frozen him to death in a single sweep. "Do you recognize him?" Melisanda asked.

"No. Oriseus must have posted him here to watch this portal." Aeron shook his head. "We'd better assume that the novices and students serve Oriseus without question. Come on—we need to get to the library. I've got to check some references."

Aeron dragged the fallen novice out of sight and carefully tried the door, peering into the corridor beyond. He retreated immediately. The Council Room was at the center of the Masters' Hall, and several students hurried past in the spartan hallway beyond the chamber. "We're going to have a hard time reaching the library undetected," he whispered. "I dressed as a servant to slip in before, but I'm sure that Oriseus will have told his people to watch for that now. Any other ideas?"

"Invisibility seems like a practical alternative," Melisanda suggested. "As long as they're not expecting us, it should work just fine."

"All right. Let's—" Aeron stopped as he detected a slow, deliberate ripple in the weave of magic. He glanced back toward the portal, where a black vapor had appeared above the rune circle. "Someone's coming through!" he said. "Quickly, Melisanda!"

The Vilhonese mage started her spell. Aeron blocked her from his mind and forced himself to relax, working the charm of invisibility. He reached down and pulled Baillegh close by him to cover her as well. It was becoming more difficult to control the spells he cast; in the heat of his battle with Dalrioc, desperation had lent him strength, but now casting a spell he knew as well as this one required far too much of his energy. Melisanda struggled even more before she faded from view.

They vanished just in time. From the darkness stepped Oriseus, with two other wizards in tow. Aeron held himself still, scarcely daring to breathe; magical invisibility was very useful, but a competent mage could easily dispel it if he thought to search for such a simple illusion. He felt Melisanda's unseen hand tighten on his arm in panic as she, too, tried not to make any suspicious movement.

"Assemble the masters and the students on the point at sundown, Helrios," Oriseus said to one sorcerer. He was the slender Mulhorandi abjurer Aeron had encountered in the chamber of the Shadow Stone. "Unless I miss my guess, we should be able to proceed by midnight at the latest."

"What of the novices?" Helrios asked.

"We'll need them to complete the ritual. They may not be much in the way of sorcerers, but where else can we find seven more on short notice? Keep the rest close at hand, in case we need to repeat the last step more than once."

The Mulhorandi nodded. "It shall be as you command."

"Good. I trust you to see to the details." Oriseus turned and faced the other wizard, a tall Chessentan woman in the tabard of a student. "Locate Dalrioc for me. I need him back here by an hour before sundown, at the latest."

"My lord, do you know where—"

"No, I do not. That's why I'm sending you," Oriseus snapped irritably. "Check the seventh platform. He may be there. Or try Akanax. Dalrioc fancies himself a warlord."

The student bowed without another word and stepped back into the dark curtain, while Oriseus and Helrios strode to the door. Aeron sighed in relief—they'd marched past without a look to the side. But abruptly Oriseus halted, turning to look at the last seat on the oaken table. White frost gleamed on the back of the chair, and danced in a sparkling pattern against the stone wall.

"What's this?" Oriseus muttered. He peered about, his dark eyes flickering out to search each corner of the room. "Where's Brennan? He's supposed to be here."

Helrios followed the trail of frost. Very quietly, Aeron guided Melisanda away, circling toward the chamber door. The Mulhorandi master suddenly grunted. "He's here, my lord. Dead."

Oriseus stormed over to the dark corner where Aeron had hidden the novice's body, his face darkening. "It seems we have a mystery on our hands," he said. "Here is Brennan, frozen to death with a spell or enchantment not unlike the scepter favored by Dalrioc Corynian, who happens to be missing at the moment. What do you make of it, Helrios?"

The Mulhorandi put his hand to his chin, thinking. "Dalrioc returned before he was supposed to and slew Brennan? Dalrioc's temper is quick, but what offense did Brennan offer to merit this response?"

Oriseus scowled. "One novice more or less is no loss, but I don't care for improvisation. I will look into this myself, I think." He wheeled and stalked out of the chamber, leaving Helrios to consider the frozen corpse.

Aeron did not hesitate. He reached down with one hand to take Baillegh by her collar and caught Melisanda by the arm with the other. As the door swung shut, he pulled them through and into the hallway beyond. Oriseus turned right to speak to the students and masters who awaited him; Aeron turned left and pulled Melisanda toward the servants' passages. Hoping that no one would notice a single door opening by itself, he slipped into the narrow hallway paralleling the main corridor and made his way to the servants' exit. He and Melisanda stumbled together as they blundered down the steps and out into the courtyard, unable to see their own feet.

"Aeron, look." Melisanda's voice whispered in his ear. Her voice was sick with fear. "The sky, it's all wrong."

He glanced up. Faint streamers of purple light twisted through the sky, each meeting over the tower. There were seven of them, arrowing toward the center from distant points spaced equally on the horizon. It's the magic trapped by the outlying shrines, Aeron realized. All the magic of Chessenta, channeled to this one point! But now it's visible in the real world. Beside him, Baillegh whimpered softly. Aeron watched for a long moment, his breath caught in his throat. "The flow of magic wasn't visible before."

"Do you remember what Oriseus said in the Council Chamber? About assembling the students and novices at dusk? Oriseus must be close to finishing his spell."

"I think you're right," Aeron said. "We're running out of time."

* * * * *

They found each of the library's doors locked and sealed with heavy chains. Aeron circled the building again, double-checking each entrance, but all had been secured against intrusion.

"Great." Aeron returned to the side door they'd first tried. "I have a spell that might disarm any magical traps here and open the door, but I'll lose my spell of invisibility if I cast it."

"Go ahead. I'll keep watch," Melisanda said. "At least we don't have to worry about anyone inside if Oriseus has decided to keep the other wizards out of here."

Casting a nervous glance around the quadrangle, Aeron waited to make sure that no one was in sight before muttering the spell of opening under his breath. He quickly slipped inside, holding the door until Melisanda and Baillegh brushed past, and quietly shut it. As far as he could tell, no one had spotted them.

He locked the door behind them, and turned to survey the vast stacks of books that towered in the gloomy chamber. The library's great windows were shuttered and secured, and it took a long moment for Aeron's eyes to adjust. Everything was covered with a fine layer of dust, indicating months, perhaps years, of disuse. But the rows of heavy tomes, scroll racks, atlases, and grimoires all seemed intact.

"What are we looking for?" Melisanda asked.

"The scrolls of Madryoch," Aeron said. "If they're here, they'll be hidden in an unmarked tube, with a scroll describing alchemical processes covering them."

"Wouldn't Oriseus have them, if they're that important?"

"Maybe, if he found them." Aeron allowed himself a small smile. "Five years ago, I hid them before I left my room. I'm hoping that Oriseus, or whoever it was who searched through my belongings, simply returned my books and scrolls to the library."

Deliberately, Aeron moved over to a scroll rack, pulled out the first unmarked case he found, and checked its contents. It was a text on Rashemite genealogy. He started to cap and replace it, then decided that time was more important than neatness. He dropped the case to the floor with a soft clatter and pulled out the next one, moving faster. At least I'll be able to see where I've been already, he thought, discarding the case. Melisanda gave him a startled look, but with a snort she copied his more direct approach, until the air seemed heavy with dust kicked up by scrolls clattering on the floor. Baillegh prowled around the library, her hackles stiff; Aeron guessed that the hound sensed the wrongness in the air and interpreted it as a threat.

It took half an hour before Aeron found the scroll he sought. "Melisanda!" he called. "I think this is it." Licking his lips, he carried it over to a nearby table and emptied out the scroll. Impatiently he brushed away the dry old alchemical treatise.

Underneath, a musty scroll of papyrus pages stitched side-to-side waited, covered with sinister whorls and runes. Brushing her hands against her skirt, the Chondathan sorceress moved closer and peered down at the ancient text.

"It's the same writing as the inscription on the Shadow Stone," she breathed. "You can make sense of this?"

"I think so." He drew the scrap of parchment from his belt pouch and laid it beside Madryoch's text. Carefully, he transcribed the Shadow Stone inscription from the meaningless marks of Madryoch's cipher into ancient Rauric, using the key he'd hidden in the Chants. It was not a long passage, and after a moment he straightened up, examining his work.

"What does it mean?" Melisanda asked, breaking the silence. "I know ancient Untheric and Thorass, but that doesn't seem familiar. Something about the powers of shadow, bound in stone?"

"That's pretty close," Aeron admitted. He leaned back from the table, looking up at Melisanda. Absently he noted that dusk was near; the gray daylight was fading outside the library's shuttered windows, and it was quite dim inside. "The old Imaskari sorcerers used knowledge they'd learned from creatures of immortal evil to record their spells. They weren't priests, really—they didn't draw their magic directly from the dark powers they served. They only used what they'd been taught to work their own sorcery. As best as I can tell, this inscription is a magical seal or bond, the keystone of an enchantment that focuses or channels the Shadow Stone's power."

"Just as we might seal a door or strengthen a tower by inscribing it with words of power," Melisanda observed.

"Exactly. The ancient sorcerers couched their invocations in different terms, but the principle is the same." Aeron stood and paced away from the table, rubbing his hands together. "So how can we use this to undo Oriseus's spell?"

"Magical writings can be erased," Melisanda pointed out. "I know several counterspells and abjurations to neutralize or destroy signs, wards, and glyphs—"

"But if you forged your counterspell from the Weave, the Shadow Stone would merely absorb it," Aeron broke in. "I'd have to craft the counterspell from shadow-magic. It may be that the stone wouldn't cancel a spell made from its own substance."

"Do you know a spell of erasure?"

"No, I don't have one prepared." Aeron swore viciously. "And Dalrioc took my spellbook when he chained me in the shadow shrine. Damn!"

Melisanda slumped against the wall, tears in her eyes. "My spellbook was taken as well. So close—"

Aeron slumped to the floor, grimacing in defeat. He leaned back against the crooked bookshelves, trying to think of a way to get at some student or master's spellbook in order to borrow the spell he needed. Wizards guarded their spellbooks well. It would be dangerous, but what choice did they have? Time was short. Baillegh pressed her nose against his face as if to console him. He scratched her neck and looked down into his lap, considering the best choice for his desperate effort.

His eye fell on the smooth blue silk of Fineghal's pouch of spell-tokens, hanging from his belt. "Of course," he muttered. He undid the drawstring and poured the smooth stones into his hand. Fineghal usually traveled with several dozen of them, water-worn pebbles and rocks marked with old elven glyphs. Aeron had learned to cast his first spell from the elf lord's tokens. He sifted through them until he found a striated stone of green and gray, marked with a double-loop and curving symbol engraved in its cool surface. "*Cuilla dheneis,*" he said, a smile beginning to play across his face. "The striker of marks."

Across the room, Melisanda looked up. "What did you say?"

"I said, I think we've got a chance," Aeron said. He crossed his legs and returned the rest of Fineghal's tokens to their pouch, holding the rune-eraser in his right hand. "I need to memorize this spell. Keep your eyes open for trouble; it may take me a while."

* * * * *

Time passed without measure, as the light slowly failed and dusk fell over Cimbar. Aeron couldn't say if it took an hour or even two to force the shape of the spell into his consciousness; he was tired, his chest still hurt from his fight with Dalrioc and his side ached from the novice's attack, and above all the driving awareness that he had to memorize Fineghal's erasure spell quickly slowed his efforts to master it. Eventually, he stirred and stood, dropping the green, smooth stone back into its pouch.

"I'm ready," he announced. "We'll have to go back to the plane of shadow. I have to be close to the stone in order to work this magic."

"That means returning to the Council Chamber."

Melisanda scowled, looking out at the college's courtyard from behind the shutters. "Someone checked the door to the library while you were studying your spell, maybe an hour ago. There were a lot of masters and students moving around the college then, but I haven't seen anyone for a long time. I don't like this."

"Probably looking for us," Aeron said grimly. "Oriseus must have found Dalrioc by—"

Before he could continue, Baillegh growled and turned toward the great double doors of the library. The white wolfhound bared her teeth, moving to stand between the mages and the entrance to the room. Aeron sensed a presence just beyond the portal, a cold hunger and filthy bloodthirst that almost stained the air he breathed. He recoiled three steps without even realizing he'd given ground.

Melisanda paled and edged away as well, sliding around the scroll-littered table. In a frightened whisper she asked, "Aeron, do you feel it?"

He licked his lips and tried to swallow. "Yes. I think Oriseus has found us."

Malice and purpose gathered beyond the stout oaken door, pressing against the magical wards that barred entry to the library. For a long moment, the doors almost seemed to bulge inward from the psychic pressure—and then they flew open with a resounding crash. Through the smoldering wreckage emerged a humped, beastlike shape, its ichorous hide gleaming in the deepening dusk. An impossibly long, barbed tongue lolled from between its double-jaws. It paused on the threshold, snuffling loudly while its tiny ears twitched and cocked in different directions; Aeron realized that the creature had no eyes. A silver band marked with whorls and runes clasped one of its clawed forelegs.

"Aeron," hissed Melisanda. The creature's heavy head swiveled unerringly to face her, fixing her position.

"It's Oriseus's yugoloth," he replied quietly. "The same one we saw kill Master Raemon, all those years ago."

As he spoke, the creature turned to face him, too. It advanced slowly into the room, blocking the door with its stocky form. The monster coughed once, a throaty sound of satisfaction.

"What's it doing here?" Melisanda moved to put the table between her and the yugoloth.

"Oriseus must have summoned it to find us. That's what yugoloth do—they find things. Once it's got your scent, you'll never throw it off your trail." Aeron pulled his eyes away from the creature for a moment, trying to locate the other doors to the library. One was only about fifteen feet past Melisanda, off to his right. There was another about thirty feet directly behind him, but with one look at the yugoloth's powerful frame he knew he'd never reach it. Quietly he asked Melisanda, "Do you know the glamour of phantasmal sound?"

"Yes, I do. What's your plan?"

"I've read a lot about these creatures over the years," Aeron told her. The yugoloth was padding closer, moving up to an easy pounce as long as Aeron showed no sign of fleeing. "They're sightless. I'll conjure a cloud of noxious vapors, which should negate its sense of smell. If you can distract it with illusory sounds, we'll effectively blind it. That's our best chance. Ready?"

The Vilhonese noblewoman nodded. "I'll follow your lead."

Aeron glanced at her, and back to the approaching monster. Muttering under his breath, he started his enchantment. The magic he sought seemed to slip away from his fingers, almost wrenched from his grasp by the proximity of the Shadow Stone. He redoubled his efforts, shouting the simple words to the spell as he tried to shape the Weave through sheer force of will. Melisanda started her enchantment and struggled as well, her voice high and cracking with strain.

The yugoloth froze for a moment as the two mages began to weave their spells, and then rocked back on its heels as if to sit up, its mouth gaping wide. From its stinking maw it shot its vile tongue like a bullwhip. Aeron tried to dodge without losing the effort to build his spell, but the yugoloth's sticky tongue caught him lasso-like, whipping around his shoulders and pinning his arms to his side. With one toss of its armored head, the yugoloth jerked him off his feet and started to drag him to its gnashing fangs. The half-formed spell in Aeron's mind vanished in panic and pain as the stinging barbs dug into his flesh.

"Melisanda!" he cried.

Melisanda held to her spell with fierce concentration, finishing the enchantment. With one gesture of her hand, she filled the library with the roaring racket of a great revel, complete with music, singing, the clatter of dishes and the loud buzz of dozens of conversations. The yugoloth growled in distaste, but it ignored the cacophonous sounds for the moment—with Aeron caught in the coils of its tongue, it didn't need to hear what was around it. Digging in its great talons, it reeled Aeron closer to its terrifying fangs.

Then, like a silver blur, Baillegh launched herself against the monster's flank, knocking it over and seizing a mouthful of its chitinous hide. The wolfhound growled and worried at the back of the yugoloth's neck, cracking its armored plates beneath her powerful jaws. The yugoloth shrieked in pain and rage, momentarily drowning out Melisanda's sound glamour, and lunged back at the hound, but it couldn't get at her while it held Aeron with its tongue. Finally, it released him in order to retract its tongue and meet Baillegh's attack. With catlike swiftness it spun and snapped at the hound, but Baillegh dodged away from its attack.

Aeron scrambled to his feet, ignoring the blood that streamed from the rough abrasions that circled his body. The yugoloth might have been deafened by Melisanda's spell, but it scrambled after Baillegh with uncanny precision, following her scent in its gaping nostrils while it whipped its tongue back and forth, trying to locate the hound by touch. Baillegh yipped and dodged, looking for an opening to dart in and resume her attack.

In the corner of his eye, he saw Melisanda snatch up a heavy book and hurl it across the room at the monster, striking it in the flank. Instinctively the yugoloth turned and snapped at empty air. In that moment Baillegh attacked from the other side, her jaws closing on the yugoloth's throat. The fiend wheeled in the air, trying to shake her off. Aeron tried to move closer, trying to decide how he could help Baillegh.

"Aeron! Try Dalrioc's wand!" shouted Melisanda over the din of her own spell. The yugoloth tried to turn toward her, but Baillegh pulled it back into the fight. With one huge paw it turned on the hound and smashed her to the ground. It broke free of Baillegh's grip and turned against the silver elf hound, its massive jaws gaping wide for the kill.

Aeron vaulted over the great table in the center of the library to give himself a clear line of fire, snatching the iron scepter from his belt. He aimed it at the yugoloth's back and shouted the weapon's command word. The tip of the scepter glowed white as a thin, pale ray sprang out to strike the monster with a blast of unbearable cold. The chitinous plates that covered its back whitened under the ray and then split with brittle cracking sounds, revealing dark meat underneath that froze solid under the wand's deadly beam. The yugoloth screeched with an awful sound, stampeding blindly through the bookshelves and wreaking awful havoc in the ancient library. Aeron pursued it, firing blast after blast into the monster while Baillegh worried at its flanks.

Enraged beyond reason, the yugoloth wheeled and sprang at Aeron—but the mage stood his ground and delivered one final blast of transarctic cold into the creature's face, spearing its head with a lance of ice. It stumbled once, wheezed, and collapsed to the ground, dark ichor seeping from its double jaws. Melisanda allowed her illusory revel to die away, leaving the room curiously silent as they watched for any sign of animation in the creature.

Aeron moved over to check on Baillegh. The hound was battered but intact, scratched and clawed all along her flanks. She looked up at Aeron and licked his face.

"Someone must have heard that racket," said Melisanda.

"I know," said Aeron. "Come on. Let's get out of here while we can. We have to get back to the plane of shadow."

Twenty

Aeron, Melisanda, and Baillegh slipped ghostlike from the college library, using one of the barricaded side doors to conceal their departure. Aeron expected another attack at any moment; the struggle against Oriseus's yugoloth had been anything but silent, and the gaping wreckage of the great double doors in the front of the library building was impossible to miss from the college quadrangle. But the open courtyard between the college buildings was empty and quiet, cloaked in a heavy ground mist. The fog clung to the sides of the building with long streamers, drifts of impure snow driven against each hall.

Aeron's breath streamed away, caught in a bitter cold that seared his nose and throat. Dusk had long since failed, and the yellow-burning lamps of the college barely flickered in the gathering gloom. He glanced up at the sky and gasped; the streams of magic overhead were ribbons of elfin light against a black and colorless sky. They circled in a silent maelstrom centering on the rebuilt obelisk, spinning more and more rapidly with each passing moment. The masters and students must be at the tower, he realized. Oriseus's masterpiece is almost complete.

"Did we step through a shadow-portal?" Melisanda asked in a small voice. "This isn't right."

"Oriseus is tearing the veil between the worlds," Aeron answered. "When he finishes his spell, there won't be a plane of shadow anymore. It will be here." He wrenched his gaze away from the horror in the sky and hurried toward the Masters' Hall.

No one remained in the building. Its paneled corridors were empty, echoing with their footfalls. The gloom was even denser indoors, thick shadows clinging to the walls despite the flickering globes of mage-light that illuminated the hall. Aeron padded quietly to the Council Chamber, checked the door for any magical seal or alarm, and let himself in. Melisanda and Baillegh followed, keeping a close watch up and down the corridor outside.

The Council room was empty, as before. The novice's body had been removed, but none of the damage to the furnishings had been repaired. Dark frost still gleamed over the swath of the room where Aeron had employed Dalrioc's ice-scepter. In the center of the floor, the faded circle of magical symbols that marked the doorway into the chamber of the Shadow Stone waited. Aeron did not hesitate; he trotted into the circle, Dalrioc's wand clasped in his hand.

"Stand close," he told Melisanda and Baillegh. "Oriseus may have left a guard to watch over the chamber this time."

Melisanda and the wolfhound crowded close behind him, joining him in the rune-marked circle, but nothing happened. They waited a long moment, taut with anticipation, before he growled in disgust. "Why isn't this working now?"

"You didn't see Oriseus use a spell or command word to trigger this portal, did you?" asked Melisanda.

"No, the student just walked right into it," Aeron replied. He frowned, thinking. Unconsciously, he wrapped his arms closer to his body, trying to stretch his battered cloak over his bony frame. The Council Chamber was freezing. "Wait a moment," he said slowly. "Maybe the portal isn't working because we're already in the plane of shadow."

"It feels like it. Have you noticed how you can hear the stone now?" said Melisanda. She was pale in the darkness. "The worlds are merging. How much power it would take to move the entire college across the barrier?"

"Why assume that Oriseus only dragged the college into the realm of shadow? It might be the entire city. Or all of Chessenta, for that matter," Aeron said bitterly. "Well, we'll have to get into the tower on foot. Come on."

They left the same way they'd come in and crossed the college grounds again, this time heading for the ruined obelisk. As they neared the monument, Aeron felt the pulsating distortions of the Shadow Stone growing stronger, until it seemed the entire world was quivering in time to the stone's menacing rhythm.

"I don't know if I can go on!" Melisanda shouted in his ear. She had her arms folded across her belly, fighting against the nauseating influence of magic poisoned by the stone. "It hurts, Aeron! The spell's too far gone!"

He caught her arm and steadied her. "We have only one chance at this!" He turned back to the angry black radiance spilling from the pyramid's stones and moved closer. It seemed that the very air and ground were caught in a heat shimmer, warping and twisting around him, but this was no mere mirage—icy daggers of unbearable cold and darkness clawed at him with every step. He dragged himself closer and fell into the stone doorway of the tower, a high, narrow chamber framed by great doors of rune-carved oak.

Two students stood in the doorway, fists clenched by their sides as they stared mindlessly into the distance, a rictus of unholy delight and terror twisting their faces. Aeron could have spread his arms to touch each one, but they ignored them, lost in their private moment of transcendent triumph. As he'd thought, the structure seemed to protect them from the stone's distorting effects.

Beyond the doorway stood the pyramid's front gallery, a great echoing chamber of dark stone. In his previous visits Aeron had turned left to follow a winding staircase to the vaults below, while the same staircase continued up to the right to climb to the monument's upper levels. The hall itself was the largest room in structure, the sanctuary of a dark cathedral. Aeron slipped through the door to the back of the room, and froze in terror.

The masters and students of the college stood before him. They were locked in the same blank attitude as the door-wardens, concentrating on a raving pillar of violet energy that crackled down from the ceiling to vanish into the marbled floor. They muttered and moaned in time to the stone's heartbeat. Aeron quickly ducked behind a pillar, seeking cover in the stairwell. Melisanda and Baillegh scrambled after him.

"What's wrong with them?" the sorceress whispered. "They must have seen us."

"They're all playing their part in Oriseus's spell," Aeron replied. "It's taking everything they've got to do it."

Melisanda rose slowly and stretched to look around the chamber before quickly drawing back. "He's here, Aeron. Right in the center of things."

She pointed, and Aeron followed her gesture. The saturnine archmage stood in the center of a half-circle of the college's most powerful wizards, intoning the words of a spell so great and terrible that it hurt Aeron's ears to hear his incantation. With each syllable the Sceptanar expelled, the column of energy that filled the center of the room grew brighter. Rings of distortion, of tortured reality, rippled away from the unchained power.

Aeron watched, transfixed by the majesty of the sight, and then wrenched his gaze away. "Let's put a stop to this."

"You don't have to ask twice," Melisanda replied under her breath. "Do you know where the chamber lies?"

Aeron thought of the first time he'd set foot in the tower, five years ago. His stomach turned at the memory of his fear and pain. "I know the way," he answered.

They came to the old door that marked the entrance to the stone's chamber. Lambent light escaped from the hairline cracks under the oaken door and shone through every seam and imperfection in the wood. Aeron reached out to open it without hesitation, but Melisanda placed her hand over his.

"Careful. Just because Oriseus left this room unguarded before doesn't mean that it's not protected now."

"So far as I know, the stone can protect itself," Aeron replied. "But you're right. Why take chances?" He drew back and cast a spell of mage-sight. To his relief, no barrier blocked their path. "It's safe," he announced.

Melisanda raised an eyebrow. "Safe?"

He repressed a bitter laugh. "Well, taking everything else into consideration . . . at least there's no trap here." Steeling himself, Aeron pushed the door open and stepped into the Shadow Stone's chamber, hand raised to cover his eyes from the painful light.

The chamber was much the same as they had left it only a few short hours ago, but the Shadow Stone had changed. It burned with a fierce radiance of black light, searing Aeron's eyes and scouring the walls with its intolerable touch. All of his senses reeled with the stone's proximity; his ears were filled with the shrieking rush of tortured air and the cracking of the tower's blasted stones, the air stank with a miasma of ozone and decay, and even through his closed eyes the stone pressed its hateful image into his mind. It pulsed in the center of a rippling blackness of floor, ceiling, and walls wrenched impossibly through a transdimensional storm that destroyed his sense of up and down, distance and form. He recoiled, toppling against the wall as his feet swept out from under him.

Melisanda fell beside him, her long brown hair flying about her face as if she were caught in a gale. "Aeron!

Speak your spell!" she shouted, huddling against the ruined stone wall.

Aeron opened his eyes a mere slit to gain his bearings, climbing to his feet with one hand on the ice rimmed stone of the chamber wall. He looked again on the Shadow Stone, gathering his strength and determination for what came next.

"Aeron! Now!" cried Melisanda.

Drawing a deep breath, Aeron barked the first syllables of the striking-spell, freeing the symbol in his mind. But instead of seeking the strength of his own spirit or the natural stone, air, and water around him to power the spell, he threw his consciousness forward into the yawning black maelstrom before him, embracing the shrieking chaos of the Shadow Stone.

From the stone one coursing stream of unfettered power lanced out to transfix Aeron, pinning him on a spear of foulness and hate that threatened to flay the flesh from his bones. He screamed as every inch of his body crawled with the malignant energy and corruption pouring into his heart. Somehow he endured it, maintaining just enough awareness and will to finish the last syllable of the erasure spell, holding on to the dark silhouette of the stone's iron banding as a dying warrior might cling to the sight of the crest of the enemy who had just struck him down. He narrowed his eyes against the agony and turned a fraction of the stone's awful power toward his spell.

The runes upon the stone's casing glowed once and faded, stricken from existence. As they vanished, the bands shifted, slipped, and then clattered to the ground, no longer clasped to the Shadow Stone. Instantly the coursing conduit of power that tore and clawed at Aeron's breast snapped away, grounding itself futilely in the walls of the chamber. It was joined a split second later by first one, then another ravening stream of power, dancing and creeping against the chamber walls and the blank archways of shadow, while the stone began to pulse brighter and brighter.

Aeron shook his head and found himself lying with his head cradled in Melisanda's lap, a cold dull ache in the center of his chest. The unbearable touch of the stone was fading, allowing him to recover his senses and sanity.

"What happened?" he asked against the rage of the storm.

"It worked!" Melisanda whispered. "The stone's out of control. It's not doing whatever it was doing before."

Aeron levered himself to his elbow and gazed at the spectacle for a long moment. The stone's pulse was growing faster, stronger, a dull booming and rocking that shook the substance of two worlds. The fierce radiance with which it had blazed before was now trapped within its uneven facets, a pinprick of light that grew larger and brighter with every passing moment, until the stone strained with the incalculable potential imprisoned within it.

"The bands didn't focus the Stone's power, they let it escape!" he realized.

"I don't think we should stay here too much longer," Melisanda said. She helped Aeron to his feet and slid his arm over her shoulder.

"No," said Aeron. "I've got to stay. Go ahead and get out of here now—take the arch that leads to Akanax, if it is working. And then move far away from the portal's exit."

Melisanda wheeled to face him. "Are you insane? If you stay here, you'll be killed!"

He offered her a weak smile. "And if I leave, Oriseus may be able to undo what I've just done. I have to make sure that the stone is destroyed, Melisanda."

The sorceress fixed her eyes on him, a fragile mix of emotions flickering across her face. "If you stay, I stay. We'll see it through together," she said.

Aeron considered what he could say to change her mind, but then he felt a deliberate ripple in the chaos around him, a noxious parody of the old delight he'd sensed when magic was woven nearby. A whirling streamer of darkness formed by the chamber door, a new shadow portal hovering in the air. He stood back, trembling in fatigue.

"Ready yourself, Melisanda. It's Oriseus."

She glanced at him and nodded. "I don't know if I can cast any spells in here," she said.

Aeron handed Dalrioc's wand to her. "This might work. I think Dalrioc crafted this scepter to draw its power from the stone." The portal was nearly complete; Aeron quickly edged away to leave plenty of space between them. "Don't hesitate when he appears. We can't give him any chance to work his spells against us."

With a thin tearing sound a form materialized in the spiraling shadow and emerged, shedding streamers of tangible darkness like a swimmer rising from the deeps. Slender and agile, the intruder sprang into motion before the curtain began to fail, crouching to aim a long bow at Aeron.

Melisanda raised Dalrioc's wand, ready to unleash its deadly ray, but Aeron shouted, "No! It's Eriale!"

He raced to catch Melisanda's hand before she struck. Melisanda looked at him, startled, while Eriale's hands blurred and the bow sang its shrill song. Aeron twisted cat-like in mid-leap, but Eriale's arrow caught him high on the hip, skewering his side. His legs seemed to turn to rubber, spilling him to the cold flagstones before the first claws of pain sank into his awareness. Gasping in shock, he turned to look at his foster-sister.

Eriale met his eyes with a look cold enough to chill his heart. No trace of emotion or recognition crossed her face. With mechanical certainty, she reached for her quiver and drew another arrow, its steel point aimed at his heart. She drew the bowstring back to her ear, death in her unblinking eyes.

"Eriale, it's me!" Aeron cried, while warm blood streamed from his wound. "Don't shoot!"

The archer hesitated for a moment, the merest hint of indecision softening her expression, but then she steeled herself and steadied her aim for the killing shot.

Melisanda barked an arcane word and swept a blinding ray of sparkling frost from the iron scepter across Eriale. Eriale winced but didn't make a sound, dropping the bow to cradle her frost-burned arms to her body. Her blank eyes still held Aeron fixed in a deadly glare. The Vilhonese sorceress dashed up to kick the bow away, and wheeled to face Aeron. "Are you—"

"I think I'll live," he answered, trying to climb to his feet. He leaned awkwardly against the chamber wall, staring at Eriale. Pressing one hand to his side, he glanced down at the arrow. He didn't know much of the healing arts and wasn't willing to take any chances with trying to pull it out or push it through. Pinning the arrow in place with his right hand, he snapped off the shaft and steeled himself to push it to the back of his mind for the moment. "She didn't get a true shot at me, thank Assuran. Let me see if I can work a countermagic to dispel Oriseus's charm over her."

Pushing himself off the wall, Aeron moved over to where

Eriale crouched and knelt beside her, seeking some indication of the type of charm or geas she'd been placed under. He winced at the blistered white streaks and glistening frost that showed where Dalrioc's wand had struck her—if Melisanda had missed by only a foot or two, Eriale might have been critically injured. He worked a simple counterspell to remove the magics that ensorceled the archer.

Eriale flinched, but a hint of color returned to her face, and the blankness fell away from her stare. "Aeron? What happened—" She gasped as the pain of her injuries flooded through her, no longer checked by the ruthless dominion that had turned her against him. She sagged to the floor, suppressing a sob.

"Eriale, I'm sorry," Aeron began. "I didn't know—"

He was interrupted by the sudden cold certainty that shadow-magic was gathering under a conscious will. His heart lurched with the sensation of magic at work. Behind him, Melisanda cried out in alarm. "The portal, Aeron!"

As the twisting shadow door through which Eriale had come faded out altogether, the streamers of darkness began to sink to the floor, coalescing into a single pool or slick of night-black shadow stuff. The pool quivered once, and then something began to rise from its depths, drawing its shape from the darkness, a tall man with cruel, fine features.

"Aeron, you fool! You have no idea what harm your interference has caused," Oriseus said, speaking as he rose from the ebon circle. "You have doomed all of us by unchaining the Shadow Stone." The sorcerer's hands turned and flashed, shaping a spell with frightening celerity.

Aeron barked out the words to a shielding-spell, covering both himself and Eriale with a shimmering green field of energy. From the raging Shadow Stone tendrils of inky darkness shot out to play along the curving sphere of force, corrupting it instantly with black veins of negative energy. Behind him, Melisanda dodged behind one of the pillars that divided the open chamber from the gallery that ringed it, raising Dalrioc's wand to attack Oriseus. But the archmage finished his spell first, directing a serpentine ray of crackling purple energy at Aeron. It sliced through Aeron's shield without the least interference and struck Aeron full in the chest. He fell to the stone floor, stunned.

Eriale recoiled in fright, but then threw herself over him, trying to protect him from Oriseus's spell. "Aeron!"

Oddly enough, he didn't seem to be injured. He shook off Eriale's attentions. "I'm all right," he told her.

Melisanda shouted the command that activated Dalrioc's deadly scepter and sent a blast of arctic air scything toward Oriseus, but the ancient sorcerer whispered another word and turned sideways, disappearing from view. Passing near the Shadow Stone, the frigid ray seemed to attract a coursing conduit of energy from the pulsating crystal, suddenly doubling and redoubling in strength until it shattered one of the stone pillars across the chamber.

"Aeron, Oriseus vanished! Can you see him?"

Aeron struggled to his knees, one hand pressed to the oddly charred patch over his heart. Oriseus's spell had done something to him, he was certain of that; he could sense black, cold energy pricking at his skin, dire potential as yet unrealized. "No, I don't, but that doesn't mean that he left. Be careful, Melisanda—the stone's influence is wreaking havoc with our spells."

"Indeed it is." Oriseus's voice was strong and confident, near Aeron yet somehow impossibly distant. "I must confine the stone's power again, or we shall all be killed. When you struck my spell from the stone's bindings, Aeron, you struck away the only thing that protects all of Chessenta from its power." Oriseus suddenly appeared before the fallen stone, an impossible caricature of a man. He was a flat image, a playing-card figure that winked into nonexistence when he happened to face them edge-on.

Aeron shook his head, astonished. He'd heard of such spells, but he'd never seen one cast before. "I don't believe you, Oriseus. And even if I did, I'm willing to make that sacrifice. Better that the three of us should die here and put a stop to this than allow you to finish what you've started."

"Your life is yours to throw away if you wish," the sorcerer said with venom in his voice, "but what of your sister's and your friend's? And you accuse me of ruthlessness." Oriseus stalked forward and then shifted sideways, vanishing. Aeron caught a glimpse of him spinning across the room, flashing in and out of reality. "We don't have much time for this debate, Aeron. The stone will decide it for us in a matter of minutes!"

In the room's center, the Shadow Stone now burned like a black star, too bright to look at directly. Its dreadful power threw stark shadows against the walls, and it seemed almost distant, as if it were sinking out of sight through the very stuff of reality. The floor and ceiling buckled and twisted toward the stone, drawn to it by a force greater than any maelstrom.

"Then that's it," Aeron replied.

Oriseus cursed in a forgotten language. He reappeared by the stone, stooping for the discarded iron bands that had circled the crystal. Aeron reacted without hesitation, raising his hands and barking out the words for the storm-strike. With no other options, he drew his strength from the Shadow Stone's awful presence, enduring its sinister touch long enough to finish his spell. From his fingertips bright electrical arcs leaped forward to stab at Oriseus—but even as they reached for the sorcerer, they doubled back on Aeron and struck him. He screamed and twisted under the assault of his own spell, caught in the throes of a dozen burning skewers of pain, before collapsing to the floor.

Oriseus looked up from his work with a bare smile. "You should have been more careful, Aeron. The first spell I cast upon you was a mage-shield I devised centuries ago, designed to turn your own spells against you. It may have lapsed . . . or it may still be intact. Why don't you cast another spell and see?" Deliberately, he inscribed a rune upon the iron strip.

Aeron groveled in agony, his vision red and hazy. His strength was failing fast; he'd pushed himself to the limits already. "Baillegh, stop him!" he gasped.

The silver hound streaked forward to leap at Oriseus. The sorcerer raised his hand and spoke a single word, catching the dog in an amber beam that froze her in mid-leap. Stiff as a statue, she crashed to the ground at his feet, imprisoned in a shimmering field of golden energy.

Eriale helped Aeron rise, her face frozen in a tight grimace of pain. "What are we going to do?" she said quietly. "How can we defeat him, Aeron?"

He shook his head. "I'm running out of ideas," he replied.

Melisanda slipped the scepter into her blouse, and silently began to work a spell. Aeron watched her, fascinated; she didn't have his ability to use the incalculable energy of the Shadow Stone and had to draw the entirety of her spell from the burning flame of her own life-force.

Before his eyes she seemed to wilt, sagging to her knees and paling with the effort, but she managed to finish her casting. A single streaking point of light soared away from her hand, arcing toward Oriseus. The sorcerer looked up just in time for the spell to detonate in a terrific blast of flame that filled the chamber with an awful roar. Aeron raised his cloak over his face and turned away to throw Eriale to the floor as searing heat washed over them.

The fiery sphere dissipated in moments, leaving behind a haze of smoke and the stink of burned clothes. The Shadow Stone still lay where it had been, untouched by Melisanda's spell. Oriseus, however, was not so fortunate. He groaned and stirred, burned black over his face and hands, while small flames smoldered over his ceremonial robe. Despite the horrible wounds he'd sustained, the sorcerer drew himself to his feet, turning a look of awful rage on Melisanda.

"You were warned," he said through cracked lips. He took a step toward her, already gathering magic for the spell that would destroy her.

At the edge of the room, Melisanda's strength gave out and she collapsed to the floor. She'd crafted too strong a spell from her own spirit. Aeron staggered to his feet, determined to help her. Oriseus's mage-shield still clung to him like thick oil. His thoughts raced as Oriseus closed in on Melisanda. He needed a counterspell; quickly he barked out the words to the dispelling enchantment.

Oriseus wheeled at the first sound of his words, and then grinned. "So you have decided to chance my rebounding shield again, Aeron? I thought you smarter than that." He turned back to Melisanda, his hands glowing with power.

Aeron finished the spell, directing it at Baillegh. If Oriseus's shield had fallen for some reason, he might be able to free her from the amber field that imprisoned her. Sparkling motes of magic danced around the trapped hound, but then they shifted and appeared around Aeron, attacking the black abjuration that tainted his magical powers. Under the assault, the curse failed, freeing Aeron.

Instantly he shaped the deadliest attack he knew, the force-missiles he'd used against Oriseus the first time they fought. Without consideration for himself, he wrenched at the raging power of the Shadow Stone and hammered three coruscating spheres of black-streaked energy at

Oriseus. The archmage wheeled just in time to catch all three in his torso. Each detonated with bone-shattering force, blasting great gaping wounds in Oriseus's body and crumpling him against the wall. Incredibly, the sorcerer slowly stood, dragging himself to his feet and turning to confront Aeron again.

"By all the gods," Aeron breathed. His knees buckled with exhaustion and he slumped to the floor. He had no more spells of attack left to him, none that could affect a mage as formidable as Oriseus. "What are you?"

"I told you before, Aeron. This body is nothing more than a shell for my consciousness." Oriseus attempted a triumphant grin, a horrible expression in his burned and damaged face. "You've treated my steed poorly, but you haven't hurt me at all. If this frame does not survive the day, I'll just find another. Perhaps your friend Melisanda here . . . or maybe even you. It's no matter to me." He reached out and summoned the Shadow Stone's metal bands to his hand, finishing the inscription he needed to restore his spell of binding and control. "Let me set this in order and finish what I came here to do, and then we'll speak of this at greater length." He laughed, a horrid rasping sound.

Aeron dropped his eyes to the floor, unable to bear the victory in Oriseus's gaze. Eriale reached out to rest her hand on his shoulder. "How can you beat something like that?" she said.

Beneath his hand he felt cool, smooth wood. He glanced down in surprise; Eriale's bow lay on the floor next to him. Slowly, he picked it up. "Do you still have your quiver?" he asked her.

"Yes, but my arms are half-frozen. I can't shoot."

"I can," Aeron said softly. "Give me one of the enchanted arrows." He held out his hand, watching Oriseus while Eriale fumbled for the rune-marked shaft. Silently she laid the wood, the good oak wood from the heart of the Maerchwood, in his hand.

At the last moment, Oriseus sensed his peril. He looked up, meeting Aeron's steel-hard eyes, the iron bands hovering in the air before him as he mouthed the words to bind the Shadow Stone to his will and control again. His hands started to work at a defensive barrier, moving quickly and certainly to their task as the iron bands clattered to the floor, the spell abandoned.

He wasn't fast enough. With all his old skill, Aeron drew Eriale's bow to his ear and released the arrow straight and true. It buried itself to within a handspan of the fletching in the hollow of Oriseus's breast, biting into the scarred stone wall behind him. The sorcerer drew in a great breath, his jaw falling open as his legs gave out. He slid about a half-foot down the wall before the arrow arrested his movement, leaving him to hang helplessly on the wall.

Aeron rose from his kneeling stance, letting the bow fall to his side with a grim smile of satisfaction. Distantly, he noticed that the eerie light from the stone was etching his shadow against the wall with fierce intensity.

He heard Eriale hiss in dismay behind him. "The stone! Aeron, look at the Shadow Stone!"

He turned his back on Oriseus and instantly threw up an arm to shield his eyes. The raging power inside the stone was no longer confined to the space inside its ebon facets; great glowing cracks had appeared in its substance, like a dam that was beginning to fail. The pounding rhythm of the stone's heartbeat shook the walls and floors, crumpling and warping the very air of the room. Intuitively he realized that it could not endure the tremendous magical energy that was being channeled into it much longer, and that he didn't want to be nearby when its tolerance was surpassed. He blinked his eyes clear and glanced around the chamber.

"Eriale! Take Baillegh and go through that archway there!"

The archer nodded and scooped up the wolfhound, tenderly working around the frost burns on her arms and torso. The amber field that encased Baillegh was fading, running out as Oriseus's life failed. Weaving under Baillegh's weight, Eriale managed to get her body under the hound and staggered toward the door that led to Boeruine.

Aeron slung Eriale's bow over his back and reached down to help Melisanda to her feet. The girl was semiconscious, pale and cold; he didn't like the way she looked, not at all. As he turned to leave, he heard a wet rattle behind him. "Leaving . . . so soon?"

Oriseus hung transfixed on the arrow, gasping for breath. Blood trickled down his chin and marked a great red stain in the center of his chest. His mouth worked futilely. "Still . . . not enough . . . to kill me," he choked.

Aeron glanced at the Shadow Stone. It seemed to writhe and twist like a mortally wounded animal, bleeding the raw stuff of magic. He returned to Oriseus. "It might be beyond my skill to kill the spirit that animates Oriseus's body, Madryoch. But I'll wager that you won't enjoy being here when the stone breaks."

With Melisanda in his arms, he ran awkwardly across the chamber and plunged headfirst into the dark doorway after Eriale.

* * * * *

Burdened by Melisanda's weight, he stumbled and fell as he emerged from the shadow portal. For a long moment, it was all that he could do to pick himself up, dragging Melisanda away from the cold stone slab they'd appeared upon. Cloud-wracked sky stretched away above him, and the hushed sound of the nearby water filled his ears. It was night here, or a day so dark that he couldn't tell the difference, and a great storm was almost on them, with howling wind and crackling violet lightning arcing from cloud to cloud.

"Aeron! Where are we?" Eriale shouted against the storm.

He took only a moment to find his bearings. The great fortress and city were still below him, a mile or so away, ringed by siege entrenchments. "This is Akanax," he told her. "Soorenar's armies are laying siege to King Gormantor's tower."

Eriale looked at him blankly. "But that's a hundred miles or more from Cimbar!"

"That's why Oriseus built his shadow doors. Here, help me with Melisanda. I want to get away from the hilltop."

"Why?"

"Because I don't know what's going to happen when the Shadow Stone shatters, and if we're standing right by the portal we're only a dozen yards from the cursed thing." Aeron didn't wait for Eriale, but staggered down the path toward the Avanite camp. Eriale carried Baillegh down behind him.

Without warning, the world broke beneath his feet.

The hilltop rocked as if it had been kicked by a titan, spilling Aeron and Eriale to the ground. From the open hilltop above and behind them, a brilliant flash of crimson light erupted, casting its eerie glow against the low, scudding clouds and throwing long shadows out and away from them. A split second later, a rolling thunderclap blasted Aeron to the ground again, a wall of air dense enough to splinter trees and pulverize boulders. Aeron was flung head-over-heels down the hillside, fetching up a long moment later in a small hollow, Melisanda sprawled beside him. The sky reeled drunkenly above him.

Overhead, the clouds began to dissipate, with slanting shafts of sunlight piercing the gloom. Aeron frowned, trying to figure out what was happening. He scrambled to his feet, looking out over the landscape. Golden rays shot through the clouds, illuminating sparkling patches of ocean beneath the stormclouds. Beside him, Melisanda drew a deep breath, the color returning to her face. Her eyes flew open.

"Oh, Aeron. Can you feel it?"

He closed his eyes, stretching out his senses. He could feel . . . magic. All around him, the Weave poured back into the land, a trickle at first that grew into a torrent, the power of life and nature reasserting itself against the wrong of the Shadow Stone. It surrounded him in a living chorus of enchantment, until he laughed in open, childlike delight. Eriale slid down the slope from the place where she'd fallen, and Baillegh yipped happily, dancing like a puppy chasing sunmotes. Even in the armed camps below them, Aeron could see soldiers staring up into the sky and wandering in incomprehensible circles. Impulsively, he caught Eriale and hugged her, and then turned to embrace Melisanda.

"You did it," she said. "The spell's broken!"

"No," he replied. "We did it."

"What now?" Eriale asked. She nodded at the great armies below. "Do we try to straighten up the mess Oriseus has made of all this?"

Aeron thought for a moment, and shook his head. "That's not our concern. Let them work it out without the machinations of mages and archmages." He turned toward the south, watching the skies clear. "By my guess, Cimbar is that way. Let's start walking."

Epilogue

Spring had come early to Cimbar, as if the forces of nature wished to make up for the failed summer of the year before and the long, dark winter wrought by Oriseus's magic. As always, the endless activity of the great city fascinated Aeron as he stood gazing out over the harbor from the old battlements. The galleons and roundships of a dozen nations rode at anchor in Cimbar's harbor, and if he looked hard enough he could make out the tiny shapes of sailors working on their decks. It was good to see the port bustling with trade again; Chessenta had had enough of war over the last ten years, and the people looked forward to a long peace.

"Are you certain you can't stay?" asked Melisanda, her arm around his waist. "We need you here, Aeron. I have only a fraction of your skill and power, and sooner or later the demagogues and the senators will see through the anonymity of the Sceptanar's title. I need a wizard like you to heal the college and back me up when I falter."

"You're being selfish," he told her, and kissed her softly to show that he didn't mean it. "I've been away from the Maerchwood far too long. And besides, you'll be a much better Sceptanar than I've been in the last five months. People like you."

She shook her head. "I'm not even Chessentan. They'll know it soon enough."

Aeron tapped the rod of silver and jet that hung at her belt. "The Sceptanar's rod of office conceals your identity. The Cimbarans are accustomed to the rulership of a faceless, voiceless lord. You'll do fine. Hold the office until you find a worthy successor, and then you can leave anytime you like."

"Well, I want to go with you then."

He smiled sadly. "Someone has to put Cimbar back together," he replied.

He turned to gaze at the ruins behind them. The Broken Pyramid had been leveled by the stone's destruction. Not a single wall remained standing. A shadow passed over his heart as he thought of the dozens upon dozens of masters and students who lay somewhere beneath the rubble, victims of the cataclysm he'd unleashed. Past the wreckage, he could see workmen scuttling around the demolished wing of the Masters' Hall. The backblast through the shadow-portals had razed the Council Chamber and a great part of the surrounding building.

Melisanda followed his gaze, and leaned her head against his shoulder. "It would have been worse if Oriseus had won," she said. "You did what had to be done, Aeron."

"Do you ever wonder if he slipped away at the last moment somehow? If he's really down under the ruins with the rest of his followers?" Aeron asked quietly. "Or if any pieces of the Shadow Stone survived the blast?"

Melisanda frowned, but she passed it off with a shrug. "No one will ever know, I suppose. I mean to leave the pyramid just like it is. It won't be rebuilt."

"A warning?"

"Yes. And a reminder."

He thought about that for a time. "Good," he said.

"Your sister's waiting for you." Melisanda nodded toward the old stone stair that led down to the college's boat landing. "You don't want to miss the tide." She reached up and caught his face in her hands, pulling him close for a long kiss. Aeron felt her warm tears dampen his face. "Goodbye, Aeron."

"Goodbye," he said huskily. "When you've got things in order here, come to the Maerchwood. I want you to see it with me." With one last kiss, he broke away and shouldered his pack, trotting across the open field to where Eriale and Baillegh waited.

"Are you ready?" Eriale asked.

Aeron took a deep breath. "Let's go home."

R.A. Salvatore

The *New York Times* best-selling author of the Dark Elf saga returns to the FORGOTTEN REALMS® with an all new novel of high adventure and intrigue!

the SILENT BLADE

Wulfgar's world is crumbling around him while the assassin Entreri and the drow mercenary Jarlaxle are gaining power in Calimport. But Entreri isn't interested in power—all he wants is a final showdown with the dark elf known as Drizzt. . . . An all new hardcover, available October 1998.

FANTASY ADVENTURE

Ed Greenwood's
The Temptation of
Elminster

The third book in the epic history of the greatest mage in the history of Faerûn.

The glory that was Cormanthyr is no more. The mighty city of Myth Drannor lies in ruin, and the still young Elminster finds himself an apprentice to a new, human mistress. A mistress with her own plans for her young student. Tempted by power, magic, and arcane knowledge, Elminster fights wizard duels, and a battle with his own conscience. Available in hardcover, December 1998!

Evermeet
Island of Elves

Elaine Cunningham

The millennia-old history of the center of elven culture. What draw does this tranquil island have on Faerûn's elves? What does the future hold for this ancient and elegant race? From the long-forgotten struggles of the elven gods to the abandonment of the forest kingdoms of Faerûn, *Evermeet* is a sweeping tale of history, destiny, and fate. Available now in hardcover.